Blue Days and Fair

Blue Days and Fair

Lorraine Bateman & Paul Cole

Copyright © 2013 Lorraine Bateman & Paul Cole

The moral right of the authors has been asserted.

Apart from any fair dealing for the purposes of research or private study, or criticism or review, as permitted under the Copyright, Designs and Patents Act 1988, this publication may only be reproduced, stored or transmitted, in any form or by any means, with the prior permission in writing of the publishers, or in the case of reprographic reproduction in accordance with the terms of licences issued by the Copyright Licensing Agency. Enquiries concerning reproduction outside those terms should be sent to the publishers.

Matador
9 Priory Business Park
Kibworth Beauchamp
Leicestershire LE8 0RX, UK
Tel: (+44) 116 279 2299
Fax: (+44) 116 279 2277
Email: books@troubador.co.uk
Web: www.troubador.co.uk/matador

ISBN 978 1783060 597

British Library Cataloguing in Publication Data.
A catalogue record for this book is available from the British Library.

Typeset in Book Antiqua by Troubador Publishing Ltd
Printed and bound in the UK by TJ International, Padstow, Cornwall

Matador is an imprint of Troubador Publishing Ltd

www.lorrainebateman.com

*To the next generation,
Dexter, Mitchell, Charlie, Marcus, Laura, Thalia, Ella, Lana,
Maya.*

When Spring comes back with rustling shade
And apple-blossoms fill the air –
I have a rendezvous with death
When Spring brings back blue days and fair …

Extract from "I have a rendezvous with death"
Alan Seeger 1888-1916

1915

1919

Brussels, September 1915

All that is missing is the drum roll.

I watch the pastor lead Edith to a wooden post. She stands with her back against the splintered wood looking into the quadrangle and away from the steep banked wall behind her. Despite the open sky, it is as if we are underground with the cold damp of the night hanging around us on this early morning. A soldier approaches and draws her arms behind her, and then ties them together. He passes a rope around her waist and the stake, and tightens it to hold her fast. Edith is speaking. I strain to hear; her voice is a whisper.

"Tell my loved ones that my soul, I believe, is safe, and that I am glad to die for my country."

The pastor presses her hand.

"May the grace of our Lord Jesus Christ be with you now and always, for ever and ever. Amen." He releases her hand and makes the sign of the cross.

I am distracted by the banging of a door as it is flung back against the wall. An officer marches through shouting orders to other soldiers who follow him, a dozen in all, armed with rifles. The men position themselves to form two lines, but keep shuffling around to get themselves onto the back row. If I put out my arm I could touch the one nearest to me. I fight the urge to give him a shove and see if the whole line topples. Edith does not see them. She has been blindfolded and stands totally still with her back straight.

Another prisoner is tied to a stake, alongside Edith. I hear the soft murmur of a voice as the priest comforting this man is reciting a longer prayer than Edith had received. Perhaps this is done to soothe his agitations. Without Edith's composure, he keeps shouting for his release. No one moves until the soldiers are brought to attention when a number of officers and clerks of the court arrive. The duty of reading out the sentences is completed in a monotone, first German, then French.

"This must stop," I shout, but am ignored.

I try to push towards her, but am unable to move. The officials step back and the soldiers step forward. Orders are rapped and rifles are raised.

Russell was suddenly awake, sitting bolt upright in his bed. Disorientated he swung his legs out of the bed and rested his head in his hands, an elbow on each thigh. His mouth was dry and his breath was rasping as he tried to work out why he felt so afraid. It was his dream. Every night the dream returned. Every day the spectre haunted him.

Exhausted, Russell threw down his pen and turned to stare out of the window, trying to rid himself of the awful feeling of despair that sat too readily upon him. Absorption in work was of little help. *Dull, dull, dull.* He had pages of an official document to summarise for the operatives in the regions. *When they know it already.* He had covered it in their induction meetings. But Mr. Whitlock's instructions were to be obeyed.

"The commission has the duty, under the conditions imposed by the (Allied) Powers, of retaining possession of the foodstuffs until their final delivery in regional warehouses ... The Germans maintain their promise of no military interference, and the Commission for the Relief of Belgium (CRB) promises justice in distribution ... in order to intelligently guide the purchasing and transportation department of the CRB, it is fundamental that certain statistical information should be secured ... this information relates to consumption and stock levels."

Russell had been working for the monitoring and audit function of the CRB for almost a year, on the staff of the American minister to Belgium, Brand Whitlock. Russell had come to his attention when he was stranded in Brussels while on holiday at the start of the war. Although American, he was a research student at Oxford University, on a highly acclaimed Rhodes scholarship. He yawned and stretched. *Oh to be back with those blue spires and my books.* The administrative work had become mundane and repetitive. *Ah, Marion, if only she was still here.* The spice had gone out of his life in the three months since she had left. *Nurse Drake, Marion Drake.* To think her name brought her close.

His days had been flat since Marion's departure, and he missed Hugh's company and banter too. The secretary to the American legation, Hugh Gibson, had used his diplomatic pass to smuggle Marion and baby Alain to England safely away from the German authorities who were searching for her. Edith Cavell had not been so lucky. *Edith.* Russell could only hope that his dream about her arose from his feeling of powerlessness and was not a premonition. *Get a grip, Russell.* He looked at his watch. He was due to visit Sister Elizabeth Wilkins, Edith's nursing deputy, at the clinic, at five o'clock, to see what she had heard from the prison. *Edith alone in cell 23.* The number of her cell was all they knew so far. Three o'clock. *Two hours to fill.* He picked up his pen, suppressed a sigh and focused on finishing the section he was on.

When Russell arrived at the clinic in Rue du Culture he was shown up to the matron's sitting room, once the domain of Edith. The room was austere, with little colour in the faded furnishings and no fire in the grate. Sister Wilkins was waiting for him.

"Has there been any further correspondence?" Sister Wilkins asked immediately.

Russell's smile of greeting left his face as he shook his head.

"No, Mr. Whitlock hasn't written again since he heard from von der Lancken. I think he wants to consult with London."

"Tell me what he said," Sister Wilkins pressed him.

"Mr. Whitlock or von der Lancken?" Russell asked, but her obvious agitation was so great he decided to relate all the correspondence that had transpired so far.

"Mr. Whitlock wrote to Baron von der Lancken at the end of August …"

"Why so late, why did he wait so long? She had been there nearly a month by then."

Russell fidgeted to make himself comfortable in the winged armchair he had been directed to, but was soon perched on the edge of the seat as the nurse moved around the room, touching a piece of paper on the desk, straightening a picture, glancing out of the window. Her edginess began to infect him.

"Whitlock had made some phone calls earlier in the month and had her arrest confirmed, but no one expressed any urgency in the matter and it is only his place to enquire, not make demands."

"Who is this baron he wrote to? What can he do to secure her release? It is ridiculous how long she's been kept in that cell."

"The baron is the German political minister here in Brussels. He is not part of the army or the local administration but he does have a close connection with High Command in Berlin. Mr. Whitlock was hoping that the diplomatic channels might secure her release."

Despite being only an intern in the embassy Russell felt a thrill in knowing who was who in the political world of occupied Belgium.

"And will they? What did he say?"

"Nothing at first. Mr. Whitlock had to write a second time."

"And this is the reply you said was bad news?"

"Yes."

Brand Whitlock had suggested Russell could take the reply in person to Sister Wilkins, so Russell had sent a message for her to expect his visit but with the hint that he would not be bringing any good news. But now she was taut with tension.

"Come and sit down and I will tell you all I know."

"You must excuse my manners, Mr. Clark." Sister Wilkins sat down, but immediately sprang to her feet again. "Would you take some tea?"

"No, no thank you. I don't want to keep you waiting any longer, ma'am. I just wish the news was better."

She sat down in the chair facing him. The arms were threadbare and her fingers worried at the worn patches. Russell explained that Mr. Whitlock had twice requested permission from the German authorities for Maitre de Leval to arrange Edith's defence. A Belgian, Leval was the legal counsel for the legation. Von der Lancken's recent reply stated that Edith had confessed to everything, that Maitre de Leval could not see her, and that she, along with other defendants, had been assigned an advocate for her defence.

"Confessed? She wouldn't do that? Why would she do that? Unless … have they tortured her? Oh no, has she suffered?"

"We have no further details, but rest assured, she would not have been tortured."

"Your words are empty of solace, although I know kindly meant. You have no more idea of what ordeals she has faced than I have."

Damn, she was right. Russell was ashamed to admit to himself that he had no knowledge about the treatment meted out to Edith or her co-conspirators. His platitudes were of no value at all. He decided plain speaking was what she deserved.

"But you say", Sister Wilkins continued, "Edith will have someone to defend her. She won't be on her own in the court. That is good news, isn't it? Why do you introduce this as bad news?"

"Because the counsel they have assigned is not one that is known to the legation. He isn't German; like our Monsieur Leval he is Belgian, but we don't know how much influence he will have with the Germans." *And we will hold no sway over him.*

"If the Germans have chosen him, then it will be to do their bidding. This is ridiculous. They can't be trusted. This cannot be. We must do something. What can be done? Where is Mr. Gibson? What is he doing for Edith?" Her questions bounced off him and she was on her feet again pacing around the room.

Russell explained that Hugh was still in London, delayed by matters for the Belgian royal family, but Mr. Whitlock had requested he go to the British government with news of Edith. She was, after all, one of theirs. *They must intervene on her behalf.*

"And will they realise she is in danger? Will they give her cause any attention? Thank goodness Marion and the baby escaped. They … are they safely home? You can tell me that at least?" She touched down on her seat again.

Russell welcomed any opportunity to dwell on Marion and told her the snippet of news he had received: that she and Alain had reached London safely with Mr. Gibson and Marion had then travelled on to her own home in Little Missenden with the baby. He had heard nothing since. The German administration allowed no correspondence into the country and Russell often had to fight the feeling of isolation. The rare appearance of a British plane in the sky caused people in the streets to cheer. They were not forgotten.

"Good, good. We must count this as a blessing. Edith will be relieved to know Marion is safe." Sister Wilkins managed a brief smile. "But what of Edith? What will the British government do? They must act quickly."

"There will be plenty of time for them to act. Edith may be confined, but she is in no immediate danger." He smiled, confident with this reassurance. "Legal wheels turn very slowly. Mr. Whitlock will be kept informed at every stage. There will be so much red tape to wade through. It is more likely she will die of boredom than retribution."

"Well really, Mr. Clark! The subject of Edith's death is not something to make light of." The sister was on her feet again, and Russell jumped up too.

"No, I'm sorry, terribly sorry, ma'am, please let me apologise." *Stupid, thoughtless.*

Sister Wilkins raised a hand as if to pardon him and sat back down, an action he mirrored.

"I was attempting to ease your mind, but it was careless of me, ma'am. But please don't worry so, there is time for all the necessary petitions to be made, I am sure." *Am I?*

"But we can't be complacent. The Germans are not to be trusted. They have made examples of so many with their firing squads. We mustn't let this happen to Edith."

Russell flinched at the mention of firing squads. *My dream.* The image was so vivid it revived his feelings of panic. He spoke slowly, as much to calm himself as her, telling her that Edith would not be shot, *of course she wouldn't*, but she must prepare herself for the likelihood that she, along with some of the others, would be detained. Brand Whitlock had assured him the Germans would not condemn a woman to death. Even they would realise this would be an insane act.

"I think we know a different enemy, Mr. Clark. I have seen what these Germans are capable of. When they first marched into Belgium, they had little consideration for anyone, regardless of their gender or station in life. They are murderers and are entirely capable of what you say they wouldn't do. I only hope one of the British politicians carries a sense of urgency about this. I am afraid for her."

There was a knock at the door and one of the orderlies brought in a tea tray. Russell accepted a cup and asked her if she had been allowed to visit Edith, but despite all her efforts she had achieved nothing more than getting a letter and some personal items of comfort to her.

"We send a roast meal in to her every Sunday, but we are not sure if it reaches her. I just want her to know she is not forgotten. I had one letter from her. She is obviously distressed and wrote to say she had had no official visit from anyone on her behalf. Who is supposed to be looking after her? Why can't we get through to her? Is this isolation allowed?"

"I wish Hugh Gibson was here, I must admit," Russell said. "I am sure he would be rattling cages more than the minister. *And thumping their desks.* Whitlock seems to believe he is dealing with gentlemen and gives them the benefit of the doubt. I had to remind him to send a second letter, and it is not my place to do that, I can assure you. He is one to take offence."

"I am not interested in your protocols and sensitivities when Edith is at risk. I do not care who I might offend if I could only speak to someone who could do something."

Russell did not doubt that she meant what she said. Marion had always described Sister Wilkins as something of a mouse, in Edith's shadow, but it was clear to him she had found her courage and was very prepared to hold anyone to account. If only they knew who to confront. Russell doubted that his demands, even if voiced, would achieve anything, but he was haunted by the lack of action and by his own impotence.

A silence hung between them for some minutes. They occupied themselves by sipping their tea, and in Russell's case eating a biscuit. The china was plain white, no fuss, but of fine quality. *A metaphor for Edith?* Sister Wilkins broke the silence.

"I feel so useless. What will I say to her when I am allowed to visit? There is no good news for her at all."

"Ma'am, it will be a great comfort to her when you do visit.

I'll raise it with Mr. Whitlock and see if he can pull some strings."

"I despair of anything happening through official channels. I shall just have to be more persistent and arrive at the prison every day until they let me in."

"Don't do that. You'll exhaust yourself and you have the clinic to run. Edith has left you in charge."

"This clinic will be nothing without Edith. I shall certainly not stay without her. She held everything together." Sister Wilkins brushed away a tear. "I cannot replace her, no one can."

Russell was out of his depth but tried to bring some comfort. He talked of the need for them to be patient, that to create a stir might work against Edith, that it was a dull time for her but not a dangerous one. If they remained optimistic he was sure they would be rewarded by her release: it was only a matter of waiting for the furore to die down. The Germans had made their point. She seemed to brighten a little as he spoke, for which he was relieved. *If only I could stop having my dream.* He was convinced they were not doing enough.

Sister Wilkins stood up and Russell thought it was a signal for him to leave but after placing her teacup on the tray she resumed her seat.

"It was good of you to come. I must not berate the messenger. Now tell me again, now my head is clearer, what did you say was the news from Marion?"

Russell repeated the message he had received of her arrival in England and they both then imagined her reunion at home.

"Her sudden return, and with baby Alain would be quite something for her parents to deal with. I can imagine their surprise," Sister Wilkins said.

"Yes," Russell agreed, "I am sure her mother will not take readily to such a disruption, the way she orders things at home." *Mightily put out.* "Marion and her mother don't enjoy the easiest of relations, a constant battle of wills I fear. But they are both safe and that is the most important fact."

"Oh yes, her parents will be reassured by that. I know they wanted her home the moment war was declared, but she refused to leave. What of your parents, do they know of your whereabouts?"

Russell often thought about his parents and had a notebook full of things to tell them. His last letter had been to tell them about his return to Brussels, and since then: silence. He had not had time to write a letter for Hugh to post in London before his hasty departure. He described his parents to Sister Wilkins and then his home in Maine, the local timber trade, and the wooden chapel his family attended. She showed great interest, particularly in his university town of Washington and encouraged him to talk about his student days. He was soon describing the day that changed his life when the provost told him of his selection for a Rhodes scholarship and how he and his parents had celebrated his success. He had to clear his throat of emotion a couple of times. Waves of homesickness washed over him. He was speaking of Oxford University when she asked him if he had plans to return there, or go back to America after the war.

"No plans at the moment. It looks like I will be staying here, for a while at least. A few months ago we thought Americans might not be needed in the CRB, but the powers that be thought it best not to change the organisation: everything seems to be working well. *Too well, there is nothing interesting to do.* The Germans have stuck to their side of the bargain: they leave the food supplies well alone."

"Well, that's something at least, and thank goodness or we would all be starving. Rations are very tight, but we do manage. And there are still no plans for American forces to enter the war?"

"No, ma'am. There has been a lot of giving to support the Belgians and French refugees, but Mr. Whitlock tells me the American public are against joining in a European fight."

"And there is nothing positive to say about war. They are probably very wise to keep out," Elizabeth said. "But it would be good to oust these Germans. It is all taking far too long. So much for it all being over before last Christmas, and now we will have another Christmas before many months. I do hope Edith is back with us by then."

Russell did not want to open up the conversation again. The topic of Edith was a seemingly bottomless pit that drained hope and fed anxiety. He stood up.

"Now, I really ought to be on my way, ma'am."

"Of course, of course." Sister Wilkins rose to walk him to the reception hall. She seemed tiny against his six-foot frame. He noticed greying hair beneath her cap as he followed her down the stairs. An administrator more than an organiser Marion had said when describing her, and it was apparent that the strain of her current responsibilities, as well as concern for Edith, sat heavily on her shoulders. He could tell she was attempting to sound brighter as they parted.

He shook her outstretched hand.

"I'll be back as soon as I hear."

"Thank you, Mr. Clark. Your support is truly appreciated. I will play my part too."

"Do try not to worry, ma'am, I'm sure this will all work out," Russell said as he released her hand. But from the tears in her eyes it was clear his words delivered no real comfort and he carried her dejection with him as he returned to the legation.

Edith's Journal, St Gilles Prison, Brussels, September 1915

I am pleased to be on my own. It gives me time to write and think. No doubt my captors think I will weaken in solitary confinement, but for me it is the reverse. After the pressures of the last few months I feel at peace in solitude. My cell is small, with the bare essentials. A bed, wooden stool, corner cupboard, and a jug with my day's water ration. There is a small high window that lets in light but no view. The only noise that carries from the corridor is the opening of a neighbour's grille or door. My gaolers don't speak. It is *"verboten"*.

There has been so much going on since the outbreak of war, too much for me to cope with. I can allow myself to say this now, now there is no one near to hear me, nor see my shoulders droop from fatigue. Running the nurses' training school and clinic is more than a full-time job, and difficulties have multiplied under the strictures of the German occupation. Put on top of this all the recent maternity cases that have come to the clinic, some with difficult births: young traumatised girls just some of the victims from the ravages of this war. But I know I could have taken all this in my stride if it wasn't for the burden I carried from hiding the soldiers. I need this rest.

In truth each prisoner is on their own, even the ones that share a cell. My interrogators have told me they have thirty-five of our organisation in custody and the might of the German administration will pick us off one-by-one to face our judgement. I didn't know we were that many. They proudly boast they have enough links in the chain to connect us together and, after Quien's betrayal, all the proof they require. I had been warned about him, but paid no heed. Why was that?

"I don't feel comfortable about him, Edith," Marion said. "He hasn't come to us through the usual contacts. He could be a spy."

"But he knows we're harbouring soldiers and getting them to the border. He is a French soldier seeking our help. Not everyone can know of the de Croys. Many come to Brussels through different routes and contacts. And even though he's not British I don't think we should turn him away. They all need our help."

"I think we are bringing trouble on ourselves." Marion was clearly agitated. "Send him away."

"He knows too much already. If he's a bad apple the harm has already been done. What will be will be. But you keep out of his way. I don't want him to know about you. I'll see to him. We have a lot of soldiers to move out this week, so he won't be with us for long."

Would the damage have been limited if I had acted in another way? I will never know, but I doubt the outcome would have been different; perhaps just the timing. For a while I had been thinking that we were living on borrowed time. The frequency of the searches at the clinic had increased. And that feeing of being watched was always with me on the streets.

I was anxious about Quien and thought that Marion was probably correct to doubt him. But what could I do? From what he said it was clear he knew about our hidden soldiers, and although he had been called poker-faced by some his stare made me nervous. To throw him out was only to invite trouble through a different route and, if I'm honest, I was tired of living with such suspense. The subterfuge of hiding and moving soldiers under the noses of the increasingly suspicious Germans, clandestine meetings with guides, and never knowing who could be trusted or who was a dupe had taken their toll. Not knowing when the next search would take place frayed my nerves. My hands have a tremor. My writing is bad.

I breathed a sigh of relief when Quien left for the border with a group but it was only a few weeks later that *Yorc,* the de Croy password, came to tell me of some arrests.

"I am here to warn you, Edith. Some of our guides have been arrested. It feels like the net is closing in on us," Prince Reginald, who was key to the escape line, said.

"Should you have come? You need to keep yourself safe. Where is Princess Marie?"

"My sister is safe, she is in hiding, and I must keep on the move." He had not sat down.

"You must leave Brussels, leave the country: they will hunt you down."

"Yes, I am heading north to the border, but there are some safe houses I must warn first." Reginald sighed. The young aristocrat had aged visibly in the short time I had been acquainted with him. He looked weary and his hair was greying at the temples.

"No, you must go. I will get messages through," Edith insisted, "although there is little that any of us can do. We are sitting targets."

"You must destroy all proof, burn any records. I'm sure you can brave it out if they take you in for questioning. It's the men they will be rough with."

"Leave the city now, don't look back, we will be fine. You have done so much, you must keep yourself safe."

The fire in my grate burned bright that evening but it pained me to feed the flames. I had kept a second set of accounts to show to the foundation that supported the clinic. I had suggested this to Dr. Depage to ensure there should be no complications with all the costs incurred on behalf of the escaping soldiers. My books were neat and correct to the nearest franc if not centime, but they were evidence in the wrong hands. I almost faltered and thought of hiding them instead. Their destruction might save me from my German accusers, but I would still have to account to the clinic financiers when this debacle was behind us.

I set fire to any contact details and locations for meetings that I had written down. Last into the flames were postcards sent by soldiers who had safely returned to England. They had been told not to do this, but sometimes gratitude will not be bound.

I said nothing of *Yorc*'s visit to Marion. Was this wrong? I had wanted to protect her from worry, but should I have done more to secure her safety? Marion was a natural choice to partner me in this so-called crime. She was level-headed, practical, and not one to be cowed by the circumstances of the occupation; the pick of the crop of nursing trainees as far as I was concerned, and she had never let me down. It was too late to do more for her now; better to try to put her to the back of my mind lest her name should pass my lips and into the interrogator's notebook.

They have taken my statement. Denial seemed a frivolous pastime that only encouraged them to delight in their cleverness as they questioned and cross-examined, to catch slips in my concentration. They caught me out very early on and then told everyone I was their star witness, or so they said. I don't actually know what was in the statement that I signed, it was written in German, but my protests were ignored. Hours of questions and answers filtered through translation and malice; but I know I made it easy for them. Before each session they made me swear on the Bible to tell the truth in front of God. I felt no shame in the truth and even held the faint hope that by shouldering the responsibility others might be set free. The Germans did not need to have their argument with all of us; I was the prize British jewel caught in their net. I felt their menace in the cold air that chilled our breath, and my bones, each time we faced each other.

I am charged with helping enemy soldiers return to their regiments and thus to the front line; a crime as defined by these invaders. I thought each soldier had done enough for king and country already and would not be sent out to fight again, and could stay at home. But the monster that is this war demanded differently. I knew my actions broke the laws of the occupation, but I also knew I was upholding the humanitarian and Christian law to which I would rather be held to account. That word: account. It was accounts that first tripped me up. I was incensed when the interrogators declared my motives for helping the soldiers were driven by financial gain. Many of the guides did demand payment, but to profit from another's hardship jarred against every value that I hold dear. In laying out the financial facts I confessed to my deeds. My captors' smug satisfaction at that stayed with me long into the night.

The dark nights are long, and do little to relieve my fatigue, and I worry. I hope they don't find Marion and bring her in. My one hope is that she escapes capture.

Hope. I still have hope as a friend. Please God let her stay free.

Three months earlier in Little Missenden, England, June 1915

Marion had been exhausted when met by her family at Amersham station. Very unlike her, she had burst into tears at the sight of her mother, father, and sister, which brought to an immediate stop the torrent of questions they looked about to ask. She had telegraphed ahead to warn of her return but had not expected such a reception committee. She had omitted mention of Alain in her brief message and the sharp intake of breath from her mother and Evelyn did not escape her notice as she stepped down from the carriage with a young baby in her arms.

It surprised her how good it felt to be home. And she really was home, back in her own bedroom. She had woken early and it had taken a few minutes to orientate herself before the floral wallpaper located her. She remembered the argument she had had with her mother over it when she was about fourteen, when she had complained about not being able to have striped paper. Now she welcomed her bedroom's familiarity and feminine touches. It was a good-sized room, as most of them were in the rectory. The house came with her father's living. Her eyes followed a runner, which traced its way up several flower stems before ending in a cascade of ivy. The wallpaper looked so British and a colourful change to the austerity of her dormitory at the nurses' training clinic in Belgium. She was surprised to think she had only been away in Brussels for a year of training. The woman who had returned felt very different indeed.

Marion threw back the bed covers and tiptoed across the cold linoleum to the window to look down at the garden. It was lush and green in the early morning light, edged with borders of shrubs and plants that she was unable to name. At one time, in her tomboyish way, she had been quite proud of not knowing about things domestic; now ignorance of any kind appalled her. *What a difference a year makes.* Her thoughts turned to Russell, and she hugged herself, imagining it was his arms that were holding her. *Oh my love.* The trauma and opportunity of her hasty departure from Belgium had propelled them into each other's arms for a whole night. *Carpe diem.* Not the only time they would consummate their love, she hoped, but it was premature in their courtship and quite unlike anything that she or others would expect of her. *I wouldn't change anything. Apart from leaving Edith.* Marion had just run away from trouble, serious trouble.

She was a fugitive from the German authorities. Since the war started she, with Edith, had been duping the Germans, helping to smuggle British soldiers out of Brussels. Then their escape line had been compromised. And to top that, if anything could, she had a baby, just weeks old, in her care. *Poor lamb, I must find him a family.* She wondered what sort of night Alain had had and immediately wanted to find him in the nursery. Her mother had won that fight hands down.

"You most certainly will not take that child to your room. I will not hear of it. Nanny has Anthony and she can accommodate another."

"Do as she says, for tonight my dear," her father had suggested, and Marion had no fight left in her. The heady few days before her departure and the pressure of her journey from Belgium had taken their toll. But now, refreshed from a night's sleep she wanted to be with Alain. She dressed hastily and went to find him.

For a makeshift nursery the rooms at the top of the house were surprisingly well equipped. Anthony's mother Evelyn was Marion's elder sister by two years and married to a cavalry officer, although, Marion had learnt the previous evening, widowed in the early months of the war. Rather than live with her husband's family, Evelyn had decided to return to her own home for the birth of her son, and the allowance from his family had helped fund some of the changes as well as Nanny's fees. Nanny, a local girl, had her own room; Anthony, and now Alain, slept in another, and there was a day room with a small annex of a kitchen area with a sink and hotplate. Marion was feeding Alain his formula milk when Nanny appeared.

"The little one took a while to settle last night," Nanny said.

"Oh, I am so sorry. You should have brought him to me."

"More important that you had your sleep. You looked done in if you don't mind me saying."

Marion and the nanny both knew each other from the village and fell into easy conversation with each other.

"You're right, I was. Anthony is awake now."

"Don't worry, I'll fetch the mite. His mother leaves him to me."

Marion was soon settled with Alain in her arms and he clutched her finger as he sucked on the bottle. She felt anchored by him, and kissed the top of his head. Even though she was in her old home she felt like a foreigner, not quite sure how well she would fit back in. *We'll have to take it day by day, little fellow.* She and Nanny spent some companionable time together as both prepared their wards for the day. Marion had always liked her. She was down to earth with no airs and graces; so often staff aped their employer's manners, a falsehood that Marion had no time for. Nanny was plain in looks, style, and speech, and clearly competent at her job. The eldest of thirteen children, she had initially learnt her craft at home, and had come to the rectory with a strong recommendation from the Sunday school superintendent at her father's church. At twenty-seven this was her first job outside her own home and she was determined to do it well. Marion took time to reassure her that she was.

Taking a seat at the dining table for breakfast with the family, Marion was conscious that conversation stopped the moment she appeared. She entered the mahogany darkened room slightly later than the others and her father lowered his newspaper to invite and accept her kiss, which she gave easily; she loved him very much. Nodding to her mother, polite pleasantries about each other's sleep quickly followed and she smiled at Evelyn in her widow's weeds. She helped herself to breakfast from the small buffet on the dresser behind her mother's chair: an affectation Marion knew was copied from the large house where her lord of the manor uncle resided.

"Beatrice has said she will call in this afternoon, without the children. Perhaps that would be a good time for us all to assemble to hear your news, Marion. Mr. Drake" – another pretension of her mother's to address her father in this way – "has to make his calls this morning and Evelyn and I have the Ladies Circle to attend. Will that suit you, Marion?"

It suited Marion a great deal. She was more fond of her eldest sister Beatrice than Evelyn, and was relieved to know she was not going to face a barrage of questions over the breakfast table. Considering the disruption caused by her premature return, and with a so-far unexplained baby in the house, exceedingly small talk followed, punctuated by her father reading snippets of news from the paper to anyone who would listen.

Mrs. Drake opined over some of the news, which was mainly about the war. Marion realised how little she knew about the progression of the war, she had been so cocooned in Brussels. Her mother soon turned her conversation to more local matters of the parish. Away a year, the country at war, her sister widowed, parishioners dead in France, but it was still the pettiness of the flower rota and contributions to the cake stalls that fired her mother's interest. *Nothing changes.* While the familiarity held some comfort for Marion she was at the same time daunted. There was nothing new in her mother's conversation. But she knew her mother was just biding time before she could focus her attention on her.

"I hope there is good news from the Baxters today, my dear." Marion's father directed his comment to his wife.

"The Baxters?" Marion asked. "Has something happened?" Firm friends of the family, she was immediately anxious for them.

"As far as they have ascertained, James has been taken as a prisoner of war."

"Oh no, how terrible." Marion looked to her father.

"Actually, my dear, this is good news. He was listed as missing in action for months after Mons. We thought we'd lost him." James had always been a favourite of her father's, and he had always been a good friend to her. Evelyn chipped in.

"The Red Cross issued a list of prisoners, but he is no longer at the prison they said. He's in Germany, but we all want to know where so we can direct our parcels and letters."

"I shall ask his mother today. She is on the committee, although quite exhausted by all this. An only son is such a pressure."

"How is the major?" Marion asked after James's father.

"Frustrated not to be serving. The Boer did him for fighting, but he's knocked on the door at Westminster only to be turned away. And what with all the horses taken he has no stock to work with and can't ride to the hounds."

"Irascible, is what Mrs. Baxter says," Her mother interrupted. The Baxters were renowned for their horsemanship and breeding of fine mounts. They, along with her uncle attracted custom from counties away. *He would hate to be idle, so would James.*

"Was James with the cavalry?" Marion asked.

"Yes, but this modern warfare doesn't suit the horse. The men have been dug into the ground for months now," her father volunteered. "The earthworks run for over a thousand miles I'm told."

"I really need to catch myself up with all that has been happening. We had so little news in Brussels, and only what the Germans printed."

"We'll take a walk in the garden later, my dear," her father said, "and I'll give you a précis."

"Thank you, Papa, thank you. I shall take Alain for a walk this morning. The fresh air will do him good," Marion said.

"You will do no such thing," her mother boomed.

"Excuse me?" Marion said, and her father lowered his newspaper.

"You are not to be seen abroad with that baby. Not until, not until …" her mother spluttered.

Marion's father stepped in. "Perhaps not until we have all had our chat this afternoon, if you wouldn't mind, Marion? The garden will give you fresh air enough, I am sure."

"Of course, Papa, as you wish."

Marion caught a glimpse of a smirk of derision on Evelyn's face and blurted out, "He's not mine, you know. The baby. Alain. He's my responsibility, but he's not mine. I hope you don't think that he is mine."

"I am sure that is exactly what the entire parish will think by eleven o'clock this morning," Mrs. Drake snorted.

Mr. Drake folded his newspaper and stood to leave the room. Marion rose with him.

"That's enough for now," he said. "We shall meet this afternoon." And that is what they did.

Marion's morning of mental preparation was wasted in the face of the questions she was being asked. She had to admit to herself that her answers did sound vague and she had to question exactly what, or who, it was that she was trying to protect by not telling them the entire truth. *Hold your nerve.* The truth was she was protecting her own future options. If she described the trouble she had got herself into and the risks she had taken with Edith and the soldiers, or hinted that Alain had been stolen from the church authorities as a personal favour to a nun, or had given them the name, nationality, and existence of her beau, she knew that any attempts at independent action in the foreseeable future would be impossible. She would have played herself straight into her mother's fears and prejudices and, having narrowly escaped one prison, would have found herself cosseted and controlled within another.

"It would seem", her father concluded, "that Alain is an orphan whom you are under instruction to place in a family in England at the wish of his mother who died after his birth?"

"Correct, Papa."

"And it was for the fulfilment of this promise that the American secretary to the legation in Brussels accompanied you on a perilous journey across the Channel to England."

"Yes, that is right."

"Most noble of the Americans," he said, "and quite a surprising mission given all that they have to deal with."

"They were most kind."

"And you have no plans to return to your training in Brussels, after you have placed the child."

"No, but I have a mind to support the war effort. I know nurses are in great demand, and although I am only part-way through my training I know I have much to offer."

"Of that I am sure, my dear." Her father smiled.

Each statement of Mr. Drake's prevented her mother from speaking. Marion was conscious of her mother's mouth opening and then slamming shut with each of his remarks. Marion knew her mother and her sisters were not at all satisfied with what they had heard but they had been unable to interrupt her father's questions with any of their own, and he had let her off lightly. *Always his favourite.* She knew they knew she was hiding more than she was telling, and that she was under some strain was evident to all in the room. Her interrogation was not over; she knew her mother would find her own opportunity to corner her.

"So we know how to describe Marion's act of Christian charity to any who ask, don't we?" Her father looked at his wife, Evelyn, and Beatrice: only Beatrice nodded.

"It is not the ones who ask who will be the problem. It will be the ones who don't ask because they think they know our business: they will cause the tittle-tattle." Mrs Drake's statement came as an outburst. "Reputations are a serious business; one can never marry without one. I will not have this house sullied. The child must go quickly."

"In time, my dear, in good time. Our dear Lord did not think of his reputation before he helped people." Reverend Drake smiled at Marion.

Mrs. Drake looked as if she had plenty more to say but Marion's father rose to his feet and asked Marion to join him in a walk around the garden. The conversation about her was closed, for that day, and Marion was grateful, but after an hour with her father her mind was full of new information and reeling from the expanse of the theatre of war. She had had no idea of the scale, or of their own losses.

It was clear that nothing was going to plan and that hopes of quick victory, for either side, had been dashed. Timetables and costs had gone disastrously wrong and new and unanticipated foes had entered the fight. Campaigns against the Serbians and the Turks demanded manpower, and even worse fighting was taking place on the Eastern Front between Russia and Germany than along the Western Front where

French and British troops were entrenched against sections of the German Army. German colonies in Africa, Egypt, and the Middle East had to be constrained and the Royal Navy was under duress to protect the high seas from the German fleets of ships and submarines.

Marion's father had sat her down on a bench seat when he broke the news of three local boys who had died, and then her cousin Jack. She was saddened to hear of the brothers Stan and Malcolm Callard, killed within months of each other, and the Weedons' son Fred lost in the first month of the war, but news of Jack's death was a body blow to her. No reprise for her aunt and uncle unlike the Baxters. Jack had died of pneumonia only six weeks after arriving in France. A postcard from him to the master of hounds arrived after the news of his death, and was the talk of the village. He was extolling the virtues of the French countryside for a hunt. *Typical Jack.* Her father explained that her Aunt Augusta had been called to the hospital in Boulogne, her Uncle William had been too unwell to travel, but she arrived too late. He touched on Charles's death, but only briefly and said that Evelyn had borne the loss of her husband well. *And will, as long as she can find another one soon.*

The war took on a different dimension for Marion now it hit this close to home. Her anxiety about Edith was always with her, but now the losses in the village and her own family sharpened her awareness of the very real dangers of the war. She shuddered at how close she had come to being captured herself, and her father, concerned that she was shocked by the news, encouraged her indoors to lie down.

Marion spent every waking moment available to her with Alain. She was upset by Jack's death and James's capture and she was ill at ease; her stomach was knotted and she had no appetite, in fact she often now felt sick at the sight of food. She tossed and turned at nights with anxious thoughts of Edith in her incarceration. The lack of information was almost impossible to bear. She had telegraphed Hugh on two occasions, but his one reply had told her nothing. And when, in the rare moments she was not worrying about Edith and she allowed herself to think of Russell, all she did was cry because she missed him so much. Their hours of intimacy before her departure had been so special. She so wished she still had her friend Gwen to confide in, but having stepped beyond the bounds of what was acceptable, Marion knew no one must ever know of her impropriety. More than anything she wanted to be with Russell, but they could not even write to each other. No letters were allowed through to the occupied territories. Hugh had promised to take a letter back with him, even though this was in breach of diplomatic agreements, but she wanted to be in a better frame of mind when she put pen to paper.

The day she wrote to Russell was the day her period started. She had not even voiced this concern to herself, that she might be pregnant from their night together, he had been so confident and in control, but nonetheless it had lurked deep within her consciousness, an unnamed worry, only fully realised when relief hit her.

> My darling Russell,
>
> Hugh has promised to deliver this letter to you, so I hope it reaches you and that you are pleased to hear from me. I know he was able to telegraph the legation so you heard we arrived safely in England. What a gentleman he is. You could not have placed me in a better pair of hands for safekeeping, and Hugh was perfectly accommodating with Alain.
>
> I cry every time I think of you waving goodbye as the car turned out of the embassy gate. And when I think of poor Edith. I do hope she is being fairly treated,

but I am sure prison is unpleasant at any time, and most of all when hosted by such an enemy.

There is such strong anti-German feeling here. The newspapers are full of the zeppelin bombing raids. I had not thought of the war reaching our shores. In some ways Belgium feels safer from the war as its battles have already been fought and lost; ours here are still ahead of us. This war is so vast.

The family are in mourning for my sister Evelyn's husband and cousin Jack. In fact there are a fair few in black in my father's congregation. I think I told you about my cousin Jack, the steeplechase champion. He signed up with the Hussars at the start of the war, and apparently they let him off his training to race his last rides before he left for France. He died just weeks later. I have been shown several of his obituaries; he really had become quite famous in racing circles.

I am sad for my sister, of course, although she does carry the melodrama of her widow's weeds a bit far. *Why do I show her so little charity?* But if I were to lose you Russell my heart would break. Why should I consider her immune to such depth of feeling? We have never been close as siblings, our views on most things are poles apart, and I have noticed she only seems to suffer from her grief when there are masculine shoulders to cry on.

Stop it, Marion, this is unkind.

I had forgotten what it is like to rub shoulders with family when I was away. Evelyn and I have always quarrelled.

What am I doing writing about this?

> Family matters are all trivial to you I am sure and what I should be penning are words of love, but I hope you hold my feelings for you in your heart just as you held me in your arms. I dare not write more about this!

Marion lifted her head from the page and sank into her memory of their night together; their only night, but one that had sealed their relationship forever. Or so she hoped. She could run the scene through her head like a newsreel. She sighed and resumed writing.

> The fact that Evelyn is at home with her baby, Anthony, who is three months older than Alain, made our arrival much easier to accommodate. There is plenty of room in this rambling rectory. The nanny seems pleased to have my company as I am in the nursery much more than Evelyn. I largely look after Alain myself.
>
> I have to tell you about my welcome. Any joy at my return or concern for the reasons for my hasty departure from Brussels were lost amid their horror at my arrival, with a babe in arms. Mother was speechless. Yes, unheard of, but she could not utter a word! I had telegraphed ahead, at Hugh's insistence, but not mentioned Alain. I would have preferred to arrive unannounced but they had all turned out to meet me at the station and I was really touched. Quite the homecoming, until Mother and Evelyn spotted Alain. They both gasped and I even thought Evelyn might faint. It took my father to step forward and bustle me into the car he had borrowed from my uncle. It was only when we were crushed together inside that they started to breath again. Mother had turned quite purple. *I really should stop finding pleasure in her discomfort.* I am told I should pay more attention to what people think as our arrival has caused quite a stir.

I want to hear that Edith will be released soon. I do so long for news of her. Hugh's correspondence has offered me little information on this front. I shouldn't have abandoned her.

I have told the truth to my family, but not all the truth. They know that Alain is an orphaned refugee and that I am under instruction to find him a home. My mother would like me to take him to an orphanage straightaway. I have had all the lectures about ruining my life and prospects, but all taunts and tactics have so far made me cling to him all the more. I actually overheard two women at church talking about me. "Well, they say the baby is a refugee, but that would be the story wouldn't it?" The problem is I care more for him than I do for their opinions, but I know this is being very unfair on my family. To her credit Mother has done her best to salvage my reputation, but I apparently undermine this at every turn with the affection I lavish on Alain. I am never out of the nursery, whilst Evelyn is almost a stranger to her own son.

I haven't dared to mention the trouble I was in with Edith and even to my ears the reasons for my sudden return sounded feeble and contrived. They know I am hiding something from them; they see there is something more behind my tension. My father barely has time to read the newspaper before I am poring over it looking for news of Edith, but there has been nothing printed at all; do the British government even know about her arrest? Does Hugh have contacts there? His job sounds very exciting. I now understand why you find it of such interest when I listened to him talking; his conversation opens a door into a world that was hitherto closed. Seems like politics is everything these days. Meanwhile our men are being killed.

I must sign off now, my love. I wish upon wish I

could walk out with you this evening, as we did in Brussels. We must be strong while we are apart. We may be on different stepping-stones, but the river is our love and it will bring us together again. Soon, I hope.

Yours forever,
Marion.

Marion sealed the envelope and then wrote a brief note to Hugh and placed them both in a larger envelope addressed to Mr. H. Gibson at the American Embassy, in London. She would post it the next day.

The weather was good. Marion took Alain with her when she walked into Amersham to post her letter to Hugh. Her path took her along the banks of the Misbourne River, a grand name for something that was little more than a shallow brook, lined by willows and birch trees, and easily vaulted by an unladylike leap. She paused at a place where some rocks straddled the water and hugged her letter to her chest, reminded of Therese and her wise words. She had told them their love was the river and sometimes they would find themselves apart, on different stepping stones, but the water would flow strong and keep them connected. She had to trust that it would.

Therese, such a friend. Marion had nursed Therese through the final stages of her confinement and had delivered Alain. It was Therese's warning that saved Marion from capture, and it was Therese who had given Alain into her safekeeping preferring for Marion to place him with a family than he be handed over to the Catholic Church and put in an institution. Marion had promised Therese that Alain would never learn of the violent night when he was conceived from rape. Nor of his father, an unknown Prussian soldier, and his mother, Therese, a nun.

And that was another one of the lies that had been woven around Alain. His mother was not dead, but had returned to a convent, a silent order, near Leuven. Therese had told Marion she wanted to focus entirely on God. Her interactions with the world and its ways had interrupted her communion and she had been keen to return to her sanctuary. Marion had been astounded that Therese's faith remained untarnished after her ordeal. She smiled at the memory of her and decided that she would write, when Alain was settled, to let her know all was well with him.

Edith's Journal, St Gilles Prison, Brussels, October 1915

I lied to my colleagues. Or did I? Can I step into the truth that I put in the letter I wrote? I am allowed to write one letter a week. I addressed my letter to my nursing colleague, sister Wilkins and asked her to tell everyone not to worry about me and that I was all right. Why did I say this? Habit probably. I asked for some blankets, towels, a toothbrush, a napkin, cup, fork, spoon and plate, and some clean linen. My stay is going to be less temporary than I first thought; they will glean this from my requests.

I did write that the days feel long and asked for some embroidery and my copy of "*Imitation of Christ*" and my prayer book. I hope they found this inspirational and not maudlin. So few turn to Him now, but I savour the meditations. She will understand my desire to have occupation for my hands. I am never one to sit idle for long, unless in the Lord's presence. I told them I would be back with them soon, once the questioning was over. That was a lie, it wasn't what I knew; it was just my hope. But I didn't write "I hope", I wrote "I will". Nothing that happens here is in service to my will. I cannot see God's hand in it either.

I also wrote out a list of instructions in the letter as if nothing had changed; all must continue with nurses' training and clinic chores. They would be followed to the letter, of that I am sure.

Thank goodness Sister Wilkins was released on the same

day of our arrest: her innocence apparent through her confusion about what she was asked, and because Quien hadn't indentified her. He fingered me straight away.

"Yes, that's her. She was the one at the clinic. Grey hair, in her fifties, not one to smile."

He had stood in front of me, with no shame, just a shoulder shrug that I imagined rattled the thirty pieces of silver in his pocket.

"The other one's not here. She was young, a real beauty."

I froze then, but he went no further.

"The one that got away." He said as he turned and left the room.

I had not looked him in the eye, because I did not know what look to convey. What was there to say to this man? He had played his part as I had mine. Jesus had known Judas was going to betray him and had told him to do his work. Had I done the same by letting him into the clinic? I was not downcast but also not ready to forgive. Instead I looked over his shoulder at a picture on the wall.

The picture was a photograph of what looked like a family group in front of a house. Not a grand house, not people of any particular standing, but many had their arms linked. Why were they here, in this place? My sister had organised a photograph of our family in a similar pose last summer, just days before my return to Brussels, from Norfolk, and war being declared. My mother had sat on a chair as the centrepiece and we had shuffled up close together to block the space where my father, may he rest in peace, ought to have stood at her side.

My mother, in her eighties, had wanted me to stay with her and not return to Belgium, and perhaps I should have listened. My life had been in service to others as governess or nurse when, like most spinster daughters, my place should have been at her side. But in her heart she knew I would not settle; that my duty to the clinic would override my sentimental dues. And in my heart I knew she did not mind. She was well cared for, but I know her fear for me was real. No one had known what was ahead. Belgium was a neutral country so should be safe. Empty words now; what would she make of this? What do I?

Will it be enough that the Germans can prove they are right; they have been wronged? Will the knowledge that they have outwitted this line of resistance be reward enough, or must punishment and example follow? They have shot people for less than this and we are fair game. I am Britannica within their grasp. I try to care about this but I am very tired. In God's hands I will rest.

I received a letter today: my first. It was from Sister Wilkins. She had perpetuated my lie; commenting she was relieved I was all right, and had parcelled up my requests. I could tell she didn't want me to know she was worried about me and so her letter was full of news from the school, nothing major, just the detail that I love, and I immersed myself in it as if by her side on one of our rounds. We were always thorough.

The nurses' training school was well run. My pride and joy. Our nurses were acclaimed throughout Brussels and before this war started our intake had been growing from strength to strength. Student nurses were from many nationalities but my favourites, I have to confess, were the British girls, and of these Marion trumped them all. That's why I chose her to help with the soldiers. She is the "one that got away".

I sagged with relief when I understood one message nestled within Sister Wilkins's penned lines. "Therese has left us and her vision on parting was of Moses safely in the bullrushes. She thanked us for all our assistance." She referred to Therese, the maternity patient Marion had attended and who then asked her to find an adoptive home for her baby; an all too familiar rejection from a victim of rape. So many raped. I no longer understand this world.

I interpreted her message to mean that Marion had eluded capture. Had she taken the baby with her? This must be what Sister Wilkins was telling me. No words could give voice to the delight I felt, and the gratitude that Marion is safe. I wondered if she had received help from our friends at the American legation. The young man she was walking out with would no doubt come to her aid and Mr. Gibson, the legation secretary, would do all that he could, I was sure. I wept tears of joy.

I don't cry easily. I didn't cry whenever I left home. I rarely do, always too excited or determined about what is ahead. That doesn't mean I don't have feelings I just don't give them much airing. But I cried for quite a long time today, more than was warranted by the news of Marion. I feel so alone.

There was no news of rescue in Sister Wilkins letter. I like to imagine the righteous indignation expressed at my arrest and detainment. Would Mr. Gibson be arraigning the governor general? Would legal representation be made on my behalf? Would funds be raised for my release? All quite fanciful, but thoughts like these help me while away some hours each day. The reality is I am no cause célèbre; I have thwarted the powers of the land in which I live, even if those powers resided against the will of the people. In the eyes of any establishment, German or British I had forged my destiny by my own actions, and it wasn't as if I had been unaware of the potential consequences. Reprisals against civilians were reported almost daily.

My readings bring me comfort. *"Remember that lost time does not return"* works as a prompt to savour and try to fill each moment with fruitful thoughts, and not descend into despair. The irony did not escape me that my companion in words, Thomas a Kempis, was himself a German, though not of our time. My well-thumbed copy of *The Imitation of Christ* has served me throughout my life and, however frenzied or disturbed some days could be, always led my meditations at the end of each day. *"First keep the peace within yourself, then you can also bring peace to others."* A big thought for me now, to help me keep my composure when under pressure from my interrogators. I heard I will be charged with a crime against Germany, and my captors delighted in telling me that I will be tried alongside all the others.

Princess Marie de Croy is now in our number. She, who started the escape line from Mons, has been arrested.

Days pass in solitude but my mind is easier now Marion is safe. With myself as my only concern I can more easily subject myself to the will of my captors. What they desire will be.

Brussels, October 1915

"Do come in, Sister Wilkins," Russell welcomed the nurse into his office.

"Now, you said you would call me Elizabeth."

"Of course, of course, ma'am. Do come in."

Russell showed her to the seat alongside his desk and manoeuvred himself around her and his desk, to the only other chair. His office was small, and the furniture overlarge. To keep it functional most of Russell's records and files were in piles around the edge of the room and his current work was neatly stacked in front of him. The room's saving grace was the almost floor to ceiling window, which gave a view of the embassy's private garden, the lawn's lush green providing a welcome contrast to the grey of the streets in the city. Their meetings had become a regular weekly visit, but this was only the second occasion Elizabeth had come to him. He was expecting Hugh back from London at any time and did not want to be absent for his return. Today Elizabeth had news of her visit to Edith to share. He could see it had been a tonic for her as she was more relaxed than at their last meeting.

"I want to tell you about my visit, but, do you have any news?" Elizabeth launched in after sitting down.

"No, well not really. You go first. Tell me how did the visit come about? How is Edith?"

Elizabeth explained that the relentless requests made by her and Edith had finally caused her captors to acquiesce and they had allowed them an hour together, although heavily chaperoned by guards.

"No time in private? That's not right," Russell queried.

"We largely ignored the guard, and I am sure he would have been bored with our conversation unless he was particularly interested in the running of nurses' training."

"Surely not? Is that what you two ladies talked about?" Russell was making notes on a sheet of paper while he listened to her.

"You know Edith, she never stops working."

"Actually, ma'am, I don't know Edith, just of her, through Marion. She certainly has spirit, that much I have gathered. But how is she?"

Elizabeth, greatly reassured by her time with Edith, reported that she was bearing up well. Most of their conversation had been about the management of the clinic, the nurses' training and the move to their new premises, a project that had largely been handled by Edith. Pages of Elizabeth's notebook, which she waved at him, had been filled by the end of the hour, with Edith's instructions and directions.

"I had taken in some account books, but they wouldn't let me have them when I was with her and I can't hold figures in my head very well so I became a bit muddled on the books."

"But did she tell you about life in the prison? How is she managing?"

"She has a room to herself, with little in it, it would seem, but at least she has solitude which she enjoys. Only a very tiny, high window", Elizabeth nodded her head towards the large expanse of glass to their side, "she can't see out."

"I don't think I could cope with the solitude," Russell reflected. "I'd need the distraction of other folks. It would bring me down to be on my own, and to miss daylight." *Awful.* Russell stood and walked to the window and looked up at the sky, before turning back to Elizabeth.

"I think I'm similar to you, Russell, but Edith has always been one for her own company. When she retired to her room in the evenings, she was happy to close her door on the world."

Elizabeth continued to tell him of her visit. Edith was allowed exercise in a small yard for half an hour each day, during which she had to wear a linen sack with slits in for her eyes. It made her stumble, but Edith had described her guards as kindly towards her. She said Edith looked pale and had lost weight, but was seemingly quite at ease with her situation.

"To see her made me feel much better," Elizabeth said. "She was delighted to hear that Marion was safely away. We didn't mention her name, of course: she called her M. The thought of Marion being captured had been the greatest of burdens on her. She seems quite resigned to whatever punishment may come her way. If that means prison until the end of the war, then so be it. She doesn't expect a fuss to be made."

"Well, that's just as well, because the only news I have is that the British don't seem inclined to interfere on her behalf."

"Really?" Elizabeth jumped to her feet. "What have you heard?"

"Nothing really, nothing official, ma'am." Russell walked around his desk and held the back of her chair to encourage her to sit down again. "Only a telex from Hugh, Mr. Gibson. The government minister in England he spoke to said, 'Edith knowingly broke the law and must face the consequences.' There was nothing they could do."

"There is plenty they could do." Elizabeth had resumed her seat, but was perched on the edge of it.

"I'm sure there is, but let's say there doesn't seem anything they are prepared to do. Hugh said he would look into it some more when he returns." *Can't be soon enough.* Russell was relying on Hugh to take action and relieve him from the anxiety that never left him. "We're expecting him today."

"I do so miss Edith." Elizabeth's shoulders sagged and she slumped down into the chair.

"Yes, Marion told me how closely you all worked together. You must be so proud of your work at the clinic. You've all helped so many people since this war began: refugees, injured women, wounded men. You've provided an oasis of care when people thought that kindness had left the world."

"We just did what needed to be done." Elizabeth blushed and pulled herself upright in the chair." And that's all Edith and Marion did with the soldiers. That can't be a crime."

"Law in times of war is a different kettle of fish to peacetime. The vanquishers write it to suit their ends. It has been the same all through history."

"Didn't Marion tell me this was your area of study, lawmakers of the past?"

Russell explained that this was one aspect of his research and the topic that had first brought him to Belgium. He had the opportunity to study the medieval manuscripts held at Leuven University just weeks before the building was destroyed. Tears pricked his eyes as he remembered he was probably the last person to touch the documents before the Germans torched the building. *Animals.* In his mind such vandalism was an unforgiveable act. He coughed to cover his emotion, and with the mention of Leuven, Elizabeth opened her handbag and took out an envelope.

"That reminds me, I have a letter here for Marion from Sister Therese. I wonder if I should give it to you? You might have more chance of getting it to her."

"I gave Marion a note from Therese before she left Brussels with Mr. Gibson. It was Therese's letter that convinced her to take Alain with her."

"Well, this is another. She left it with me before she went back to the convent. But actually when I think of her instructions she was quite clear that I had to give it to Marion myself. When I told her that might not be for years, she said that when we next met it would be exactly the right time."

"Then you must keep it for her, ma'am. Therese had an uncanny way of being right about so much."

"Yes, she's a remarkable woman. When you think of what happened to her, such a vicious attack, even worse somehow on a nun, and yet she was always radiant."

"And so wise. She put me straight on a few things, I can tell you."

"Can I show you another letter?" Elizabeth asked as she placed the envelope back in her handbag and pulled out a sheet of paper, which she unfolded. "If you wouldn't mind reading this through? It's more of a petition really. All of us at the clinic will sign and we want to give it to the governor general. We have to feel we are doing something to support Edith."

"Of course. I would be delighted to read it. *A petition?* And I am sure no efforts will be wasted." *It's probably futile.* Russell took the piece of paper and swivelled his chair towards the light and started to read.

The letter was addressed to Baron von Bissing, the German governor general in Belgium. Russell was studying it when Hugh walked in. He was immediately apologetic for interrupting them but Russell jumped to his feet and pumped his hand in greeting. Quick introductions were made, with a promise from Hugh to catch up with Russell as soon as his debrief with Whitlock was over. *Make it quick.* Russell returned to the letter, which was written in heavy prose and obsequious terms but he thought it was a waste of time to suggest changes.

"I'm told it reads better in German," Elizabeth explained. "This was translated back into English for us to keep as our own record."

She sounded very proud and Russell wanted to inflict no doubt in her mind about the worthiness of her efforts to secure Edith's release, so he nodded and smiled.

"Each of the nurses will sign their names. He must pay attention to such a request. We will put the Red Cross stamp on the letter too."

"I am sure he will be in no doubt as to the sincerity behind the words and your request for her release." Russell was impressed with his own diplomacy. "No harm can come from sending it. And hopefully it will trigger something good," he added as he handed the letter back to Elizabeth and watched her as she put it away in her handbag. "And as you say, you are at least doing something." *Not like the rest of us.* "I'll inform Mr. Whitlock, but he has not been in the best of health recently. Hugh will take over now I am sure." *He must.*

He stood up and guided Elizabeth to the door and then walked with her along the corridor to the reception area.

"I'll be in touch with you before next week if there is further news," he said, and Elizabeth agreed to do the same.

They made their farewells and Russell returned to his office but found it impossible to settle at his work. *Come on Hugh.* He was relieved and excited by Hugh's arrival and waited impatiently for him to return.

"Good to see you, young fella," Hugh said as he walked back into Russell's office, two hours later. "It's good to be back."

"It's seemed a long time," Russell said as he leant back in his chair and looked up at him. *Forever.* Hugh perched on the corner of his desk.

"Yes, I even had time to get some tailoring done whilst I was in London." Russell suddenly became aware of his own crumpled look against Hugh's pressed edges. "It felt more like a secondment than a visit. Page and Hoover had me working on all sorts of things. I don't think those two get along. Ambassador Page favours the British view too much for Hoover's liking. I heard some ructions between them."

"And I'd heard you were delayed sorting some things out for the Belgian royals." Russell performed a mock bow, but was constrained by the desk and his seat.

"Cover story, 'old boy', as those Brits would say." Hugh tapped the side of his nose and laughed. "Page wanted me to stay on over there but Whitlock wouldn't hear of it. Quite tried his patience the time I was away."

Tell me something I don't know.

"He gave me short shrift at times this morning."

"He hasn't been in the best of health and has been cranky with everyone. Don't think it's just you. I've been on the wrong side of him several times."

"Always best to just keep your head down."

"Yes, but I couldn't always. I had to keep reminding him of Nurse Cavell. He's done next to nothing, I've been so frustrated." *Don't rant.* Russell stood up and moved to the window. "Marion will be on my back about this. I'm so pleased you're back here. Perhaps now you can rattle some cages." *And quick.*

"Even the Brits aren't prepared to do that," Hugh said as he settled himself in the chair recently vacated by Elizabeth. "They've washed their hands of her. At least that's what I picked up in Westminster. Those establishment boys have quite a downer on women. The suffragettes have them really stirred up.

"But surely they …"

Hugh held up his hand to silence Russell.

"The Brits have no interest in seeking favours from the Germans. They are still smarting from their losses at Loos: it was a disaster apparently, and they have no trust in a tête-à-tête with the enemy. Their view is Nurse Cavell knew what risks she was taking and if she faces time in prison, then so be it." Hugh shrugged his shoulders to mimic the words.

"Yes, thank you, I just updated Sister Wilkins on your news."

"Well, I hope you wrapped it up a bit sweeter than that for her."

"I, well, no, I ..." *Damn that was dumb.*

"Never mind. I'll smooth the waters with my diplomatic charm when I meet with her." Hugh adjusted his tie and pulled down his jacket that had crumpled slightly.

"You can try," Russell said recovering his poise, "but the truth is no one is doing anything to help Edith, and Elizabeth can see straight through rhetoric. *Even yours.* Marion would be so angry if she knew."

"Ah, yes, Nurse Drake. Quite a gal you have there, young fella, quite a gal."

Hugh adjusted his tie again. *He's preening himself.* For a moment Russell was torn between pursuing his case for Edith and enquiring about Marion. Marion won.

"How is she? Have you seen her? Do you have any letters from her?" *Slow down.* Russell couldn't stem his questions. Hugh laughed.

"Yes I have some letters. I'll find them in my suitcase for you – I've yet to unpack, but no, I haven't seen her. Not since I put her on a train at Marylebone. She's one gutsy lady."

Russell welcomed any opportunity to dwell on Marion, but he was less comfortable hearing Hugh use her name, particularly as Hugh and Marion's hasty departure from Belgium had been an escapade that Russell knew little of and felt separated from. The flutter in his stomach reminded him of the suspicions he had once held of Marion and Hugh. *He hasn't visited her.* Hugh resumed his seat and took his time reliving his journey to London with his two wards: the border checkpoints; the slow Channel crossing with its zigzag route, the train to London. It was clear he had enjoyed Marion's company.

"There was a little awkwardness as we only had one cabin allocated to us on the boat ..."

Russell stood up and butted in.

"I hope you gave all the privacy to Marion and Alain." Russell moved towards Hugh. "She is compromised enough already with that child …"

"Whoa, whoa, fella, let me finish," Hugh said. "I was going to say that I was able to share with a fellow traveller, a journalist actually, so all was fine. And anyway she seemed very comfortable with the baby. He was as good as gold and I heard her telling a couple he was a refugee and she was taking him for adoption. Unnecessary really. I thought she and I passed off as a fine looking couple."

Hugh stood up and turned to face Russell, who was close to him with his fists clenched at his sides.

Hugh laughed.

"Cool down, hothead. I just said it to excite you." Russell threw a mock punch. "She's as good as married to you. You were all she wanted to talk about," Hugh said.

"Me?" *Me!* The smile on Russell's face showed his forgiveness and relief. "What did she say?"

"Oh no, I'm not going to be the messenger boy. You can read her letters. I'll go fetch them. But what's this you say about Brand not doing anything for Nurse Cavell? He's just handed me the file. Looks to me like he has it all covered."

"It just feels too passive. Yes he's made phone calls and written letters. I can't fault him on that, but he's relying on the Germans to keep him informed and they are playing everything very close to their chests. We must be able to do something more than this?"

"I have some thoughts on that already. Sit down."

"Oh good. What?" Russell said as he perched on the window ledge.

Hugh described his plan to arrange for Monsieur Leval and himself to meet with Monsieur Kirschen, the attorney assigned to Edith's defence, and the offer of assistance they would make to help prepare her case. In return he would be asked to keep them informed at every turn. Russell immediately offered to accompany, as note-taker if nothing else, but Hugh said he would not be needed. *At last, some action.* The relief Russell felt with Hugh now on the case was immediate.

Russell was rereading Marion's letter for what seemed like the fiftieth time when Hugh knocked and entered his office. It was Friday evening, the end of the week of Hugh's return and they had seen very little of each other, hence their plans to dine together that evening. Russell smiled but Hugh was in a sombre mood as he sat down.

"It seems you might have been right, Mr. Clark, our dinner must be cancelled. We have things to attend to this evening."

"What do you mean? What's happened?"

"It would appear we are too late to assist with the defence of Nurse Cavell."

"Monsieur 'Kitchen' has it ready does he?" *So why is dinner cancelled?*

"Monsieur Kirschen has no need of it, her case has already been heard. The prisoners were in court, yesterday and today."

Russell was on his feet immediately. *What?*

"Yesterday? Today? That's impossible. We knew nothing about it. We were to be told. We should have been there. How did that happen?"

"Kirschen had been impossible to find until just now, but he did say it was better that we weren't at court and if we had spoken ahead of today his advice would have been to stay away. The Germans are determined to attack the British, and any supporters would have only inflamed them further. That's his view, anyway."

"Do you agree?" Russell was striding up and down the small room.

"Whether I agree or not is irrelevant. What's done is done. It is what might happen next that is my concern."

"Why? What do you mean? What will happen next? Will she go to prison?"

"You are the same as Marion, Russell," Hugh said as he stood up and moved his chair out of his way. "Three questions at a time. Don't rush. Give me time to attend to the first."

"Yes, of course. But she's been tried already, without any of us there. She must feel totally abandoned." *Oh God!* "Marion will never forgive me." Russell flung himself into the chair.

"Well, now is our time to 'rattle some cages' as you put it."

"What can we do? Will they reduce her prison sentence?"

"She hasn't been sentenced yet. That decision is still to come, and when it is made then we can appeal. But I want to make sure we are the first to hear, so we have some calls to make this evening."

"Before the weekend? It's that urgent then?" Russell sat up straight.

"Yes it is, my friend. The sentence the prosecutors asked for is the death penalty. We have much to do."

"The what? Did you say death penalty?" Russell stood up but was immediately drawn into the scene of his nightmare and felt quite light-headed. He steadied himself with a hand on the desk. "Sentenced to death? That's impossible." *Please God, it's impossible.*

"Not sentenced, no. Her death is what the prosecutors have requested. It is for the judges to decide the sentence."

"When, how, what will they decide? When will we know?"

"That is exactly what we need to go and find out. I am assured by Leval that the legal wheels will turn slowly, and no doubt there is a large amount of posturing at play. I am convinced they won't want to enrage public opinion by delivering the death penalty, they wouldn't be that stupid, but I want to be sure we are on top of things."

Events had suddenly moved very quickly and they had been caught off guard. *Just what I feared.*

"Proposing such a punishment", Hugh continued to talk as Russell picked up his jacket and followed him from his office and along the polished wood corridors of the embassy, "will deter any other patriots, and will certainly put the wind up the British government. We'll use the car to go to Kirschen. He said he would be at his office."

"I am sorry to butt in on you Hugh, but Sister Wilkins is here, in reception, in a very agitated state. Can I bring her in?" It was Monday afternoon and Russell guessed his interruption would be unwelcome.

"Why? What's her problem? I have Brand breathing down my neck at the moment. Can it wait until tomorrow?

"Not from what she has told me, but I'd rather you hear it straight from her. It's about Edith and it's not good news."

"There is no news about Nurse Cavell. You know that. We were assured on Friday evening that Monsieur Kirschen will keep us abreast of developments, and I've heard nothing. The court session only finished on Friday and here we are on Monday. No sentencing would have happened in that time and that's the only information we are waiting on."

"I only hope you are right, but let me bring her in. She has asked to speak to you." *Demanded*.

All right, give me five minutes to telephone Leval and Kirschen, just to check, and then I'll see her."

Russell nodded as Hugh reached for the telephone, the newfangled gadget that they were both in awe of but Minister Whitlock abhorred. Russell left the room to fetch Elizabeth.

After their greetings were over and Elizabeth was sitting facing Hugh with Russell beside her, Hugh asked her what news she had.

"The guard at the prison, he's always been kind, always made sure Edith received her Sunday dinners from us. He had overheard that the prisoners had been sentenced and Edith is to be executed at dawn tomorrow. The information reached me half an hour ago and I came straight here." Elizabeth darted anxious looks between the two men. "I didn't know where else to go. What can we do? We mustn't let this happen. Can't you stop them?"

"Well, we don't know this is true yet. I have Monsieur Leval on his way to Kirschen's offices. We have heard nothing, and we have been promised to be kept informed." Hugh said in a practised diplomatic tone.

"And you still think Germans keep promises?" Elizabeth snapped at him, clearly agitated.

"We can only work within the official channels, Sister Wilkins …"

Hugh was interrupted by the ring of the telephone which startled all in the room. From the conversation Russell and Elizabeth listened to it was clear that Monsieur Kirschen could not be located, and that no further news was available from the prison. Hugh asked Monsieur Leval, the caller, to join them at the legation.

"It is most unlikely that a sentencing decision would have been made over the weekend, and let me assure you she will not be sentenced to death; incarceration will be a sufficient deterrent. The Germans have made their point and need go no further," Hugh announced with certainty.

"I do not share your confidence, Mr. Gibson." Elizabeth stood up to face him, and Russell rose too. "I am most afraid for Edith. Will you please enquire further?" Elizabeth drew herself up to her full height. "Now is not the hour to rely on gentlemen's agreements, but to find the facts."

"It was no gentleman's handshake on Friday, let me assure you." Hugh also stood. "We demanded to be kept informed of all developments immediately they happened. They know they will have us to answer to if they act prematurely."

"With all due respect, Mr. Gibson, you being angry if you

hear they have executed Edith prematurely will be too late for her. She needs our support now."

She's right. "What can we do, Hugh?" Russell agitated.

"Precious time is passing," Sister Wilkins added.

"We must do something," Russell insisted and was rewarded by a glare from Hugh.

"Will you excuse us a moment, Sister Wilkins? Mr. Clark and I will endeavour to find some answers from the prison. When we know the true situation, then we can act. Russell, please take Sister Wilkins to your office. It is more private for her there than the reception hall; then please return."

Half an hour passed before they rejoined her.

"They all say the same, ma'am," Hugh told her. "Whoever we speak to says the same. I have been repeatedly assured that no sentence has as yet been pronounced. I hope this offers you some reassurance, Sister Wilkins."

Elizabeth who had been standing by the window, turned as they entered, but appeared to take no consolation from Hugh's announcement.

"I still fear the worst for Edith. I have no trust in the word of Germans."

"These are not minor matters, ma'am. The Germans cannot dispense their own form of justice without due process being followed," Russell said in an effort to reassure her. "Even if, or when, such a sentence is pronounced there would be an appeals process, wouldn't there, Hugh, so time is on our side."

"Yes, of course there would. Now, ma'am, I suggest you return to the clinic and we will be in contact as soon as we hear anything through the official channels. There is nothing more to be done now." Hugh moved to the door, which he opened, walked through and waited for Sister Wilkins and Russell to follow. He led them along the corridor and back towards reception. Hugh was interrupted from bidding her farewell by an aide, approaching him with a lady hot on his heels. She was known to Sister Wilkins and they greeted each other. Elizabeth made the introductions.

"Mr. Gibson, Mr. Clark, this is Mrs. Stirling Gahan, Reverend Gahan's wife. He is the pastor at the English church Edith and I attend."

"I am so pleased to find you all here. Has your intervention been accepted? Perhaps I can take my husband the news?" Mrs. Gahan said.

"Excuse me, what intervention is that. ma'am?" Hugh asked.

"To secure a reprieve for Edith. To save her life."

"We have just been discussing that matter, but it is a little premature for interventions. We are still waiting to be notified when her sentence will be pronounced. We anticipate hearing something over the next few days," Hugh said and began moving both ladies towards the entrance door.

"But it has been pronounced, it has. She is to die. She is to die tomorrow," Mrs. Gahan said. "Oh Elizabeth, I am so sorry. I thought as you were here you knew."

Mrs. Gahan's apology had been prompted by a gasp from Elizabeth. Russell looked at Elizabeth and saw the colour drain out of her face. He quickly stepped forward to catch her before she slipped into his arms in a faint. Hugh helped them both to a chair and Mrs. Gahan waved her hands in front of Elizabeth's face to give her air. Russell spoke for Elizabeth.

"Yes, Sister Wilkins brought us the same news, but we have been unable to verify it. We are waiting to hear through the official channels."

"But my husband has been called to the prison this evening to deliver the sacrament and the last rites. How much more 'official' do you need. She will be shot tomorrow."

Another gasp from Elizabeth showed that she had heard

these words, and tears fell down her face. Russell held onto her, for himself as much as for her.

"Excuse me, ladies," Hugh said as he bowed. "Join me as soon as you can, Russell," he called and turned to run up the stairs that swept around the reception to the first floor. Russell heard him knocking on the minister's door and the door open and close behind him.

Russell was having little success in calming the women so, at Elizabeth's encouragement and on the arrival of Monsieur Leval he extricated himself, and took Monsieur Leval to find and join Hugh. He was back in his office completing a letter to the German authorities for Minister Whitlock to sign.

"We didn't agree on the words," Hugh said. "Brand will only go so far as to ask them to take pity on her. I have a lot more that I want to say, but he has to sign it. We'll go in person to make our points when we deliver the formal plea for clemency to von Lancken. This will be a long night."

"What can we do for Elizabeth? She is devastated," Russell asked.

"Yes, I'm sure she is." Hugh wiped his hand across his eyes and then looked back at Russell. "They can't come with us. Suggest to Mrs. Gahan she returns to the clinic with Sister Wilkins, and tell her I would like to speak with her husband this evening once he has seen Nurse Cavell, to hear how she is. Perhaps he would also inform Edith we are working on her behalf and will be through the night. See what you can arrange Russell, while Monsieur Leval and I complete the appropriate documentation. The Germans have forms for everything."

An hour later with paperwork intact, Hugh, Monsieur Leval, and Russell headed out in the embassy car to find the Spanish minister, Villobar, the only other neutral voice in town with any weight. Villobar was dining with Baron Lambert but when told of the reason for the interruption agreed at once to accompany them to find Baron von Lancken and plead for Edith's life, or at least a delay until her case could be reconsidered. Hugh was profusely apologetic at Mr. Whitlock's absence, but the poor man really was unwell. Due to the late hour von Lancken and his staff were no longer at their offices, and messengers were sent to have them return. *Oh God please.* Russell prayed that they would.

Edith's Journal, St Gilles Prison, Brussels, October 1915

"Will you please send me my blue coat and skirt, white muslin blouse, grey gloves and fur stole."

I want to look my best for the formalities in the courtroom: neither crumpled nor austere. "Sunday best" is what my mother would say. What would I say if I could write to her? Thank her for the life she led and for the life she gave to me. My father was a sombre man, and sober too. Not an easy husband, his rule was firm. As rector of Swardeston he had to have a certain formality, but he was kind to the poor as were we, my brother and sisters. We had family prayers at eight o'clock every morning and we could not sit down to our own Sunday dinner until we had fed a poor and needy family or two in the village. It was quite a ritual, but they liked the food. At least they had theirs hot, ours was often cold by the time we faced each other across the dining room table. I can smell the furniture polish now. I still begin each day with prayer and thoughts of others. It is second nature now to put the needs of others first.

… So that was my trial, the first day.

Why didn't I wear my nurse's uniform? Because I wanted them to see me: the person who committed the crime, the woman who stood against them. I lay my clothes carefully over the back of the chair I have in my cell, ready to wear again. As a nurse I have no opinion and no choice as to the patients I tend. My actions are uniform as well as my dress when I don my apron and gown in service to the humanitarian vows of the Corps. But today I stood before them as an individual and sought no sympathy, no softness in their stance towards me. I wanted them to direct their bile towards me, the imperial enemy, and hopefully find more favour towards the Belgians who surely they need trample no further into the ground.

My day in court and all thirty-five of us shared it.

One after another the same charges were made and questions asked. The defence knew none of us, apart from Princess Marie de Croy whose own eloquence was matched by the legal virtuoso who accompanied her. She blamed the whole escapade on her brother's influence, whose will she was not in a position to resist, and he was – who knows where? London in fact, was the joyous news that passed through our ranks in mumbled moments. Safe.

After so many weeks in solitude I was disorientated to be transported with the others to the Belgian National Palace for the trial. It was a grand room with galleries of seats, but no Belgian governance was at home, ousted by the invaders the year before and in their place puppet German judges. Beyond my fellow conspirators I saw no faces I recognised in the room. All were foe.

The procedures were long and mostly in German; I understood very little. The words washed over me like a sermon that had lost its thread until that jolt of awakening when the last hymn is announced: in this case when a question was translated and directed into our midst. We each had an advocate for our defence, but they offered little and I held my own counsel and said nothing. What was there to say? "I only wanted to save lives?" But this was war, a battlefield of sorts. Our motives were unwelcome and no idealism can survive against such an onslaught of twisted hatred. Within my defence would be the unspoken attack, "... so that they could fight against you". We were cornered and guilty and they had proof and God on their side. At least this is what their military belt buckles told us, with *Gott mit uns* inscribed.

I hope He isn't on their side. I always believed God followed conscience, or does conscience follow Him? Either way, my conscience is clean, but laws had been broken. We would be punished: I had freedoms to lose. The lavish courtroom pantomime had to have a finale, a closing act that justified the pomp and fuss and told the world who was in charge. It is their will that will be done.

Day two in court was different. The prosecutor talked and talked. There was little to understand because he spoke in German and what was translated made no real sense. He spoke to the judges anyway, not to us. Our part was walk-on only today. The story he told involved us all at different times. He would come and point at one of us from time to time during his speech. A different room today and it was hot and stuffy. When the judges left for lunch the guards kept us in our seats and we had to make quite a fuss to be brought some water. Two of the women fainted. Real or not, it helped our cause and food arrived.

I have never had a premonition, but a feeling of doom began to penetrate the general despair that had been with me for some days. Even so I was still shocked when towards the end of the day the call for the death penalty for eight of the thirty-five was translated into French. Mine was the second name on the list. They mispronounced it: Cavell should rhyme with travel, but they were not to know. This was the fanfare for the finale; this show demanded a brutal climax. The reprieve would come in the last act, it always did, but I was in sombre mood.

I return my clothes to the chair, positioned as if I was still wearing them, pencil thin. I look at them as an observer might look in on my life, in that surreal way of separation. This is happening, it is real, but not to me, surely not to me: it could not be my flesh and blood that is at risk. And for what? For doing what any decent citizen would do: helping another in duress. The message drummed into me from my father's pulpit each week. But this fight was against human nature.

I do not understand the ways of people. Women pout and men posture. Women subordinate and men want to be lords of their domains, however humble that territory might be. Women defuse while men defend and stand side by side in shows of strength to intimidate all challengers. I would rather be a woman, living without the ever-present threats that keep men on their guard: will another hurt me, or mine, or take from us? I would not want to take up arms and fight. I have no man to fight for me either, no husband, though Eddy will weep when news of my incarceration reaches him. Our family will bring him support and solace.

Thoughts of Eddy lift my mood. My cousin, a favourite of mine, is the nearest I came to a lover. We could have been companions for life, but his nerves were bad. He stayed farming close to home, but we think of each other and have always corresponded. A pity our letters can no longer get through. I think of our childhood games when life was fresh and innocent and before we had to measure up against the adult world and he found himself unequal to it. I write with him in mind in the front page of my copy of *Imitation to Christ*. It is a notation of events:

Arrested: 5 August 1915
Brussels Prison St Gilles: 7 August 1915
Court martialled: 7 Oct 1915
" " 8 " "
Condemned to death 8 Oct in the Salle des deputes. The prosecutor's words.

More will follow, so I leave space.

The prosecutor demanded the death penalty for a few and imprisonment for the remainder. Breaking this chain of resistance is not going to satisfy them; they want to make an example of us. The sentences will need to be long to deter the spirit of determinism that simmers in the city, and the death penalties will no doubt be commuted to the longest of these. I can't believe they will kill us, not with the world watching. Boredom, inactivity, and incarceration look to be the curse of my future years, with poor diet, cold, and damp to add to the duress. I try to resign myself to this fate, but it sits heavily with me. Homesickness heaves within me.

I write letters that will be sent after the weekend. For once there is a lot to tell as I describe the events of the last two days, and make several requests to prepare my personal affairs, the clinic, and school for my prolonged absence. I ask for my dog Jack to remain at the clinic.

It has taken ten weeks from my arrest to be brought to court. I wonder how many weeks will pass before the prosecutor's demands are reviewed and we will be sentenced, or perhaps we will all remain here in obscurity. Until I know the details hope still holds on, but by a perilously thin thread.

Little Missenden, October 1915

Marion felt quite strange. Her days had established themselves into something of a routine, but she had the feeling that life was on hold. And she was tense, waiting, but for what? Her mother remained keen for Alain's departure, but they had quickly reached a stalemate. Apart from the now weekly ritual of her mother asking if Alain would be leaving them that week and Marion's standard reply that he would not, the subject between them was avoided. Her mother's disapproval required no words; she conveyed it in every muscle of her face. Marion frequently escaped to the nursery where Evelyn, on one of her rare visits, found her cuddling Alain. She erupted.

"What do you think you are doing?" Evelyn shouted.

"What do you mean, what am I doing? You can see what I am doing." Marion was sitting in a chair holding Alain. He had been fed and changed and his eyelids were looking heavy. One hand clutched her thumb.

"Don't be so obtuse. I don't mean this precise minute; I mean the totality of what you are doing: unmarried, and bringing a baby into the house. The gossip is all over the parish, just as Mother said it would be. You are ruined. No one will marry you now. I only hope my reputation is not sullied by your antics." Evelyn flounced around the nursery, picking things up to examine them before putting them down and moving her attention on.

"Antics? I thought an act of Christian kindness would bear better witness than that."

"Christian kindness, my foot. You are up to something, that I do know. The only thing I don't know is what, but Christian kindness it isn't. You are on edge, I'd even say jumpy, it's as if you're expecting something to happen. Is the father coming for you, is that what you're waiting for? You are making Mother ill with all this. Her headaches have been terrible."

"Poor Mother."

"You can't even say that with kindness."

"Well really, she does make an awful fuss." Marion was losing her patience with Evelyn and their querulous exchange was disturbing Alain. She tried to keep her own tone calm.

"A fuss?" Evelyn bit back. "Do you have any idea what you have done to her? She has lost her standing …"

"You mean her morally superior position in life," Marion interrupted. *Nasty.*

"Don't be cruel. To be held in high esteem means everything to her, and should mean more to you."

She's right, she's right.

"How can she, or Father too for that matter, hold the moral compass for the parish when one of their daughters is a fallen woman."

"A fallen woman? I'm not a fallen woman. For the umpteenth time, Alain is not my child."

"You say that, but the way you act he might just as well be. Why is he still here? He should be in an orphanage by now. You've been home for months and have done nothing about him leaving."

I know, I know. "Actually I have, quite a bit if you must know."

"Of course we 'must know'. Anything would give some respite to Mother. You are so stubborn with her."

"As she is with me." *Stop it Marion.*

"Yes, you make it bad for each other but, come on Marion, give a little towards her." Evelyn sat down on the other chair and faced Marion. "I learnt to give in to her years ago." Evelyn softened to a pleading tone. "It makes for a much more pleasant life, for all of us."

Yes, yes, I know.

"So tell me what arrangements have you made?"

"None yet but ...", Marion raised her hand to stop Evelyn interrupting, "I have found the name of a couple of organisations who might be able to help me. I'll need to make appointments to visit them."

"Barnados will take him."

"Barnados are always advertising for money. I see their adverts in *The Times*. They say the war is seriously affecting their income. I don't like the sound of that. But there is plenty of time. He is too little to be away from me yet."

Marion looked down at Alain's face and then over to Evelyn.

"I am all he knows, Evelyn. I delivered him and I have looked after him since then. They look so vulnerable when they are so little, don't they?"

Evelyn rose and walked over to the cot that held Anthony. He was sleeping through the raised voices.

"I never really took to mine. I felt wretched throughout my time of carrying him."

"Was it a difficult confinement?"

"Of course it was difficult. I had just lost Charles," Evelyn snapped at her. For once Marion did not bite back.

"I'm sorry. Losing Charles must have been very hard. You had hardly started your life together. He was a fine man." *That's better.* Marion smiled at Evelyn when she returned to sit near her again and she listened while Evelyn described her life with Charles, full of parties and dances and freedoms she had not enjoyed before. They both preferred not to have children immediately, they were having too much fun, so they had been disappointed by news of her pregnancy, but then life was dashed by the war anyway.

"Look at me now: no husband, no parties, all invitations have stopped since you arrived home, living with my parents and this ...", Evelyn looked across to Anthony, "this responsibility. I can't think why you want to tie yourself up with one."

"I ..." *Keep quiet Marion.* For a moment Marion imagined herself confiding in Evelyn, but too many years of sisterly back-stabbing held her back. "I can't really say."

"What happened to you over there? You were always so definite about what you were and weren't going to do and I remember babies were high up on your list of things to avoid. Now look at you."

Does she really want to know? Evelyn seemed genuinely interested in her for the first time since her return and Marion had to work hard to combat the desire to spill the beans and tell her sister all that had happened in Brussels. *I want to talk about Russell.* When Evelyn turned on her charm, she could be difficult to resist.

"I really can't say." *Not too much.* "But I did promise his mother I would look after Alain, and I am not going back on my word. Not for my mother or my reputation."

"Be it on your head," Evelyn said, pulling back. "But the longer you keep him, the harder relinquishing him will be for you. They actually pay sparse attention to anyone when they are little, so Mother says. He won't mind where he is, or with whom. Nanny does a fine job for me."

"Is that why you spend so little time with Anthony?" Marion had obviously touched a nerve. Evelyn bristled at this.

"Are you implying I ignore my child?"

You do.

Evelyn stood and walked over to the cot. "He is well looked after. Nanny manages much better than I would at this age.

Alain would be better off if you meddled less. They need a routine."

At that moment Alain moved, stretched his arms and sought out Marion's hand. He gripped her finger and took it to his mouth.

"Look, he knows I am here."

"He wants food, that's all. I cannot believe you are being sentimental over a baby, you of all people. Don't let Mother see you, it really is very common behaviour."

Luckily Nanny chose that moment to return to the nursery and Evelyn departed before Marion's reaction to her put-down could be voiced.

"Nice to see Mrs. Huxworth in the nursery," Nanny said.

For a moment Marion was confused as she never thought of and rarely heard her sister's married name. *Mrs. Clark, that was how she wanted to be called, Mrs. Russell Clark. Would that ever happen?*

"Yes it was." *Sort of.* "She was just passing through to lecture me on the rights and wrongs of my behaviour." *And there weren't many rights.* "Excuse me, Nanny, it is entirely inappropriate for me to criticise my sister, but we are quite opposite in our thinking."

"Yes, you are different, in your looks too, with her so blonde and you so brown. Both fine looking though, that I will say, as will all of my brothers."

Marion kissed Alain to cover her embarrassment. She stood and moved towards his cot to lie him down.

"But don't you worry so over Alain; babies and children are resilient. They make the best of where they are and what's available to them."

"Don't you start, please. That's exactly what Evelyn was saying: that Alain would adapt well without me. The problem is, I am not so sure I would manage without him." *That's the truth.* Marion tucked his blanket over him.

"You could go abroad again. The newspapers are full of wanting volunteers. You shouldn't be stuck here with a bairn. He's a happy soul; he'll be fine wherever he goes. You'll soon forget about Alain when you are nursing again. And them gossipmongers will be hushed. You have ruffled some feathers, you know. The Proper Way is not to be messed with."

"I've always thought myself something of a rebel against social convention."

"Are you a suffragette then, miss? They're the rebels, they say."

"They've been quiet recently. I believe they pledged to behave themselves while the men were away fighting. Quite laudable considering the trouble they have caused. No, not a suffragette, but I would say I'm a suffragist. I think all able-minded people should have a say in the affairs of the country and should have the means to vote, regardless of their wealth or sex. Naïve I know, but worth the dream."

"That's if there will be anything left of the country. There were fires in London again last night. All over the papers it was, and Scarborough bombed too."

"Yes, I saw. I was scouring the papers for news from Brussels, but all I found was an appeal for money to support the Belgian relief fund."

Marion had confided in Nanny that her matron had been arrested by the Germans, but had not furnished her with the reasons why. It helped Marion to have someone to share her anxiety with. There were no words that could be said to make her feel less anxious, but her exchanges with Nanny released some tension. Two of Nanny's brothers were out in France, she had told Marion. She was used to worry. Many of Marion's cousins and family friends were over there too, but it was the need for news of Edith that gripped her the most.

She needed to know Edith had been released and was safe. *That's what I'm waiting for.* Everything was in abeyance until this happened; only then would her conscience be relieved of guilt: *I ran away.* She had thought of her own safety and abandoned Edith. She could not imagine how she would ever face her again. What could she possibly say after such a cowardly act? The only thing that appeased her conscience was when she looked at Alain. He was safe because of her. Perversely, she actually welcomed the social discomfort that her return had created and the damage to her reputation. It was right that she should suffer and not come through this unscathed. Edith should not be alone in her punishment. Marion also had to bear her separation from Russell, and most days this felt the hardest burden of all. *Alain will stay with me until Edith is free.* She told herself this was her penance, but when candid she knew it was because of the comfort she received from his presence. Marion remained in the nursery until it was time for her to dress for dinner, a formality her mother still insisted upon, war or no war.

Marion stood in the doorway of the drawing room. Evelyn was sitting next to her mother, and her father was resting his arm on the mantel of the fireplace; the unusually mild weather meant there was no need for a fire. The curtains over the French doors to the garden were drawn closed and side lamps lit the room. Marion's mother looked beautiful and poised. Life had turned out well for her, better than she ever expected, but then society always opens its doors to the beautiful. Despite her looks she captivated Bernard with her riding seat, or so the story went. She and Evelyn were listening to her father report on a visit he had made that day. They had not noticed her.

Marrying one of the Drake brothers was a coup for her mother, a social entrée, but not to a luxurious life. Marion's Papa had few means of his own. He once confessed to her that he was not a great catch, with his expensive habit of hunting and little ambition beyond the next ride out. Uncle William saved him with the living here, and it had worked out fine for them. It had all gone better when he found a good source of sermons to buy, their family secret.

But whatever he might lack spiritually he made up for with his philosophy of common decency towards others. "Do unto others what you would have them do to you" was what he taught her and a principle, he repeatedly now said, that was sadly lacking among the European powers at play through war.

Her father saw her and smiled. He looked well, still trim. His pose next to the fireplace with his arm on the mantel suited him. She and he were the same height: five foot seven at the last measure. Marion smiled back, walked in and sat down, but let their conversation wash over her.

Her father was a kind man and they as a family were lucky that Uncle William liked him so much. Her uncle had been very generous towards them. Evelyn's and Beatrice's husbands were found on the back of his introductions. What plans had she ruined, she wondered?

Marion's mother's voice was querulous and it cut across her thoughts.

"We have been overlooked by your brother, and it is not the first time," her mother directed to her husband. "They hosted a dinner party last weekend too. We would normally have been at the table. You must talk to William, Bernard. It is most unhelpful. We wouldn't include Marion of course, that I do understand for the time being, but *we* should be there. If we are not at their table, we will all become social pariahs."

Evelyn patted her arm in sympathy. Marion sat still in her wing back chair in the hope that it might shelter her from an onslaught if one was to be directed at her.

"I will raise the topic with William when I next see him, but I am sure you are reading something into nothing. He was asking after Marion just the other day."

"You didn't mention that to me. What? What was he asking? Her circumstances are obviously of concern to him. I keep telling you that baby looks bad for all of us. People are talking."

"People always talk. One would hope with a real fight on our hands people would forget such pettiness, but in fact I think it makes them worse."

"Not everyone has your kindness, Papa," Evelyn said.

"It would seem", Marion interjected, "that there is a code for kindness that I have misunderstood. Offering a start in life to an orphan child appears to be beyond the bounds of Christian compassion in these quarters."

"Don't be ridiculous," her mother retorted. "It is you who have traversed beyond the bounds of what is reasonable, creating this consternation for all of us. If you had passed the child on immediately the situation could have been more easily salvaged, but it is apparent you now have an emotional attachment to the child which is entirely inappropriate." Marion glared at Evelyn, feeling betrayed. "You hang on to him through sentimentality alone. You've lost any sound judgement you might once have had."

"Ah, dinner is called. Shall we go through?" Evelyn said as she rose. For once, Evelyn saved, rather than stirred the moment, perhaps chastened by the look Marion had given her.

Bernard managed a wink to Marion as they walked through to the dining room, always the coldest room in the house with its north facing window, and gloomy with its dark mahogany furniture, mostly oversized cast-offs from the big house. Marion braced herself for another broadside from her mother, but it was not forthcoming. She did seem genuinely upset and Marion felt a hint of remorse. *Too high-handed again.* Once settled at the table, and with their first course served, she offered an olive branch.

"I have received a reply from an organisation in London who are willing to talk to me about Alain and his placement.

They found my request unusual and did say these were difficult times. Apparently most babies go to the foundling hospitals and then on to orphanages, but they did sometimes hear of families who want to take in a baby."

"Hrrumph," was the only sound emitted from her mother, as if she trusted herself to say no more.

"He is such a sunny child," her father volunteered, "he will bring happiness to any household, I am sure."

"But not this one?" Marion asked.

"Indeed not," her mother retorted. "I do not understand why you don't just hand him in to the church orphanage. They are equipped for such circumstances. They can look after him."

"Because I promised his mother that would not happen."

"She obviously had no appreciation of what she was asking from you. Matters are not handled in this way in our society. Who does she think will want to take on an extra mouth to feed? And it is not as if you owe this woman anything."

"My word," Marion said, "I gave her my word." Marion knew just how much she owed Therese, her freedom, though this was not a story she was ready to tell her family. "And some more good news for you is that I shall be progressing my application to join the volunteer auxiliaries as a nurse. It will be a wonderful way to continue my training and support the war effort." *And will remove me from the social battleground here.*

"You will do no such thing," her mother replied. "You are far too headstrong, always have been. I gave in too easily to you before. This time you will follow my instruction every step of the way. Despite your antics I still intend to have you settled."

Marion opened her mouth to protest, but her father raised his hand and out of respect for him she kept silent.

"We will have plenty of time to discuss futures once the little fellow is settled. Let's leave it there for now," and he moved the conversation on to discuss the harvest supper due in two weeks' time, announcing that would be a good time for them to be seen *en famille* in the parish.

By the time Marion looked in on Alain at the end of the evening she was exhausted. Dinner conversation had been a minefield of topics to avoid, *don't upset Mother*, and the effort to hold back her rebuttal to her mother's plans for her future had sapped her too. She needed news of Edith's release and then she could let Alain go to a family who would nurture him in the way Therese had asked. Marion stroked the side of Alain's face as he slept; her mother was right about one thing: she loved him. How could she ever give him up?

Edith's Journal, St Gilles Prison, Brussels, October 1915

I have been sitting for a long time and haven't moved. Or has it just been minutes? I cannot tell. My brain is unable to transmit messages for my muscles to move. I cannot recall how I returned to my cell. I remember very little after the screams and gasps that followed each announcement. I have been sentenced, we all have. Already? So quick.

They gathered us all in a room at three o'clock. There were no chairs so we stood shuffling in a semi-circle. No one spoke. There was some good news. The first eight prisoners named were acquitted. Gasps of relief were released into the room. Perhaps this would be over sooner than we thought? But the sweetness was short-lived.

Those who faced minor charges were next and more gasps and tears followed the announcement of the time they were to face in hard labour: the range from two to eight years seemed arbitrary. I found it impossible to breathe and my short breaths came faster and faster as I desperately tried to inhale. I didn't know which person belonged to which sentence until each head bowed with the weight of their news as each prison term was announced.

I watched Princess Marie de Croy as she received her sentence of ten years' hard labour. She was as frail as a sparrow now, and had suffered ill health during her imprisonment. Her legs gave way and she sank to the floor. How could she survive? But I had begun to take heart. The prosecution's request for the death penalty had been denied. Perhaps there was hope and after all prison would be more arduous and less sedentary than I thought: the term hard labour after all did not convey idle incarceration.

Herman Capaiu, the man who brought the first two wounded British soldiers to me, and three others bowed their heads in turn: fifteen years of hard labour each.

I hadn't liked the rush to resolution. The momentum felt unstoppable, no time for intermediaries to apply the brakes. The judges must have worked over the weekend. Why? Why couldn't our fortunes wait another month or more? They could broadcast our demise at any time to stop others from doing the same; our capture would make most think twice. Would it have stopped me? I'm glad I won't be tested to find out. To put oneself at risk when the chances of exposure are high and the punishments harsh, will most likely intimidate even the most hardened activist.

There were five of us left with our heads still held high, but not for long. A loud cry filled the room, and someone screamed. I do not think it was me. We were all to die. Philippe Baucq, Jeanne de Belleville, Louis Severin, Louise Thuiliez, and I. I found I was sitting on the ground without realising I had moved. Others collapsed around me. The Germans were unmoved. They have meted out so much death since they stepped onto Belgian soil, what difference were a few more lives to them?

Did I want to place an appeal? The others all answered yes to the question asked after each death sentence was announced. Now the wheels of bureaucracy would start to turn. For me I feared there was little point. The others pleaded with me, but I answered no. Brave? Stubborn? Or stupid? If the Germans are sure of one victim perhaps the others will be spared. I will not beg. They have no clemency in their hearts for the British. It was our forces that stepped into the fray to support the Belgians and the French against them, frustrating their plan to subordinate these nations and reign supreme. They want their turn at world domination: they have seen how rich and powerful it made us.

The others insisted I was a fool and tried to turn my resolve, but I refused. Will my stubbornness be the death of me? My mother used to say it would.

London and Little Missenden, October 1915

The woman, primly dressed in puritanical grey, probably in her mid-forties, smiled at her. Marion had found it difficult to find the Humanistic Services, situated in Tottenham Court Road. They were above a run of shops and she had walked past several times before spotting the dark blue door. Everything in the office had the look of hand-me-downs, cast-offs from a previous era, but the ideas of the organisation were modern and appealing to Marion.

"Call me Maddie" Mrs. Upton had said with a smile which invited Marion's openness. "I can appreciate that you wish to keep him away from the church institutions, but he is rather young to place with most families."

"I had thought a couple might prefer a young baby. To bring up as their own."

"Oh no, rarely as their own, but they can settle into a family and make themselves useful. We are more likely to get him fostered, but if that didn't work out he would be returned to an institution."

"It all seems so harsh." Marion's shoulders sagged.

"It wasn't so long ago that children were apprenticed from the orphanages. Slave labour, I call it. Under their self-righteous banners of doing good no one spoke up for the children. That's why older children are more popular for placements; families don't have to feed them for so long before they can be made to work for them. There is little room for sentiment with orphans. If you can find a family who want to give a home to a child and expect nothing back in return you will have found a rare thing. I am not sure what you expected but in this country we do keep orphans largely off the streets now, and that, my dear is progress."

What had she taken on? Marion began to doubt the wisdom of returning to England with Alain. Brussels now seemed far less problematic. The Ladies Committee who oversaw the clinic and training school had put forward names of several families but none had seemed the right choice for him at the time. This conversation made her regret those hasty rejections.

"I had no idea it would be so difficult. I turned down some opportunities for him in Brussels. I didn't think the households were educated enough, but there was plenty of love in them. How rash I was."

In the cramped confines of Maddie's office, Marion felt more despondent with every turn in the conversation.

"I'm not saying it will be impossible to find a family for him, but you would have to leave all aspects of his placement to us. Once he is signed over you say goodbye and your dealings with him will be finished."

Oh no! Marion grimaced.

"Most women are relieved to be told this." Maddie smiled.

"I can imagine they might be, but I promised his mother I would make sure he was going to be with the right family. I would want to be more involved."

"I can assure you that our scrutiny will be sufficient to ensure a good placement for him," Maddie intoned the company line, but then softened, "but I can appreciate how you feel. It is a big responsibility. I suggest I make some enquiries and that we meet again when I have some possibilities in mind. I will not be able to be specific, but perhaps I can tell you enough to hearten you."

"Thank you, most kind. It really is a lot for me to consider." *That's enough for now, I need to leave.*

"Perhaps, if you don't mind me saying," Maddie paused, and waited until Marion was looking at her, "you might want to consider keeping the child yourself. You do seem to have a strong bond with him, and with the support of your family ..."

"Without the support of my family," Marion corrected her. "For all their Christian talk, they are more concerned with how people will look upon us, than about Alain himself."

"I see, yes very difficult for you, but my advice, for what it is worth ..."

"No please, I welcome your thoughts," Marion said to encourage her.

"My advice would be for you not to be in a rush. I will make my enquiries, but perhaps your family will come around."

"I very much doubt it," Marion said. "And thank you for your time. Your information has been helpful, but I've found it a lot to take in. The situation wasn't quite as I expected. I need to think it all through."

"We will keep in touch." Maddie rose from her seat and walked around the desk to shake her hand. "Alain is lucky to have such a strong advocate in you."

Marion bade her farewell, walked back out onto the street and straight to the nearest Lyons Teashop on Oxford Street. She ordered and then sat stirring her tea waiting for the conversation with Maddie to sink in. The more it did, the more she despaired and berated herself.

I've done it again: rushed into something without thinking it through. Edith told me not to get involved, and leave Alain to the authorities. Russell had tried to say the same. But I didn't listen. My loyalty to Therese and my own stubbornness meant more. And Mother is right about Therese; she knows nothing of what she has asked of me. And how could she? She's a nun and knows nothing of English society. And how soppy have I become about him? Far too close. It's ridiculous to care for him. Evelyn is right. He can't tell who he is with as long as he's fed and warm. His day with Nanny today will be no different than if I was there. I am making a fool of myself. Of course Maddie can find a family for him. As long as they keep him away from the Church and their institutions. I have to trust them, let him go and start my life afresh. But this mustn't be rushed, it must be right.

Marion looked at her watch, drank her tea, attracted the attention of a waitress to pay, and was soon out on the street. She set off to walk to her second interview of the day at the Volunteer recruiting offices. Equipped with her test results, curriculum, and testimonial from Sister Wilkins, she knew she would not be turned away as a nursing assistant. The only difficult questions that she anticipated would be about how far afield she was prepared to travel and when she could start.

By five o'clock Marion was on the train home and let herself relax into the clack and rattle of metal on rails. The soporific rhythm numbed her mind. It was what she needed as the information gathered from conversations throughout the day was jumbled in her head. She felt pulled in different directions and unable to think her way through the conflicting scenarios. Normally she would avoid thinking and follow her first impulse, but this was what had got her into deep water recently and she really did want to give the decisions she faced proper consideration. *Take your time.* If she was honest with herself, she did not know how to do this. *Easier not to think.* Instead she let her mind wander as the countryside rushed past the window of the carriage.

"We plough the fields and scatter, the good seed on the land, …"

The church was full to capacity as far as Marion could see. She knew all the words to her favourite hymn so was able to look around at the festive decorations that festooned every possible surface. She had been roped in to assist with various window displays, but to see the full effect of everyone's efforts was quite spectacular. She smiled and nodded as several people caught her eye.

"And it is fed and w-a-tered by God's almighty hand."

Her mother had not wanted her to participate in the preparations, but her father had persisted and won the day. The rest had been down to Marion. She put herself out to be helpful and was soon back into easier relations with most of the matrons of the parish, despite the gossip she knew they had been circulating about her. It was Mrs. Emerson, her old Sunday school teacher, who helped clear her mind.

"All good gifts around us, are sent from heaven above,
Then thank the Lord, O thank the Lord,
For a-a-all His love."

Mrs. Emerson had been showing her how to position carrots, beetroot, and parsnips in a way that mimicked the union flag. She'd gently probed Marion's plans, and Marion, who had remained troubled since her visit to London, welcomed the opportunity to talk especially as there was no one else working near them and they were unlikely to be overheard. With echoes of previous confidences between them, Marion had opened up about the dilemmas she faced.

"I just want to be the most useful I can, and support the war effort," she concluded, "but I want the best for Alain too. The two seem to be mutually exclusive, at present."

Marion had not signed up as a volunteer after her interview. She told them she intended to, and wanted to work close to the action but only after sorting out some personal arrangements.

"And what is right for your own family too," Mrs. Emerson had stated rather than asked as she reached for another bunch of carrots that she began to separate. "They were beside themselves with worry when you were in Belgium after the war started."

Were they? "Of course," Marion said, but as an afterthought, surprised to learn the extent of her family's past concern. *Mother only shows annoyance to me.* She brushed the mud off some parsnips and passed them to Mrs. Emerson, who passed them back and pointed to a space for them on the window ledge.

"We don't always have to think big, Marion. The difference we can make to one life is of as great importance as touching many. Perhaps giving Alain a good start in life is what you are meant to be doing. But have you asked God? Do you know what He wants from you?"

"I've rather got out of the habit of doing that."

"Perhaps that is why your mind is struggling. Ask Him for a sign. Pack those parsnips a little tighter."

"How will a bolt of lightning help my decisions?" Marion tugged on the parsnips and then quickly apologised for being flippant, but Mrs. Emerson laughed.

"Not all signs are dramatic. Ask Him to show you the way that is for you."

"How will I know when He has answered?" Marion asked, and then immediately answered herself, "Actually I know the answer to that. Therese, a friend of mine in Brussels, she's a nun, told me: that you know what is right when the decision feels easy."

"There you are then. Pass me some more carrots. You just have to wait for that time to come, and trust that it will. Now have you spoken to Mrs. Baxter yet? She is arranging flowers in front of the pulpit. Do have a word with her. She has still heard nothing from her son James. It is so distressing to think of him in prison in Germany."

"Yes, I've seen her already. At least she knows he is safe and out of the war. She had thought him dead. He was missing in action for months. There, is that the parsnips finished?"

"But being starved from what I read in the papers. Yes they're fine, now the beetroot. How dare those Germans treat our men so badly? Oh, your mother is calling you. Now remember what I said, hand your decisions to the Lord; and feel His guidance."

Marion had tried to heed Mrs. Emerson's counsel and stop worrying. She did keep going over the pros and cons of every possible permutation in her mind, handing over Alain, working abroad, keeping him, but she had lost the feeling of anxiety and no longer struggled for resolution within herself. She just waited. Even when she received two letters, two days apart, to return to Maddie's offices and the VAD recruiting office, both offering meetings on the same day, one at ten o'clock and the other at two o'clock, she held back from drawing conclusions. The appointments were two weeks away. *Plenty of time for decisions to become clear.*

Marion enjoyed feeling part of the larger community again at the harvest supper. Most households in the neighbourhood were represented in some way or another. *Country living at its best.* The barbed tongues were silent and goodwill prevailed; even her mother was relaxed, enjoying her moment of glory as she was showered with compliments and thanks at the end of the supper for her role in orchestrating the meal. She demurred to all her helpers, but in rather a regal way. But then, often overshadowed by events at the big house, Marion thought it was nice for her mother to receive her moment of local adulation. The role of a rector's wife was largely that of an unsung hero, and even though her mother did tend to wear her sufferance on a long sleeve, she did work tirelessly to support Marion's father and the parish. Marion was delighted by the warm feelings she found herself harbouring towards her mother, and with the genuine smile that she passed on to her when they caught each other's eye. Her mother looked quizzical in return, such was her apparent surprise.

The family conversation over breakfast the next day was buoyant after the success of the service and supper. Plaudits abounded as all had played their part. Each complimented another, as appreciation, that was more often absent than present between the women of the family, was expressed.

"Splendid, all splendid," volunteered Reverend Drake who even beamed at his wife. Did you see that William stuck his head in? He didn't want to stay, but he did leave an invitation with me. They are celebrating the harvest with a dance at the house and we are all invited, and I mean all," he added looking at Marion. Next Saturday, after his shoot, there'll be quite a party I should imagine."

Marion was surprised to feel uplifted at the thought. She could see the frisson of excitement that rippled through Evelyn, and her mother looked delighted and immediately began to plan.

"You must wear your finest black, Evelyn, and we can dress your hair. Marion, your jade will complement nicely, it is dark enough, as is my brown. Do you approve, Mr. Drake?"

"What? Yes, yes, of course my dear, as you say, as you say."

Marion was convinced her father had not heard a word about their proposed outfits, but her mother was only seeking confirmation, so seemed satisfied with his response. During the morning Marion took Alain out for a walk, and thought about the party at the coming weekend. It was late to be invited only one week ahead; many would have had the function in their appointment book for several months. Perhaps Mrs. Emerson had been working behind the scenes. Certainly her approval of Marion, although of no great social merit, was something of a spiritual yardstick. She had repeatedly stationed herself beside Marion at the harvest supper to show solidarity. If Mrs. Emerson had accepted her, then others would be less quick to judge. The wind of approval must have reached the big house.

Thoughts of attending a party and the prospect of enjoying the company both of strangers and acquaintances of old lifted her spirits. Her social world had remained very small since her return and she suddenly found herself wanting some fun and laughter, and perhaps even mild flirtation. *When Mother wasn't watching.* For the first time she was struck by the burden of her responsibility for Alain. Would any man want to flirt with a woman who was responsible for another's child? And for some her virtue might still remain in doubt. Worse, she shuddered, what if some of the men considered her easy game and didn't mind their manners? She had felt a prickle of this at the harvest supper when a couple of the labourers had brushed past her a little too close. *Absurd.* In mannered company all would be well; she was just feeling nervous. And what was she thinking of anyway? She had Russell to dream of; she needed no attentions from anyone else. But she still determined to look her best on the evening, to better Evelyn, if nothing else.

Edith's Journal, St Gilles Prison, Brussels, October 1915

Why do I so readily accept the Germans' will? Why do I not fight to save my life? Because I am stubborn? Because I am tired? Because I see this as God's will? Perhaps it is a little of each. Thomas a Kempis brings me comfort.

"*Happy is the soul which heareth the Lord speaking within her, and receiveth from His mouth the word of comfort.*"

When I feel God's love is with me, in me, then I bear my captors no malice. Then I have no hatred or bitterness towards the Germans. Borders have no place in heaven where we are all the same despite our different creeds, colour, and languages.

"*Happy ears which receive the breathings of the Divine whisper, and take no notice of the whisperings of this world.*"

In some way now I wish my death to come soon, but I know before the order can be given there will be some diplomatic rumpus to see if the punishment fits the crime. The Germans will tell the British politicians that within their jurisdiction, it does: that I confessed and knew the perils of my actions. And after a token hullabaloo I will slip into political obscurity. I grieve for my friends and family.

The Germans are about to make a terrible mistake. It is all happening too fast. I, and one other, are to be shot tomorrow morning at 7.00. Tomorrow morning? Tomorrow? The tremor in my hands has returned. Philippe Baucq and I are to stand side by side at our stakes. Appeals for the others are under review. I was too hasty and stubborn in accepting my fate; it is too late now.

My death will come too fast for the diplomats and national pride will be affronted. Of the German monsters much will be made. I fear the British will make a martyr of me, and ask for more volunteers to join up to avenge my death. And all I have ever wanted is to save lives. There is no injustice here that needs revenge; let my words of love and responsibility inspire peace.

I had a visit from Reverend Gahan, my English pastor. I meant no offence to refuse the German Lutheran priest they sent, but he doesn't know our ways, or me. It will be Belgian Pastor le Seur who will officiate tomorrow. I do not know him and that will be best. I took the sacrament and gave Pastor Gahan letters I have written to pass to family and friends, my last dialogues; so much and yet so little to say. I ask him to give my Thomas a Kempis and prayer book to my family, but not now, I will need their comfort through the night.

I tell him I have no fear. I have seen death so often it is not strange or fearful to me. This time of imprisonment has been a time of deep meditation for me, and everyone here has been very kind. I tell him I realise that patriotism is not enough. I must have no hatred or bitterness towards anyone.

These words to my pastor are the last I will ever speak in English. They are for my mother and family, for Eddy to hear. He will pass them on and tell them of my stoicism and peace. This will calm their fears of my suffering.

"Help me, O my God, and I will not fear, how much soever I may be distressed."

Now that I know the death sentence is to be carried out, the sooner is the better for me. The grief that settles on me only expands with each hour. I do not like to countenance the pain that my family will suffer from my death. I wish my mother could be spared this news. She thought no good would come of my return to Belgium, but I knew best.

It is impossible for me to sleep.

Brussels, October 1915

No one was going to have any sleep that night. Russell stood in the background and Hugh presented all their documentation to the duty officer to be passed to the German governor general for Belgium. Von Lancken had swept through the vestibule of the building just minutes earlier. His annoyance at being disturbed reverberated with each step as he stamped his way up the stairs to his office and slammed his door.

"This case must be reviewed now," Hugh demanded of the officer who, without saying a word, marched stiff-backed up the stairway, with the papers under his arm. Russell wandered around the hallway, looking at nothing in particular and noticing very little, but then it was stark in its decoration and barren of furniture. There was nowhere for them to sit, not that any of them would have managed this for long in their agitated state. After what seemed like an age they were escorted to see von Lancken who launched into a tirade ahead of any polite protocols. They were all standing in front of his desk, with no invitation to take a chair.

"But this is ridiculous; at this hour? What you say is improbable. I cannot believe that sentence has been pronounced and even if it had it would not be executed so swiftly." Von Lancken slapped his hand down on the papers in front of him.

Russell winced at his choice of words and the statements were all too familiar. Only a few hours before, Hugh was saying the same, in the face of Elizabeth's concerns.

"I can assure you the facts are correct," Hugh asserted.

"But you haven't heard through any official channels, have you?" von Lancken barked at him.

"Gentlemen," Villobar the Spanish emissary stepped forward, "perhaps the facts are only a telephone call away. Baron von Lancken, if you were to speak to the justice who presided over the court, he could tell you the situation, and we could all be advised."

"Very well. I will see what I can find out, but it will have to wait until the morning."

"Tomorrow", Russell who could stand the tension no longer, shouted, "will be too late. To be of use, we must act now. Please sir, I beg you to make the call."

Hugh coughed and caught Russell's attention and delivered a censorious frown. Russell had stepped beyond the bounds of protocol, but von Lancken did not appear to take any offence; in fact he stood up.

"Very well, wait here."

They did not have to wait for long.

"It would appear, gentlemen, you are correct." Von Lancken had returned after only a few minutes' absence. "Edith Cavell, along with one other prisoner is due to be executed before morning. I share your surprise that this is so swift, but there must be reasons."

"But this is entirely wrong," said Hugh. "On all counts this is wrong."

"It is decided," von Lancken said.

"It must be stopped, delayed, reconsidered. This cannot happen. It is madness to execute a woman. Surely you can see how this would look to the world at large? Even espionage has only warranted a custodial sentence. You Germans are treating this woman badly because she is British, but she is not the enemy. She is a nurse, she saves lives. Her trial was a farce. She had no defence. This must be stopped," Hugh emphasised each point with a dramatic wave of his arms.

"I do not know the details of the charges, but I did hear she confessed. She discounted her own defence."

"But you can't want her death on your country's conscience? Whatever the circumstances there is no need for this rush. We all need time to look at the court's decision. We must have time to appeal."

"I have no jurisdiction on military matters. There is little I can do."

"But is there not something?" Villobar suggested. "Could you not phone the military governor and see if he has signed the orders? He may be open to your influence. It is in no one's interest to create an upset over this."

"He would be as displeased to be disturbed at this hour, as I was," von Lancken said. But he made to leave the room and this time asked them all to be seated. Russell opened his mouth to speak to Hugh, but Hugh lifted his hand to silence him. Not a word passed between them as the minutes ticked by.

Russell fixed his eyes on the clock and watched the hands jerk through each second and minute. He dare not close his eyes in fear of a return to the nightmare scene that was never far from his thoughts. *Edith was going to die and I can't stop it.* The panic that would wake him from sleep now rose within him and he felt bile rise with it. He was concentrating all his efforts on not vomiting when the door opened quietly and von Lancken returned. He had been away for half an hour and was sombre. They all stood for his pronouncement.

"It will be done. The order for her execution will be carried through. I have spoken personally to the military governor and he said that after deliberating he has ratified the orders. She will be shot at seven o'clock, at dawn."

Russell slumped down onto the nearest chair and put his head between his knees.

Von Lancken collected together the paperwork that Hugh had deposited on the desk.

"Please take these with you, gentlemen. There is nothing further for us to discuss. I bid you goodnight."

"No," Hugh shouted, and then more softly, "they must stay with you. This is an official visit and I want our plea for clemency registered."

"Then you must do this tomorrow when the offices are open."

"And when it is too late," Russell, who had lifted his head to take in some air, said with some bitterness.

"Let me read you this, young man," von Lancken said as he lifted a piece of paper off his desk. "Paragraph 58 of the German Military Code says: 'Will be sentenced to death for treason any person who with the intention of helping the hostile power or of causing harm to the German or allied troops, is guilty of one of the crimes, such as, conducting soldiers to the enemy.' I need not read more. Nurse Cavell condemned herself to death by her actions. Good night, gentlemen."

They were in Edith's room in the clinic and it was three o'clock in the morning. Reverend Gahan had just finished telling them of his moments with Edith and there was a hushed silence broken only by Elizabeth's sobs. No one spoke.

"Her spirit was remarkable," Reverend Gahan added. "It was she putting me at ease. In the circumstances I was the one that felt more despairing, I fear. She was at peace, and wants it over."

If Russell had not been feeling so wretched, he might have laughed at the absurdity of these words. Hugh, Villobar, Leval, and he were anguished by their failure to create any delay, and the Reverend was telling them that Edith now wanted it over quickly. But she would be the only one not in despair when the triggers were pulled.

What will Marion say? Russell was frightened at the thought of Marion's reaction when she heard the news. The injustice, as she would see it, as they all saw it.

"Is there nothing we can do?" Russell asked, knowing he would have to account for Edith's last moments to Marion. "Have we tried everything?" *I feel so useless.* "We must have missed something?"

"They are moving fast to prevent us stopping them. They do not intend to be thwarted," Hugh said.

"They are making a big mistake," Villobar added. "No one will accept such treatment of a woman. They are showing themselves to be uncivilised savages."

"At least the world will see their true colours." Russell jumped at this sudden outburst from Elizabeth. "They won't be able to hide behind their rhetoric on this one. They have been savages ever since they arrived in Belgium. Edith is defenceless like all the other women they have killed, maimed, and attacked. I don't know how Edith can speak of forgiveness. I hate them." She collapsed back into her tears.

Her words hung in the air.

"I want to see her," Elizabeth said moments later, pulling herself together.

"They are not allowing visitors," Hugh said. "We did try and insist. The only dispensation they allowed was for Reverend Gahan to visit and they will bend no further."

"She will have the prison pastor with her," Russell added, but as soon as he said it he realised how feeble it sounded.

"Where will it happen? Will they shoot her in the prison?" Elizabeth asked.

"No, they will take her to the edge of the city, to the old fortress, Tir National," Villobar offered.

"Can we go there? I want her to know she is not forgotten," she continued.

"It is fortified there, ma'am. No point in going; we wouldn't get close to her. They'll not let us in," Hugh said.

"Then I shall go to the prison. If they won't let me in, I will wait for them to bring her out. Even if she only has a glimpse; I want her to see a friendly face on the day she dies."

"That is a very generous and kind thought, ma'am," Hugh said.

"I would like to join you, if I may?" Russell asked.

"I think we should all accompany you," Villobar said. "How might we organise that, Hugh?"

"Can we collect your car from your embassy?" Hugh asked the Spanish ambassador. "That way we can all fit in, what with my car too. Would you join us, Reverend? Mrs. Gahan?"

With nods all around a plan started to form and Russell felt better for having a task. Elizabeth and Mrs. Gahan went to the kitchens to make hot drinks and sandwiches for everyone. Russell accompanied Villobar to collect his car and to brief Hugh's driver to be ready. Hugh asked for the use of a telephone to make contact with Brand Whitlock. The hours before their departure passed quickly and Russell welcomed the food and hot coffee Mrs. Gahan pressed him to take. Elizabeth ate nothing but was persuaded to drink a cup of sweet tea.

"We don't want to risk missing her. We have no idea what time they will be moving the prisoners," Hugh said as he wiped the residue of a sandwich from his mouth. Russell took him to one side to ask whether Minister Whitock had anything useful to say.

"Not really. Only that he wants me in his office at nine o'clock to debrief him."

"Well, it will all be over by then," Russell said, "that's for sure. I still can't take it in. I have no idea how I am going to face Marion after this. She won't believe we couldn't stop this happening."

"Neither can I. If only we had more hours on our side. Perhaps then we could brief the press and create an international scandal. That might well stop them."

"Like it did with Leuven?" Russell asked.

"Yes, exactly."

"They had three days to do their worst though. They devastated that city. To fire that precious library; it makes my blood boil."

"Hard to fathom," Hugh agreed, "and they are misjudging this event too. Executing a woman will backfire on them. The press will make a martyr of her." Hugh looked around and saw that the rest of the party were starting to gather. "Russell, why don't you bring Sister Wilkins and Mrs. Gahan along to our car and I'll direct the reverend to travel with Villobar."

No one spoke on their drive to the prison. Russell tried to imagine what Edith's last journey would feel like, but found it impossible to envisage. *At least we will be there, and she will see us.* He hoped this was true. It might offer some solace to Marion. The only comfort for him was that Marion was far away from this drama. The thought that she might have been captured and executed was unbearable. Relief washed through him that she was safe; not quite the feeling that was in keeping with his travelling companions so he looked out into the dark through the window and kept his thoughts silent. Marion had played with fire and had come dangerously close to the flames. He hoped she had learnt her lesson and would now play safe. He feared any rebellion against her mother's expectations could lead her into trouble again.

Not being in communication with Marion was excruciatingly difficult. He wanted her close to him. When he held her in his arms the night before she left Brussels he had felt strong and protective. A feeling that Marion's feisty and headstrong ways did not typically inspire, attract, or reward. She was always ready to fight to defend her own independence. He loved her and knew he was lost to her, and what made him happy, even on a day such as this, were the words of love he had memorised from her letter. The car drew to a halt and Hugh interrupted his thoughts.

"Russell, would you mind seeing if you can find anything out. Looks like there is someone at the gatepost."

Russell was quick to return.

"The prisoners are due very soon. The sentry asked for the cars to be moved and told me where we can stand. Shall we, ladies?"

Before long they were all gathered in a line and, as if choreographed, all took a step forward when the gates of the prison began to grind open. Four vehicles passed slowly through and for a moment Russell panicked, that he might not see Edith, but his attention was caught by a shout from Elizabeth and he followed her gaze. He only caught a fleeting view of Edith, a white face, but he was sure she saw them, and Elizabeth glimpsed her too. But she was gone in an instant. Afterwards they all stood with their heads bowed, and when Russell heard sobs escaping from Elizabeth he slipped his arm around her shoulders and held her close.

Edith's Journal, Tir National, Brussels, 12th October, 1915

My light was on all night and my door opened every fifteen minutes. It is called a suicide watch. The Germans did not want to be robbed of my final moments; it has to be them who take my life away. My will subordinated to theirs.

Pastor le Seur travelled with me from the prison and I welcomed his company, but I feel prepared and ready to pass through the veil. Does it salve my executioner's conscience to see the clergy with me; my spiritual journey is in his hands and not on their conscience.

Perhaps fanciful, but I think I saw Elizabeth as we passed out through the prison gate. A true friend.

I complete my inscription:

"died at 7.00 a.m. on Oct 12th 1915"

and sign my name and dedicate the book with my love to E. D. Cavell: my Eddy.

"Then am I weary of longer life, and wisheth death to come, that I may be dissolved and be with Christ."

I hand the pastor my journal and books. He tells me the shots will be quick and clean and I will feel no pain.

"Behold, O Beloved Father, I am in Thy hands."

1916 & 1917

London, January 1916

Marion felt flat. As she settled herself on the train she remembered her last trip to London and almost could not recognise the person she had been then: excited to find out about nursing opportunities abroad and somewhat trepidatious about her meeting with the adoption agency. Today she should be ecstatic; her journey was to meet Russell. His telegraph had arrived out of the blue and had caused quite a stir at home, but she was not even excited. She was numb.

"Who is Mr. Clark and why have you been summoned to London to meet him?"

"I haven't been summoned, Mother, I have been informed that he will be in London for twenty-four hours and have been invited to meet him, if it is convenient for me."

"And is it? Are you going? Who is he? And please do not avoid my questions."

"I am surprised you can't recall him, Mother. He was a student at Oxford when he paid you and Papa a visit. You gave him letters and all sorts of home comforts to bring out to me in Brussels, soon after the occupation began."

"You mean the young American? I had forgotten his name. I'd heard nothing of him since. Does this mean you remain in contact?"

"No, this is the first contact since my return; no letters can get through, and he is still based in Belgium. This is only a quick visit."

"Well then it is presumptuous of him to demand your attendance in London. The man must be refused."

"He has demanded nothing, merely invited. People don't include polite niceties in telegraphs, they get to the point as cheaply as possible."

"And what need does he have of you? I thought that Brussels business was all behind you?"

Unfortunately Marion had been handed her telegraph whilst at breakfast and had no reason not to pass it to her mother to read.

"Perhaps the matter of his visit is a private one, my dear." Marion's father drew himself away from his newspaper to pass this comment on to his wife. Before retreating again he looked at Marion.

"Might it not be a good idea to visit him? Could well buck you up a bit, my dear. I remember Mr. Clark: I found him most enjoyable company."

As did I. Marion looked idly out of the carriage window and tried to locate what she now felt for Russell, but every emotion that it was possible for her to feel was overwhelmed by a suppressed rage that had tightened every sinew in her body. She was suffocating: her ribcage locked into a rigid frame that would release no sobs. *Sobs!* It was a primeval scream that sat within her, waiting for its moment of liberation to howl. But still, she was on her way to see him despite her mother's comments. After the shocking news of Edith's death Marion had been moody and morose. She knew her parents were concerned, so unusual was it for her to be desolate.

She had been at the party hosted by her uncle to celebrate the year's harvest when she had overheard a snippet of conversation that had sent her running to scour the newspaper the minute she and her family returned home, some agonisingly slow hours later. And there it had been, just a brief piece on page eight of *The Times*, the words, read so often, now forever etched in her mind.

> **Englishwoman Executed in Belgium.**
> **Charge of Helping our Soldiers**
> *The following communication has been received from the Press Bureau:*
> The Foreign Office are informed by the United States Ambassador that Miss Edith Cavell, lately the head of a large training school for nurses at Brussels, who was arrested on August 5 last by the German authorities at that place, after sentence of death had been passed on her, was on the 12th inst. executed.
> It is understood that the charge against Miss Cavell was that she had harboured fugitive British and French soldiers and Belgians of military age, and had assisted them to escape from Belgium in order to join their colours.
> So far as the Foreign Office are aware, no charge of espionage was brought against her.

The shock had frozen her. She continued with the motions of living, but in the early days she was merely observing life around her through the wrong end of a telescope. Everything and everyone felt distant and she often had to concentrate very hard to make sense of what people were saying to her and to offer the appropriate response. Her only comfort was Alain. He became quiet and still, never pushing her for a response, but always ready to give and receive a cuddle, quite the angel. They spent hours together. Gradually, as Marion read more editorials in *The Times* about Edith's life and fate the ice in her melted, but only to be replaced by a furnace stoked by rage.

Now that she was dead Edith had become the *casus belli* of the British government. Too late they claimed her as their heroine and were exhorting more men to join the army to avenge her death. In Marion's mind the ministers who had done nothing to save her were milking her demise as a propaganda coup. She read snippets of correspondence in *The Times* from Brand Whitlock describing the useless protestations they had put forward, but Marion could not forgive them their failure. It was unfathomable to her that the Germans had been allowed to assign and carry out such a sentence, but equally unforgiveable that the Americans had not prevented it. Her own guilt at abandoning Edith and surviving her was buried too deeply for her to recognise it.

"Take me through it, everything, every conversation. Don't miss out any details, and don't try to spare me. You must tell me everything." Marion was sitting up in a double bed with a sheet pulled around her, facing Russell as he sprawled beside her. The room, in a small hotel near Marylebone station, was entirely taken up with the bed and two bedside cabinets. With no space for a chair their clothes were abandoned on the floor in one corner. With curtains pulled the light was dim, but the room looked freshly decorated and the furnishings, although plain, were not drab.

"I will, I will, but come and lie back down with me. I want to hold you."

"No, no. We have to talk, we have to talk now. We shouldn't have, you know, we should have waited until after we've talked. You rushed me." *I shouldn't have let you.*

"I didn't rush you. We, we made love." Their coming together had been passionate. "It's our reunion. We've waited weeks, months to be together and only have a few hours. Don't let's spoil it. Come here, I want to enjoy you, breathe you in, we can talk later."

"Is that what happened in Brussels?" Her tone was suddenly sharp.

"What? What on earth do you mean?"

"Everyone just thinking of themselves. Did anyone make any

real effort for Edith? She would have been saved if they had, if you had. I cannot believe you all just let her die. I should have stayed, or left Alain here and returned. I thought I could trust you and Hugh to defend her. I didn't think she was going to die."

"None of us thought she was going to die."

"So no one thought it was urgent and did nothing. Is that how it was?"

Marion's agitation increased with each outburst and Russell gave up on his picture of him holding her gently in his arms while he talked her through the events surrounding Edith's death. He wanted to give her comfort, but she was poised for a fight. After all the discreet efforts Hugh had made to secure them a room for the afternoon, he could not believe they were going to spend the time talking; he wanted to devour her.

"No, that wasn't how it was. We kept pressure on the Germans all the time. They played their cards very close to their chests. We were wrong-footed at every turn."

"Tell me then, tell me all that you did," she challenged him.

"All right, I can see you are determined. Wait a moment, I need to sit up."

Russell rearranged himself on the bed so that his head was at the same level as Marion's, and he could look her directly in the eye. He was about to be held to account. He had always known this moment of reckoning would come with Marion, but he had hoped the thrill of being together would have pushed it into the background. But Marion was as coiled as a tight spring. Making love had been more of a wrestle as they grappled each other, rather than a melding together; but the fire in both of them had, at least, extinguished any inhibitions. She had certainly not melted into his arms as she had in his numerous fantasies and, now they were talking, she was definitely frosty.

Russell explained that the morning she left Brussels Mr. Whitlock had written a letter to the German authorities requesting that he be kept informed of their proceedings.

"He gave them the name of Monsieur Leval, the legal council Brand wanted to appoint for Edith's defence," Russell explained.

"Why didn't he demand her release immediately? Why didn't he go and see them rather than write a letter. Where is the authority behind that? It is too easy to ignore a letter. What was their reply?"

"There wasn't one. They didn't reply."

"Exactly: my point exactly. How could you sit around and let nothing happen? How could you?"

"Believe me, Marion, I was very anxious for Edith. I checked our messages and mail and asked Mr. Whitlock about her every day, and I can assure you he was not pleased being harried by me. I did the best I could."

"Well, it wasn't good enough, was it?"

"No, it wasn't, but her death wasn't my fault."

"Then whose fault was it? Why didn't you Americans save her? It should have been easy for you to get the Germans to see sense. You have dinner with them often enough, for God's sakes."

A long-standing bone of contention that lay between them was his behaviour as a neutral American, fraternising, as she saw it, and forming friendships with the German aggressors. Russell did not rise to the bait but emphasised the pressure he had put Mr. Whitlock under to visit the governor general to plead Edith's case.

"He told me in no uncertain terms that this was not the way things were done and that if I continued to appear so obdurate the road of diplomacy would not be the one I would be following in the future. He said he would pen another letter, and to this one we received a reply, almost immediately."

"Diplomacy, my foot. It is nothing more than men failing to hold one another to account. What are they frightened of? Being bullied? It's pathetic. It makes my blood boil."

"He wanted to make sure he did nothing to upset the Germans and the more he pressed them on Edith, the more they would see her as a prize. Feigning indifference might have meant they would lose interest in her themselves."

Russell was struggling to keep his exasperation under control. Marion's tone was testing. He breathed in deeply and awaited the next onslaught. It came quickly.

"They didn't though, did they? They saw harming her as a way of getting at the British. They should be ashamed of themselves, but we know that they aren't. They don't care who they hurt. What was their reply?"

Russell told her that the German authorities had said that Leval would not be needed as the court had already appointed defence counsel for all the prisoners and that they would keep the legation informed. They had also stated that no visitors were permitted. Despite Russell's own protestations Mr. Whitlock had not progressed matters further. He seemed satisfied that he had done as much as he could.

"Satisfied? How could he be satisfied? That is outrageous. It's worse than I ever thought."

He had made the wrong choice of word. Marion was leaping on each statement as an admission of ineptitude.

"He knew he had to bide his time. He was also unwell and had taken to his bed. There was nothing he could do."

"Banging on doors and desks for a start."

"But that could have made it much more difficult for Edith. He didn't want them to think she was a special case."

"But she was special, so special. She was a woman, a nurse. Allowances should have been made. Her death was cold-blooded murder. They should have been stopped. What did Leval say her defence should be?"

"I don't know. I didn't see him." Russell was feeling more and more inadequate with every response. All his attempts now seemed feeble, even to him, against the loss of Edith's life, and certainly didn't appear to stack up to much in Marion's eyes. "It wasn't discussed with Leval until Hugh returned and took up the case, but by then it was too late. We only heard what was happening after the death sentence had been passed."

Marion's only response was a withering glare. He endeavoured to salvage something by reminding her that the international furore they stirred up over her execution did stop other sentences being carried out. They had saved lives but, tragically, not Edith's.

"And have you seen the posters here?" Marion snapped. "Pictures of Edith are everywhere. The government is encouraging men to sign up to avenge her death. And they are. It's so awful. This is the last thing she would have wanted. I just can't bear it."

"She would want to be remembered," Russell said.

"Maybe, but not like this, as a rallying call for more violence. If Hugh had been there to help her, she may well still be alive. Instead I dragged him away. He could have saved her, I'm sure of it."

Marion picked up the nearest pillow and started to beat it with her fist. Russell was relieved that her frustration, for the moment, was focused on feathers rather than him, and he told her about Elizabeth's contact with Edith which he hoped would bring some comfort. He spoke of their letter exchange and the meals she had sent in to her and described her visit. He caught her attention when he said Edith's only concern was that she, Marion, was safe.

"I know, Elizabeth wrote to me, to say she was home. I will go and visit her, but I'll leave it a while. It's all a bit too raw, for both of us."

"Did you go to the memorial service at St Paul's? We heard they had a special requiem for her when her death was announced. I imagined you there."

"No I didn't. I couldn't, I wouldn't go."

"No, I can see that it would have been too upsetting."

"Upsetting? You have no idea. I am eaten up by the thought of government ministers who had not lifted a finger to save her, pontificating about her to gain public sympathies. It incenses me. It seems to me that Hugh Gibson was the only person who put himself out for her."

"Well, I, I did all I could." Russell bristled at the mention of Hugh, the only person who Marion seemed to hold in any esteem in the whole affair. "You would have been a frustrated observer too, if you had been there."

"I could not have stood by and watched this happen," she said indignantly.

"Marion, that is exactly what you would have had to do." Russell was tiring of her high-handedness. "I don't know what fantasies you carry about the difference you could have made. There was nothing we could do."

"You just didn't care enough."

Russell was hurt by this and hit out. "And perhaps you care too much. She was a grown woman who knew the risks. Just as you did, and you both still went ahead with your foolhardy scheme. I told you it was madness."

"So she brought it on herself. Is that what you are saying?"

"You were lucky to escape. And it was those that you now criticise who made that happen."

"And why? Why did you save me? So you can use me as a whore in a seedy hotel in a London backstreet? Is that why?"

"You have pushed me too far. You don't mean that? You can't mean that?"

"Don't I?" Of course she did not. "You must have known I would be upset about Edith; that I would want to talk about her death, to understand what happened. It was all over our newspapers, but I wanted to hear the truth, from you. Instead you, you seduced me." *Stop this, Marion.*

Russell felt dizzy and started to shake. He did not know whether it was from anger or fear, perhaps both. The urgency in him had been overwhelming but he thought it had matched her desire. It had.

"I thought you wanted me too. I thought you felt the same. I have ached for you, to hold you, to feel you close. We entered this room and bed in love, at least I thought we did."

Russell moved away from her and swung his legs over the side of the bed. He rested his elbows on his thighs and held his head in his hands. His head was swimming. He was bewildered and about to lose the most precious thing in his life: Marion and their love. It took a while for him to realise that the bed was shaking. He turned to see Marion prostrated on the bed sobbing and groaning into her pillow. His first instinct was to reach out to her, but he felt so attacked that he dared not touch her. Instead he reached for his shirt and held it to his chest before starting to dress.

Russell had never imagined that Marion might not want the same intimacy. Now he felt lost, disorientated, and suddenly conscious of how far away from any sense of home he was. For the last months thoughts of Marion had anchored him and motivated him to continue with his work in Brussels. She had become the centre of his universe, a magnetic force that drew his thoughts and dreams towards her, and with this gravitational pull abruptly severed he felt adrift.

Russell turned back towards her but her face was towards the wall and she had curled into a foetal position. This was not petulance, he realised, she was wailing with grief. Her body was racked as the sobs seized her and it was only when he put a hand gently on her back that she seemed able to take in a gasp of air. She turned towards him and he pulled her into his arms and held her. They stayed this way for at least half an hour until she quietened. He thought she had fallen asleep, but she spoke as soon as he moved to stretch his arm.

"I'm sorry. That was unforgiveable."

"You don't need to apologise for crying. You never need do that."

"Not for crying; for what I said. I'm sorry. Truly, truly sorry."

"It was the heat of the moment," Russell said as he stroked a lock of her hair off her forehead, but he was relieved to hear her words all the same.

"No, it wasn't. I wanted to hurt you. I wanted to hit out. I have done since I heard of Edith's death. This is the first time I have been able to cry; I have been so locked up. I have been impossible these last months."

"I hope I never do anything to induce such an upset again."

"I've missed you and ..."

"And?"

"And I am glad to have had Alain with me. He has been such a comfort."

Marion was calm now and her anger completely spent. Her breathing was back to normal, and she even managed a quick smile when she mentioned Alain.

"How is that little man?"

"He is delightful. I can see Therese's smile. He has her dimples."

"All babies have dimples."

"Since when did you become an expert?" Marion smiled and Russell's relief meant he had to swallow back tears of his own.

"I'm glad you are together. I can imagine the comfort he brings. He is a lucky boy."

Russell kissed the top of Marion's head and she lifted her face to his and they kissed, gently at first and then with more passion they made love. He, this time, with less urgency.

Russell was startled awake by a banging on the door to their room. Both of them had drifted into a light doze with limbs wrapped around each other and sheets tangled in between.

Russell had asked the concierge to alert him when it was four o'clock, a sensible precaution as he had completely lost track of the time. Marion stirred when he called out his thanks and disentangled himself. He was half dressed by the time she was fully alert.

"Oh, must you leave?" Marion put on a pout.

"'fraid so, but what an afternoon."

"Rather ruined by my tirade." Marion looked rueful.

"I forget how gutsy you can be."

"And I forget how smug and self-satisfied you can be."

"We're not heading for another fight are we?" Russell laughed.

"Not enough time, it seems," and Marion joined his laughter, which lapsed into giggles, as she watched him fighting to put his second leg into his trousers and becoming tangled in his braces.

"Now that's better," Russell said when he had straightened himself out. "I've missed your laughter and your smiles."

"I can't just produce them to order. It has been a ghastly time. I have felt so wretched about Edith. And there is no one who would understand at home. They don't know the half of it."

"What about Gwen, your friend from Brussels? Is she close by? Wouldn't she understand?"

"I haven't seen her. She is nursing in north London but we've grown quite distant."

"North London's not that far from you. Look at us here today. It was an easy journey you said. Why don't you visit her?"

"I don't mean distant in miles. I've been very absorbed with Alain since my return, and she, well, in her only letter seemed very keen on a chap, and she's working long hours. We have less in common now that we don't share our routine at the clinic. She knew nothing about Edith and me helping the soldiers anyway and would have told me I was mad to be involved. She can be short on sympathy."

"Well, you know I thought you were mad."

"And you know I would do the same again."

"I don't want you getting into any scrapes here. Please promise me you won't."

"I shall promise no such thing," but she softened this with a grin.

"Stay at home and look after Alain. That's a worthwhile task. I know you'll be safe there."

"Is that what you think? That I am going to put my life on hold, and for him? No thank you, Mr. Clark. I intend to return to nursing."

"Where? Not with the troops? You will stay in England won't you?" There was alarm in Russell's voice.

"Will I? What puts you in a position to tell me what to do?" Marion threw her pillow at him.

"Don't my wishes hold any sway at all?" Russell caught the pillow and sat down next to her. She took his hand.

"Of course they do; truly I would never want to upset you, but you really must trust me to make decisions for myself."

"But what about Alain?"

"We really don't have time to discuss Alain now. You have to leave."

"That reminds me. Sister Wilkins told me she had a letter for you from Therese, but she wanted to give it to you personally."

"I'll arrange to see her soon. When did Therese write the letter?"

"Before she left for the convent, I believe."

"I do miss her, such a wise one. Alain calms me so much I sometimes feel that Therese is in the nursery with us. Fanciful aren't I?"

"Fanciable," Russell said and leant over to kiss her.

"Enough, Mr. Clark, you must leave and if you kiss me again, I can't promise that I shall let you. I daren't ask when we might see each other again."

"And to that unasked question I have no reply. As soon as possible is all I can commit to."

"If only we could write to each other."

"It does feel impossibly hard, doesn't it? I am becoming very tired with my work, and the sparkle left Brussels when you did. Perhaps I can orchestrate my release and return to Oxford. Then we will be closer and with a postal service that works too. I can't promise, but I'll start working on it. But now, my darling, I must leave."

Marion cried a little more when Russell shut the door behind him, but soon fell into a deep sleep. She was exhausted from the emotional release. It was early evening when she awoke and she was tempted to remain at the hotel for the night, but her need to see Alain outweighed that idea, and she decided to head home. Despite her sadness at once again being parted from Russell, and fatigue, she felt lightened by her tears and conscious that she could breathe deeply again; her diaphragm was no longer rigid. The rage locked within her for so many weeks had dissolved.

She looked into a mirror and smiled as she stood brushing her hair. *You're quite a girl, Miss Drake, quite a girl. You pushed him a bit hard today.* She and Russell walked a tightrope in their relationship and, while she liked the interplay that kept the rope taut between them, she realised she had placed Russell under significant pressure. *Next time, be sweetness and light.* She could only hope that he carried the highs and not the lows of their encounter with him. *Next time, when would that be?*

London, Spring 1916

The news was wretched. Marion, like everyone else, was drawn to the casualty list the papers updated daily. There had been more losses in her local area. She had recently attended a memorial service for her cousin Jack on the first anniversary of his death. His brother Edward's health was of great concern for the family, nervous trouble and dysentery from Egypt, and Marion had been shocked to see her cousin looking so thin and agitated at the service. Her father had led the service beautifully; Jack had been such a favourite of his. She felt sad for her uncle William, with one son dead and another who had almost lost his senses.

It was the effects of the war on soldiers' minds that occupied Marion's thoughts. Edward's nerves were shot to pieces even though his body was still whole. There had been many and varied comments in the newspapers that had caught her interest. The Press called nervous reactions "the coward's wound". She knew Edward was no coward, but he was a wreck now, and his brother's death must have hit him hard. It hurt them all.

Marion put the newspaper to one side and checked her watch. She was waiting for Elizabeth as arranged, in the Lyons teashop at Piccadilly Circus. It seemed the most convenient place, with one coming into London from the north-west and the other from the south-east, but it had proved quite an expedition for Marion with the baby. Very early into her journey she had regretted her decision to bring Alain and wished Nanny had travelled with her. He was sleeping beside her. Sister Wilkins and she had corresponded a little since Elizabeth returned to England the previous November but, in truth, Marion had mixed feelings about this reunion. Her mother had been incensed that she wanted to take baby Alain with her, telling her how ridiculous it was to be taking an infant to London. So Marion had lied and said she was going to visit an adoption organisation after meeting Sister Wilkins, and her mother was then slightly appeased.

"He's a darling," Sister Wilkins said as she looked at a sleeping Alain.

"He will need changing and feeding. I haven't thought all this through. I have everything with me, but I'm not quite sure where to take him," Marion replied.

"Leave that to me," Elizabeth said and went to talk to the manager of the restaurant who soon offered to take Marion through to a back room where she could see to Alain, while his food and milk were mixed and warmed.

"May I hold him?" Elizabeth asked as she stretched out her arms and took him and the bottle off Marion. Alain snuggled into her and sucked his way through eight ounces without even opening his eyes. He still had smudges of his baby food around his mouth.

"Enjoy him while he is quiet, he can be such a fidget, he likes to roll himself around on the floor when he has a chance, but he rarely cries."

Marion and Elizabeth were at a table in the corner of the restaurant, furthest away from the door. The place was bustling with people and Marion loved the noise and the random snatches of conversations she could overhear. She had a clear view of the door which dinged a bell each time it opened and each new customer would either head towards a table or to the counter to select their cakes. The regular ring of the cashier's register added to the feeling of activity. Most of the clientele were women as were all the serving staff.

"Don't they look smart, the waitresses?" Marion said. "With their little hats and cuffs they could almost be nurses," Elizabeth replied. "These really are such pleasant establishments."

"It quite reminds me of the cafés in Brussels, but with the cakes on display I think this tops even them."

"What are we going to have to eat? Travelling always makes me hungry."

"Savoury before sweet?" Marion asked.

"You sound like my mother," Elizabeth replied, and they were laughing when their waitress came to take their order.

"No family for Alain yet then?" Elizabeth asked.

"No, and I haven't really tried. I did make enquiries with one agency last year, but didn't follow through. I was so shaken by the news of Edith, it forestalled all my plans, and Alain was a great comfort to me. He was too young to be passed on to other people anyway, he needed to be with me; I'm the person he knows."

"But he's taking his milk from me without any problem." Both women watched as Alain sucked on the bottle. "I am sure he will quickly adapt. At this age all they need is warmth and food."

"Now you sound just like my mother. She wants shot of him. The way I have upset the social order in our local community has been devastating for her."

"So do you have plans?"

Marion explained that she was ready to find a job and return to nursing, to which Elizabeth replied that she had meant plans for Alain, not her. Marion reached over for him when the waitress delivered their order, cleaned his face and settled him on her lap. He immediately gripped her thumb and smiled up at her. The noise around them had increased and every table was taken.

"I don't think I could bear to be parted from him, Elizabeth. I never saw myself as sentimental, but I love him dearly, and I fundamentally disagree with you about warmth and food being sufficient. They might suffice his body, but not his spirit. Nanny tells me he is very different on the days when I have not been with him."

"Don't mind what I say. I have no experience of children. It was just the practical side of me coming out."

"I may sound whimsical, but when he looks into my eyes I'm sure he knows what I feel for him. I'd like to think that as he gets older, it is my eyes that will reflect back to him the person he is. We have a deep bond, and I want nothing to damage that."

"You make me feel quite envious. Perhaps if more mothers connected with their sons we would have fewer brutes leading us into wars. He is a lucky boy and Therese was a wise woman to choose you. That reminds me," Elizabeth drew an envelope out of her handbag, "I must give you a letter. Therese asked me to pass it to you when we next met."

Marion thanked her and tucked the letter carefully into her pocket before giving her attention back to Elizabeth.

"Thank you, I'll read it on the train. Now please, Elizabeth, I want to ask you about Edith. Russell, Mr. Clark, said that you saw her, at the prison. How was she? Please tell me everything. You were so brief in your letters."

Interrupted only by the waitress who brought them a fresh pot of tea and then made a fuss of Alain, until tutted at by her supervisor, Elizabeth gave a full and frank account of the weeks that led up to Edith's execution. It took some time.

"Mr. Clark was a true gentleman. His hands were tied like everyone else's and we all were just groping around in the dark, but his support to me was of immeasurable value."

"Was it?" Marion said more than asked. "That is good to hear. I gave him a hard time for not doing more for Edith." *A really hard time.*

"Poor chap, he didn't deserve that, Marion. He visited me very regularly and kept me informed, as did I with him. It was such a difficult and frustrating time and I was so fearful for Edith. Sometimes I was quite paralysed and Mr. Clark would always know how to nudge me forward. He was a great help."

"But it was Mr. Gibson that created the stir wasn't it? I thought it was him that managed to get answers?"

"Yes, Mr. Gibson was wonderful. He made Edith his cause as soon as he returned to Brussels; but Mr. Clark would have allowed him no other priority. But we were always too late, always one step behind the Germans. They wrong-footed us."

"I have felt so wretched about Edith. I can't forgive myself for leaving her."

"But that is what gave her the most relief, that you were away and safe."

"And it is what burdens me the most," Marion sighed. "I should have helped her. One of my uncles is an MP. I should have made her his cause célèbre. I could have done more than I did."

"The British authorities felt no sympathy at all. Don't forget Mr. Gibson brought her situation to their attention when he was in London and was cold shouldered."

"They soon changed their tune afterwards. There was a public outcry here, true outrage that the Germans should do such a thing. And then our government used her death to drum up more men for the army. Edith would have hated that," Marion said.

"But she would have been delighted," Elizabeth responded, "with the new hospital wards and nurses' homes bearing her name. I can't open the newspaper without spotting another medical establishment that has honoured her, and don't forget she was never against men doing their duty."

Emotions were still raw for both of them, so Marion diverted Elizabeth from further talk about Edith with questions about her fellow trainees at the Brussels clinic, but Elizabeth had remained in contact with only a few since her return to England, so had little news to offer. She was more forthcoming when Marion enquired about her own work.

"It's lucky that nurses are in such demand, otherwise, at my age, I might have found it more difficult. They won't have me as a matron anywhere, but I am satisfied with just being a ward sister. The hospital I am in receives a number of war casualties. They have been patched up overseas and then come to us for recuperation, or in many cases amputation. It seems they can do little more than stem the bleeding in these field hospitals. Many are in quite a state by the time they arrive with us. My head never seems to be clear of the smell of gangrene."

Alain was sleeping again so needed none of her attention and Marion really enjoyed her conversation with Elizabeth. It was much more companionable than their working relationship had ever been. She was the only person Marion could talk to who shared her experience with Edith, understood her professional desire to nurse, and who knew Russell. They could talk all day, she realised.

"And what of Mr. Clark?" Elizabeth asked. "There is a man smitten if ever I saw one."

Marion could not help smiling at this observation. She wondered if her own feelings were so evident.

"We are miles apart and with no means of contact."

"But you saw him in January?"

"Yes. Mr. Gibson sent him over on an errand, on a diplomatic pass, but I spent most of what was a short visit anyway berating him about Edith. It might have been too much for him."

"And what does he think about Alain?"

"We didn't have time to discuss him."

"So you don't know how accommodating he would be about taking him on."

"No, no idea, and that's probably why I avoided the subject when he was over."

"Impertinent for me to ask, but would you choose Alain ahead of Mr. Clark?"

Marion paused. This question had come to mind many times but she had suppressed it. The rational response was to protect her independence, but the emotional pull drew her towards Alain all the time.

"I don't find it impertinent in the least, but I have no idea how to answer you. It's a choice I never want to be presented with. Ideally I would like a future with them both, and with me also able to pursue my work interests. Does that define me as modern woman?"

"Or a fantasist," Elizabeth said and they both laughed. "In my opinion you are quite within your rights to want all three and there are so many more opportunities for women now. But, Marion, is this the time in your life to be constrained by the responsibility for a child?"

The question was left hanging while the waitress cleared their plates and Marion encouraged Elizabeth to go and choose them a cake each from the counter display.

"No other man I have met is as appealing to me as Russell. I feel able to be myself with him," Marion said as she tucked into an egg custard, "even if this means he sees the rough side of me."

"He spoke of you at every turn in Brussels, but he was very nervous that you would hold him to account for Edith's demise. He really did push the others very hard. Mr. Gibson told me that Mr. Whitlock was quite put out by Russell's impatience on several occasions, and it was you he didn't want to let down."

"He told me nothing of this." *Perhaps he did.* "Or I just wasn't listening. I was ready for a fight, and he became my target. I can only hope I didn't push him too far."

"Better to be true to oneself, I'm sure. But then who am I to say? I have never considered marriage for myself. I prefer work as my companion. At least work allows me some days off; marriages are simply years of endless conversations. The thought of all that talking quite exhausts me."

Marion opened up about nursing opportunities and explained she had turned down an opportunity with the VAD to work in Malta.

"I must find some work for myself close to home, but when Alain is a bit older. A local manor house I could reach easily from home has converted to a hospital. It's only temporary, for the war, but I heard they have several wards with wounded patients, many with head injuries and nervous disorders, and are looking for help."

"You, of all people, definitely shouldn't be idle."

"That sounds like something Edith would say." Marion immediately regretted raising Edith's name again.

"Yes, she would. She looked so solemn on her final journey. Luckily she didn't have months to contemplate her death. We have to think it was a blessing for her that it all happened in such a rush. We had not been long at the gates of the prison that morning when the cavalcade of vehicles came out. We only caught a glimpse of her, but she was looking our way, so I am sure she saw us. That was all I wanted, for her to know she was not alone."

Marion had to stop eating her pastry as her eyes stung with tears. Elizabeth's description was so stark, the flash of Edith on her way to face the firing squad. She could not speak.

"They refused to let us take her body for a Christian burial. They told Mr. Gibson that had all been taken care of, and we were not allowed to visit her grave."

"One injustice upon another. It is so awful to think about her punishment, and for what? How can it be considered wrong to save men's lives?"

"No, it wasn't for that she was shot. The Germans were very particular on this matter. Her crime was assisting soldiers to return to their regiments and so to fight against their enemy. It was for aiding and abetting the war effort that she was executed, not for her nursing. You were lucky to get away."

"And for this I have Therese to thank. If not for her warning I would have been captured. I wish I could talk to her now, about Alain. She always had such a wonderful way of knowing what would turn out for the best, but she was insistent he went to a family and not an orphanage."

"Perhaps her letter will help you. She was a canny one. You'll work it out. It was that spark in you that Edith most admired."

"Spark? Is that what she said?"

"And more. She held you in the highest regard. Do what you think would make her proud, if that thought helps."

"That thought would have me on the first troopship to Malta. She put duty to others first."

"Duty takes many forms, Marion, many forms."

The sun was shining and the sky a clear bright blue when they stepped out of the teashop. Encouraged, Marion and Elizabeth took a short stroll together in Green Park before they set off on their journeys home. Spring was definitely in the air with a first hint of blossom on the trees that lined the paths. Elizabeth quoted a line of poetry.

"And apple-blossoms fill the air,
When Spring brings back
Blue days and fair."

"Pretty words, Elizabeth. Hard to think we are at war on a day such as this." Marion sighed. "Let's hope it is all over soon." They hugged, and agreed to meet again.

Later, on the train Marion wanted to reflect on her conversation with Elizabeth, and read her letter from Therese, but both proved difficult. The carriage was full and people kept asking her questions about Alain and wanting to fuss him. She could see he was enjoying all the attention. Therese's letter remained in her pocket. It would have to wait until she was home.

Brussels, Summer 1916

Russell felt elated; this week had been long awaited. He had first voiced his desire to return to Oxford in January but Hugh had been quite dismissive of the idea, putting his restlessness down to missing Marion, and making fun of him as a result. Russell knew this was definitely a part of it but the malaise within him ran deeper than Marion. He was desperately bored with his work and was fearful of what he might do to provide some recreation. Hugh made sure there was no shortage of invitations for him as the social calendar slowly grew again and flirtations had been open to him. Now that Hugh had finally arranged for him to return to England he felt relief more than disappointment at these missed opportunities. He had remained true to Marion, and was thankful. He knew she would smell an indiscretion a mile off, and he could never lie to her. He hoped the same would be true of her.

Life in an occupied country was dull. The embassy staff were better off for food than most, but even their choice was severely limited, and the repetition of dishes added to the monotony of his days. Outside the embassy, and without the security and relative freedoms afforded by a diplomatic pass, the civilian atmosphere was distinctly tense. To the people of Brussels the Germans were the enemy and many rebelled against the heavy load of rules posted almost daily. Punishments were severe for those who stepped out of line and favours generous to those who reported on their neighbour's activities; everyone was on edge.

Russell was particularly relieved to be leaving Mr. Whitlock behind. Relations with him had never recovered after "the Cavell Affair", which was the way the minister referred to the whole episode. He was equally delighted to be travelling with Hugh who had been allowed a placement in London; they might even be able to see something of each other in England.

Russell was satisfied that he had completed the necessary handover of his work to a fellow American who had been transferred from their embassy in Spain. He had been tickled by his enthusiasm. The man, in his thirties, seemed excited to be close to the action, as he saw this posting. Russell did not avail him of the truth and tried to make his audit trips around the country sound exciting rather than the tiresome task he found them. The briefings had been straightforward, but this was in no small measure due to the organised way in which Russell worked; he made the job look and sound easy.

"You've forgotten how much you have learnt, my friend. Pass me that box please." Russell had wandered into Hugh's office to find him indexing papers and packing them into boxes. "You take for granted the conversations you manage each day, and to have been a part of this programme and seen how it has developed from the genesis of an idea to the organisation it is today, is an experience to be envied."

Russell nodded his head in agreement. *Yes, he was right.* He had been fortunate enough to take part in a truly remarkable humanitarian effort that had undoubtedly saved many lives, and continued to. He cleared some papers off a seat and sat down.

"He does seem keen to take over and I sped him through the entirely dull parts of the job. I hope he fares well."

"What is dull to you may be comfortable routine for another. We're not all made the same, Russell. Off that seat please, I need the space. Where did you put the papers that were on the chair?"

"I know that." Russell stood up and handed Hugh the papers. "It's not for me to assume how he'll find the job. Who is taking over from you? I thought they would have arrived by now. You're not going to have any time left to brief them, are you?"

"That's a sore point, and the reason Brand has been even more disagreeable these past few weeks. I am not being replaced. Washington doesn't plan to send anyone. Mr. Whitlock will have to take on more himself. He is not pleased with that, as you might guess. I'm curbing my enthusiasm for London. He mustn't know how delighted I am to be taking this assignment. If we are mutually commiserating all is well between us. This is not the time for my eagerness to show." Hugh smiled and held his finger to his lips. Russell grinned back.

"You have been rather muted. I thought you were having second thoughts!"

"It's an act and now you know the reason. I can't wait to be in England. Now what's next?" Hugh moved to a large stack of papers and began to leaf through them.

"The only sobering part for me is the Channel crossing," Russell said. "Three ships were hit last week, unless that's German propaganda. With the Germans running the newspapers it's hard to know what the truth is. Can I help with any of this?" Russell placed his hand on a pile of papers in front of him.

"That's the same whoever is running the newspapers," Hugh laughed. "I agree about the boat trip. We'll be holding on to our hats until we are across, and then we can celebrate in style. Yes, they can all go into a new box. There is one behind the door. Will Marion be meeting you in London?"

Russell described his plans to Hugh as they methodically worked through the papers. After the upset with Marion on his last flying visit to London, Russell wanted to make sure there was no margin for error so he planned to go and visit her at home.

"I want to do it all properly this time," he explained.

"Won't that cramp your style with her mama breathing down your neck?" Hugh quizzed.

"Yes, it probably will, but I want Marion to know I am serious about her. I'm prepared to take my time."

"Very laudable. You'll have to take her on lots of country walks and get her lost in the woods. I don't imagine your resolve will last very long once you two lovebirds are on your own."

"We'll see. It was a bit ornery between us in London. I think I might have assumed too much."

"I thought it was Edith she was fighting you about?"

"Yes it was, mostly, but I shouldn't have assumed we would continue where we had left off here. It was all rather heady when she left Brussels, and we had both taken advantage of the moment. I think I need to take things more slowly this time. The English way."

"Yes. Always better to be invited in than pushed away, that's for sure."

The next few days were full of intense activity and the hours flew by for Russell. Even though he could be as daunted as the next person by new challenges he needed them to fire his motivation. The thought of days filled with repetitive tasks, stretching into the years of a working life filled him with dread. He enjoyed creating order out of chaos and had developed a penchant for crisis situations with problems to solve. How this new appetite was to be fed was the question that had started to disturb him.

Hugh was correct. He had been thrilled to be in at the start of this venture, but the administration that had settled on him had now lost its appeal. He still delighted in reading all the correspondence that his office received from Hoover; he was filing some now as one of his final acts. Hoover was a master with a pen and Russell found his eloquent letters provided lesson after lesson in diplomacy. He reread one of the letters to Lord Eustace before putting it in the file.

"I think you may take it that these measures will settle the business once and for all and that the strenuous tone of your note calling attention to this matter has done the world of good: still, I do not feel that in the midst of our other difficulties and complexities the matter merits further pursuit."

That told you.

It was obvious to Russell that Hoover had a quest, and was tireless in its pursuit. He never took no for an answer. Letter after letter of his that Russell read showed the man just saw difficulties as the next hurdle to overcome. It was the troubleshooting which Hoover was embroiled in, and his determination to succeed, that inspired Russell. The only activity that came close for him was his research and his own ambition to learn and master his subject. This had satisfied him before, which was why his keenness to return to it had surfaced. But the slightest niggle of doubt kept nagging at him, which so far he had pushed away, afraid of a chasm this might open up if he explored it. But the unasked question remained in the shadows of his mind: after two years of vital work in wartime, would his research still satisfy him?

Russell stepped off the train at Amersham and was almost knocked over by the woman who flung her arms around him. He had not had time to see her before her face was pressed against his cheek, and she was holding him tight, but he knew her voice immediately. He took hold of both her arms and by straightening his own managed to hold her back to enable him to see Marion's face, which was streaming with tears, but with a happy smile.

"Now that's something of a welcome," he said, beaming back at her.

"You've no idea how pleased I am that you are here."

"So it would seem. You almost knocked me over. Let me look at you."

Marion released her hold on him and pirouetted on her heel. She was wearing a cotton dress, with a fitted bodice which showed off her slim waist to great advantage. She drew admiring glances from more than just Russell.

"Enough. Come here," he said, laughing from happiness and relief at his reception.

Russell tried to draw her back into a hug, but Marion, now conscious of people around her, took his arm instead.

"I have a cart waiting outside. Where is your luggage?"

"I had most of my things sent on to Oxford, so I've only this valise. I can manage, we don't need to find a porter."

"That's just as well. This is Amersham, not London. We have to make do out here. If we don't need the cart I can let it go and we can walk if you are up for it. My home is a few miles."

"I would love to walk, but could we put my bag on the cart. Or is that too much trouble?"

"No, the carrier has a list of things to collect and take back to the house. No journey serves only one purpose these days. My parents have lost their horses to the war. Everyone around here was heartbroken when the horses were corralled for the army. Poor things, I hate to think of where they are now. I doubt we'll see them again."

Russell deposited his bag on the cart. The carrier doffed his cap and clicked the old horse forward. Russell took Marion's arm again and at a leisurely pace they started their walk.

"This weather is perfect," Russell said.

"It's been like this for days. Just right. Not too hot, but big blue skies. Our farmers want rain, but there always has to be a grumble somewhere," Marion replied.

The station was at the top of a long hill, and Missenden was along the valley at the bottom. Russell took in the surroundings as they walked and Marion pointed out several local features.

"That is St Mary's Church you can see below us."

They had skirted some woods and were striking downhill on a path across a field. He could see the roofs of the town houses nestling below and, majestic among them, the church.

"It looks idyllic. I love your old English towns. My mom would love to see this."

"Just wait until you see how old some of the buildings are. Many date from the 1500s."

"And is this all part of your uncle's kingdom?"

"His estate, not kingdom; sorry to disappoint m'lud. Yes, I think he owns probably half the town houses and public houses and most of the surrounding land. But bits and pieces are being sold off now I believe. I can't say I pay much attention to family affairs, but Mother always has something to say on the topic."

When they reached the town Marion stopped outside one or two of the houses to tell him something about their history. He liked the way the houses butted into each other, up close together but with no symmetry at all. He tended to be one for straight lines but he could feel the passage of time in the sagging roofs. Marion exchanged greetings with several people who passed them, but was not forthcoming with introductions.

"Let them wait to find out who you are," she said. "The gossip will be all around the area by teatime tomorrow. They can make of you what they will. My reputation is already tarnished."

"Is it that damaging for you to be seen walking arm in arm with a man?"

"I'm sure my mother would prefer a gap between us the size of a church aisle."

"Then we must respect that in her company. I don't want to be the cause of any upset while I am here, Marion."

"No, it's Alain that has caused the blemish on my character. And will continue to do so for a while, I am sure."

"He's still with you then?"

"Yes, yes he is."

Russell thought Marion was going to say something more, but instead she stopped and gave him the history of the market hall, built by one of the Drakes in the 1700s, and then she added, "It seems the right thing to do. For now anyway."

She glanced at him, as if to gauge his reaction to this. They continued walking and after a short while he responded.

"For him, yes, but for you?" Russell asked, picking up the thread.

"I'm prepared to keep an open mind about that for now. Christian charity seems very rigid in its definitions around here. Alms remain at arm's length. Turn a project into something you care about and it suddenly becomes something different, certainly for my mother."

"I'm sure she is just wanting to protect you. She has your best interests at heart. You have your life ahead of you."

"Nobly spoken. I'll see if you hold the same view of her after 'enjoying' her company for a few days."

"It's your company I have come here to 'enjoy'. I hope there will be plenty of that."

"Of course there will, but I do have chores to do too, and Alain, of course. We all have to contribute to the running of the house. Help is terribly difficult to hold onto these days."

"Perhaps I can be put to work too. Will there be something I can attend to, perhaps for your father?"

"That is a kind and generous thought. I am sure there will be something, but you are not with us long enough to be working. You will be our honoured guest."

The sweep of the farmland accentuated the depth of the valley as they left the high street behind them and walked along an old lane, beside a lake and then the river Misbourne. The banks were lush and green and populated with birch trees but Russell thought the title of "river" rather grand for a flow of water he considered to be the size of a stream back home.

"We skate on the lake in the winter," Marion said. "It really is great fun. The house at the top of the hill", Marion pointed to a cream Palladian styled mansion up the steep slope to her left, "is my uncle's home, the seat of the estate. Poor Uncle William: his eldest is dead and his younger son Edward is suffering. Uncle lives for horses and most of those have gone. He really is a broken man."

"I think more people are going to have their hearts broken soon. Did you see in the newspaper about the battle in France? Thousands have been killed."

"Yes, Father was reading about it at breakfast. Some place near the river Somme, in France. It sounded unbelievable."

"Quite. The guns failed to break open the German defences and the soldiers walked into machine gun fire. They were mown down in droves. This has turned into a war like no other."

"Oh don't, I can't bear to hear it. Father was extremely upset this morning. It will take days or weeks for the names of the casualties to filter through, so every family who has a son in France will be anxious. I am so thankful not to have a brother at times like this."

"Your family must have been pleased that you returned safely from Brussels. They must have been worried for you there."

"Yes," Marion nodded, "but needlessly. We were quite safe."

"Do they still not know of your escapades with Edith? I am assuming the answer is no."

"Of course they don't. It would bring on my mother's palpitations. You mustn't breathe a word. Please, Russell," she pleaded.

"I wouldn't dream of it, unless of course …" He tailed off.

"Unless what?" Marion replied sharply.

"Unless there are insufficient kisses from you in a day to keep me distracted."

"That sounds like blackmail to me, Mr. Clark," Marion laughed.

"I can assure you, Miss Drake, that is exactly what it is."

Marion took his hand and pulled him into some shade by a cluster of horse chestnut trees.

"We had better stop here for a few minutes then. All too soon we will be in my village and I won't dare to even take your arm there."

Russell needed no further encouragement.

The house was as Russell had remembered with its regular features of windows on either side of a porched front door, but it looked new compared to the properties they had walked past in the village, and larger than most. He had not been invited into the dining room on his previous visit to the house. On that occasion, almost two years before, afternoon tea had been served to him in the salon when he had brought news of Marion for the family. He had left Brussels just before the Germans had marched in, but Marion had turned down the opportunity to return to England, preferring to stay and face the consequences of the occupation. If she had returned, he would most likely have stayed in Oxford too. He would now have been nearing the end of his studies and they might be planning to wed soon. And there would have been no child to add any complications. Marion had left him alone in the dark room, with its heavy furniture, while she went to fetch Alain.

"I'm sure he recognises you," she said once she had returned and both Russell and the child eyed each other curiously.

"Don't be absurd. Of course he doesn't. He hardly had his eyes open when you left Brussels. You must have been feeding him well. He's glowing with health. My, he's grown!"

"It must be your voice he recognises. Look at that smile for you. Do you want to hold him? Take his hands, he likes to try to stand." Marion bent down to put Alain on the carpet.

"No really, let him stay with you. I ..."

"Of course Mr. Clark doesn't wish to hold him, Marion. That is what Nanny is for; really my girl, the way you moon over that child is unhealthy. Mr. Clark, good day to you." Mrs. Drake stretched out her hand in greeting as she swept into the room. "I am sorry my husband is not here to meet you, but he has been called out to one of our parishioners. Another lost son, I believe. It is so nice to meet a young man not in uniform, a rare sight these days, at least one with all his limbs. You look quite the athlete. Do you ride?"

Russell shook hands with his hostess, thanked her for her welcome and to make up for his equestrian shortcomings he began to describe his love for a game of tennis. Mrs. Drake cut across him.

"I shall look forward to hearing more over luncheon, but I must be excused to check on the arrangements. One cannot rely on staff these days. Does your mother find the same? Of course she wouldn't, you're not fighting a war, are you. It is so tiresome. Marion, luncheon will be served at one o'clock. Do show our guest to his room. He might wish to change from his travel clothes. Until one o'clock, Mr. Clark."

The door closed behind her and Marion giggled at the look on Russell's face.

"Had you forgotten how imperious Mother is?" Marion asked.

"I don't think she was when we last met. She really was concerned for you then."

"Not any more. I'm largely an irritation and an embarrassment. Still," she said, turning her attention back to Alain, "you're worth every minute of the heartache from her, aren't you young man?"

She bent down and put his feet on the floor. He grasped a finger from each of her hands and bent his knees in a bobbing motion.

"Can he walk?"

"No, but he likes to stand, and he can crawl at quite a speed. Since his first birthday in May he is on the move most of the time when given the chance."

"I can see Therese in him."

"Can you?"

"Yes, he has fine hands like hers, and her blonde hair and blue eyes. And he has her mouth."

"I hope he has her nature and not that of his father. I have never seen Alain in a temper. If he wants something he will just wait. He makes his cousin Anthony look like a tyrant. Not that I mind that."

"Anthony? Your sister's son?"

"Yes, you'll meet Evelyn at luncheon."

"Are you getting along better?"

"Not exactly. We have our moments, but she agrees with Mother: I have shamed the family and reduced her chances of a new husband, and she is not even finished mourning the last one yet."

"Well, I look forward to meeting her all the same, and particularly to meeting your father again."

"Yes, he said the same at breakfast. Let me show you your room. And don't worry about Mother's pretensions about changing for luncheon from your limited wardrobe. If you need to borrow anything for dinner I am sure my father will oblige. Come on, young man," Marion lifted Alain, "we have stairs to climb."

Left in his room while she went to supervise Alain's lunch, Russell lay on the bed and thought of Marion and the pressure of her lips on his from when they kissed underneath the shady branches of the tree. He wanted to marry her. The warmth of her welcome at the station had cast aside any doubts that had lingered from his last visit. She was spontaneous and warm and beautiful. Tendrils of her brown hair still escaped any attempt to bring them to order. The confident way she carried herself always put him at ease. When she was relaxed and open he could not imagine a more entrancing person to partner him in life. He had almost proposed to her under the tree, but protocol had held him back. He must speak to her father first. Hugh had warned him how stiff the British could be about manners. He loved her and knew they would be happy together and surely their engagement would solve the problem of her social standing. No wonder she had wanted to escape all these strictures and live in Belgium. The anonymity there must have held enormous appeal.

She was gutsy and he loved that about her. Sometimes rash and hot-blooded but he could surely hope that she would grow to trust his judgement before rushing into decisions once they were together.

She was certainly a prize filly. Russell chuckled to himself as he started to apply equestrian language to his thoughts of her. Got to brush up on the lingo before lunch, he said to himself. They were such a horsey crowd, but with not a ride left between them. *Brush yourself down boy, and go ride the storm.* Russell washed his face and combed his hair, but then rifled his fingers through it again, remembering that Marion preferred his hair wavy to straight. He took a deep breath and walked down to the dining room.

He met Marion and her father at the bottom of the stairs.

"Bernard Drake, delighted to meet you again," said the Reverend warmly as they shook hands. "I hope you have been made comfortable. Sorry it will be such a short visit. You're off to Oxford I hear. Picking up the reins of your studies I believe?

Keen to get back into the saddle I'm sure. You sit here next to me," Bernard led them both into the dining room and was settling Russell to his right at the table, "and you can tell me all about your studies. Medieval law isn't it, or have I remembered incorrectly?"

"Yes, sir. Oxford again, but its not medieval law. Its …"

"Ahh, here they all come. Come along. Evelyn, have you met Mr. Clark, Marion's guest? No, well here you are both of you." Russell jumped to his feet. "My daughter Evelyn, Mr. Clark, and you have met my wife again, I believe?" Russell nodded to Mrs. Drake and shook hands with Evelyn. Mr. Drake then directed his attentions to his wife. "Yes, dear, we are sitting down. No, we don't want the food to spoil, and yes, I will say the grace."

While Mr. Drake was distracted by his family, Russell studied Evelyn who was sitting directly opposite him. She was exquisite. Not as tall as Marion and the opposite in colouring: blonde, blue eyed, and graceful. Every movement of her hands was balletic and he found himself mesmerised as they fluttered with her napkin and passed dishes around the table. Mr. Drake had to repeat himself to gain Russell's attention.

"You were telling me about your studies, Mr. Clark."

"Russell, please call me Russell, sir, and yes, I was, but perhaps we can talk more later. It is a dry subject for such a jolly table as this."

Russell nodded his head to Evelyn and her mother and turned to Marion too to include everyone in his comment. Evelyn was the first to respond.

"Mr. Clark, sorry, Russell, Marion has told us so little about you; she is quite the dark horse. We would enjoy hearing more about you and your country. Do tell us, are you from a city or the country?" She smiled at Russell and looked directly into his eyes in a frank manner that startled him as she plumbed him with her questions.

It was only later that Marion described Evelyn's special smiles to Russell. Most of the mealtime conversation was taken up with him answering Evelyn's questions. He spoke his answers to the whole of the table and wherever he could he introduced Marion's name, but it was clear he was being totally monopolised by Evelyn. By the time dessert was served Russell felt distinctly uncomfortable and was fearful of an eruption from Marion, but when he glanced her way and managed to catch her eye all she did was offer an amused smile. He did not know if he was supposed to pay court to Evelyn, or whether he should attempt to direct the conversation himself, but no one else attempted any diversion, so he faltered from one question to the next making valiant attempts to eat something at the same time. His only respite came when Mr. Drake intervened.

"Thank you, Evelyn, for giving Mr. Clark such a grilling. I am sure he must feel there is nothing left to reveal about his life or his country. It has been quite an education, and a wonderful diversion from our usual dialogue about the war. You have entertained us well, Mr. Clark, Russell, but I promise no further interrogations."

Russell was relieved when the conversation moved from him, but he had to admit to feeling just a little wistful when Evelyn's attention shifted away too. He had enjoyed her undivided attention; in fact it had quite captivated him. Later, when he and Marion were alone he pretended to cajole her.

"You might have given me some warning, Marion."

"About what?"

"About Evelyn. I had no idea."

"No idea about what? That she planned a charm offensive? That she would monopolise you?"

"That she was so, so, umm ..."

"Is attractive, the word you are looking for? Mr. Clark, or may I call you Russell?"

Russell ignored her teasing. "She is certainly very comely," he said.

"And she has a foul temper, can be spiteful, and ignores her child. But yes, she has charms."

"Luckily for you I prefer brunettes."

"Luckily for you, you mean. I would warn any man off Evelyn. She has been too carefully schooled by my mother."

Russell and Marion were sitting side by side in the garden on the south side of the rectory enjoying the late afternoon sun and each other's company. He was pleased to have Marion to himself, without her family and, even more, without Alain. Her attention was taken when the baby was present.

"Now this is pleasant, very pleasant," Russell said. "This moment could only be improved if I was able to kiss the back of your neck, with no fear of your mother barrelling down on me."

"Not a chance. I saw the curtains twitch a moment ago. You'll have to restrain yourself. I will try and find some private time for us later."

"I need a conversation with your father too. When is the best time to catch him?"

"After breakfast is generally a good time. Mother is directing the household for the day so he disappears into his study. What do you want to see him about?"

"Oh, just a chat. He wanted to hear more about what I am doing at Oxford. It's too dull for a mealtime conversation."

"You didn't used to think that. When we first met it was all you talked about. Are you looking forward to returning to your studies? I like the thought of you in Oxford. It's not too far away at all."

"I share that thought with you. Being separated for so long has felt very hard at times, and at least now our letters will be sure to reach each other. Altogether better."

"It's a good job I've decided not to join up then, or we would have been ships that passed in the night. As you arrived, I would have been departing."

"What do you mean, join up? Join what? Go where?"

"The Voluntary Auxiliary Division."

"The what?"

"Nurses. VAD nurses. They need them overseas. I was exploring going to Malta: they have several hospitals there. Or even to France."

Russell sat bolt upright and turned to look at her.

"Are you mad?" he sounded alarmed.

"Excuse me?"

"Haven't you been in enough trouble already? Don't you think it would be wise to sit out the rest of this war? France is no place for women. I would much rather know you were safe, here. I told you that before."

"It's a good job I didn't wait to discuss it with you. If I hadn't made up my own mind, for my own good reasons, I would definitely join now, just to prick your pompous assumptions about women. Why is it that only men can have all the fun?"

"Fun? Fun? When are you going to lose this recklessness of yours? Look at the trouble that attitude caused in Brussels. You seem to think this war is a game. It isn't."

"Don't be so patronising, Russell, and don't tell me what I should and shouldn't be doing. Of course I know the dangers are real. Too many have sacrificed their lives not to know that." Marion turned on the bench to face him. "But this war is a game: a politician's game. They should lock the politicians from all the fighting countries into a room and not let them out until they can agree a peace. The use of guns can never bring things to a satisfactory conclusion. Leave it to the generals and they'll keep fighting until the last man is left standing. It's all utterly ridiculous, but that doesn't mean I shouldn't play my part in helping those who have no choice but to fight."

"And I don't want to fight with you, Marion," Russell reached to take her hand, but hastily withdrew when Marion gave a very slight shake of her head to remind him they might well be being observed. "But thank goodness you saw sense and have decided not to go," he concluded.

"It was not about seeing sense, as you put it. I have responsibilities. I have Alain to consider."

"And what about me? Didn't I feature in your thinking?"

"You are quite capable of looking after yourself, but I am still the best person to care for Alain."

"Well, that puts me in my place." Russell felt quite put out at where this private moment had taken them. He stood up, put his hands in his pockets and adopted a relaxed stance leaning against a tree, just in case other eyes were indeed on them. But Marion had managed to unsettle him considerably.

"I am going to work at a local hospital. When I say hospital, it is a country house, similar to my uncle's, that has been made available for patients. They specialise in injuries to the head and nervous disorders. I have been to visit and will be interviewed soon. They are checking my references."

"That sounds more like it. Close to home and away from the battlefields." Russell felt encouraged and walked back towards her on the seat and sat down again.

"From the screams that resound in the corridors, I don't think the nightmares of the battlefields are far away. The orderly who showed me around said she found it quite harrowing. My cousin Edward has nightmares. He says when he wakes every morning his bed is drenched with sweat. Poor Teddy, he is so cut up about losing his brother."

"It must be dreadful," Russell said wishing he could hold her, such was his relief at her decision. "Will you be able to visit me in Oxford? Do you know anyone you could stay with? Women aren't allowed in our rooms. I would love to show you around the colleges."

"I am sure I can, but let me see how arrangements work out at the hospital first. I will need to know my routines, but yes, I would love to visit. Now it's time I saw to Alain's meal. Will you come with me?"

"If it's all right with you, I think I'll sit here a bit longer. What time is dinner called?"

"Eight o'clock: prompt." Marion's tone was brusque when she replied. "I think we have some guests joining us so Evelyn's attention will be distracted from you. I'll see you at dinner. We'll be in the nursery if you change your mind."

Marion was clearly disappointed he was not joining her with Alain and the minute she had left his side Russell regretted his decision. He was being churlish and he knew it. He should enjoy just being with her even if her attention was on another, but he was greedy for that attention for himself. An hour slipped by while he stubbornly remained on the seat. Marion did not return and his spirits were lowered when he went in to change for dinner and an evening with the family.

The Rectory, Little Missenden, July 1916

Marion was with Alain but for once he did not have her full attention; her mind kept straying to Russell. She had looked out of the window a couple of times to see him sitting on the seat in the garden. He had not moved since she had left him to come to the nursery. They had been apart for months and yet it seemed he would rather sit on his own than spend every minute with her. *Why?* She felt confused and was conscious of a concern that was nagging at the back of her mind: would Russell accept her plan to keep Alain. He had not been as warm towards him as she had imagined he might.

She had been so excited about his visit, but had kept her emotions to herself to avoid her mother's censorship. To Evelyn she had referred to him only as a friend from Brussels which, in her sister's eyes made him fair play for her. Evelyn had certainly turned on the charm at lunchtime and had been as flirtatious as she dared in her mother's company. Fortunately Marion had no fear that he would be ensnared. Evelyn was pretty, but dim. He would tire of her attention in an instant, she was sure.

She wished she and Russell did not quarrel quite so easily. Not that they really argued, but she could feel herself rebel whenever she experienced his attempts at control. She considered her decisions were hers to own, but then this was the independent streak her mother had tried to batter out of her since she was a child. She never readily acquiesced to another's way or will and according to her mother this characteristic would be her downfall. She always pushed back against expectations when they were counter to hers. But the draw to each other was still strong. That is what this evening needed more of, the pull of attraction, she decided. Determined not to be outshone by Evelyn at the table that evening Marion began to think through her attire until her attention was drawn back to Alain who was in the mood to play. She handed him into Nanny's care earlier than planned. Tonight she wanted to make sure she had plenty of time to dress.

Marion knew she had her outfit just right when she met her father at the bottom of the stairs. He was waiting for her mother. It was a tradition they had and Marion was gratified when he smiled and nodded his head.

"You look especially beautiful this evening, my dear girl," her father said as Marion stopped and kissed him on the cheek. "Quite beautiful."

Marion had to admit she was pleased with the effect she had managed. Her hair was usually tied back, but this evening she had put it up, loosely pinned so that it looked soft around her face. Her gown flattered her figure with its slim waist. The colour, a deep purple, looked luxurious against the brown of her hair. She had never been one to fuss over her looks and had been forced into various dresses for family occasions in the past, but tonight she had prepared herself for a man's eyes, for Russell, and she liked the way it made her feel.

She saw the effect the minute he walked into the room. The Austen phrase, "Darcy was struck by her beauty" came to her mind and she had to stop herself from giggling when she saw the look on Russell's face.

"You look beautiful," he said, and he raised her hand and put it to his lips.

"Don't I always?" Marion sparred before regretting it instantly. This was not the moment for banter. "Thank you," she acquiesced, "I dressed for you."

"I feel honoured," Russell said and only released her hand when her mother entered the room.

"Have introductions been made?" Marion's mother asked before taking Russell to the other side of the room to meet the couple who were joining them for dinner, together with a middle-aged gentleman.

Marion watched Evelyn turn her charms onto Mr. Bazzard. He was a widower of the parish and very partial to her. Marion knew he occupied a back-stop position in Evelyn's mind should she fail to secure a more fashionable second husband. He was a charming man, a farmer, and with not insignificant holdings. He beamed at Evelyn every time she turned her attention onto him. Marion knew Russell was watching her and he winked at her several times when table conversation or a new serving had distracted everyone. She was glowing and had to stop herself smiling several times when she caught her mother looking at her.

"That was a delightful evening," Russell said to Marion as they sat next to each other in the salon after the guests had departed, "and you looked divine across the table in the candlelight."

"Thank you, kind sir. You looked the part too." And he did. "We make a handsome pair I hope."

"We do. Do you think it is obvious to everyone, what we feel for each other?"

"I suspect so. My mother has never seen me pay so much attention to my appearance before. She even paid me a compliment. But we must not remain downstairs for long. Everyone is turning in for the night. I wondered if we might take a picnic tomorrow. There is a wonderful vantage point on the Icknield Way, close by. Just the two of us; I can arrange for Alain to stay with Nanny for the day."

"What a marvelous plan. I will look forward to it immensely. You're quite a girl, Miss Drake and you're my girl too. I hope you know how happy that makes me feel."

They parted at the top of the stairs and both made sure they closed their bedroom doors in a way that the family would hear.

The day was not going as Marion planned. Breakfast had been fine. All seemed to be in good cheer. She had left Russell heading off to speak to her father while she went to the kitchen to prepare their picnic, but when they met up again he seemed distracted and withdrawn. She was extremely surprised when he insisted they took Alain along on the picnic with them. On this occasion her ward acted as her unwelcome chaperone and Marion's own spirits were dampened. Alain was receiving more of Russell's attention than she was and she was beginning to resent it. She had imagined a romantic time and even anticipated that he might talk to her of the future, their future. She was quite ready to marry him. Last night before sleep came she had convinced herself that she could enter into a partnership with him, and could learn to accept more of his counsel on her decisions. If they were decisions that determined their joint future, then they would be entirely different anyway. But no proposal was forthcoming. In fact the reverse, he hardly engaged in a proper conversation at all.

"Did you enjoy talking to Father this morning? Did you catch him in his study?"

"What? Oh yes, I did."

"What did you talk about?"

"He was very distressed by the mess of the Somme battle. We spoke about that and my return to Oxford. He was interested in my studies. It was good to talk about them again. It fired up my enthusiasm. I can't wait to get back into it again. I miss other students too. It's always stimulating to hear what others are doing. I'm looking forward to seeing those blue spires again. If it is all right with you, I will get the train this evening. I don't want to overstay my welcome with your folks. They have been most kind."

"But I thought you were staying at least until tomorrow? Why the change in plan?"

"I am keen to get back. It has been a long break from my work."

"So one more day won't make much of a difference then. I had hoped that this evening, I mean tonight, that we could spend time together, in your room. I was going to come to you."

"No, I couldn't, Marion. Not under your parents' roof, not at all."

"Then when are we going to, to have time together?"

"We are having time together now."

"You know what I mean. I thought …"

"And what are you thinking, young man?" Russell interrupted Marion by burrowing his face into Alain's tummy, which brought forward a rush of giggles.

Alain's chortles were irresistible and infectious and soon lightened the mood, but, even so, Marion was left with a deep feeling of disappointment. His attraction to her the previous evening seemed to have been forgotten by Russell and some of her old doubts about not being bright enough for him returned. His sights were set on Oxford and his intellectual set. Perhaps he saw her now more as a country simpleton, stripped of the glamour of her uniform and her city confidence? She feared she was diminished in his eyes and he seemed oblivious of her desire for his affection and avoided her touch at every turn. She felt confused by the change in him, and then she remembered he preferred his own company yesterday, in the garden, to hers in the nursery. Perhaps the signs had been there all along and she just had not seen them, or wanted to see them. Yesterday she would have been thrilled to see him so engaged with Alain: it was what she wanted, the three of them together, as a family, but as the day lengthened and the distance between the two of them grew she began to fear that he had a different destiny in view and her dreams were to be assigned to fantasy.

Russell had gathered his things together when they returned to the house and Marion offered no resistance when her father offered to accompany him to the station. How had she lost him in the space of a day? He said all the right things as they parted, promised to write and have her to Oxford as soon as they could manage it, but she knew his heart was not behind the words. She could not work out why. In all conscience she was unable to blame anything on her mother. Even to Marion's sensitivities, her mother had not put a foot wrong. Her father seemed his usual friendly self despite his recent melancholy over the recent casualties.

"Let me know how it goes with the hospital," Russell said, "and do take good care of yourself and that young man. Write soon."

"I will, on all counts. And I hope Oxford is as you left it, and you can find all your books, Russell." He turned his head to her and she planted a kiss soundly on his lips. "I love you." He squeezed her arm in return and climbed onto the cart beside her father. She watched them down the drive and felt a flicker of hope when he turned and blew her a kiss, just before they disappeared out of sight. Never had she felt so separated from him. The last thing she wanted was to find Evelyn in the nursery.

"He seems a nice boy," Evelyn said to her as she entered the room.

"He is more than a boy. He is twenty-five."

"But he seems so young compared to the soldiers we meet. Battle does mature men. Don't you agree?"

"The ones it doesn't kill you mean?"

"So will he make an honest woman of you? Are you to wed?" Evelyn asked raising her eyebrows.

"Evelyn, really. Mind your own business." Marion busied herself with Alain and turned her back on Evelyn.

"I take it that means no then? He's not quite ready to play happy families just yet. I see he didn't spend much time with baby Alain. Not quite the doting father."

"He is not the father," Marion replied with some weariness, "and actually", she turned back to face Evelyn, "he asked that we take Alain on our picnic today. He was wonderful with him. He played with him the whole time."

"Not quite what you had in mind, I'm sure. Stop," Evelyn raised her hand to interrupt Marion's riposte, "don't fight me, Marion. He's handsome. I wouldn't have wanted a baby on a picnic with me if I was out with him, that's for sure. And you quite captivated him over dinner last evening. I was left entirely to Mr. Bazzard."

"Who you seemed to handle in your usual way. He would have eaten dinner off your hand if he had been allowed."

"Oh, really? He is no challenge at all. He is sweet and most attentive. But why has Russell left us already? I was looking forward to hearing more about America at dinner this evening." Evelyn moved across the room to sit on the window ledge. "Not a lover's tiff I hope?" Evelyn looked at Marion but received no reaction. "Mother will be disappointed. She thinks he is your only salvation. She was quite taken by your look for dinner. I have to say, sis, you did look rather good, quite the turn."

"Thank you for the compliment, Evelyn," Marion said, ignoring her questions, "if you mean it as one, but I do wish you would stay out of my business."

"You are family business. You cannot live at home and expect to be independent. You forfeited that when you returned with your tail between your legs. It is obvious to us all that you were thrown out of the nursing school. And what have you done since your return? Nothing but moon over that baby." Marion was changing Alain and playing with his legs. "Anyone would believe he is yours the fuss you make of him."

"He has no one but me, Evelyn. Where is your Christian charity?"

"In the alms box. That's enough."

"And I am going to return to nursing. I did not leave Brussels a failure. I have excellent references and am about to put them to good use. I have an interview next week." Marion was struggling to control her temper.

"Back to Belgium? That boyfriend and you are never in the same place. That is not the way to catch a man."

"I don't want to catch a man. I'm not like you. And no, not back in Belgium, at Bachelor House. I will see if they will take me."

"From what I understand they will take anyone."

"Then perhaps you should avail yourself as well."

"I shall do no such thing. This war has had everything it is going to get from me. You do not know how I have suffered. To lose one's husband is a terrible bind."

"And to find a new one, even harder?"

"Don't be beastly, Marion. I cannot ignore the fact that the numbers of men are greatly reduced. I have to use what God has given me to advantage …"

"Before it sags." *Nasty, Marion.*

"I can see you don't want to be friends, but I will not stoop to your level. I shall tell you what I wanted to say and leave you to your infant." Evelyn stood and moved towards the door, with a glance in Anthony's direction, asleep in his cot. "Have you remembered we have a cousin with a house in Oxford? He and his family are not always there, but I am sure they would accept you as a guest, should you wish to visit your young man."

Marion was taken aback by this gesture from Evelyn. She had forgotten about her cousin Robert. He was considerably older than her, and not a member of the family with whom she shared any familiarity or friendship. It really was generous of Evelyn to offer such a suggestion. *What a brick.*

"Thank you, Evelyn. It's kind of you to think of that. I'll make enquiries and talk to Mother."

"No need. It was Mother who told me to mention him. You see we do have your best interests at heart; however much you doubt us. I will see you at dinner."

Once Alain was settled Marion's thoughts returned to Oxford. She had not expected her mother to facilitate her courtship with Russell and in normal circumstances would have been extremely appreciative, but, after what she concluded was a distinct cooling in his feelings towards her, she now wondered whether any such efforts might be too late. She had taken her place in his affections for granted. She had thought their night together in Brussels and the afternoon in London had sealed their bond forever. She had trusted he would always want her and she needed that certainty to allow her to push against him without concern that he would back away, that he would hold fast their love. *I shouldn't have argued.* Perhaps she had been too headstrong, and undermined his confidence that she would be open to his views? She thought she had considered his opinions more, but she had fought against her mother's interference for so long that her instinctive response was always to dig in her heels. She needed to take and make opportunities for him to see her differently if this was the fear he carried. *Soften up, Marion.* She must be more malleable and give consideration to his wishes more readily, and not leave him in Oxford too long on his own. She still wanted to believe in their future, but at the moment the path ahead was distinctly unclear.

Her preparations for dinner were more sober than the evening before. To give herself a boost of confidence before she went downstairs she drew out of her drawer the letter Sister Wilkins had given her from Therese and reread it for the hundredth time. She had learnt the translation by heart.

> My dear Marion,
> There will come a day when this letter will be placed in your hands, by Sister Wilkins. This means you are safe and that Alain remains in your care and I thank God for this. I know my love for him is carried by you, and that through your nurture and protection he will thrive. He will be a messenger for God of that I am sure. Why else would I have been asked to bear him?

The first time Marion had read the letter she thought Therese was announcing Alain was the next Messiah until she had read on.

> Only you will understand his sensitivities and will encourage him to find his way of telling people what God wants them to hear. I had no such guidance and struggled with myself for years. You will see the gift that he is sure to have, for what it is, and will encourage it.
> I see you with a compass in your hand. Your decisions when made will always keep you on your true path. You will always know what is the right decision, and you will take Alain on this journey with you. You will not be swayed by others: this is your independent path, but you will not be on your own. Ultimately another will join you and you will be a family.

Marion was unsure of the exact translation for "ultimately"; perhaps Therese meant eventually, but the message was the same: an inference that this would not be immediate. It was her own impatience and perhaps even insecurity that had sought certainty with Russell now. She had a niggling concern that Therese had not named Russell in this picture of her future. She found this unsettling. For her he was her North Star and she had no intention of deviating from him. He felt right and that was what Therese had written: that she would always know. She also felt at ease about her decision to have Alain remain with her and not to have joined the VAD overseas. She would attend the hospital at Bachelor House next week and hopefully be accepted. More than anything she needed to keep busy. Tonight she would tell her parents of her plans. Having let it slip out in her conversation with Evelyn, she now had no choice.

> I will hold you and Alain in my prayers every day, and whenever you need to feel God's hand in your life, step into the sunshine and His presence. Therese.

Marion looked out of her bedroom window and saw a shaft of evening sunlight dance on the garden seat she and Russell had sat on the day before. She went down to dinner with a smile on her face, and reassurance in her heart.

Bachelor House, Summer 1916

"You couldn't have arrived at a better time," Doctor Ambrose said to Marion. He had met her in the reception room at the hour of her appointment. Tall, early forties she guessed, and strikingly handsome with a strong jaw and a full head of dark hair. "Your credentials are excellent and we are expecting a big influx of patients from the battlefields of the Somme. Matron said you interviewed well. We need strong nerves for some of our patients. Many have lost their wits and need a strong hand if we are to return them to the battlefields."

"Return them? Haven't they done enough?" Marion was so surprised to hear patients would be sent back she spoke out before thinking.

"It depends on their condition." Doctor Ambrose appeared to take no offence. "Many of the head injuries will never fully recover. But the nervous dispositions, these can be cured. Enough to join the ranks again."

"War is barbaric. You must think the same with the injuries you deal with?"

"What I or you think is of little account. Our job is to patch and mend, nurse."

"Yes doctor, of course."

Marion had stepped out of line, but it was the immediate ease she felt with Doctor Ambrose that led her to speak her mind. He invited candour with his open face and warm smile, and he had held her hand for longer than was strictly necessary when they met, or so she had thought.

"No, I'm being tetchy. I agree with you, Nurse Drake. That is one of matron's sayings: to patch and mend. We face a human tragedy every day. Bring the politicians in through these doors. See what they have to say then. That's what I really think."

"And the generals too," Marion felt encouraged to say. "They need to be chastened." The doctor smiled.

"I can see that you and I could put the world to rights, Nurse Drake. I look forward to working with you. We will make a strong team. As long as we keep on the right side of matron, that is. I hope that skill has been part of your training?"

"My last matron was Edith Cavell, in Brussels. She was strict but always fair. She made her expectations clear and I never experienced any difficulty with her. We worked together very well. I was often in her confidence."

"And what a tragedy her death was. How can men lose their senses like that? It must have upset you to lose her. Is that why you returned?"

"Well, it was all connected, but not exactly straightforward. Perhaps that's a story for another time."

"I look forward to another occasion then. Ahh, here are the others. Let the ward round commence. Keep by my side, Nurse Drake. I would like to hear your views. It will give me a better idea of where to place you when you start with us. When is that to be by the way?"

"Nurse Drake will begin the day after tomorrow, Doctor Ambrose. She can only work day shifts, but will no doubt make herself extremely useful." Matron had approached behind Marion and her voice took her by surprise. Management by stealth was the best trick of a matron. Marion realised she would have to watch herself and win matron over, but all such thoughts soon left her as they approached bed after bed of patients with horrific head and facial injuries. It astounded Marion that one man in particular had survived. He had lost his lower jaw and part of the back of his head. She looked at and into his eyes, which stared blankly back at her. Before she left his bedside she patted his hand. She caught Doctor Ambrose looking at her and withdrew her hand, but he smiled and nodded before proceeding to the next bed. At the end of the round he took her and matron to one side.

"Nurse Drake handled that admirably, matron. Some of our patients are not pretty sights. Not everyone can see past the damage to the man, but I see that you can. Admirable, admirable."

Matron looked pleased. "Very well, Doctor Ambrose. Nurse Drake will be assigned to the ground floor. Come along with me to arrange your uniform and I will introduce you to the rest of the team on your wards. We are short of staff so they won't have much time to talk, but you will know where to come on Wednesday."

Whilst on her way home with her uniform under her arm, Marion took stock of what she had only intended to be a fact-finding day. She had not expected to be needed immediately. At least she would be away from the dull routines of home and the complaints of her mother, but it unnerved her to realise that she would be leaving Alain in Nanny's care, all day, each day. She would have to talk Nanny through all the things he liked and how to interpret his needs. There was so much to cover and so little time for him to adjust. She felt rushed and slightly panicked and sorry that she had allowed herself to be talked into starting that very week, but it had been a heady experience at the hospital, and the decision had simply felt the right one to make.

She had amazed herself at how well she had accepted the injuries of the patients and still glowed at the praise from Doctor Ambrose. If she was honest she had been somewhat intoxicated by his attentions. It was obvious that he had taken a liking to her instantly. He was a good-looking fit man and she could not help wondering how it was that he was not in France. Perhaps with his pacifist views he was a conscientious objector. No doubt he had his own story to tell. She looked forward to finding out more.

That evening she wrote to Russell to tell him of her new job.

> Dear Russell,
> I have yet to hear that you have returned safely to Oxford, but I do hope all was in order when you arrived. Do you have the same rooms, and neighbours, or has all changed?
> Much is different for me! I visited the hospital today for my interview and they have signed me up immediately, even before all the paperwork has been completed. I still don't know all my terms, but they are short of experienced staff and Doctor Ambrose seemed to be delighted with my approach. He is mid-forties and I do not understand how he has evaded France. I will find out his story and he wants to hear more of Edith Cavell. She's already a heroic figure in people's eyes.
> The patients are a sorry sight, the few I have seen. I wasn't taken to the wards for those with nervous disorders, but I saw some of them walking in the grounds. Cousin Edward looks fit compared to them. They cannot control their limbs. I have no idea how they are to be helped. I have much to learn, but after so long away from nursing I will be happy to be of use again and employing my training. I have to confess that I didn't welcome your impatience to return to Oxford. I wanted more time with you. But now I am to be working again I understand better. You wanted to be absorbed again and I am sure your studies will quickly consume you.

I have agreed to work days only. I couldn't bear to leave Alain at night. He still wakes up sometimes and no one else would provide him the same comfort. Even though I have much to organise, and there is no time for both of us to get used to the idea, I cannot wait until Wednesday to start work. Mother is disgusted, but she is with all my decisions.

I hope all was well with you during your visit here? You seemed quite withdrawn when you left. Perhaps too much exposure to family is not a good thing? Was everything fine with Father when you spoke to him? Feel free to ignore all these questions. I do understand your impatience to return to Oxford and should just thank you for your diversion to visit me.

Let me know how things are for you,

I remain your loving Marion.

"He wrinkles his nose when he wants a cuddle, and frowns when he needs to be changed. He has a particular face when he has had enough to eat and will move the minute you put him on the floor. He likes to stand and …"

"Thank you, Miss Marion, I think I can work out the rest. I will keep him to his usual routine. Don't you worry about a thing; he is such a good little boy, always has been, and will be a delight for me to spend more time with. Between us we will manage. You can begin and end each day with him, as long as you don't tire yourself."

Marion was breakfasting with Alain in the nursery and was telling Nanny of her new working arrangements. She ran her fingers through his mop of unbrushed blonde hair.

"I will still probably see more of you than I do of your sister Evelyn," Nanny quipped.

"And you are sure that looking after two isn't too much for you?" Marion asked.

"I have had five at home before, all under the age of five too. Don't tell anyone, but this feels easy."

"Your secret is safe with me." Marion buttered Alain some bread. "I am not going to leave you today at all."

"How was news of your job received by madam?"

Marion sighed.

"Mother despairs of ever hearing good news from me. She has been fishing around since Russell's visit and when I said I had some news I think she was expecting or hoping for my engagement announcement. Her hopes were dashed once again. I'm only pleased I have escaped any form of interrogation about him. I haven't felt ready for that."

"Is everything all right? I thought you said Mr. Clark was going to be staying for a few days. His visit seemed very brief. I hope you don't mind my asking?"

"Not at all, Nanny, I consider you my friend. I'm sure all is fine. It was my hope he would stay for longer, but I'm sure our family ways can be quite stultifying and he was impatient to be back at Oxford. His studies have been on hold for a year. He has made an enormous sacrifice. I can understand his enthusiasm now that I am returning to nursing, but I must admit I wasn't that happy with him when he left. He just seemed to withdraw completely, and I had thought he might want to cement our relationship. Nothing formal. But he offered no thoughts about our future at all. Perhaps Mother is right, Alain has become too important to me and perhaps Russell felt put out."

"There's none so queer as men and what they think," Nanny said. "They are a mystery to me. I intend to steer clear of them. And you need a man who is sure of himself, to match you, miss. You could run circles around most, and then boredom would set in. I admire the way you stand up for yourself."

"Thank you. It's nice to hear this quality complimented when I am so often chastised for being stubborn and headstrong. Mother does turn everything into a battle of wills. Russell calls me feisty, but says he likes that about me. I do have to watch myself though. I flared up when he said I was not to consider active service abroad. I had decided against it anyway, because of Alain, but I do hate to be told what I can and cannot do. If that's a fault I just can't help it, I'm afraid."

"Give and take, that's what is needed for an easy life."

"Should life be easy? Is that what we can expect of it?" Marion had moved Alain on her lap and she looked at him. "We seem to be messing the world up for you at the moment, young man."

"Easy relations yes, I don't think we should be looking for fights all the time."

Marion mock punched the air using Alain's fists, which she held in each of her hands; he started to giggle.

"And what do you plan for today with Alain? Nanny asked. "Do you want Anthony and me along, or do you want to enjoy a day with Alain?"

"Let's take a picnic and all go out," Marion suggested. "I took Russell to the Icknield Way. From the vantage point there I can imagine I can see the blue haze of Oxford. We could even invite Evelyn."

"You go and find her, miss, and I will organise the boys' things. The weather looks bright enough."

Every part of Marion's body ached after her first day at work. She had caught the sun a little too much on her picnic the day before and her face now felt unusually hot as she soaked in the bath tub.

"A healthy glow, Nurse Drake," Doctor Ambrose had said after greeting her. "Just the tonic these boys need, and such a pretty face too. The patients are not the only ones who will be perked up by having you around." Marion giggled to herself as she remembered his words and the wink that accompanied them.

She had been on her feet all day. Moving men out of their beds to strip and remake them with fresh sheets. Her back and arms ached. There were twenty beds in each of the main rooms on the ground floor of the house, ten along each side. The carpets, which usually adorned the floors, were rolled up at one end of each room and the floorboards had been roughly stained to try to improve the look of the now bare spaces. The sweep of the main staircase in the grand hall was simple in its design, and Marion imagined it followed what had been a flourish of the architect's pen on the plans. All other floors opened onto the staircase and the hallway acted as an echo chamber. Marion heard screams several times that day as she crossed between her two wards. They all emanated from the treatment rooms on the second floor.

Overall, she generally liked the other nurses and auxiliary staff she had met so far. Most of the help was local, but a couple of the nurses were from the Midlands and were lodging in the hospital grounds. It became apparent to Marion that her training put her ahead of the others, apart from matron and the sisters of course. Marion knew how to think when she was on the ward and never stood around waiting for instructions. By the end of her first shift she already had others looking to her to direct their efforts. She was going to enjoy herself.

Alain had not seemed to suffer from her absence, but made clear his pleasure on her return. He had raced across the floor of the nursery with his funny shuffle on his bottom, and laughed the moment she had picked him up to give him a hug and a big kiss, which had turned into a raspberry blowing game, his favourite. She had stayed with him until he settled down for the night and was now enjoying her own private moment of luxury before a quick supper and bed. Her uncle had installed a bath at the rectory when he was upgrading the plumbing and putting in electricity at the big house. On this day in particular she was grateful for his largesse.

There had been no post for her, still no letter from Russell. She felt too tired to write to him about her first day at work. Instead she fell into bed exhausted, but not too tired to recapture in her mind all the glimpses of Doctor Ambrose she had managed throughout the day. *It had been a wink.* She admired the doctor's easy confidence, and already enjoyed the way he treated her as a partner equal to the task, with none of the superior airs employed by matron. And, so far, she had made no mistakes.

Prior to her uniformed arrival at Bachelor House she had not considered the social side of working at all, but she now realised how introspective and dulled she had become since her return home and how much she looked forward to striking up new friendships. It suddenly struck her just how unlike her former self Russell must have found her: domestic, maternal even, and steeped in small parochial and family matters. *No wonder he fled.*

Doctor Ambrose's appreciative eye had reignited her playful nature and she knew she must fan these flames to be able to attract and keep Russell's attention when they next met. *Time to visit Oxford.* Her final thought before sleep overtook her.

The Cherwell, Oxford, October 1916

"Horatio."

"Horatio?" Russell said.

"Yes, that is Doctor Ambrose's name," Marion replied.

"No wonder he keeps that quiet."

"Now don't be mean about him. He is a very nice man."

"And all I seem to have heard about since you arrived."

Marion's long-awaited visit to Russell was happening. She was staying at her cousin's home in Summertown for the weekend, close enough to Russell's college which made time together easy.

"Don't be ridiculous. I've only mentioned him when I've been telling you about my work."

"In which he seems to play a big part."

"Well, yes, he does; we are quite the team matron says. I don't get tongue-tied around him like many of the other nurses."

"So he can be an ogre then?"

"No, quite the opposite. He is always charming, but he is handsome and he flusters some of the nurses. It's matron who has perfected the art of intimidation."

Marion was sitting with Russell on the banks of the river Cherwell in the grounds of his college, beside the remains of their picnic and her cousin's hamper. Lying side by side on a tartan rug, also provided by her cousin, with the fingers of their hands, his right and her left, entwined, lazing in the warmth of an Indian summer. Many people were taking advantage of this late glimpse of summer. Marion was aware of the chatter of other voices close by.

"Who is looking after Alain this weekend? And how is the little chap?" Russell asked.

"Nanny, she is such a top, and Alain seems very happy with her."

They were interrupted as a shadow fell across them.

"Did you drop this?" A young boy was standing next to them holding out his hand. Marion and Russell both sat up.

"I beg your pardon?" Marion said. She shaded her eyes to see him better in the bright sunshine.

"Dropped what?" Russell asked.

The young boy said nothing else but dropped a white feather that floated down onto Russell and ran off. Russell jumped to his feet and Marion moved to stand beside him. The boy had joined two women sitting in the shade of a nearby tree. Both were looking in their direction.

"How dare they? Marion said. "Come on, I have something to say to those ladies."

"Now don't you go getting upset on my account; this has happened to me before and no doubt will again." Russell brushed down his trousers.

"Of course I am upset. How dare they give you a white feather? Are you coming?"

"Marion, please. Do not cause a scene; it isn't worth it."

"Don't be ridiculous. You must stand up for yourself. Come on."

Marion strode off towards the two women, and had covered half the distance before she realised that Russell had stayed behind. She paused and watched him bend to pick up the blanket and for a moment considered returning to him, but instead she approached the group by the tree.

"Look at this. He can't even fight his own battles. He sent this young woman to speak for him. What do you make of that, Edward?"

The two women had got to their feet as Marion approached, and the young boy, who Marion now knew to be Edward, tucked himself into the edge of the skirts of the taller of the two women.

"Is he your son?" Marion said as she pointed to him.

"And what of it if he is, may I ask?"

"He just delivered a white feather to my, to my guest."

"Yes, he did just run an errand for us. It is disgraceful to see young men not in uniform. He should be fighting."

"Don't be so ridiculous. You know nothing about him. How dare you give him, anyone for that matter, a white feather?"

"We can give them to any man not in uniform, or unbadged, unless he's wounded of course, and he looks fit to me." The woman nodded in Russell's direction and they all turned to watch him give the blanket she and he had been sitting on a final shake before folding it and laying it on top of the hamper. He looked across to Marion.

"Too humiliated to come over himself, I see?" said the mother of the boy.

"Too disgusted would be nearer the truth. You are stupid indeed if you think that sending more men into battle is going to solve anything. And, not that it is your business, my friend is a guest of our country. He's an American, and I am humiliated that he should receive such treatment whilst here."

"Oh, yes, well," the woman paused, clearly put off her stride, but her friend came to her rescue.

"And you, young lady are not in a position to call us stupid. Our efforts to prick the consciences of shirkers and cowards have been lauded in the press."

"Your efforts would be better spent at the hospitals, putting back together the wounded, or raising funds for the widows and their families. And as for cowardice, you even had to send a child over to do your work for you, too scared to look us in the face yourselves. You obviously have no idea of the conditions men face in battle."

"We do not need to be lectured by you."

"You like to hand it out, but not have an opinion meted out to you. You are despicable."

Marion turned on her heel and walked back towards Russell without allowing either woman to speak again. Russell was livid when she reached him.

"I don't need you to speak for me, Marion. I am quite capable of defending myself when I need to." He picked up the hamper and the rug and started to walk away from the river.

"It's not just about you, Russell," Marion said as she collected her handbag and caught up with him. "The slight was to me too, for being with a so-called shirker. It was a horrible thing to have happen."

"It is not the first time," Russell snapped, and then more reasonably, "I have felt out of place since I've been back here. The war is something you have to be for, and be active in one's support, or against and be vociferous for the pacifist cause. This is no place for neutrality."

"Well, yes, you can't hide behind your country's stance here, that's for sure." Marion's own annoyance flared. "There is resentment for those countries who stand on the sidelines and watch the bloodbath continue."

"Is that what you think too?" Russell stopped and turned to her. "Do you resent America's position?"

"Probably, if I thought about it." Marion stood and faced him. "We had no choice in this country. Our loyalty determined our actions; we had to step in and fight. America, it seems, is still deciding how loyal it feels towards us, and our cause." Marion turned to walk and flung her next comment over her shoulder. "Meanwhile America's making plenty of money out of the war." *Enough, Marion.*

"What? What did you say?" Russell walked briskly to catch up with her. "So if you resent my neutrality, perhaps I should go and fight, make my own contribution?"

"What you personally could contribute to this war," Marion said with all the put-down she could muster, "is not going to make the slightest bit of difference to the outcome." *High and mighty Marion, calm down.* She immediately relented. "Russell, why put yourself at risk? You have already sacrificed a year of your studies. You've done enough. Those women made my blood boil."

"You can't call a delay a sacrifice, not compared to men giving their lives." They were now walking in step with each other. Marion reached out to take the blanket and Russell changed the hamper to his other hand. It was bulky and kept banging against his leg.

"Russell, you can hold onto your life, and I suggest that you do. You don't have to join up, so don't. In fact it would be egotistical, thinking you could make a difference." *Ridiculous.* "You men and your heroics."

"You don't give me much room to manoeuvre, Marion. I am damned if I support the war and damned if I don't."

"And you say you want to work in politics?" Marion laughed. "Time to get used to the reality that you can never please everyone. You just have to decide who or what is most important to you and plough your own furrow." *Stop pushing him, Marion.*

"I think I can manage myself, Marion, without any more of your platitudes." Russell was not in the mood to listen, or respond.

"I'm sure you can, Russell but, I have to say, I'm not sure you know what is important to you. I thought you did once, but you seem so unsettled now."

They continued in silence as they walked along St Giles towards her cousin's house. Marion did not want their time together to be soured by the feather incident, nor by a spat between them. She softened her tone.

"These are difficult times for everybody."

"Yes, they are, but", Russell relented, "you are right about me, Marion. Thoughts of life and my future did seem much more straightforward in the past, in Brussels. Now my life feels like a jersey with a loose thread that is being slowly unravelled." Russell stopped to put down the hamper and flex his arms.

"Well, you have to decide what you want to knit up next." Marion planted a kiss on his cheek, and they moved on.

"I used to think it was simple," Russell continued. "Map your own course through life and stick to it. Keep in blissful ignorance of whatever is going on around you and what others think. But, my sweet one," Russell looked at Marion and smiled, "life has proved to be more complicated; plans can be thwarted by the interests, or the needs, of others. Well, that's the way it feels to me at the moment."

"I'm not sure I know what you are talking about, but you haven't settled back here at all have you?"

"No, not yet, but it was a lot to expect that I would. Oxford has changed. The war has done that. And I'm different. Brussels and you have done that. My life just doesn't fit me any more. Sorry to sound gloomy, but I can't lift myself out of it. Bit pathetic but I feel a bit lost, sorry to say." Russell gave her a wry smile.

"I think I've known that, since you returned from Brussels." Marion squeezed his arm. "You've been a fish out of water. I had convinced myself it was me you had tired of; now I see that it is more than that. I'm not sure if that is better or worse."

"For better or worse, for richer or poorer, in sickness or in health, easy words that hide a mammoth commitment, and not one that I am good enough for it would seem."

"Russell, you are talking in riddles. What do you mean?"

"Nothing, nothing, just playing with words. Enough of my maudlin mood. Come on, sweetheart, we have five hours before your train. What do you suggest we do?"

"You're right, we're talking too much again. Let's drop these things at my cousin's house, and if they are out, well, if they are out, we can decide if we want to stay in."

Marion missed Russell the moment she had settled on the train. They had not made love, but Marion relished the feeling of his arms around her as they had lain together on her bed. They had been delighted to find the house empty, and Russell's mood had lifted. Once again she was conscious that the distance which so easily developed between them when they disagreed, disappeared when they physically touched. Their shared endearments forged a bond where conversation sometimes divided. The world seemed simple when she was in his arms, but the further the train took her away from Oxford, the more she imagined difficulties ahead.

Russell had said nothing that offered her any feeling of certainty about their future together. He had not mentioned returning to America, but he was more unsettled than she had anticipated. She had not broached the topic and did not like that she was fearful to do this. She preferred to hold on to the promises he made when she left Brussels for England but perhaps him saying they would be a family had been spoken in the heat of the moment after their night of passion, when he was fearful for her and Alain's safety. Now he offered nothing. *Has he changed his mind?* And this was where she was confused. Deep inside she was sure he felt the same. She knew this about him, but there was a reticence in him that she did not understand. He had not wanted to make love, *why?* And often she felt sure he was going to say something but then he held back and some instinct told her not to push him. They were certainly on different stepping stones at the moment. She just had to trust that the river would keep them strong.

Recalling Therese's words about the river of love reminded her of Therese's letter: *ultimately another will join you and you will be a family*. Why had Therese not said Russell will join you, why a nameless other? Therese had told both of them a love would always exist between them, and she had taken this to mean they would always be together. But Russell was no longer declaring notions about this, and she was beginning to doubt his commitment to her and Alain. He had asked very little about Alain; in fact, when she thought about their time together she realised he had asked her very little about anything at all.

Marion shuddered at the thought that what she was clinging to might be a false and a convenient hope that provided a comfortable ruse and permission to hold onto Alain. Perhaps she was making a dreadful mistake, and Alain really should be introduced to a family of his own. Was it her own stubbornness that had got in the way once again, and this time damaged her own as well as a secure future for him? Marion felt appalled at the thought that her mother might be right. If she and Russell did not have plans to unite then perhaps she had no choice but to let Alain go.

All thoughts of Therese's letter were pushed to the back of her mind, and by the time she reached Missenden she had created all the arguments in her head as to why having Alain adopted was the right plan to follow. She knew who to speak to and how to make it happen. She had to place Alain in the hands of people who could make dispassionate decisions, and this would let her take hold of the reins of her own life once again. Then perhaps she and Russell could find in each other the people they were before. She would write a letter to Maddie Smith the moment she arrived home. But when she arrived home, she did no such thing: the house was in chaos.

She walked into the rectory to be told the doctor had been called several times over the weekend for Alain, who had been running a temperature. The source, the doctor told her, when she rushed to the nursery, was an infected throat, but Alain had been unable to keep his medicine and food down and was like a rag doll. Marion immediately went to tend him. Nanny looked quite exhausted.

"I thought he was pining for you," Nanny explained, "off his food a bit, but then his cheeks became pinker and pinker, and I thought he was teething but your father thought it best to fetch the doctor."

"I am grateful that he did. Poor little mite. I'll take over now."

"Look, he's perked up with your voice, but he didn't sleep much last night. He'll be tired now as much as anything."

"And you must be too. Take yourself off, Nanny. I'll stay here with him. We'll be fine."

After the household had closed down for the night, Marion took Alain from the nursery to her bedroom and put him in bed with her. He slept most of the night alongside her as she dozed, sent to sleep by his breathing. Her heart had overturned when she had seen him weak and vulnerable. Even though her head may have been trying to lead her in another direction, she knew that night that her heart would always win. *Heartstrong instead of headstrong.* That was a new thought for her. She was also now sure of her answer, if a choice had to be made, to that question posed by Elizabeth some weeks before: Alain would come first, even before Russell. Realising this made her feel lighter, her mind freed from chasing down so many different avenues of thoughts and decisions which had been nagging at her for months.

Despite her lack of sleep Marion felt fresh and alert in the morning and was delighted to see how greatly recovered Alain was, but she decided to stay with him that day and not report to work. She telephoned her apologies through to Bachelor

House, and was relieved to leave a message for matron rather than speak to her directly. By the afternoon she and Alain were enjoying fresh air in the garden and his cheeks were rosy from the sunshine, all signs of fever gone.

London, October 1916

Russell boarded the train from Oxford to London and settled into his seat with a sigh. Once underway, he was soon lulled by the carriage's gentle rhythmic motion and he sunk into a deep contemplation. He was confused about his life.

Before the upheaval caused by the war his future had been free of doubt or uncertainty. But from August 1914 it seemed as if a giant, malevolent hand had wrenched control of his destiny from him and was determined to extract a high price for his golden start to adulthood. He tried to analyse his conflicting feelings in a logical manner, more befitting the supposedly gifted scholar he was. He knew he should be in a good mood at the prospect of seeing his friend Hugh Gibson; and he should be much more enthusiastic and curious at the prospect of meeting Herbert Hoover again.

Russell was in awe of Hoover's single-minded drive and determination, which was now legendary. Hoover had secured the funding for a continuous supply of food to Belgium. He had cajoled, negotiated, and navigated with apparent calm neutrality, through the politically treacherous terrain of the governments of Britain, France, America, and Germany. His accomplishment had been an astounding display of organisation in a wartime crisis; and so, when Hugh had written to ask whether Russell would like to join him and Hoover for lunch, he had fired off his delighted acceptance within a few minutes of opening the envelope.

So why was he now feeling so flat? It was a mood he had slipped into since arriving back at Oxford at the end of the summer. His return to England and Marion had been full of high hopes and he was not prepared for this deterioration of spirit. He thought by now his future would be certain. He and Marion engaged, and a plan in hand to locate her, Alain if necessary, and him in America, and with the notion of a job to be ready for him at the end of his studies. Instead he had been made to feel foolish and even foolhardy by her father. Being in love with Mr. Drake's daughter was not, it seemed, enough to secure his agreement for their engagement or marriage. Russell still smarted at their conversation during his visit.

"Mr. Drake, may I talk to you, in private?"

Russell had knocked on Marion's father's study door after breakfast while she was completing some chores for her mother. The room was lined with bookshelves and had a fusty smell. Nostalgia for the library at Oxford struck Russell.

"Of course, come in, sit down." Mr. Drake waved his arm towards a chair and Russell bent to lift off some pamphlets, which Mr. Drake took from him and placed on top of a precarious pile of documents. "I am reading more reports of that awful battle at the Somme. Tens of thousands killed in a day. I've never known the like before. What did those generals think they were doing? I call it murder sending all our young men over the top like that. Our guns had achieved nothing apparently, and they had been firing for days." Mr. Drake folded his newspaper and took off his glasses. "The Germans were waiting for their advance with machine guns. Dreadful. Truly dreadful, quite distressing."

"Yes, I read about it when I arrived in London. It was a bad show by all accounts."

"Count yourself lucky not to be in it, my boy. It's not your fight; stay well clear. Do something useful with your life. Mind you, we could do with some help to shift these Germans. They seem so well dug in."

"I thought America would have been more active in the fight by now," Russell said, "but I don't think enough support the thought of entering the war and the politicians don't want to risk losing votes. But", Russell pointed to Mr. Drake's newspaper, "the number of casualties is astonishing. Seems the Somme battle was a massacre."

"Everything is so uncertain. It doesn't look like this push is going to solve anything. We could be at this for years. But enough talk of the war, what was it I can help you with?"

Russell took a breath and tried to remain calm.

"I, er, want to ask you about Marion."

"Ah, Marion." Mr. Drake picked up his glasses and opened and closed them in his lap.

"I would like to ask if you would consider me as a husband for Marion. I am asking for her hand in marriage."

"I see. I see. And this is what Marion wants?" Mr. Drake placed his glasses on top of the newspaper on his desk.

"I haven't asked her. I thought I should speak to you first."

"Ah, I see." Mr. Drake picked up his glasses again, pulled a handkerchief from his pocket and began rubbing each lens. "I, Mr. Clark, Russell, have learnt not to speak for Marion."

Russell did not know what to say next and indeed whether it was even his turn to speak. Bernard continued.

"But tell me, as we are talking, do you think it wise to be taking on commitments, when times are so unstable?" He tapped the folded newspaper. "Can you even tell me where you will be in a year's time? I thought not." Mr. Drake had caught a slight shake of Russell's head to his question. "Why don't you wait until this war is over, and all has quietened down. At least you might know on what side of the ocean you will intend to be. I would leave it a while, not say anything to

Marion just yet. It would only unsettle her." Mr. Drake nodded in agreement to his own words.

Russell had not expected this response and leapt to his feet. He thought the conversation was a mere formality, and next they would be shaking hands, even slapping each other on the back. He tried to gather his thoughts as he walked to the bookshelves. He wanted to give a good account of himself, but he was completely thrown off balance. He returned to his chair and faced Mr. Drake again.

"I am truly disappointed to hear this, sir. Perhaps it would please you if Marion and I become engaged now but delay our wedding until after the war, when as you say, I will know my future with more certainty. Wouldn't it help you all, and Marion, if we are engaged? She says that tongues wag so much about Alain."

"Tongues will always wag when there are women about. I do not know how they find so much to talk about."

"Yes, sir," Russell still wanted to plead his case, "but I would like Marion to feel secure in my feelings for her, and for our future."

"And would that future include Alain?"

"Well, yes it could, it would. Yes I'm sure it would." Russell was conscious that his words sounded hesitant, so he continued more boldly. "Marion is very attached to him. He is a bonny baby. Seems to smile all the time. If that is how Marion would have it, then so be it."

"Am I right to understand the child is not yours?"

Russell was stunned by the question and sat open-mouthed.

"Forgive me," Mr. Drake apologised, "but I think in the circumstances I am able to enquire."

Russell was emphatic. "Absolutely right, he is not my child. Nor, may I make clear, is he Marion's. In the physical way, I mean, but she is clearly a mother to him."

"Indeed, indeed. I felt sure this was the case, but was

compelled to ask. Excuse me for putting you on the spot, old chap. But, Mr. Clark, Russell, to start a marriage with a child, with someone else's child, you must be aware, takes far more provision than just taking on a wife. If I were you, I would want to be sure about what size of commitment I could fund, and where I would provide a home, before I broached the subject with Marion. She's as practical as she might be romantic, that one."

"Are you saying you are unsure of my suitability, sir?" Russell rose to his feet but Mr. Drake beckoned for him to sit. He resumed his seat.

"I am sure of the companionship I see when you and Marion are together. It delights me. I had despaired of her ever finding the type of spark she wanted in a man. Her mother has introduced her to too many milksops. But, and I realise you do not want to hear this, I do not entirely think you are in a position to secure her hand. I will be able to contribute very little when Marion marries and she will have no allowance, so it will be down to you to provide and I, as you have given me the courtesy of asking me, would like to see a little more stability from you first. And you must appreciate, your, and your family's true circumstances are unknown to us." Mr. Drake gave a slightly apologetic shrug, which he lightened with a brief smile.

Russell's feelings of foreignness increased with each sentence spoken.

"Perhaps when you know what will happen after your scholarship," Mr. Drake continued, "when you know from where your income will indeed come, we could talk of this again. How much longer does your scholarship run and, it is incumbent on me to enquire, what will your prospects be at its finish?"

"A minimum of twelve months." Russell felt so deflated he had to work hard to answer Mr. Drake's questions. "The start has been disrupted so I am almost only at the start of it. And you are quite right, I am unsettled and unsure of what path I shall then follow. I had thought to go into academia, but my brush with politics has inspired and interested me recently."

"Well then, I am sure you will agree this is not the time to rush into any formal arrangements. Indeed, young man, college life should be free from such trappings." Mr. Drake laughed as he said this, and Russell had no idea how to respond, so said nothing.

"Marion", Mr. Drake continued, "remains unsettled herself. She has told us very little about the goings-on in Brussels, but I have deduced for myself that she must have been involved in the Cavell matter. Am I right?"

"Like you, Mr. Drake, I have also learnt not to speak for Marion." Russell was quick with his reply.

"I like that. Touché, touché." Mr. Drake brought his hands together in mock applause. "Marion's mind is not made up about the child, nor, I might add, am I yet convinced of the right path for Alain, but I would not want Marion to feel obliged in any direction. She needs time to sort herself out, and being promised may confuse her emotions. She took the news of Nurse Cavell's death very hard."

"Yes, and she was hard on me about this too. She felt we, the Americans, should have been able to stop the execution. Believe me, sir, we tried."

"I'm sure you did. I'm sure you did, my friend. A complex matter, no doubt. Now," Mr. Drake rose to his feet and walked around his desk to Russell, who immediately stood up, "now, young man, I must thank you for doing me the honour of asking my permission, and I can see you are disappointed that this has not been forthcoming. In time, I am sure all will come good, so do not be downhearted on account of today."

Russell felt panic rise in him. Mr. Drake was closing down their conversation, when surely there was much more he could say to press his suit, but he could think of nothing appropriate. Too much of what Marion's father had referred to was accurate and he felt mortified by his gauche naivety and obviously inadequate circumstances. Mr. Drake was right: he had not thought it through.

"We both know Marion is of an age to go against the wishes of her parents," Mr. Drake continued as he stretched out his hand, "but I would wholeheartedly prefer that this did not create a rift between Marion and myself, or indeed her family. Up to you but I would ask that you do not repeat this conversation to her. In fact I would, as I suggest, put the whole topic to one side for at least a year. She has decisions of her own to make about her work, and Alain. Let her have a clear head, when you make your proposal. This is a mournful time, with so much loss; it is too easy to grasp at a happiness that might flounder at the first obstacle."

Russell reluctantly shook his host's hand, aware that, in so doing he had silently agreed to his terms. He had kept to the handshake and had said nothing to Marion.

Taken aback by the rejection, Russell decided that what he had previously experienced as a warm welcome from Marion's family was, in truth, nothing more than the British mannered response to an interloper. He had been tempted to ignore her father and make his proposal direct to Marion but, however churlish he felt, he did not want to force her to choose him against her family's wishes, and Mr. Drake's objections had rankled with him; they were too close to the truth for comfort. He knew that he would have heard the same cautions from his own parents if he had been in a position to broach the subject with them. None of this had added up to the romantic proposal he had imagined.

Russell's thoughts were interrupted when the carriage door was abruptly pulled open and a ticket inspector appeared from the corridor. The cost of railway travel, like so much else, had risen rapidly since war began but Russell had dipped into his reserves to secure a first class ticket in the hope of a more isolated and peaceable journey than he might have expected in other parts of the train. And so far he had been the only occupant of the six-seat compartment.

With so many men away fighting, Russell was unsurprised to meet a bulky middle-aged woman in a shapeless ticket inspector's uniform, with untidy curls framing a flushed face. As she studied him he saw her amiable expression turn into an ugly sneer and he felt himself stiffen. She sniffed theatrically loudly and slowly, and wrinkled her nose as if she had walked into a foul smell.

"Your ticket, *sir*," she said in tone devoid of any respect.

These were the moments Russell had begun to dread. He turned away from the window and, in so doing, deliberately exposed the small Stars and Stripes badge he had pinned onto his jacket lapel for just this reason. He reached into his pocket and forced a friendly smile.

"Of course, ma'am. There you go." And just to make the point he could not help but exaggerate his American accent to a caricature drawl. The woman's aggression was instantly punctured.

"Thank you, sir," she said, flustered as she clipped his ticket and bustled away.

Her disdainful attitude to him had not been unusual. Since returning to England Russell had been subjected to regular taunts, muttered comments and sometimes, outright hostility. Several times well-dressed young ladies had thrust white feathers at him. It had happened when he was with Marion and she had soon seen them off, but somehow that had humiliated him even further.

What else should he have expected when he returned to Britain? He felt embarrassed at his naivety. Stupidly, he had somehow assumed Oxford would be much as he left it before war was declared. The ancient city was timeless to him, but he now saw it was the presence of the students, with their boundless optimism and energy that had made the colleges such beguiling and invigorating places. Returning from Brussels, with the war in full swing, he found college life, as he knew it, had evaporated. From what he gleaned, many of the student body had volunteered in the early days of the war, or had soon felt compelled to follow the flow and join the forces; and of the reluctant young men left behind most had now been conscripted.

Despite the recent introduction of conscription Russell noticed there was little or no let-up in the persecution of men who were judged to be avoiding their duty. Indeed, Marion had told him that attitudes seemed even more spiteful and hostile than at the start of the war, with most families having their kinsfolk in uniform, or already having sacrificed a loved one. For conscientious objectors it was even worse. One such, a student with rooms close to Russell's, had departed the college in the middle of one night without notice, having found himself the focus of continual taunts and abuse. Before he had become so wretched he had talked to Russell about his persecutors: from dons to domestics, all, he said, being egged on by the relentless invective hurled down from establishment pulpits. Russell's liberal American instincts had been provoked by this episode and he had felt his foreignness more than at any previous time in England.

He had read in his newspaper of the government's attempt to limit the harassment of men who had been discharged from service due to wounds or illness and were now out of uniform and back at home. They were issued a silver *King and Country* pin to wear on their jacket lapels. It was this that had given Russell the notion of wearing his Stars and Stripes badge whenever he ventured out. He felt somewhat shamefaced at resorting to this tactic but he reasoned that any forestalling of aggression was no bad thing. And it seemed to work. There was certainly less animosity directed at him, although on a number of occasions he had been challenged to reply to a meaningless question, doubtless thrown at him so that his accent and nationality could be confirmed.

Thankfully the rest of the journey was without a further confrontation. An elderly couple joined him for part of the trip, the man exchanging a polite enough "Good day" to him. His wife ignored Russell's presence altogether and spent her time snuffling tearfully into a handkerchief while leaning on her husband's arm. Dressed in mourning, such a pair was a common sight nowadays, and their forlorn aura permeated the compartment.

"Our son. France. Just heard," The man said. Russell nodded his understanding, but said nothing. Once they had left the train, stooping under the heavy burden of their loss, Russell noticed that he was within two stops of London.

He tried to lift his mood; the last thing he wanted was Hugh admonishing him for moping and he turned his mind to Marion and her visit to see him in Oxford. Seemingly oblivious to any underlying tension between them, she had tried to recoup the spirit of their time together in Brussels. *But was this enough?* He stepped onto the platform at Paddington glad to leave his thoughts behind.

Café Royal in Piccadilly, October 1916

Russell took a bus to Piccadilly. When he had passed through the capital on his way from Brussels to see Marion a few months before, he had noticed little of his surroundings, absorbed with thoughts of their reunion. Now he was more attentive to the traffic, buildings in need of a lick of paint, and men in khaki who were everywhere, as well as wounded soldiers in their distinctive blue uniforms, many on crutches. He saw no evidence of the zeppelin raids but the look and feel of the drab streets were in contrast to the optimistic and bellicose chauvinism of his newspaper.

Russell's destination was the Café Royal, where he was not surprised to find himself greeted by a female doorman, or "doorwoman", he now supposed she would be called. He deposited his coat and made his way into the dining room and almost gasped: the room shimmered. Glittering under chandeliers, and with mirrors and gilt reflecting a red and gold plush interior, the windowless room was in stark contrast to the atmosphere on the streets and a mood of conviviality enveloped him. *Troubles can be forgotten in here.* He spotted plenty of uniforms and the animated officers were contributing in no short order to the noisy hubbub in the restaurant.

As the *maître d'* headed towards him Russell spotted Hugh sitting alone at a table in a far corner. He politely indicated where he was heading and approached his friend, who was now standing and beaming at him.

"Well, hullo, young man. Grand to see you again." Hugh,

dapper as ever, clasped Russell's outstretched hand with both his own and they shook vigorously.

"Come and sit down. Hoover's not here yet and I'm taking the chance to have a scotch. This must be the only place in town that isn't selling the watered-down stuff. Have one yourself while supplies last?"

"No, no, I'm fine thanks, Hugh. A juice though." Russell had little taste for hard liquor and, aware of his very junior status at this meeting thought accepting alcohol would be presumptuous.

"Well, I'm sure going to grab the opportunity for another. There'll be little enough chance when the chief gets here." Hugh ordered their drinks from a passing waiter and then smiled at Russell.

"I see you're advertising for the nation," he said, pointing at Russell's lapel badge. Russell had forgotten his Stars and Stripes emblem, and now felt somewhat foolish. As he fumbled to remove it Hugh, ever the diplomat, put him at ease.

"Oh, don't worry. I think you're being smart. I get it a bit easier as I'm usually running around the so-called corridors of power where they're still plenty of us not in uniform and we don't stand out. Still, now I think about it I might copy you and wear one myself. Now, tell me, how's Marion? You mentioned in your letter she's still looking after the baby; Alain, wasn't it? How old is he now?"

"He's nearly eighteen months. He has started walking but he falls over a great deal, and I am sure talking won't be far behind. He certainly makes his wishes known. He's a dandy little chap, always smiling."

"And the lovely Nurse Drake herself, how is she?"

"Still lovely and with a mind of her own."

"Not bending to your will then?"

"No, too busy taking on the world. She is working at a local stately home. It's being used as a hospital. She seems happy, always better when she's busy."

"Did you two recover from the Cavell business?"

"Yes, I think so. She made me very welcome on my return and it's much easier now that we can visit each other, and correspond too." Russell opened his mouth as if to continue, but fell silent.

"I hear a 'but' coming. Am I right?" Hugh asked.

"We haven't seen that much of each other. The thing is her father refused my proposal of marriage." The words rushed out before Russell could check himself. "He implied I hadn't thought it through and in effect had nothing to offer Marion."

"Heck, I'm not surprised. It is rather quick and he hardly knows you. You can't rush the British. You should have waited until he started dropping hints, inviting you into his study for a man-to-man."

"Easy for you to say now." Russell was annoyed at once again being made to feel gauche. "The problem is, I'm sure Marion is expecting me to say something to her. Yes, I was stupid," Russell spoke against himself to quash any comment from Hugh. "I spoke to her father before saying anything to her, and he was adamant that I should wait at least a year; he is very unsettled by the uncertainties of the war. I don't feel I can raise the subject with her now, without going against his wishes, or putting her up against him, and I know she feels let down."

"She doesn't know you want to marry her?" Hugh was trying to follow what Russell was saying.

"No, her father suggested, or should I say instructed, that our conversation remained just between the two of us."

"So you are keeping secrets from her too. Now that's a tricky one, but I can see your dilemma." Hugh was distracted as the waiter arrived with their drinks. He raised his glass to Russell. "Ease up, you have plenty of time ahead of you to wed. Now tell me, how is student life in Oxford? Giving you the boost you were needing?"

"Actually not quite as I thought it would. Not yet anyway."

"Oh well, you can't expect to settle in immediately. Give it time."

Russell was more interested to hear from Hugh, about his assignment in London and some unbiased and perhaps even unique insights into the war. He changed the subject from himself.

"Tell me what is going on. I've only been able to get news from the press here," Russell said, "and jingoistic doesn't begin to describe the editorials."

Hugh explained that he had been in Germany for a couple of weeks. As an official of a powerful, yet still neutral America he was able to travel through the belligerent countries on his diplomatic pass. He talked about the open disagreement between the armed forces and government in Germany as to whether their submarine warfare should go on unrestricted, and even of the whispers that some thought the time was right to try for an all-out push, but others were sensitive to this bringing America into the war.

"They hinted that they want us to broker a peace deal but whether that's part of some great poker game, or seriously meant, I'm just not sure," Hugh said.

"Are they hurting as much as the British?" asked Russell.

"Well, the atmosphere in Berlin isn't dissimilar to London," Hugh replied. "The ladies are running more of that city than here, mind; I reckon just about every man is serving now. Things are a bit tougher there, generally, I would say. More food shortages, meat's hard to find, that sort of thing. But they're not starving yet and, the thing is, I just don't see them giving up either. They're tired and weary like the Brits, but they're just as pig-headed; maybe even more so. The more men they lose the more these two countries refuse to consider anything less than full-blown victory over the other, and nothing less. Got to be victory, even if there's just a handful of goddam men left standing at the end to celebrate it."

Hugh's voice tailed off and he fixed his gaze across the room. Russell looked up and saw that Hoover had entered the room, and was standing by one of the tables, engaged in earnest conversation with a diner who had interrupted his own meal to talk to him. After a couple of minutes he watched him head in their direction, only to be stopped at another, larger table of half a dozen men.

Russell studied Hoover, struck again by how young he appeared, almost baby-faced. He was about six foot tall, the same as himself, though Hoover was more thickset. Dressed in a plain, somewhat tired, dark suit there was outwardly nothing about his looks to make him stand out from anyone else, but here he was quite the celebrity. His arrival was causing a stir in the dining room, though Hoover seemed oblivious to the glances he received. His manner was serious, if not stern, and his conversations were brief.

"Hugh, old pal, good to see you," Hoover said, when at last he reached them. Hugh and Russell were on their feet.

"And you too, Herbert, always a pleasure. This is the young man I told you I would bring along, Mr. Clark, the Rhodes scholar. He did us proud in Brussels in those early days when all the other American tourists were running around like headless chickens, and he continued working for us in the CRB. I think you two met briefly on one of your early visits to Brussels?"

"Well done, young man. Thank you for your help." Hoover shook Russell's hand, sat down at the table, and without further preliminaries engaged Hugh in the matters that most immediately concerned him.

Russell was sidelined but listened intently as Hoover described the dilemma he faced with a shortage of supply ships. The twenty ships working full-time under the Commission's flag could deliver about 60,000 tons of foodstuffs every month to Belgium but it was still not enough to feed nine million people. Another 40,000 tons a month were needed and something different from just beans and rice. Getting more ships chartered was his problem, and the British would not release the Belgian ships they were holding even though the Admiralty were not using them.

"I need you guys at the embassy to put pressure on the British government." Hoover signalled to the waiter and asked for a jug of water.

"Well," Hugh said, "I'm sure you're aware that Ambassador Page here is in close touch with all sides ..." Hoover interrupted him.

"Walter Page will probably be applying for a British passport soon. He only seems interested in making sure America joins this war. It's about time he put more energy into helping the innocent victims. After all, even if he doesn't like it, we're still a neutral country. Dammit, *the* neutral country."

Russell had read that American ambassador Page was a strong anglophile, criticised by the American press for being too close to the British. Hugh, evidently familiar with Hoover's blunt ways, proceeded to mollify him with assurances that he would do what he could. He also gestured to their waiter and arranged their order: soup and lamb cutlets. Hoover seemed to have no interest in what he would be eating and Russell was not consulted.

Hoover pumped Hugh for new information. Both men were knowledgeable about every major figure on the wartime stage. Hoover's focus on the welfare of non-combatants in Belgium was unwavering and he showed as much contempt for parts of the Allied establishment as for the German. The British Admiralty, in particular, attracted his wrath.

"It's full of vengeful old Tories who want to starve innocent Belgians in the dumb belief this will make it more difficult for the Germans to feed their own men. Believe me, it won't, and the Belgians will just die all the sooner. You know what I just saw in Belgium, gentlemen?"

His own answer was delayed as the soup arrived. Hoover treated this as an inconvenience and, having speedily bolted his down, continued talking while the other two men were only halfway through theirs.

"This was only a few weeks ago. By the way, it was almost my last trip too. My ship was stopped by German torpedo boats, even though I was on a Dutch steamer out of Holland. They forced us to the Belgian coast and took off at least fifty passengers. I'm sure some were escaping British prisoners. And while we were anchored an airplane came over and bombed us. They told me it was a Frenchie, can you believe it? The guy next to me was hit by some shrapnel; anyway, he'll live and I was lucky."

"The *New York Times* covered it, Herbert," Hugh said. "Quite a fuss they made of your near miss. They wondered how many people would starve if they'd killed you."

"Yes, well they didn't and the speculation was stupid," responded Hoover, before returning to his narrative.

"I visited one of our relief stations. There were hundreds of kids, all standing in line for a meal. Suddenly this relief worker was dragging one of them out of the queue, and this child got all upset and started screaming. I went up and asked the woman why she was doing this. You know what she said?"

"What was that, sir?" ventured Russell, to show he was engaged, though he knew that Hoover's questions were probably all rhetorical.

"She told me, and get this," Hoover's tone was bitter. "She told me that the kid looked of *normal* weight. Sure, he looked normal to me, except he was a damn hungry normal kind of kid. They were only going to feed underweight children that day, ones showing signs of starvation. Not enough food to go round for everyone."

Just then their main course arrived. Hoover treated eating

it as a bothersome interruption and then explored with Hugh the committee's latest fundraising efforts in the USA.

Russell felt privileged to be included in this meeting. It brought back that sense of exhilaration he had experienced in Brussels when he was working for Hugh setting up the initial relief efforts during the summer and autumn of 1914. This was the world of real drama, where lives were at risk, an intoxicating place to be even if he was only in the background chorus.

The two men spoke openly, appearing to trust his discretion. He was unable to contribute much, although when Hoover asked him for his impressions of British sentiments outside London his answer was listened to with attention and respect. Eventually the relentless pace of the exchanges slackened. Hoover sighed. And his tone changed.

"This war is unlike any other, you know," Hoover said. Until now Hoover had avoided much eye contact with either man. Now he looked slowly and deliberately; first at Hugh, and then at Russell. "The Germans reckon the British are losing two men to every one of theirs so everything is going just swell." They all shook their heads in disbelief. Hoover suddenly turned his attention to Russell.

"So, what about you, Mr. Clark, are you wanting to work for the Commission? I'm not sure how much longer I'm going to be here myself but I daresay there'll be some use for you somewhere."

Hugh interjected. "Actually, chief, I think my young friend here could do with some advice. I have the feeling he's not sure what to do at the moment. It's difficult being a foreigner in this country right now. This war is all consuming, and I don't think Russell finds it easy being stuck up at Oxford while everyone else is engaged in this great struggle. Is that right, Russell?"

"Well, sir," Russell paused, to gather his thoughts, feeling that Hugh had pushed him into something of a corner, "it's true I guess, I'm at a bit of a loss. This country is no place for a neutral now. No disrespect intended of course, Hugh. A diplomat's position is different." Hugh grinned and gave a brief nod to show he understood. Russell continued.

"Studying here doesn't seem the right thing to be doing when everyone around me only thinks and talks of the war. I must have been kind of nuts in thinking Oxford would be just like before. I've seen what the Germans are capable of in Belgium and I feel pretty useless sitting on the sidelines. I don't mean to sound pompous but I'm not sure I'm cut out for a clerk's job here in London surrounded by all the British at war. I feel I should be doing something more."

"You didn't feel like joining the Glory Boys then?" asked Hoover.

"Sir …?" Russell asked.

"The Glory Boys," repeated Hoover. "All those American boys who are throwing their lives away with the French and British. Dreamers who think war is all dash and glory and they'll actually make a difference."

Hoover was referring to the many thousands from his country who had volunteered. Some of the press viewed them as romantic idealists fired up by the idea of liberating France but Russell knew that intelligent young men from Ivy League colleges had also gone. He had also recently spotted details of a volunteer air squadron, staffed by Americans and in combat under French command.

"No, I hadn't. Hugh always advised me not to rush to have a rifle in my hand, and I have to admit I had been keen to resume my research, but it is true, I am finding it hard to settle back into it."

Hoover pursed his lips and stared at Russell.

"Well, Mr. Clark, let me tell you something. America will likely come into this war. I don't think we should, and I don't think President Wilson wants to. I think we should avoid this vicious dogfight and have the moral and economic strength to stay out of it and bang those warring heads together. I worry that the loudest voices in the States come from people with exactly the same mentality as the ones fighting over here. I fear we'll be dragged in and be forced to sort this out the only way these blockheaded Europeans seem to understand. Wilson's resolve is wavering, I can feel it."

Russell and Hugh looked at each other and then back to Hoover.

"There's only going to be one place for an intelligent fit young man like yourself. Get yourself back home and join the army. You're a Rhodes scholar, I believe? They could likely do with someone like you. The only fighting any of our generals saw was chasing Indians, and I expect most of them couldn't find Belgium on a map."

As Russell smiled and Hugh laughed a waiter arrived; eyebrows were raised in query, but no one was interested in dessert.

"Compared to the Brits and the Germans," Hoover continued, "we don't even have an army yet. But I'm reckoning we're going to have to find one. And when we do that army could sure use people who know what's been happening on the ground in Europe already. I don't want to see American boys being marched off to the slaughter by the same kind of jackass generals running the show so far."

Hoover slapped his hand down on the table.

"The French and the British just want us to give them American soldiers, with rifles, for them to direct as they decide. Our men would be wasted. It won't happen that way, for sure, but it does mean we'll need a commander who's going to have to stand up to them. He's certainly going to be arguing a great deal with his so-called allies, take my word on it. A liaison role, that's the job for you."

"The British and French both like to feel themselves in charge," Hugh said to Russell.

"The American Army will need bright young guys who know the language and their way around this part of the world. Have a think about it," Hoover suggested. "I know enough people in Washington to make sure you don't end up administering some supply depot on the East Coast, and I'll be happy to put in a word. Just let Hugh know how you decide. You could get your basic training over by Christmas if you went soon. Then you'd be primed for action."

Hoover smiled at Russell for the first time, and then turned his attention back to Hugh to discuss the worrying issue of the forced removal of Belgian workers to Germany. After another ten minutes or so Hoover looked at his watch and took his leave, though not without being stopped at one more table on his way out.

Russell exhaled.

"Wow. Why do I feel like I've just played a few hours of hard tennis?"

Hugh chuckled, "Oh yeah, I know exactly what you mean. Kind of exhausting company, isn't he? He never switches off, you know. He had some strong views about your immediate future. Sorry if I put you on the spot, I hadn't seen that response coming."

"No, no. That's okay, Hugh. Actually, I think you might have done me a favour. He put into words a new possibility for me. He seemed clear that we are going to join the war. I think that surprised me, but it excited me too."

"And why did that excite you?"

"Because I think I know what I want to do. I am going to join the army, Hugh."

"Whoaahhh, young man," Hugh said, and held up both his hands as if to slow him down. The usual breeziness he displayed to Russell had suddenly vanished. "You need to think hard a moment, my young friend. This is no decision to make so quickly. Herbert Hoover makes his mind up in no time, and he doesn't deal in shades of grey either. He's nearly always right, sure, but he's not infallible. No one is. There's a lot at stake here for you, and that might include your life."

Hugh was right, Russell had been swept along by Hoover's rhetoric but Hugh was a pragmatist by profession, and clearly a good one to have risen so far through the ranks of public service while still only in his early thirties.

"Well, I realise I'm risking my forehand, Hugh, or worse." Russell and Hugh had enjoyed several sparring matches on the tennis courts in Brussels. "Hoover's right though, it is a chance to do something worthwhile. I can't sit apart from the only thing that matters in this world right now. Being in Oxford has been suffocating me."

"But what about your studies? I thought they were so important to you."

"They are, they were, but I just can't get fired up about them in the way I did. And there's certainly something ironic about studying medieval law in Europe while those same laws are being rewritten in blood all around you. I think my research can wait."

"You're a Rhodes man. That makes you one of our intellectual elite. You should continue your research."

"I can pick it up again in the future. I can choose my time."

"Well, why not join the relief effort again? I know you became bored with the administrative stuff in Brussels towards the end, but I can make sure you get more varied work, and you could be based in London."

"That's kind of you, Hugh, but Hoover's got the Commission working fine. It's not the organisation I knew in Brussels any more. We were reacting to an emergency situation back then and they were exciting times. I don't want to sound arrogant but I need more of a challenge. As for London, it's hard to see where the appeal is at the moment. You've got to be British and in uniform to feel like you've a right to be on the streets."

Hugh changed tack.

"Marion?" he asked, "what about Marion, and as if to labour the point he added, "and her family? I'm not sure her father will be too impressed. Won't it make you look fickle, even irresponsible if you join in the war?"

Russell did not have such a quick answer to this.

"Yes, you're right, it may do. I guess I'm just going to hope she understands somehow. Don't forget, she's got her work now, as well as Alain to look after. Everyone's priorities seem to be changing. With any luck she knows me well enough to see my reasons are worthwhile. It does seem like normal life is on hold while this war lasts. We just have to get through it and see what's, or who's left at the end and pick up the pieces then."

Hugh smiled at him. "You have me beat. But it feels like a snap decision to me. Do me a favour, call it a payback for this lunch?"

"Of course," said Russell.

"Sleep on it, just for, say, three days, okay? Then let me know. And by the way, Hoover won't forget what he said about helping you, and he'll do it because he really does think you would be useful. He's straight as an arrow and wouldn't give anyone a break unless they'd earned it, or he thought they deserved to be given a go for a genuine reason. Now, let's take some coffee, and I might just see if there's a good armagnac down in the cellar here. Two brandies I mean, you need one too after today."

When they parted outside the restaurant Russell felt more alive than he had for a long time. He had been connected to events and issues that really mattered. He would give Hugh his three days but he knew his decision would be the same. The life he had resumed at Oxford now looked somnolent and aimless, at a time when all around him people were living theirs at a nerve-wracking intensity. His too would have a purpose again.

He was going to step back into the real world and go where he could contribute to the best of his abilities. Russell knew he had made a life-changing decision but, now that it had been made, he was elated by how simply right it felt.

He was smiling as he stepped into Regent Street and turned towards Piccadilly. Crossing the road, just in front of him was a middle-aged woman who was slowly pushing an ancient invalid's bath chair, within which a shrunken figure was staring vacantly ahead. As she tried to push the chair over the kerbstone, Russell was horrified to watch the man fall out of the chair and land on the pavement. Russell rushed over to help and it was then that he saw the occupant of the chair lacked both legs as well as one arm, and the blue jacket draped round his shoulders revealed that he was, or rather, had been, a soldier. What shocked Russell the most was looking into the face of someone who was little more than a teenager. He was light to lift back into his seat, and, with their thanks ringing his ears, Russell continued to the station, but he had lost his smile.

Little Missenden, October 1916

"Russell, I really don't want to quarrel with you."

"Nor do I. That's the last thing I want."

"But why have you decided this, and why tell me in this way?" Marion was on her feet in the salon at the rectory. The family were out and Alain asleep, with the nanny. Russell remained sitting on the sofa, but he was ill at ease, perched on the edge of the seat.

"What other way could I have done it? I couldn't just send you a letter."

"But here, at the rectory? We have no privacy here. I can't really take it in. It wasn't what I was expecting at all, quite the opposite in fact."

Marion had been excited when she had received a letter from Russell saying he was going to call on her, and could she please be at home on Saturday. She had thought that the ambiguity in their relationship was to be decided, and he was going to propose. Primed from their time together in Oxford she was ready to accept, but that was not what he had done.

"What is the point of you going back to America to join the army? America isn't going into the war anyway. Isn't that how your president was re-elected, by standing against the war? You've given yourself no time at all to settle back into Oxford. You will get back into your studies, I'm sure. Just give it time. *Stop pleading, Marion.* And what about us? What does this mean for us? Is this the end of us or are you expecting me to wait for you until the war is over?" Marion fired her questions at him as they came into her mind. "I feel so let down."

Marion, who had been pacing as she spoke returned to Russell's side on the sofa and put her head in her hands, but soon lifted her head and continued with her tirade.

"I'll beg if you want me to, if that will make a difference. I'll go to America with you and set up home there while you work out what you want to do. Just tell me what I can do that will make you change your mind. *Toughen up, Marion.* It is unfair of you to arrive and announce your plans in this way. You have given me no say at all. Why on earth do you want to go and fight?"

"I want to be relevant. The world is changing and I want to feel a part of it. Oxford is a dead end right now."

"And being killed is more relevant than your research? Are you really that bored? What happened to the passion you had for it? Where has that gone? Can't you stick with anything?" *Stop attacking him.* Marion was on her feet again. "You were bored in Brussels and now Oxford is the same." She walked away from him and stood by the fireplace. "I suppose Alain and I will go the same way. When will it be our turn, or is that what this conversation is really about?" She turned back to face him and spoke again before he could answer. "You don't need to take such drastic measures to be rid of me, Russell. Just tell me if that is what you want and you'll never be troubled by me again, but Russell," Marion bowed her head as she fought her emotions, "don't go and get killed." Marion was pleading now. *Please don't.*

"Of course I don't want this to be the end of us." Russell was on his feet and across the room to her. "I don't plan to get myself killed either, not even hurt." Russell put his arms around her and for a moment she allowed herself to feel his comfort, but pulled away as he continued to speak. "I just want to make a contribution. I need to be closer to where the action is when America comes to Europe. I can return to my studies and to you."

"But America isn't coming to Europe. Your country is not going to help us. It doesn't seem to matter how much havoc the German submarines wreak, you just turn your heads away. This war could have been over by now if your army had already given support. Now look at the stalemate we are in. The battle at the Somme continued all summer, for no progress at all, and the French at Verdun have been decimated." Marion had thrown herself onto the settee as she voiced her grievances. *Don't go, don't leave me.*

"I know, Marion, I read the same papers. But when I was with Hugh in London we met with Mr. Hoover who says we will be in the war soon, and he can put a word in for me to be put to good use. He thought my languages and knowledge of Europe would be a great help."

"You mean he recruited you. This isn't really your decision at all." *He's been hoodwinked.* "Hoover piled on the flattery and you succumbed."

"I know you are sore about this, Marion, but don't patronise me. I am quite capable of making up my own mind about things. This is my decision, even after Hugh tried to talk me out of it."

"You surprise me, I would have thought the gallant Mr. Gibson would have been waving the patriotic flag on high." *Don't be sarcastic, Marion.*

"He was as concerned about you as he was about me."

Me? Marion paused but could not let herself be mollified. "So he can see what a ridiculous decision this is, what you will be throwing away, just to satisfy, what, some heroic misconception that you can make a difference? Exactly how big has your ego become Russell?"

Russell tried to sit down again beside Marion, but she made no room for him. He walked to the fireplace.

"On the contrary," Russell said as he rebutted her question. "I don't believe I will make a difference to the outcome of the war, but my involvement will help me. We are the same in this. It's what you described to me."

"And the difference is you stopped me going abroad to nurse, and yet without any consideration to me, you make this decision." *It's so unfair.*

"I didn't stop you, Marion. You know you made the decision not to go for yourself. Alain was the reason you stayed, not my wishes."

"That's not true."

"Isn't it? Be honest."

I don't know. I don't know. Marion let a silence hang between them before she managed a somewhat mellowed response.

"Well, not entirely." She moved so he had more space on the settee. He took this as an invitation and sat down beside her. "I did know what you wanted, and it seemed silly to be leaving the country just as you were arriving. But I expected us to be spending far more time together than we have managed. I've been very disappointed. We saw so much of each other in Brussels."

"I'm not sure it was that different. Remember all those evenings when you wouldn't see me. You told me you were working when you were actually having clandestine meetings. I had begun to think you had another beau."

"No, Russell, only ever you. And the few hundred soldiers I was smuggling out of Belgium."

Despite the tension in their exchange, they both managed a smile and he reached and took hold of her hand.

"When might you leave?"

"Now."

"Now? Why now?" Marion snatched her hand away. "Can't you wait at least until after Christmas? Why are you in such a rush?"

"To get through my basic army training before things start to kick off. I want to be with the first soldiers who come over."

"You seem very certain this is going to happen."

"Yes, Hoover says it is inevitable, so I want to be ready."

"Hoover says does he," Marion sneered. *Control yourself.*

Russell ignored her jibe. "It will be a comfort to know you are safe here and not getting yourself into any difficulties."

"Oh good, whilst I'm left to worry about you." *Don't be churlish.* "How reasonable is that?" Marion moved to one end of the sofa, picked up a cushion which she hugged into herself and turned her face away from him. Nothing further was said for a long time until Russell broke the silence by looking at his watch and telling her he needed to leave soon to catch his train.

A great battle had been raging in Marion since he announced news of his departure. All she could hear was that he was abandoning her, and Alain. She had given herself to him and here he was, walking away. On top of this she resented his freedom and the choices he could so easily make. *I hate that he can do this to me. I want him to love me more than this. I wish he was holding me*, but she was unable to make herself turn towards him. They had not spoken for half an hour, and now he was about to leave. She could not summon a kind word to say to him, and this appalled her. *Tell him you love him.* She had been sitting hugging the cushion in upset silence with him beside her. She turned and saw distress in his pained expression. *We are both hurting.*

She did not disagree when he suggested that he leave. She gave him no encouragement when he offered to write. She did not even see him to the door and the moment he left she ran to her room, only just shutting the door before the first sobs were wrenched out of her body. *Russell, you are a fool.*

Not wanting to draw her family's attention to her upset she prepared herself as best she could and joined them for dinner. Her mother missed nothing and was soon on the attack.

"I was expecting Mr. Clark to be joining us for dinner, Marion."

"No, Mother, his visit was only ever planned to be short. He was on his way to London. He asked me to pass on his sincerest wishes to you all."

"Is everything alright with you, Marion? You seem a little dull." Evelyn joined the fray.

"Thank you, Evelyn, I'm feeling tired and may be starting with a cold."

"Picked up from that hospital, no doubt. I don't know why you insist on going there," her mother continued.

"As Marion is feeling off colour, I suggest we give her a rest from our table conversation. Are we all set for the harvest supper tomorrow, my dear?" *Thank you, Papa.*

Marion was appreciative of her father's efforts to turn the spotlight off her and he and her mother were soon discussing the arrangements for the next day, with her mother bemoaning the shortage of food contributions. The realisation that it was almost the first anniversary of Edith's death brought Marion close to tears. She saw Evelyn looking quite keenly at her a couple of times, but she engaged in no further conversation and left the table as soon as they finished eating. She was surprised when Evelyn knocked on her door and joined her half an hour later.

"Did you have a falling out, you and lover boy? Mother and I saw him walking into Amersham when we were on our way back. He didn't see us, but he looked dejected and I would guess you have been crying."

"And you have come to gloat have you, Evelyn?"

"I thought I might bring you some comfort. We can be kind to each other you know, we could be friends."

"I am sorry, Evelyn. I've had all the fights I want to have today. Thank you for asking. Russell came to say goodbye. He is returning to America and intends to join the army. If America comes into this war he will fight."

"My goodness, that's a turn-up. I can remember my tears when Charles went off to war, and I hadn't imagined that he wouldn't return. Such partings are heartbreaking."

"Yes they are. Yes, of course you would understand. I am more upset that we quarrelled. I thought the whole notion of him going ridiculous: entirely unnecessary and quite selfish." *I want him here with me.*

"Marion, it is not our place to question the decisions our menfolk might make: we are here to support and to please. I hope you made up before he left."

"No, not really. He is determined to see his plan through. I don't know whether that means we will see each other again. I don't know if I want to see him again. He gave little consideration to me in his arrangements."

"War is a man's business, it's not for us to meddle in. Did he say he would be back?"

"Yes, yes he did, but I didn't hint that he would be welcome."

"He will forget your sulks and heated words. Charles never let our little spats disturb us for long; don't you concern yourself. He may be going off to fight a war but you can be assured of his affection for you. I can read the way men look at women, and he is clearly very taken with you. Knowing your attitude towards paramours Mr. Clark has done very well to advance his cause this far. Don't be too hard on him, Marion. Let him go off on his jaunt, he'll be back soon enough."

"Charles didn't come back." *Clumsy.* Marion regretted saying this the moment she did.

"No, you're quite right, Marion, he didn't. Not in body, but he is with me in spirit. Whenever I look at my reflection in a mirror, I can imagine the look of admiration there would have been in his eyes."

For once Marion conceded this was not the time to chide Evelyn on her vanity. She found herself truly appreciative of Evelyn's words of support, and offered some in return.

"You always look beautiful. He would be so proud of you."

They parted with the warmest hug they had ever shared, both confident that normal relations would be resumed in the morning.

Marion felt confused. She could not refute that she loved Russell, but she was piqued that he could make his pronouncements and expect her to meekly accept them. She had never expected to join the multitude of women waiting for their man to return from war. She did not know if she could do it, or if she wanted to. Her disappointment in him ran deep.

Little Missenden, Christmas 1916

Looking around the salon, Marion counted her blessings. Her family had returned from the Christmas Day church service to a delicious luncheon. Her uncle had supplied a goose, which her father had carved with great gusto. Alain had almost toppled the Christmas tree twice, so taken was he with the glittering decorations. Still unsteady on his feet he had crashed into it several times, and Marion was concerned that her mother would have him sent to the nursery. She had managed to encourage him onto her lap and for a moment he had stopped fidgeting. He and Anthony were too young to understand the significance of the festivities, but they had been excited throughout the day. She kissed the top of Alain's head and smiled at her father who caught her eye and winked.

"I hear your American friend was the giver of the drum, Marion. Such a generous thought." Her father spoke to her from across the room.

Russell had sent gifts, cards, and a letter over from America. The gift for Alain had been a drum with two pairs of sticks. Anthony had broken one of the sticks almost immediately and Marion had confiscated the other leaving Alain with a pair that had soft mallets at the end. Even with these bafflers the reduction in sound was not quite enough and he had been restricted in the amount of attention he could give this toy. She would have to write to Russell and tell him how popular his choice had been, as was his gift for her, a beautiful shawl. She felt quite guilty. Although she had sent him a Christmas card with her greetings, she had been quite perfunctory and had sent no gifts. She had not forgiven him his departure. His letter had been friendly, but nothing more.

"Yes, it was most kind of Mr. Clark. Alain is quite delighted with it," Marion replied.

"We, less so," said her mother as Alain, who had slipped off Marion's lap, banged the drum close to where she was seated.

"Luncheon was delicious, Mother," Marion said as a distraction, and her father chipped in.

"Yes, fulsome and delicious, that was quite the bird."

"Yes, I have to concede your brother is always generous toward us at Christmas and it has been appreciated even more this year than most. We have been short of nothing, but the prices are becoming quite outrageous."

"Will we be turning the gardens over to growing vegetables, Father? It is in all the newspapers that we must." Evelyn, who had no interest in the news or the garden, surprised them all with her question.

"Damned stupid time, excuse me, to suggest this in the middle of winter," he responded, "the ground will be too hard to break. But yes, in the spring, if this warfare continues I suggest we turn over some of the lawn to produce."

"Well, I don't know who you think will manage that work," Mrs. Drake was quick to retort.

"Women," Marion offered. "There are plenty of women who can be employed: they are only too keen to have the work. We have them in the grounds at the hospital; they manage very well."

"The hospital may be able to afford them, with all the fund-raising that is done on its behalf, but we can't. Your uncle has not seen fit to increase your father's stipend for some years and the household is more expensive to run. We need some of you girls in homes of your own. Now that would be a great help."

"Today is a day of celebration, my dear, not for talk of household matters," Mr. Drake said. "Isn't it time for some entertainment, charades perhaps?"

"Charades indeed. We have had enough charades this year already: with Marion playing happy families and scaring off the only man who showed the slightest interest in her."

"If, Mother, you are referring to Mr. Clark, I did not scare him off, he made up his own mind to depart for America and the army. True, I was unable to dissuade him, but there was no promise between us. I had nothing to hold him."

"He has proven himself unreliable and fickle and is best forgotten," Mrs. Drake concluded for the room. "Now, Mrs. Baxter was telling me more of her son, James. He will be safe from battle dangers in his prisoner of war camp, and when he returns, we must invite him over. Despite Alain, she thinks very highly of you."

"Oh no, my dear, we must not write off Mr. Clark," Mr. Drake said, causing the women to turn and look at him, surprise on all their faces.

"He will be back. I only advised him to delay until after the war, until he has his future secured. I think he and Marion are entirely suited."

For a moment his words remained suspended in the air before the assault began.

"Delay what?" Mrs. Drake, Evelyn, and Marion all cried in unison. Marion sprang to her feet and her father took a step back and held onto the mantel over the fireplace.

"Um, his proposal, of course."

Alain stopped playing with his drum and toddled over to Mr. Drake and clung onto to his trouser leg. Marion watched this movement in the seconds it took for her father's words to penetrate.

"He is quite taken with our girl, my dear." Mr. Drake directed this comment to his wife and supported it with a smile, which quickly disappeared when his wife, the first to gather her wits, assailed him with her rapid-fire questions.

"Proposal? When was this, when did he speak to you? Why do I know nothing of this?"

"Ah, yes, I see. Well, it was um, in the summer. Poor chap, he was quite put out when I advised him to wait, but he was not in a position to take on responsibilities. He'll be back."

"Oh, Papa, what have you done?"

Marion sat down on the nearest seat and held her head in her hands. Hands that were soon covered by Alain's who had toddled in her direction the moment she had slumped down.

"Why didn't you tell me?" Marion implored her father. "I had no idea that he had spoken to you. I thought he had changed his mind about our future because of Alain." Marion ruffled the young boy's hair and then pulled him up onto her lap and hugged him.

"Well, maybe he did change his mind. My conversation about providing for a family was a sobering one. He said nothing to you?" her father asked.

"Nothing at all." Alain wriggled to be put down. "I don't think I feature in thoughts of his future any more." *Nor he in mine.*

"But your gifts?" her mother said. "He sent you Christmas gifts, he must still consider you friends."

"Friends, maybe, but nothing more. We didn't part on the best of terms, and I believe, *for once*, Mother, you are correct. He has proved himself to be fickle and has no idea about the path he wants to follow."

"The war will be over soon. Didn't you say, my dear," Marion's mother addressed her husband, "that Germany have put their terms forward? Perhaps the fighting will stop and our lives can return to normal, and Mr. Clark will return."

"Um, yes I did say that but the Germans want to redraw their borders and keep the land they have won, and that won't be acceptable to anyone. I fear it will mean an even bigger push is needed. We will need the Americans to support us to break this deadlock. Mr. Clark might be back in Europe soon, but in khaki," Mr. Drake replied.

"Blue," Marion said, and they all looked at her. "In his letter he said his uniform is blue."

"Such a silly boy to rush into things," Mrs. Drake said. "There was no need for that, he is too young to know his own mind."

"These are unsettling times my dear, so do not be harsh on him. He is pulled in many directions, but he kept his word to me, and in my book that is admirable. He is a worthy suitor, once his means are secured." Mr. Drake, who was not known for shows of affection, walked over to Marion and squeezed her arm. "Come on, my dear, what about that game of charades?"

Later that night when the house was quiet, Marion, unable to sleep, tried to make sense of the churning thoughts in her head. Russell had wanted to propose and Papa had refused him. No wonder he had been so dejected and returned to Oxford in such a hurry. He must have been mortified to appear so inadequate in her father's eyes. *Why, oh why hadn't he spoken to her?* However romantic the notion, Marion wanted a relationship where both parties determined their future. *Together.* All the talk about Russell's standard of living having to pass muster with her father made her seethe. She felt patronised by both of them and ready to rebel. She would remain single rather than be discussed as chattel. *Oh, Russell.*

In Brussels, Edith and Elizabeth seemed to be entirely fulfilled in their lives through nursing, and Marion could not imagine either of them playing second fiddle to a man. The audacity of men to still think that marriage arrangements were something they determined, in ignorance of the woman's wishes. *Oh why hadn't she known?* But then her father was no different from most men who had their lives organised with their wives coming first, after them. Perhaps this was a universal truth, honoured from the Garden of Eden. No wonder the suffragettes had created so much masculine opposition: the current order suited men well.

She had felt deeply rejected by Russell's unilateral decision to join the American Army, but now at least she understood the rejection he carried with him from her father. *No wonder he had been withdrawn. But what has he gone away to prove? I would have gone to America with him as he is.* If they lived in America she knew they would enjoy freedoms from the corsetry of uptight expectations that governed so much social behaviour here. And it was protocols that had damned them. Russell had approached her father, not her, and had been so humiliated by his rejection that he had not even told her of his intentions.

Perhaps it was better this way: him gone and her free to do as she wished. Well, as free as her commitment to Alain allowed. It saddened her they had not parted on better terms. *He did want to marry me. He did. If only I had known.* She had no grounds to carry a grudge now. But what a fool for not telling her.

But would she be foolish to wait for him? He might not survive the war, or come back the same man. And even if he did come back the quarrels between them might never stop. Long gone were the heady days of their times together in Brussels; since then they always seemed to be disagreeing about something. But somehow she was convinced this was because their lives were pulling in different directions. Once they were united, then an easy understanding of each other would prevail. But he had chosen America and the army ahead of a life with her, and the resentment still ran deep.

She had a restless night and was up early, so she started the letter to Therese she had promised herself she would write.

Dear Therese,

I hope this letter reaches you and finds you well. Its route will no doubt have been circuitous, but Mr. Gibson promised to do all he could to have it delivered and I trust his intentions.

I want to write and tell you that all is well with Alain. He is walking now and starting to say some words very well, his favourite is "ball", and he has the most delightful sunny disposition. His cousin is quite grumpy in comparison. Yes his cousin! Alain remains at home with me, in my care. I describe him to people as my ward, but I am afraid to say in some quarters my reputation is in tatters as many choose to believe I am his mother. He calls me Mama and indeed I am by my actions and my love. He will never lack my attention and protective care. I will keep him with me always [*there it was, decided*], despite the best efforts of my own mother to divest me of what she sees as an inappropriate responsibility. But how can I expect her to understand when, true to my word, I have told her nothing of his start in life?

I must tell you this. On our walk a few days past, Alain was toddling along, but was soon on his knees digging in the dirt and he produced a stone that had broken in two, ridden over by a cart most probably. He gave me a piece and then held my hand and pressed his half of the stone against mine, making it whole again, and as he did this a ray of sunlight fell onto us. It was otherwise a grey scene. I have to say I felt touched. It was as if he was telling me that we belonged together, and the sun sealed our love, and perhaps fate.

Fanciful perhaps, but it was you who taught me to believe in signs, and I will encourage Alain whenever he shows me he has something to say.

Mr. Clark, Russell, has returned to America. It

seems we will need them in this war to curtail the German Army and convince them to return home. Russell will be in uniform soon. I fear for him. None of our futures are secure, but I wanted you to know of Alain's home with me, and perhaps this will be no surprise to you.

Therese, I send you love and eternal gratitude. You saved my life. I am sure you will have learnt of Edith's death. Without you I would have shared the same fate. God bless you and keep you safe and well.

Marion.

Evelyn was in the nursery tending to Anthony when Marion arrived with warmed milk for both the boys. Nanny had been given the day off and had just left to see her own family for the day, and rare as it was, she and Evelyn worked companionably together, at first in silence and then Evelyn directed her attention to Marion.

"That was quite the surprise yesterday: fancy Papa keeping that one under his hat. No doubt Mother tore a strip off him last night. She will never forgive him for turning away a suitor. Will you lovebirds mend your broken hearts now, or is it too little too late?"

"I wanted to tear a strip off him as well, and Russell too for that matter. He should have spoken to me, not Papa."

"Don't be ridiculous, of course he had to speak to Father first."

"No he didn't. It is for me to decide what I want, and who I might want to consider marrying."

"The boy has manners, at least. Even if he is American," Evelyn said.

"He should at least have told me afterwards. We could have determined our own future, instead of him sulking and heading off to the army. It's all ridiculous, and yes, it may well be too late."

"I am truly sorry, Marion. Like Papa I think you are well suited. Perhaps he will be back."

"Who knows, and it is probably stupid of me to hold out hope, but thank you Evelyn." *I think she means it.*

"Anyway, you might meet someone you like more at the hospital. I am making some new acquaintances there myself."

"You? When have you been to the hospital?"

"Not yet to the hospital, but to the house. The stables are one of the collection centres for Queen Mary's clothing for the troops. I am often there when I can escape Mother's committees. I have passed a rather gorgeous man several times and I know there is a conversation brewing between us."

"If I know him, perhaps I can make the necessary introductions," Marion offered.

"No thank you, no introductions are needed. I much prefer the cat and mouse to be at play. We will speak when we are ready to. For now, noticing each other will suffice."

"I have to confess to enjoying the company of one of my colleagues at Bachelor House. He's quite the charmer."

"Tell me more," Evelyn encouraged, but Marion would not be drawn any further.

She marvelled at this exchange of confidences, and at herself for considering Doctor Ambrose a flirtation. She had become conscious that their break times often seemed to coincide when he would single her out for conversation and his attentions had not gone unnoticed by the other nurses. Marion had been embarrassed by their nudges on more than one occasion, but if he saw them he paid them no heed. *A flirtation, that would lift my spirits.* But which was she, the cat or the mouse? Perhaps she should ask Evelyn for some tips, and maybe 1917, she mused, would be the year when sibling rivalry would change to sisterly accord.

Bachelor House, June 1917

Marion was exhausted. The pressure on the hospital had been phenomenal: swamped by a high number of patients from the battlefield at Arras. Many of the men had already been operated on in London and had come for their recuperation. Some did not last the journey. The casualty lists from the carnage in France kept growing, but she found spirits among the officers were high. The Germans had been pushed back and America, having declared war against Germany, was soon to join the fray.

"What can you do for them?" Marion nodded towards two shell-shocked patients on chairs underneath a nearby tree. She was enjoying a break from her work and was sitting on a bench outside where she had been joined by Doctor Ambrose. This had become the part of her working day she looked forward to. The air was warming up, but was fresh after the stuffiness of the wards kept at a constant temperature for the patients.

"The doctors try to settle their nerves, to stop them jumping. Their nervous system has been overstimulated and is sending too many impulses to the muscles."

"Or none at all. I've heard that some of them have lost the ability to speak or walk."

"When you see unspeakable horrors, it can lock the brain."

"How do you settle their nerves?" Marion turned back to face him after she had watched a patient and an orderly walk past. "Mine are frayed when I hear some of the screams emanating from the second floor. What goes on up there?"

"It's a shock treatment. They send electric current through the nervous system to jolt it out of the haphazard rhythms and back into a normal state."

"And does it work?"

"Not always, they are still experimenting, but that's why you hear some screams. The ones that have to return for a second or third time are the screamers. They know what's coming."

"Does it hurt then, this treatment?" Marion asked as she shuddered.

"Of course it hurts. It's an electric shock through the brain. They have to put thick leather between their teeth to stop them biting through their tongues."

"How awful. How absolutely awful."

"But so is the condition they have. Involuntary spasms are exhausting. They will feel as if they have brought in the harvest each day. Their body allows them no respite. That's why they become so thin."

"And when they are recovered they return to their units to fight, you said?"

"Yes they do." Doctor Ambrose stood up to stretch his legs and sat down again. He stood at about five foot ten inches and, while not muscular, was toned and fit. "The army still needs every man it can muster. There is little patience for this condition in the army, nor among many of my medical colleagues. The generals think they are shirkers; that the condition is self-induced. And in a way it is. Their system is saying I cannot take any more of this fear, but it is not something they consciously decide. We all have different amounts of trauma that we can tolerate. Most of them want to return to their companies, they don't want to be seen as weak, or at least that is what they say when the top brass are around. Not that it would make any difference if they didn't. They are in the army and must do as ordered. Or be shot for desertion. Now, shall we take a stroll?"

"Were you in the army?" Marion asked as she stood to join him.

"Here it comes. The question that always comes. What you mean is, why aren't you in the army? Am I right?"

"Well if you want me to be direct, yes, that is my question."

"And you haven't wanted to ask me before now?" Doctor Ambrose stopped walking and faced her.

"I feel I know you well enough to ask you now."

"They wouldn't have me," he said and began walking again, "Asthma. Always suffered from it. I think I make up for it with my duties here, but if this war goes on for much longer they might let me in."

"I had no idea. You seem healthy to me and anyway you more than make up for it with the hours you put in. This way?" Marion pointed to a path between some flowerbeds that now contained vegetables. Doctor Ambrose followed.

"I wouldn't go for the fight, but to help the troops, perhaps save a few more lives, rather than the patching up we do here."

"Would you want to go? This hospital wouldn't be the same if you left." Marion paused. "You are such a good doctor. The patients adore you."

"Just the patients?" Doctor Ambrose smiled his question and Marion blushed but before she could take advantage of his overture, he continued.

"Not everyone feels the same about a man not in uniform. I have a jam jar full of white feathers that have been sent my way."

"How awful for you. I tore two women off a strip when they dropped one on a friend of mine. But the Earl of Derby even encourages wives and girlfriends to hand them to their men. I read one of his speeches in *The Times*."

"You're not taken with the war are you, but I'm sure like all our countrymen you don't want the Germans on our shores. We have no choice but to fight. It's the only language this aggressor understands. Thank goodness the Americans are on their way, we need their help. As does matron, by the looks of her: I think she is looking for me. Must dash." They had reached the front entrance of the house, and there was matron waving to them. Doctor Ambrose strode off.

So does he like me or not? Marion continued her walk. She was expecting an invitation from him to meet outside work but on this he remained elusive. His manner was often flirtatious with her, and she was sure that some of the accidental touching of their hands was not unplanned. He was attentive, and their chats, although more cosy than intimate, were nonetheless ongoing and clearly the envy of the other nurses. Matron had warned her just recently that he was a man of mystery and not one that she should attempt to solve, but that did nothing to quash her growing interest in him.

Despite her notion that she and Evelyn might continue with their confidences they had swiftly retreated to their normal exchanges, with nothing more forthcoming. And the truth was she had nothing to share, other than her growing fancy for Dr. Ambrose. And even that was sporadic. Some days he did nothing for her, and all she could think of was Russell and her nostalgia for the dizzying feelings they both experienced in the early days of their relationship. But seeing Dr. Ambrose at work was no hardship at all, and he was often the boost she needed to overcome her tiredness. And when she reached home, there was Alain.

Now two, he was quite a chatterbox, although sometimes unintelligibly. She treasured his smiles and hugs. Mrs. Emerson had spoken to her as they left church the previous week

"He's an old soul, Marion. He's been here before."

"I think just the same the way he looks at me sometimes, as if he's waiting for me to catch up."

Alain had smiled at both of them.

He did have a way about him that was hard for Marion to

describe. She loved that he was able to calm Anthony, and that boy's tantrums were becoming legend. She had once watched Alain take hold of Anthony's flailing fists and within minutes calm had ensued. When Marion had copied this Anthony had bitten her.

Marion did not want to think that Alain might be the reason for Dr. Ambrose's reticence toward her. *You're being too serious, girl.* There were so many widows in the country now, with children or a child in their care, she could not imagine that her situation looked any different. Unless of course it was the doubts about her reputation, but she hoped that tittle-tattle was long in the past. And then one of her nursing colleagues had asked her, just that morning, whether her American boyfriend would be joining the fight. Perhaps Dr. Ambrose thought she was engaged. She would have to find the right moment to put him straight.

Pleased with this thought, Marion, who had continued her walk back to her usual bench, bent to collect her teacup and then eased herself upright. Lifting and moving patients to change their bedding was taking its toll on her. The work was generally more physical than mental; some days she thought she did not call on her medical training at all and a housemaid would have done as good a job, and probably would have been sturdier, but she loved the patient contact. She stepped inside the house through the patio window and was soon back on the ward, absorbed in her duties.

Marion enjoyed conversations with her patients and she was good with them, putting them immediately at ease. The downside of this for her was that they talked quite openly and often about the traumas of battle, and some tales were very hard to stomach. She was surprised that afternoon to stumble across an argument between three officers in the recreation room. In chairs circling the unlit fireplace they all turned towards her as she approached and one beckoned her over.

"Just what we need, a referee, to put this argument to bed."

Marion asked what the problem was.

"The Angels of Mons," Captain Wiseman said.

"The so-called 'Angels of Mons'," Webber added and Goff said nothing but gave her a lovely smile to show there was no real tension in the air. His wound had left his face lopsided, but his eyes were clear and always had a sparkle when she was around.

"I thought it was a fairy story?" Marion volunteered.

"My point exactly, that's settled." Webber grinned.

"It's not settled, not for those who were there and my gunner was, and he's a mature bloke, not one for fancy ideas," Wiseman continued.

"What does he say?" Marion asked as she pulled up a chair and Goff shuffled his to make room for her.

Wiseman took the floor and told them the tale as he had been told, even though they had all read it in the newspapers. There had been quite a splash and much editorial comment as the story caught people's imaginations. Reminiscent of a campfire story, he set the scene of the British Expeditionary Force in retreat at the battle of Mons in the early weeks of the war.

"The Germans were chasing our boys and they were running ragged, when suddenly in the sky above them they saw angelic hosts. The sky was full of them, riding horses and the angels had helmets on, like warriors. Some say you could hear the sound of the horse's hooves thundering above them. Apparently my gunner said it stopped the Germans in their tracks and hundreds of British soldiers made it to safety."

"To fight another day," Goff said, echoing the thought in Marion's mind.

"Sounds like a load of tosh to me," Webber said.

"We know what you think, Webber, but what do you make of it, Nurse Drake?" Wiseman asked.

"Well, from what I read, it seemed like a miracle that so many of our soldiers survived that battle, so angels or not, Lady Luck was on their side."

"I thought the same," Wiseman admitted. "Except when my gunner told me about it, his face shone. I can't forget that. He's called Lucky by his mates and they all stick close to him."

"Let's hope he stays lucky and makes it home. He'll have a story to tell his grandchildren in years to come. He believes he saw them and perhaps that's all that matters, particularly if it keeps him safe," Marion said as she stood up. Matron was beckoning her from the doorway. "Must go."

"You're quiet Goff, what do you think …?"

Marion heard Captain Wiseman ask the question as she left them and attended to the patient matron had called her for. A new arrival, he had just recovered consciousness and Marion had a battery of tests to run. It was an easy way to build a rapport while taking the man's temperature and checking wounds. Marion was never quite sure why she needed to note the height of her patients, nor the colour of their eyes, but if the question was on the admission form, it had to be answered.

Doctor Ambrose called by to ask her what time she was taking her lunch and they agreed to meet later.

"Boyfriend, miss?" the soldier asked.

Used to this question, Marion reeled off her now familiar reply. "Purely professional," and was starting to regret that this remained the truth.

"Do you believe in angels?" Marion asked him as they shared a sandwich lunch later.

"Of course, I do. I am surrounded by them." Doctor Ambrose waved his arm to take in her and several other nurses seated around the patio on garden benches.

"No, I meant real angels, angelic host type angels."

"I don't expect I do, no, not really. Does that disappoint you? I will try and believe if that will make you happier."

"Always the tease," Marion replied, laughing.

"Why the question?" he prompted as he bit into a raw carrot.

"Oh, just something to ask. It came up with some of the officers today: they were talking about Mons and the vision of angels."

"I thought that story had been created by a journalist."

"Me too, but those who believe the story do seem to have something that us doubters don't."

"Delusions?" Now it was his turn to laugh. "Or do you mean God on their side?"

"Very funny. I was being serious," Marion said. "It seems to me that believers can enjoy endless possibilities. Anything can happen if you believe in the spiritual realm, and everything can be accounted for and explained."

"So if anything was possible what would you have happen, Nurse Drake?"

Marion pondered his question, but for only a moment.

"This war to be over."

"Yes of course, that goes without saying. What else?"

"Are you probing for my secret desires?"

"Professional interest only, you understand," Doctor Ambrose said and adopted a stance as if she was a new patient to be diagnosed.

And that was her problem, she never knew when to take him seriously and whether he was ever serious. He seemed to enjoy teasing her and seeing her blushes. She felt like a schoolgirl with a crush. *Enough, do it, Marion.* She decided to break through the banter and turned towards him.

"Your interest would be welcome if it was more personal than professional." Marion held his gaze until he coughed on the carrot he was chewing and looked away.

"That felt like an invitation, Nurse Drake, and I thought you would have taken matron's warnings seriously."

"Should I?" Marion asked, fearing they were back to banter again.

"She is a wise, all-seeing woman, and should be heeded at all times. Especially now, here she comes."

Matron approached and sat down without waiting for an invitation to join them and launched into a conversation with Doctor Ambrose about a particular medical protocol. Superfluous, Marion stood up and made her exit. Too unsettled to return to the ward she walked briskly down to the end of the drive and back to try to release the scream of frustration within her.

So close, so close. She could say no more. How could she say so much? She had all but offered herself to him. No she hadn't, she hadn't, she had only hinted at moving from professional to personal. She hadn't hinted, she was direct. Had he looked relieved when matron arrived? He didn't seem disappointed. When would he stop playing with her? He was toying with her. Had she spoilt the game? Would he tire of her now? When would he ask her out? What was wrong with him? Or was it her: was a nurse too menial for him and did she bore him? Stop it, stop it, you were good enough for Russell, and he is brighter than Ambrose. It was so straightforward with Russell. Russell? What was she doing?

Marion turned the corner of the house and bumped straight into Doctor Ambrose. He put his arms out to steady her and did not let go.

"Where did you dash off to?" he asked.

"Oh, just a quick burst of exercise," Marion said, but she felt flustered, and stepped back out of his reach.

"Matron was only with me for a minute, I had hoped we could continue our conversation."

"It wasn't a conversation, you were toying with me." Marion surprised herself with her outburst. *Shut up, shut up.*

"Ah, yes, I am a damned nuisance at that. Been told that before. Don't give up on me, Marion. You never know when I might come cantering over the hill on my white horse to sweep you up."

"There you go again." *Shut up.*

"You're quite right to upbraid me. When my pillion is free, I'll be yours, and that's a promise. There, how is that for being straightforward."

"Oh, I see, I think I see." *Say nothing.*

"From professional to personal, I like the sound of that. Um, jolly nice. We'll see; we'll have to see."

Marion was mystified, and his mixed metaphors had not helped. Cantering to collect her on his white horse but only when his pillion was available? Well, who was riding with him now? And why was he encouraging her if he was already seeing someone else? If this was the cat and mouse game she hated it, and he was beginning to look more of a rat than a cat. Marion felt out of her depth and even a little humiliated. She should have heeded matron.

The good thing was, nothing seemed changed between them after their conversation. He did not avoid her, in fact, if anything, she thought he sought her out even more and her confidence when with him grew. He obviously just liked taking his time, but she had an idea that she thought he might like. She put forward her proposal at one break, explaining that she had an appointment in London on Saturday and that perhaps, if he was going into town, they could meet up. For the first time ever she thought he was flustered. *Too much, too fast.*

"A, a lovely idea, Marion, but I am afraid I am, um, working on Saturday: so sorry not to oblige."

"No, well, it is short notice, and probably a silly idea anyway."

"Not at all, another time, perhaps. When will you be travelling?"

"The half past ten train."

"It was a lovely thought. I hope your appointment works out. Not a job interview I hope?"

"No, I am meeting an old friend from Brussels days. Hugh Gibson, he was the secretary to the American legation."

"Ah, yes, I heard mention of an American and you."

"No, no, that isn't Hugh, wasn't Hugh, isn't anyone, any more, not really. But there was an American, yes, but no, not him." Marion tripped over her words and he laughed.

"Not meaning to pry. Everyone can have their secrets." He raised his hand, as she was about to start a longer explanation. "Even if you have more than most."

London, June 1917

Russell felt a thrill of excitement as he stared down over the side of the *SS Baltic*, a majestic ocean liner that had carried him from New York to Liverpool. The day was overcast; the sky, the sea, and the huge bustling port could only offer him depressing shades of an ambient grey. However, he did think the few flags and coloured standards fluttering in the melee on the dock below brought some brightness to the occasion. *Which is, just now, about all my fellow colonists and I can offer to this country anyway.* He shivered in the cool, damp breeze.

He knew he was privileged to be watching an historic event in the making but, never a strong sailor, after ten days at sea Russell longed to feel land under his feet again. On this return to Britain though, the decision on when to disembark was no longer his to make: he was now an army man.

Unfortunately the ceremonials seemed to be taking forever. The cause of them was his army commander, General Pershing, who was now on the quayside inspecting the third line of a guard of honour. To Russell, the sight of the battalion mascot, a goat as lavishly decorated as any of the most senior British officers in the welcoming party, gave the scene a touch of vaudeville. Despite the constant reminder of his stiff new lieutenant's uniform he still found it hard to take all aspects of military life seriously.

"Don't you worry, gents. The cavalry's arrived."

The words, inaudible to any of the British officials or soldiers down on the dock but clearly aimed in their direction, were spoken by one of his fellow American junior officers, and they caused some merriment. Russell and the other younger lieutenants had quickly gelled during the voyage and the extrovert Lester Greenley had appointed himself the team's humorist. He followed on.

"Hey, Russ, who's the miserable little guy with Pershing? The one with more whiskers than my grandmother and half a scrapyard pinned to his chest."

Russell joined in with the laughter. It had refreshed him no end being surrounded by bountiful American optimism and enthusiasm this year, even though they had been preparing for war. He was one of the first contingents of the American Expeditionary Force. They numbered under 200 officers and ranks, but few had ever been to Europe, let alone spoke French. His European experience meant his peers saw him as the authority for all things this side of the Atlantic, and he enjoyed the easy status this gave him. Indeed, it was his experience and languages that had catapulted him to the position of liaison officer on Pershing's staff; aided to no lesser extent, he was prepared to admit, by a reference from a most senior officer, Major General Franklin Bell, who, in turn, had responded to a letter of recommendation from Herbert Hoover. The great man had kept his word.

"I'm pretty sure that's General French," Russell replied. "Only before you say anything, Lester, French isn't French; he's British as you can see. He led the British Expeditionary Force into France at the beginning of the war, and not very well it seems. General French didn't get on with the French. So now they've got a nice British sounding general in charge, called Haig. Only he too has got a bit stuck. And that's why we're here."

Further raillery was stalled by the appearance of a merchant seaman who had been sent to inform them that they would be leaving the ship within the hour to train down to London. The cheerful young Americans promptly dispersed to collect their equipment, though Russell knew that it would not take them more than a few minutes to pack the meagre quantity of personal possessions that army life allowed. What a contrast to his first visit to this country as a student: by comparison he had arrived in Oxford before the war with the travel necessities of a minor royal.

"Well, well, Lieutenant Clark, look at you. I do declare you make me proud to be American."

The last time Russell had met with Hugh Gibson was when the two of them had lunched with Herbert Hoover at the Café Royal all of nine months before. Seeing Hugh once again rising from a chair to greet him, he realised what a changed man he must appear since that time. No, more than that, what a changed man he *was*.

The two men shook hands and slapped each other's shoulders. They sat themselves in the lounge of the Great Central Hotel and Hugh ordered a pot of coffee. Russell had been locked in briefings at the War Office since his arrival two days before but, having made contact with Hugh at the embassy, had gratefully accepted his friend's invitation to join him and surprisingly, Marion too for luncheon. Hugh was soon to leave London for a position within the State Department in Washington, and without any knowledge of Russell's arrival had arranged a farewell meeting for himself with Marion. They had agreed on the Central, the hotel alongside Marylebone station, which was where Marion's train from Amersham would be arriving.

Despite the strained, or should he more honestly say estranged relations between himself and Marion, Russell had not been able to stop the jealousy that stabbed at him when he heard of these plans. Marion and he had written letters to each other, quite regularly in fact, each with news of their activities, but no endearments had populated the pages. There was no let-up in her antipathy towards his departure. His hands felt sweaty as he anticipated seeing her again, and he had to concentrate on dragging his attention back to Hugh.

"I telegraphed Marion yesterday suggesting she catch a later train, to give you and me some time to catch up. She should be in just after noon. That gives us an hour."

"Was she okay about my joining you?"

"Oh, she'll be fine, she'll take it in her stride." Despite his confident words, he looked a little nervous.

"She doesn't know, does she? You haven't told her I'll be here, have you?"

"No, I didn't, but I did tell her I had a surprise for her."

"It will certainly be that. We didn't exactly part on speaking terms."

"Oh, you lovebirds will soon make up. There's a war on, no time to waste. Now tell me, I'll bet you're feeling a lot easier in London than the last time we met? That's some smart uniform," Hugh said, as they settled into large armchairs.

"No question," stated Russell. "It's like I've come back here as someone else."

His blue uniform was uncomfortable and impractical. The high collar dug into his neck and was especially unwelcome in the warm room. The long jacket lacked proper pockets, and the stiff Sam Browne belt always seemed to be in the way. Pershing insisted his officers dress in this manner, but Russell knew it made him look impressively smart.

He had walked along the streets with his head high and from the long stares he received he knew he was a novelty. He was conscious of the contrast to his last visit, when he had felt so uncomfortable and out of place in civilian clothes. Now, as one of the long-awaited American Army, he felt very special. Some strangers across the street had even shouted greetings to him; and a few had applauded. The very same sort of young ladies who had scowled at him before and handed out white feathers were now throwing admiring glances his way. He described this to Hugh.

"You're seen as a saviour, not just a novelty act," Hugh replied. "Or rather, the first of hundreds of thousands of saviours. The British and French have been getting impatient, and are at their wits' end. Now that American troops have actually arrived, even if it's just the headquarters staff, they'll feel their prayers have been answered. They're betting the bank on us. Or at least what they have left in the bank, which isn't much, we reckon. You won't believe what they're spending to fund this fight."

A waiter arrived with cups and a coffee pot and served them in an unduly deferential style. The man's obsequiousness was theatrical; either he was mocking them or he had mistaken Hugh for an exceptionally high-ranking dignitary. But Hugh winked at Russell behind the waiter's back before rolling his eyes towards the reception area. Russell turned his head to see what his friend was pointing out. There stood a group of about half a dozen men and women by the desk, talking together in an animated fashion and looking in their direction. It became apparent it was he who was the centre of their attention. This is getting ridiculous, he thought. I'm beginning to feel like some newly discovered species. He sank deeper into his chair to be less visible from the hotel lobby and sipped his coffee. Russell's palate had re-acclimatised to American coffee and he grimaced at the strength of his first sip.

"There might be some wishful thinking on their part, Hugh. We met some British and French officers on the ship. I was mainly talking to the French, but it seems both of our allies have some pretty crazy notions about us; and a huge list of demands."

"Don't tell me …" Hugh said. "I can guess what they were. They want the sun, moon, and stars. Oh, and I hear the king wants fifty thousand airplanes as well!"

"You heard about that, did you? Didn't take long to reach us both did it?"

Pershing had been to a reception at Buckingham Palace the day before, and over breakfast Russell had heard reports, filtered down through his colleagues, that the king, like his subjects, seemed to have an absurdly exaggerated notion of American military capabilities.

"I'm a diplomat, young fellow, it's my job to have my ear to the ground. Mind you in this case the news wasn't hard to pick up. I was there."

"I should have guessed," Russell smiled.

Hugh sipped his drink and shuddered. "It's worth going back to the US just to get a real brew," he said. "First thing I'm going to do is order a gallon of our finest, and I'll be thinking of you stuck with this moonshine."

"Black Jack will make sure we've got our own supplies, I'm sure," Russell said, using Pershing's nickname. "What did you think of him, by the way?"

Hugh took his time to answer, to give Russell his complete read. He assured Russell that Pershing looked the part and was snappy and vigorous compared to the more bellicose British generals, hinting that he looked half their age. He had managed to stay pretty tight-lipped at the reception, saying the right things and not much more, but he oozed quiet confidence and competence. Even if he proved to be no good, in Hugh's opinion he had already boosted morale at least.

"I would reckon on him being pretty demanding as a boss, and he doesn't give the impression he'd be very forgiving. But I didn't see much sign of arrogance. So I reckon he's one of those leaders whose men will blindly follow to hell and beyond. That tie in?" Hugh concluded.

"Pretty much, at least from what I know of him so far. As you can imagine, I'm not one of his intimates. He's a hard taskmaster, that's for sure. Expects everyone to be busy all the time; has us running around every minute of the day. I'm sure the senior officers, who really know him, would hand over their entire worldly goods to him if he asked them, and probably throw in their wives and children too. So I think he's the real deal." Russell frowned, and added, "Mind you I think he'll be fighting a diplomatic war as much as a military one."

"I'm not at all surprised to hear you say that," Hugh said.

"Yes, looks like Mr. Hoover was spot on. The British and the French officers I've met all seem to believe we'll be handing over thousands of troops for them to use wherever and whenever they think fit. Pershing says he's going to operate his own independent command. I think I'm going to have my work cut out stuck in the middle. I already get the feeling I'll be saying 'Ce n'est pas possible' all the time."

Hugh laughed. "And after that it'll just be *Non, non, et non.* I'll be glad to get them all off my back, that's for sure."

"And Pershing's thinking big. Seems he's talking of at least half a million men over here before he'll make much of a move; and he wants all his own support and logistics to go with that. We've got railwaymen, engineers, and shipping people with us, some in uniform and some not. We're just the tip of the iceberg. The whole thing's gonna be huge."

"Yes, and the iceberg will need towing across the Atlantic. It's not going to float on its own, and there's the problem. It all comes back to the same old question. Ships, ships, and more ships. Now who's got all the ships?"

Hugh opened his hands in a gesture that explained that the answer was here, where they were, in Britain.

"Sounds familiar," Russell said ruefully. "Just like it ever was. Right from the very beginning in Brussels."

He and Hugh had gone through troubled times together in the early days of the occupation and they always reminisced at some point, every time they met. While dull for an eavesdropper, for Russell each telling was as fresh and vivid as the last, and he was happy to relive those early months of the war. To him their experiences were like precious secrets, spoken in a code that only they could decipher and appreciate. Or at least they and one other person, Russell suddenly remembered. He dragged himself out of the comfort of their mutual nostalgia and looked at his watch.

"Hey, Marion's train will be here in ten minutes. We'd better walk across and meet her."

For the first time ever, he saw Hugh Gibson flustered.

"Look, I'll go get her," Hugh volunteered. "It's probably best you stay here, what with your uniform and everything. You'll get a load of attention and won't be able to greet her without a big audience gawping at you. If things aren't easy between you, she might not appreciate the sideshow."

"Are you thinking your surprise might not have been the best idea?"

"Well, perhaps."

"Look, I know Marion better than that. Here's the deal. You stay here and keep our seats and check on our table reservation for lunch. I'll go get her and clear the air, and if she's too punchy with me, well you two can have lunch on your own as you had always planned." Not waiting for a rebuttal, Russell stood, pulled down his jacket and shook hands with Hugh.

"Just in case this is goodbye."

"Don't forget she might not recognise you. She won't be looking for a man in uniform. She will be expecting me." Russell turned smartly on his heel and walked to the station concourse, just across from the back entrance of the hotel.

It was impossible for him to stand still while he waited for the train to come to a stop and for Marion to disembark. He did not know which carriage to watch as the doors were flung open and passengers alighted and a torrent of people came towards him. Despite his confidence with Hugh he felt a slight panic that he might miss her in the crowd. He spotted someone he recognised, but it was not Marion, it was her sister Evelyn. He watched her as a tall handsome man who tucked her arm in a proprietorial way through his helped her from the train. They walked along the platform towards the barrier, and Russell. He stepped forward as they navigated the ticket gate and called out to attract her attention.

"Miss Drake? Evelyn?"

She turned on hearing her name, just as Russell saw Marion approaching. He was about to call to her when he saw the colour drain out of her face. She was staring at Evelyn and the man beside her. Evelyn followed Russell's gaze.

"Our secret is out," Evelyn said as she squeezed Doctor Ambrose's arm. "Horatio, here is my sister Marion, Marion meet Doctor Ambrose, the gentleman I told you about from Bachelor House. You have probably seen each other at the hospital. Do I need to introduce you?"

"No, no you don't," said Marion taking steps backwards, much to the consternation of passengers behind her.

"Then you must introduce Doctor Ambrose to Mr. Clark. She is a sly one, Horatio," Evelyn said. "We all thought he was consigned to the past."

"No, no, it's Mr. Gibson I am meeting, not Russell."

"But it is Russell who is here." Evelyn said as she stepped aside and Russell moved forward.

"Marion?" and before Russell could utter another word Marion had flung herself into his arms.

It was ten minutes before they made their way to the hotel to meet with Hugh. After the briefest of introductions between Russell and Doctor Ambrose, Evelyn and her companion left for their London excursions. Marion had returned to her embrace with Russell, and although concerned to see the tears that ran down her face he was pleased to see that her colour had returned. In fact she was clearly flushed. Never in his wildest dreams, of which there had been many, had he ever envisioned such a welcome from her. He was shaking, and not far from tears himself. When she could speak her first question was about Hugh.

"Where is Hugh? Does he know you are here? He must do? I am so pleased to see you. How much time do you have free?"

"Yes, Hugh is here and waiting to see you. He is at the hotel checking on our lunch reservation. We had better join him?"

"Let me go to the powder room first. You go on, I'll be with you in a few minutes, I just need to freshen my face."

"It looks beautiful to me. I'll wait."

"You didn't travel up with Evelyn then?" Russell asked as they left the station.

"No, I didn't know she was on the train. I didn't see her board. She left home after breakfast. I had no idea what she had planned for her day."

"So that is your Doctor Ambrose. He is very dashing. Quite a catch for Evelyn."

"Yes he is," Marion said, but she sounded flat to him.

"You didn't tell me they were together, or did I miss that in one of your letters?"

"No, you didn't. I hadn't mentioned it."

"Marion, is everything alright? You look shaken."

"Yes, fine. No, no, of course I am shocked. I had no idea to expect you today. Forget how Doctor Ambrose looks, you are the dashing one in your uniform. Can you see how everyone is looking at you?"

She was right, they were.

"Not at me," Russell said, "at the stars and stripes, and the fact that I have a beautiful girl on my arm."

They were laughing when they came across Hugh who was standing in reception.

"There you are. I was beginning to think you had missed the train. Put him down for a moment and say hello to me, and then let's have our lunch." Russell stepped aside for Hugh and Marion to greet each other.

Any old edginess Russell felt about relations between Hugh and Marion quickly disappeared. All three of them enjoyed a wonderfully companionable lunch. They encouraged Hugh to talk about his new job in Washington. It was a promotion and Russell was proud and excited for him, but the thrill for Russell was the feeling of Marion's hand in his underneath the table.

Just as they were about to order their desserts, the wine waiter came to tell them that guests on a nearby table had offered to pay for their wine.

"Is this what being famous is like? Marion asked. "I could become used to this." They raised their glasses to their benefactors, who burst into spontaneous applause. Russell flushed with embarrassment.

"Very appropriate, they have gooseberry fool on the dessert menu," Hugh said, "and I have no intention of continuing as a gooseberry, so I will bid a hasty retreat. But before I go, take this." Hugh put an envelope on the table. "Do quote me as your chaperone."

They all stood for his departure. Marion and Hugh hugged and he and Russell shook hands and slapped each other on the back several times.

"Take care, old boy, as the Brits say," Hugh said.

"Cocktails in Washington DC, when the fight is over," Russell said. "On you."

Marion and Russell returned to their seats, and the envelope. Hugh had obviously been busy while Russell was at the station and had booked a bedroom for a meeting in his name. The number and key were in front of them. With one look at each other they abandoned all thought of dessert and left the restaurant.

Great Central Hotel, London, June 1917

Marion kicked her legs free of the tangled sheets and looked at the clock. Russell had been gone an hour, she had just woken up, and it was time for her move. Part of her dread for leaving the room and returning to the station was in case she bumped into Evelyn and Doctor Ambrose again. *Evelyn and Doctor Ambrose. Evelyn and Doctor Ambrose.* The moment of realisation returned: *he was Evelyn's beau.*

She had wanted the ground to swallow her, to be anywhere but where she was when she spotted them. Evelyn in her totally self-absorbed state would have noticed nothing of her reaction, but it was not Evelyn that mattered to her. *It was him.* She had not been able to look at him, which she now regretted. Now she wished she had stared at him and made him look at her: she wanted him to feel uncomfortable. *How dare he lead me on with all his flirtations?*

But was that not all they were to him: flirtations? She was the silly one to have read intent behind them. *No better than a schoolgirl with a crush.* She felt foolish, embarrassed. Russell had accepted her tears as her being overwhelmed at seeing him and she had not disabused him. *Thank goodness for Russell. He saved the day.* Without him at the station her humiliation would have been crushing; instead she almost crushed his ribs when she flung herself at him. The nearest harbour was his arms. *I showed Ambrose.*

Russell. What had she done? Taken the lid off that Pandora's box again. He had thought her greeting had been all about him;

of course he would, and had responded in kind. Their lovemaking had been passionate. It was easier for her to be physical than to talk, at the outset at least. He had been thrilled, and gradually she had melted.

"This time together is beyond my wildest dreams," Russell said after their lovemaking. "And to be forgiven by you, makes me feel complete."

"Who says I have forgiven you?" Marion asked.

"This says you have forgiven me." Russell held her tight and they enjoyed a lingering kiss.

"It's not my place to be churlish, or bear a grudge when you are going off to fight, and anyway, Papa told me everything," Marion said as she caught her breath.

"He did? Why didn't you say in your letters?" Russell lifted his head from the pillow to look at her.

"Because it was water under the bridge by then. But don't be so sure that I have forgiven you."

"Is there anything I can do to persuade the lady?" Russell asked as he moved closer.

"No, seriously Russell, you fouled up good and proper. You decided on a future that doesn't include me. I'm not sure I should be here with you now."

"I know, I know, but it was a difficult time." Russell laid his head back on the pillow. "I deeply resented your father's rejection of me. I was humiliated. But the joke of it is I proved him right, didn't I."

"Some joke."

Marion lifted herself away from him, plumped up her pillows, drew the sheet around her and folded her arms across her chest. Russell copied her and they remained in silence for some minutes.

"I'm sorry."

"Pardon?" Marion said.

"I'm sorry," Russell repeated.

"Yes, well, that's easy to say isn't it, when it is too late to change anything." *Don't be horrid, Marion.*

"It's never too late, not for us Marion."

"So you won't go and fight then? You'll come out of the army?" She looked at him, but his face had not moved. "No, I didn't think so. You've chosen your path, and it's a solitary one."

"But I want it to include you. When the war is over we can be together, how and where you want." Russell turned to face her and took one of her hands in his.

"Meanwhile I'm supposed to sit on the sidelines and wait; *and worry*, like every spouse and sweetheart with a soldier abroad."

"I wanted us to be engaged but your father thought that everything was too unsettled. You were deciding Alain's future. I was sorting out mine. He was right, wise and right, but we are only talking of timing: when we will be together, not if."

"And do you include Alain in these plans?"

"Of course I do. He is a part of you, an inseparable part of the package. I wouldn't want it to be any other way. Us, all together, a family. I told my parents about both of you. They can't wait to meet you."

"Oh you didn't? Oh Russell, I don't know. Perhaps it's too late for us, our moment has passed?"

"You don't mean that. I know you love me. You have just loved me." He reached out to pull her towards him, and she let him take her in his arms.

"All this waiting, I hate it. I want us to get on with our lives. The whole country is weighed down by this war. We could have escaped it, gone to America. You didn't have to join up." Marion sighed.

"Perhaps not when I did, no, but since President Wilson decided to enter the fray, the pressure at home on the boys is as great as here. I couldn't have escaped the call for long. And I don't believe you would have wanted me to dodge my duty."

"Perhaps, perhaps not. I can't help but think the ones who avoid the fight are the sensible ones. They're not cowards in my eyes."

"I only ever want you to be proud of me, but for that I must respect myself too."

Marion understood his actions more than she would like to admit. Without Alain she would have accepted a posting abroad to nurse without giving his objections a second thought. She believed him when he talked of their future together and when she was totally honest with herself she recognised that part of her resentment for the choice he made was that she was jealous of the adventure he was now on. *Don't be hard on him. You'd be the same.*

"You will come back, won't you?"

"Now, that I can't guarantee, honey," Russell said, "I can't promise that I will come back alive, but it is more likely for me than for most in uniform."

Russell explained his role to her, in as much as he understood it himself, and she was relieved to hear that he would be sorting out in-fighting between the allies and not engaging with the real enemy at all. *Be safe, please be safe.*

"But I do want to be tested," he added.

"Tested? What do you mean?"

"I need to know that I am good enough."

"Good enough? At what?"

"Strong enough; strong enough to stand up and be counted. To meet the demands of a situation and not be found lacking."

"Sounds like a load of schoolboy tosh to me. Of course you are. You stepped into things in Belgium; they relied on you very quickly."

"To push paper around, yes, but you took more risks in

Brussels than I have and probably ever will. You have proved these things to yourself already; I still have them to learn."

"Don't you think taking Alain and me on is test enough for anyone's stamina?"

"Yes, you have a point."

"I was joking," Marion said as she playfully made to punch him. He grabbed her fist and uncurled and kissed each of her fingers.

"I hope you learn quickly and come back safe," she said as they kissed and while their kisses continued, conversation stopped.

When they did talk again she was startled by him raising Doctor Ambrose.

"Doctor Ambrose?" Marion repeated.

"Yes, he is all you write about in your letters, and I saw your face today, at the station, when you saw him and Evelyn together. You hadn't told me they were an item." Russell paused and looked intently at Marion, and then challenged her, "Because you didn't know did you? Why was seeing them together so awkward for you? What is he to you?"

"Nothing, he's nothing. Well, he's a colleague, purely professional."

"That isn't what your face told me. You looked quite put out. Has Evelyn stolen him from you?"

"No, no, but I had no idea they knew each other. I just feel, I felt a bit embarrassed, what with me working with him. I don't know what I might have let slip about her. I'd hate to think they have been talking and laughing about me. That's all. Now," Marion was keen to change the subject, "what did you tell your parents about me, and Alain, and what did they say?"

Russell described his time at home with his parents and their reactions to all he had been involved in since the start of the war. They had been relieved to have him home for a time and were proud of him in uniform.

"They always find it hard to describe to people what I do, but a picture of me in my regimental blues speaks for itself. My father said the same as yours about an early marriage, but my mother said you sounded perfect and I was to bring you home as soon as I possibly could. And by the way," Russell took her face in his hands and kissed her on the end of her nose, "Ambrose is a fool if he thinks Evelyn is a better choice than you."

"You were taken in by her charms, don't forget."

"He will tire of her. So watch out for when this happens, he'll be after you: that you can count on."

"And can I count on you?" Marion asked.

"You can count on me one hundred per cent," Russell said.

"If you come back alive."

Russell rolled off the bed and rummaged in his trouser pocket.

"This is my parents' address." Russell handed her a piece of paper. He did not get back into bed but started to arrange his uniform to get dressed. "They already have your details and a copy of my will."

"I thought you said you would be safe ..."

Russell interrupted her. "Just in case it should be needed. It's standard army procedure. They will keep all my pay packets, but I will write to them and tell them to expect to hear from you. You must ask them for anything that you need. Mother will be delighted that we have made up. She was disappointed for me. Mind you, she did say that if you were half the person I had described she knew you wouldn't let a misunderstanding come between us for long. True love will out, she said.

"This is the address to write to me," Russell continued as he handed over another piece of paper. "Your letters have been great to receive. I have kept them all, even the ones when you were shirty with me. But it might not be so easy from now on. I'm sure the post will get through but they may take a time and I won't be able to write much to you. The censors will be tough."

"We'll manage, I'm sure. I don't know how to say goodbye to someone who is going off to war." Marion looked close to tears and Russell stopped buttoning his shirt and held her.

"We will just have to remember these moments. Providence has played her part bringing us together today, and I will be forever thankful for this good fortune, and Hugh. From now on we can be sure of each other."

"When you come back, Russell," Marion said as she pulled away and climbed back onto the bed and pulled the sheets around her, "let's meet first in London. I couldn't bear the restraint again of meeting you at my home. It just didn't work last summer."

"It's a deal. When I'm on my way back I'll telegraph the date and I'll book a room for us here."

"That's a day I shall look forward to."

"More than one day, I would hope."

She could see his eyes were watering as he said his final goodbye and left her snuggled in the tangled sheets. She had started to cry the moment the door shut behind him. Whether her sobs were for Russell and her concerns for what faced him, or for herself for the fearful wait ahead, or even partially for the loss of Ambrose's attentions, she could not say before she fell into a light sleep.

Marion rolled herself out of the bed, used the bathroom, dressed, and readied herself to leave the hotel room. If she was quick she could catch the train that was due to depart in ten minutes. She did not want to be hanging around on the concourse in case she bumped into Ambrose and Evelyn. One fateful meeting was enough for the day, but unfortunately the Doctor was the first person Marion saw as she entered the station. He was selecting a bunch of flowers from the stall. Evelyn was nowhere in sight.

"Well, what a day of coincidences," Doctor Ambrose said. "Evelyn's in the Ladies room," he added, answering her unasked question. "Have you had a lovely day with your American?"

"What? Is she? Yes, yes, thank you. Have you had a good day with my sister?"

"Rather. I must say though, I had assumed you knew I was seeing your sister. I hope you're all right with it. I've told her what a fantastic nurse you are. Here she is. Shall we catch this train?"

Luckily for Marion, Evelyn did not look best pleased to see her, so when they reached the train Marion breezily announced that she would go into another carriage to give them privacy. Evelyn quickly silenced Doctor Ambrose's polite remonstration, but she did have the grace to mouth thank you to Marion, before she stepped onto the train with him in tow.

Evelyn was all smiles when they met again on the platform at Amersham. She took Marion's arm and led the way with Doctor Ambrose following behind.

"How lovely that we can all be friends now," Evelyn said, adopting what Marion recognised as one of her charm offensives. Evelyn patted Marion's arm. "But not a word at home: mum's the word. Horatio", Doctor Ambrose was by now walking level with them, beside Evelyn, "tells me you work on the same wards at the hospital: lucky you to see him every day. There will be nothing left in my wardrobe, the number of clothes I have donated to Queen Mary's charity. I must find another ruse for coming to Bachelor House."

"The patients have few visitors and love to be read to. Perhaps volunteering to read would provide the entrée you seek," Marion offered.

"Yes, well of course, but it is my place of work," Doctor Ambrose countered. "I wouldn't be able to pay you any attention there, my dear. Every day is busy, isn't it Marion."

"Yes, but there are breaks in the day which you could take

advantage of if Evelyn was there." Marion was unable to stop herself from adding, "You do little of any real value with your breaks now, I believe."

"We'll see, we'll see," Evelyn said, oblivious to the undercurrents. "Marion, it's a lovely evening, shall we walk back home together? Doctor Ambrose needs to leave us here."

"You dark horse, Marion. You kept very quiet about Mr. Clark," Evelyn said as the two sisters walked home from the station together. "When did he come back on the scene? You threw me off that scent with your talk of someone you had your eye on at the hospital. He looked very dashing in his uniform. Lucky you."

Evelyn offered no pauses, and Marion no answers, but her responses were not required, or missed. Evelyn continued to talk as if Marion had replied and indeed had asked questions in return.

"I could have said something about Horatio sooner, but I didn't realise you worked so closely together. He's a funny old boot. He assumed you knew all about us, sisters sharing secrets and all that comic book myth. He was quite put out that you didn't, I don't quite know why. But then your relationship is purely professional, it's not for you to know his business, and I intend to keep it that way, despite today's revelations." Evelyn paused to manoeuvre herself through a gate that Marion held open for her, but then immediately continued.

"You must say nothing to Mama. Nor to Papa in one of your cosy chats; she can wheedle anything out of him. Did Papa know of Russell's return? You covered your tracks well on that one. You just need to watch that your glow doesn't give you away. Doctor Ambrose wanted to know all about him. Interested in his uniform, I expect. To know an American officer is quite the thing at the moment; I think he was impressed and it was good for him to realise he is not the only cosmopolitan."

It was only when Evelyn stumbled and stopped to balance herself and catch her breath that Marion had the opportunity to speak.

"I wasn't expecting him."

"Who?"

"Russell. I was meeting Hugh Gibson, which we did, at the hotel. Russell was a surprise to me."

"One that obviously delighted you. You almost knocked him over. I was quite embarrassed by the show, and Horatio quite put out. I told him of your impulsiveness, but he said he had only seen you nicely considered at work. I soon put him right about you. So you sweethearts have made up then?"

Yes they had made up, and made love, and made promises to wait for each other, but Marion wanted time to catch up with all the events and to let her feelings settle before any public declarations were made. And she was not about to confide in Evelyn. *What did she mean: she had put Doctor Ambrose right about her?*

"We are good friends, and we understand each other better now," Marion replied.

"Have you forgiven him for leaving you for the army?"

"It is unchristian to send someone off to war, holding grudges. He is forgiven."

"Mama will be pleased. At least I think she will, although she rather has her sights set on you and James Baxter."

"Mama must know nothing."

"Well really, you are impossible."

"I promise not to say anything about Doctor Ambrose, and you must do the same."

"Our situations are entirely different."

"How are they different? We both want confidences to be kept."

"Yes, but I still want Mother to find a good match for me."

"And she wouldn't consider Doctor Ambrose a good match?"

"Exactly, she might well do."

"And you don't?"

"Well, for now, yes, as a flirtation. There are so few handsome and whole men around. But he is rather too worthy for me and apparently would want to continue to work even if we weren't at war. I prefer gentlemen who make recreation their pastime. He's not much fun for the long haul, I'd say."

"But Doctor Ambrose is a wonderful man. It is wrong for you to play with his feelings, Evelyn," Marion said with some irritation.

"He speaks very highly of you too. Perhaps it is the two of you who should be together. No, that is a ridiculous thought." Evelyn laughed. "He had heard all about Alain. Your story is known at the hospital. Mother would be mortified if she knew."

"Mother isn't going to know anything is she?" Marion demanded.

"No, no, have it your way. My lips are sealed."

With the agreement made, and both too tired to spar, the sisters walked the rest of the way home in silence and Marion welcomed being left with her thoughts.

France, June 1917

Five days after landing in Britain Russell once again found himself sailing into a foreign port facing the prospect of another formal reception. This time, rather than peering down from the towering side of a transatlantic liner, he was looking from the more modest height of a swift and elegant cross-Channel steamer, and it was French, not British, officials who were lined up on the quay at Boulogne. He could hear the band playing the American national anthem, and with crowds of civilians cheering and waving flags Russell found the atmosphere much more uplifting than his arrival at Liverpool. The exhilarating feeling from the quayside was contagious and he and his fellow junior officers were soon returning the hurrahs to the crowd. *If only Marion could see this welcome.* He felt heroic before even stepping onto French soil.

Russell watched General Pershing accompanied by his senior officers walk down the gangplank. The cheering erupted once again and Pershing raised his hand to the crowd. Any doubts Russell harboured about leaving his studies to join the army were dispelled in that moment. It had been impossible for Marion to understand his desire to join the fight, but he knew if she was standing beside him now, absorbing the scene, she would. He tried to commit each sight and sound to memory to write to her all about it later, his parents too. He was proud to be there and felt noble in his uniform.

Soon after leaving Dover, Russell and the American military staff onboard ship had been summoned before General

Pershing. Even though they met in the largest room, which could be shut off from the rest of the passengers and crew, space was in short supply. Russell was getting used to the army ways and knew there would be no jostling for seats; the men instinctively positioned themselves in the room in order of seniority. That left Russell, Lester Greenley, and two other lieutenants without chairs having to stand against the back wall.

After a brief wait the three members of Pershing's personal staff, followed by the man himself, entered from the single door at the rear of the room, next to Russell and his colleagues. Every man stood to attention. Fortunately, the general expressed no irritation when he had to twist his frame to squeeze through; in fact he nodded to Russell as he nudged past. Pershing exuded a natural and absolute authority buttressed by an upright and broad-shouldered physique so that now, finding himself so close to the man, Russell was surprised to find that he was the taller of the two, by some inches.

The general appraised his audience from the front of the room.

"Sit down, gentlemen." There was a brief pause while those with seats resumed them.

"I wanted to take this opportunity to have a word with you before we land in France. We are an hour or so away from a momentous time in our nation's history. You are the vanguard of the first American army to set foot in Europe. A lot is expected of us, and our performance on this mission will determine the world's view of our country in years to come. I will not allow that view to be anything but outstanding. Whatever it takes."

The words were efficient and no nonsense. Russell approved; it matched the can-do attitude he loved in the American character.

"One thing I want to make clear," Pershing continued, "when I said American army, I meant American army. Our soldiers are going to stay under my control. There is to be no agreement by any officer to hand over any unit, however small, to our allies' command without my express agreement. Do I make myself clear?"

"Yes, sir," was the instant reply across the room.

"Good. Now understand that does not mean you have any right to be less than correct and respectful to our French and British allies. They have suffered grievously. We must learn everything we can from them, and use their knowledge in preparing our own troops. Training them is vital. I aim to bring a million soldiers over here and I don't intend to waste a single one of them."

A million? Russell was amazed at the number, and he obviously was not alone; judging by the many intakes of breath it seemed that only a few of those present were previously aware of the scale of Pershing's ambitions.

"This will be major undertaking. We will be building our own logistical supply lines from new ports. Some of you have already come across the first of the railway and shipping engineers with us."

Russell and his colleagues had of course been aware of the handful of specialist civilians travelling with them, but had assumed they would be coordinating transport on existing French and British systems, not pioneering a separate American arrangement. The grand design Pershing was laying out dwarfed any previous suppositions.

"So there is much groundwork to be done, and I want to make it clear that anyone found wanting will not last long. I will be demanding one hundred and ten per cent from each and every one of you. First impressions matter, and I want our allies to be impressed. I expect you to do your country proud."

"We will fight a new way, and we will win," he concluded before handing over to one of his captains to brief them all on the disembarkation logistics, which was to include an inspection of uniforms by Captain Holt.

Russell inwardly groaned at the thought of the inspection. Uniforms were a bugbear of Pershing's who was a strict disciplinarian for appearances. Anyone with a loose jacket would be publicly rebuked; he considered a correct turnout essential. Russell and the junior officers moved further into the corner of the room to allow their seniors to exit first. Lester Greenley moved close to Russell to whisper.

"Nothing from Dr. Dose today? Maybe the general thinks the language gap will be *protection* enough? Moi thinks non."

"Your French has come on, Lester. All of two words now." Russell whispered back.

Lester had been referring to the medical officer on the staff. Dr. Young was an expert on venereal disease and soon after sailing from New York he had given several graphic lectures on the perils of this condition. Pershing had made attendance compulsory for all ranks and the zealous gravity with which he treated this issue was the one subject of preparation for the war that Russell and his colleagues could not take seriously.

"Is it true what they say about the French dames, Russell?" Eugene asked.

Eugene Arno was a gangling bespectacled signals officer who was forever fizzing with excitement at his overseas adventure and looking to Russell for answers to his insatiable curiosity about all things European.

"Well, they're certainly very pretty, Eugene, but I can't say I've had the pleasure of walking out with any of them," Russell replied, as the four junior officers filed out of the room and made their way to the open deck.

"Hey Russ, what the hell kind of expert are you," the fourth member of their group said with a wide grin, "if you can't tell us the most important facts 'bout where we goin'? I don't want you taking us to see some damn fancy churches in France now.

You're the liaison man after all, so I reckon you've got to do some of that liaising for us big strong American soldiers and all those poor little French ladies left behind; leastways before we find ourselves sitting alongside their boyfriends in five feet of mud."

Walter Sheldon was a Southerner, as tall as Russell but much more muscular. He was an aide to the colonel of engineers but liked to portray himself to the others as something of a hick mechanic. From the few times Russell had found himself alone with him, and the conversation turned more serious, Russell had concluded that Walter was one of the smartest people he had ever met.

"I would have thought a redneck like you would feel quite at home up to your armpits in mud, Walt?" Lester threw in.

Walter opened his mouth to respond when Eugene cut him short by hissing a warning that the inspection officer was working his way down the men on the railings, and would be upon them shortly. The four men pulled their uniforms straight and began a fastidious audit of one another's appearance.

Russell had been exhilarated by their reception in Boulogne but he was completely overwhelmed by the reaction of the citizens of Paris who were on the streets to greet the American cavalcade. The emotion of the crowds bordered on the hysterical, with some people weeping openly. Flowers were thrown their way, and a solid mass of people pressed in on their convoy as it crawled from the railway station to the hotel reserved for General Pershing and his staff. Russell heard cries of *Vive l'Amerique* all along the route and handshakes were offered and kisses blown by people running alongside their vehicles. *I want Marion to see this.*

They had set off in strict order of seniority, which placed Russell and the other three lieutenants in an old taxi at the back of the motorcade, sharing their transport with a French officer designated to accompany them.

"This is my kind of war, buddy." Walter had to shout to make his voice heard over the noise. His beaming smile, which never left his face during the half hour journey, was infectious and Russell, too, caught himself grinning like a simpleton while the words and music of *See the Conquering Hero* went round and round in his head. He felt on top of the world.

It was after three weeks of frenetic activity that the four junior officers found an opportunity to all meet together again. Pershing had established his staff headquarters in two adjoining five storey town houses overlooking Les Invalides. Cramped compared to their baroque neighbours, the rooms they used as offices were bursting at the seams and desks had to be shared. Whenever Russell left a work area he had thought his for the day, no matter how dingy a corner, he would usually return to find it commandeered by a more senior officer. He surprised himself by how calmly he accepted these frequent interruptions, realising he had fallen into military ways where the courtesies of civilian life could be swept aside by a superior rank. Despite the often petty inconveniences this caused, he quite liked the simple efficiency of a command structure: it offered an appealing contrast to the more opaque academic world he had left behind. He had selected a local café for their get-together which started with much backslapping.

Russell described to his friends how he had spent most of his time in Paris arranging innumerable conferences for his superiors with the French army officers. Between them they were to orchestrate the training for the American troops, the first of whom had just arrived in France. Lester Greenley told them he had been cloistered with the intelligence section being briefed by the British. Eugene Arno had been away to the front line with the British, studying how miles of communication wiring was being laid. Walter Sheldon had also been absent all this time, and as they sat at a corner table in a tired-looking café he explained what he had been doing.

"I've been just about all over this damn country, fellas. Me and Major Johnson have done France. You name a port and I've seen it. Never stopped for three weeks and made more notes than I did in all my years at school."

"More luck than me, Walt," said Lester. "Wish I'd been touristing instead of being lectured to by a load of Brits. Mind you, I can't understand half of what they say. Reckon you've got it easy Russ. At least with the French you can just wave your arms about to make yourself understood."

"Ah, you've noticed the right way to speak French, have you?" Russell laughed and then asked Walt: "Seriously, what's it like outside Paris?"

"You've gotta understand," Walter explained, "basically I moved from one depot to another finding big problems with supplies. The Brits want to have everything coming through their ports but they're choking with their own supply fleets and what's left of the main railroads are being used by the French. The major reckons we're gonna have to build it all ourselves: wharves, dockyards, freight cars, you name it. And, can you believe it, the French military are communicating by mail most of the time: a load of their army offices haven't even got access to a damn phone."

"Any good news?" Lester asked.

Walter laughed. "Thinking in particular of you, Lester, there are lots and lots of ladyfolk about, that I did notice, and old men and children. Now, what have you found?"

"Well," Lester replied, "the French Army is falling apart, mutinies everywhere. They hate the British almost as much as the Germans, and they want us to make up for all the soldiers they've wasted already. They can't wait to send us all to join the dead, seems to me. Nothing you can't guess."

Walter turned to Eugene. "Hey, what about you, Eugene?

Haven't seen you in a while, too. You've been mighty quiet for a change. How're the Brits doing in all that mud?"

It was true, Russell thought, he had said little. Eugene removed his spectacles and began cleaning them vigorously with a small cloth, a recognisable sign to Russell and his friends that he was uncomfortable. They waited patiently until, with his glasses back in place, Eugene started to speak.

"We've got a lot to learn. And I mean, lots and lots. They're living like rats up in the front line. But they have to. If anyone sticks their head out of a hole they get it blown off. You guys have no idea how tough it is. It stinks and it's foul and we've all been living in dreamland!" Eugene took off his glasses and rubbed them again. "All those magazine pictures of the front line? That's horseshit compared to what it's really like. Sure, they show trenches and mud but that doesn't tell you the half of it. It's completely nuts out there, I tell you!"

The atmosphere at the table sobered. This was not the buoyant Eugene Arno Russell had come to know.

"What is the other half, Eugene?" Russell asked softly, though he guessed he might have a better idea than the other two.

"What?" Eugene asked. He had been staring at his glasses in his hand. He looked at Russell who repeated his question.

"The other half, Eugene? You said no one's seeing the full picture, only one half of it. Do you want to tell us what the other half is like?"

Eugene shuddered and Russell could almost feel the chill that spread over his friend even though the night was warm.

"The Brits know what they're doing y'know. They're not the useless assholes some of our guys seem to think. Sure, they're a bit stiff-necked and they have a lot more stupid rules than our army's going to put up with; but this idea that they're sitting there just because they don't want to move ain't right."

Lester looked like he was going to say something but Russell lifted his hand to stop him and Eugene continued.

"It's pretty much one big stalemate. Every so often one side or other moves the front line a bit, but they never seem to get very far before it's back to business as usual. And all the time they're losing men. Hell, they even lose men when they're not moving anywhere. There are always shells coming over. Might be quiet for a bit then they get bombed to bits like there's an attack coming any minute. Every night there's patrols going out. Sometimes no one comes back at all. Other nights there might be Germans coming over to kill you. Then comes daytime, but you still can't relax for a minute, even if nothing's coming down on top of you from enemy guns. There are snipers everywhere. They get the slightest chance and you're gone. One guy got the top of his head blown off not far from where I stood."

The waitress arrived at the table ready to renew their order but no one paid her any attention and she withdrew.

"New guy; seems it's usually the new guys," Eugene continued. "His body just lay there waiting for someone to take it away. People were just stepping over it like it was a piece of junk on the floor. Even the guys in his outfit were just getting on with their day like nothing had happened a few minutes ago. Mind you, bodies and bits of bodies are everywhere."

"Goddammit, Eugene that's terrible. How did you …?"

"I went past fresh graveyards the size of half a dozen football pitches." Eugene ignored Lester's question and carried on. "All this talk from our generals about moving fast and shooting straight and how we're going to show everyone how to fight, it's all a crock of bull I reckon. We're all just the new guys … A million new guys …"

Eugene tailed off and shuddered again. Russell pushed his own brandy across the table to Eugene who downed the drink in one go and then gasped as the fiery liquor hit his throat.

Russell was not surprised by what Eugene had said, but Walter and Lester looked taken aback by their friend's descriptions.

"Black Jack won't let us fill in on their lines," Russell said.

"This war will be over by the time we've gotten our men ready anyway," Walter added.

"Better find us some ladies quick, guys." But for once Lester's attempt to inject some humour failed and the party broke up soon after.

Russell was convinced that Pershing would protect his troops from trench warfare. He knew his plan was for a significant offensive to push back and break through the German line, but he was not going to contemplate this until all his men were over and well schooled and trained, and that would take months, or even a year: 1919 had even been mooted for their push, they had so much preparation to do. Russell, back at his digs, decided to finish his letter to Marion. There was no place in correspondence to discuss such matters and he was relieved that he did not have to defend the American military strategy to her. The Europeans had expected torrents of Americans to pour into the trenches and push back the Germans, but Pershing had political as well as military objectives in mind, and Russell knew Marion would dismiss such posturing out of hand.

Despite the sobering tales from Eugene, Russell admitted to himself a degree of disappointment with his war, so far. He felt ready for the test of a fighting man but yet again found himself pushing paper, translating words and meaning from and for the French and administrating logistics. It was easy for him to reassure Marion he was safe: he felt too safe.

Bachelor House, October 1917

Marion folded Russell's letter and put it in her pocket, picked up her cup of tea, and took in the view over the far hills. Russell's letter, like many of the others she had received since his departure, contained several descriptions of his surroundings, and very little else. She was gaining the impression that his adventure was not turning out quite as he had hoped, and once again it was his boredom threshold that was being tested more than his courage. His letters were short and conveyed very little of his actual circumstances, but he had warned her to expect this. She knew more from the daily press, who, whilst impressed by the war machine that the Americans had set in motion, were making clear the country's frustration that no American soldiers were joining the ranks of their own fighting soldiers. Pictures of the American cavalry, riding over the hill to push the enemy back, remained in the derisory cartoons in *Punch* magazine, to which her father subscribed.

The gardens of Bachelor House were all now dug over for vegetables, a venture mirrored across the country and at her own home too. Only that morning Evelyn and her mother were discussing what might be added to pumpkins to improve their flavour when served, and what of the surfeit they might take into the village. Marion looked up as Doctor Ambrose's shadow blocked the last rays of the sun.

"May I?" he asked pointing to the space on the bench beside her.

"Of course," Marion replied. "It's a free country."

"Not as free as we had hoped for," he said as he sat down. "The reconciliation talks have broken down, the German authorities are asking for too much consideration. It will be another winter in the trenches, I fear."

"For some," Marion said.

"Is that a dig at me?" Doctor Ambrose turned to face her.

"No, of course not. I was thinking of the patients here. Not all of them will return to fight, and thank goodness for that."

"Has Evelyn told you our news?"

"News? No. We exchange very little. Are you to be wed?"

"No, entirely the opposite. Our dalliance is over."

"Over? When? I saw her here only yesterday. I presumed to see you."

"No, she threw me over some weeks ago, distracted by the new intake of officers. She found one with a title and land. Poor chap, it would have been safer for him to stay in France. She is something of a predator, your sister."

"I could have warned you, if I had known what was 'going on'." *Don't bite, Marion.*

"And I thought you knew, being sisters and all that."

"Let's not go over that again. It is truly none of my business." Marion smiled to soften her words.

Relations in the months since Marion's discovery at Marylebone Station had been slightly strained between them and there had been none of their relaxed conversations at break times. It was unusual for him to join her like this. *Time to move on.*

The Monday morning after their paths had crossed in London, he asked if they might clear the air before they arrived on the wards. The knowledge that she had flirted with him when he was already courting Evelyn humiliated her. Awkward and embarrassed, she would rather have avoided him entirely but knew they needed to be cordial and it was clear he wanted to talk. He explained he thought she knew he was seeing her sister, and apologised for not telling her himself, but also confessed to enjoying the sport of sisterly competitiveness for his attentions, as he saw it.

Despite her anger and further humiliation from his casual suppositions, and with herself for having found him attractive, she had restrained herself and, for once, had not picked a fight. Her professionalism came to the fore and she wished him every happiness with Evelyn, and told him nothing more needed to be said. But he had sought an explanation from her too, as to why she had kept her relationship with the American lieutenant secret from him. At this she had told him it was best they kept their personal lives private and their relations professional, and this was how it had been for months, until today.

"How is Lieutenant Clark? Well, I hope?"

Marion smiled at his question, and the opportunity of talking about Russell.

"Yes, he is. I had a letter from him yesterday. He is still in Paris."

"A distance from the fighting then. I've heard the American soldiers are raw recruits, not trained for war at all."

"If you mean they are volunteers, who are not yet ready, you may be right. But Russell said General Pershing wasn't going to engage them until they can make a big push and drive the Germans back." *That's a turn-up.* Marion was not used to defending the Americans.

"We can only hope the Germans comply with their plan and don't push through the line while the Americans build their roads, docks and railways. We may not be able to hold them back until the Americans deign themselves to be ready."

"Russell went out there to fight and I am sure he feels as thwarted by the delays, as we do. But then," Marion endeavoured to take the fight out of her words, "I can't imagine what it is like to manage a war. Organising the Sunday school picnic was a big enough feat, this harvest time. What it must be like to supply and feed an army, in a foreign land, where would you start?"

"Moving men and machines, I suppose."

"All the way across the Atlantic. No wonder they have to build docks and roads."

"We have managed to supply our men for three years. I can't believe it has gone on so long, with no end in sight. Anyway, this is what I wanted to tell you, I have put myself forward to the medical board. I am volunteering for active service again."

"To go and fight?"

"In the medical corps."

"You no longer value the work you do here?"

"It's not as much fun any more," Dr. Ambrose winked at her. "No seriously, I think I can save more lives if I am nearer the battlefields. If they take me in this time. I will miss this place, and working with you. You are an excellent nurse, and I'd like to think a good friend, despite our recent reserve."

"While you were courting my sister, you mean."

"Um, yes. All a bit crass of me, I fear. And forgive me for saying but she isn't a patch on you. She remains rather proud on her pedestal, and adoring isn't a particular strength of mine. Give me your spirit any day."

"So, as a spurned lover, you are running off to war, and it seems you want to take my sympathies with you."

"I would like to think of us as friends."

"Of course we are." *But don't worry, Russell, only friends.* "When will you know if you are accepted?"

"My board is in London in two weeks. I wondered if you might like to accompany me. We could go to the theatre. Make a day of it. The bombers only come over at night, we would be back safe by then."

"And how would I explain that to my sister?"

"Oh, um, yes I see, but nothing need be said. Believe me I am no longer of any interest to her. What I do is of no matter to her. Would you tell her?"

"And would taking her sister to London provide the snub you want to show her you are not affected by her withdrawal. I think I see what's behind your invitation and my answer is no."

"You have us wrong Marion. Your sister and I enjoyed getting to know each other but we both knew we were not suited, not for anything serious. I lost count the number of times she said that I should be courting you. She thinks we would be well suited, that we could build a good and worthwhile life together."

You warned me, Russell.

"Evelyn does have a way of making the worthwhile sound very dull."

"I think she might have a point. We work very well together and …"

"And", Marion interrupted, "you are heading off to war, or at least trying to. Say nothing more."

He nodded and the subject was closed.

While Marion's life was established in a rhythm that on the surface suited her, her work, Alain, and seemingly her family, her inner world was often in a state of turmoil, and Doctor Ambrose's intention to be closer to the action sparked the questions that were never far from Marion's own mind: could she be doing more? She knew she was more capable than many of her colleagues, and as Russell would have put it, had already been tested and come up trumps, so surely she could be living more dangerously than nursing in a manorial house in middle England. A large part of her wanted challenge and excitement, just as a major part of her baulked at the feeling that life was on hold until the war ended, and like a railway engine in a siding she was building up quite a head of steam as her impatience with the world and its ways grew. Why were the Americans not finishing off the Germans?

Her only relief from all this head chatter was when she was with Alain; then all the conflicting voices within her were silenced and she felt anchored. No one else understood him like she did: the connection between them was so intimate and their responses to each other so finely honed as to be telepathic. They had a bond that she would never break, and when with him, she knew she could never leave him to work abroad. The rush of emotion that swept over her as she greeted him each morning, or watched him sleeping, or as they embraced on her return from work was overwhelming and triggered a complex mix of intense feelings, to which she had become quite addicted. They were heady moments when she felt her response to his neediness and dependency, when his innocence lit up his face and called forth every ounce of protectiveness within her being. And she was always rewarded. He was never moody or withdrawn; he could be quiet, but this was normally a forewarning of a childhood illness, and thankfully these had all been short-lived. He also had the uncanny ability to sense and even anticipate her moods: if she was down, he would give her his favourite teddy bear to cuddle; if she was bouncy and full of fun, he would find his drum and march and bang and laugh with her. He absorbed her totally and when he ran towards her with his arms out wide, and they hugged, she felt her world was complete.

On the anniversary of Edith's death they had both wrapped up warm and taken a walk. Marion's emotions about Edith, which were never far from the surface, bubbled through and having seen her brush some tears away Alain had hugged her leg and held her tight.

"The lady sends her love," Alain said when he pulled away.
"What? Who? Which lady?"

"That lady over there." Alain pointed to a tree silhouetted by a stream of autumn sunlight."
Edith?
"She says she is proud of you, and you should be proud too. What does proud mean?"
"Um, well it can mean puffed up or pleased."
"She means pleased."
"Where is she, Alain? I can't see her or hear her."
"She's gone now. Come on, let's run." And he had run off kicking up a shower of leaves as he went.
Thank you, Edith.

Rather than always missing Russell she quite often found herself enjoying the luxury of being alone with Alain. She could give him her undivided attention without fear of causing a slight or offence or a jealous reaction, and sometimes the thought niggled her as to how two would become three with harmony maintained. Her mother had much to say on the subject of her parenting, not that she would ever consent to such a role for Marion with Alain, and she had never given up hope that he would be adopted. She regularly threw criticisms at Marion for "indulging" and "spoiling" and "mollycoddling", and not "disciplining" "that boy" enough, which Marion routinely ignored. Her father was happy to be called Grandpa, but her mother's resistance was unbreachable and she insisted, if he had call to address her at all, on Mrs. Drake in company, and ma'am within the family. Alain seemed unbothered, but Marion overheard him putting his toys to bed one night and he was telling his teddy to cuddle a wooden doll: "This is Grandmama and she needs lots of hugs." It had made Marion cry.

"I'm in. I have been accepted."
"Oh," Marion said.
Doctor Ambrose had been waiting for her as she arrived at

work. His beaming smile showed her how delighted he was with his news and she fancied she understood what it meant for a man to have a pumped-up chest. He seemed bigger and stronger as he stood in front of her, and yet in his enthusiasm she saw more vulnerability in him than she had ever before.

"I'm pleased for you."

"Thank you for saying so, but you don't look pleased."

"No, well, you know what I think about war, but I know you want this. When will you leave?"

"End of the week. There is some training they want me to have for a month or so and then I will hear where I am being sent. They need nurses too. Perhaps we could be stationed somewhere together. Malta is my hot favourite. What do you think?"

That tug-of-war returned. Marion was drawn to the idea of working abroad, while knowing she would not leave Alain. Perhaps Alain, in his funny way, had known what was ahead in her day. He had given her one of his favourite marbles that morning and told her to keep it in her pocket. When she had asked why, he said when she held the marble she was holding his hand. She put her hand in her pocket and enclosed the marble in her palm.

"I can't leave Alain. Much as I would like to sail to Malta he is my first responsibility," Marion replied.

"But everyone has to make sacrifices at times like this. Perhaps he is yours? Do come. I am sure I could secure the same assignment for us. We make such a good team."

"Believe me, the impulsive me would love to, but I know the right decision is to stay here with him. I do good work here and it is important. These men matter."

"But it's not life-saving."

"Maybe not. I'm not stopping soldiers from dying, but I do help those who are injured and hideously scarred to want to live."

"Seeing you is a good reason for anyone to want to live."

"Just because you are leaving at the end of the week doesn't mean you need to start a charm offensive."

"Indeed not," matron said as she approached them. "Congratulations are in order, I understand Doctor Ambrose, but we have much to do to prepare for your departure. Shall we proceed?"

Doctor Ambrose was marched off and marshalled by matron for most of the week, but a note from him in her locker had secured dinner with her at The Crown hotel in Amersham on his last evening. She had not told Evelyn.

The meal was quite ordinary, made pleasant in large part by the freshness of the vegetables, all locally grown. Their conversation had differed in no great part from one of their more recent shared breaks, now their former easy relations had been re-established. But Marion was slightly disconcerted with this. He had made such an occasion of them dining together that she had anticipated an onslaught of flirtation from him but nothing had been forthcoming, *you were wrong, Russell*, until dessert.

"I have saved the best until last," he said as he ordered a slice of apple pie for each of them.

"I didn't think you had a sweet tooth?" Marion commented.

"I didn't mean the best of the meal. I meant the best of my week, my last week here, for a while, at least: an evening with you. Only sorry there couldn't be more."

"Will you come back to see us before you are posted?"

"That depends."

"On what?"

"On whether you mean come back to see 'you' before I am posted, or 'us' at the hospital, and before you dodge me, Marion, you know what it is I mean. I know you have your American friend, but who knows where he will land up at the end of the war, may he reach that far. I just want to hear if there could be a chance for me, Marion? Could it be that you could hold me in your affections?"

"I already hold you in my affections. You are very dear to me and I shall want to hear that you are safe and untroubled."

"I will write, I promise I will write."

"But", Marion held his gaze, "I have to tell you, I am promised to Russell."

"Mr. Clark?"

"Lieutenant Clark, yes."

"Yes, yes, I see, but let me say this. We none of us know what is ahead with this bloody war, nor how we will fare. Promise me this, if you will: if Mr. Clark doesn't return," Marion flinched at the thought, "do give me a chance. Can you hold this promise? Will you?"

It was simple for Marion to say yes and he reached across the table, took her hand and kissed it by way of acknowledgement.

When they left the restaurant, Dr. Ambrose helped her on with her coat, but her sleeve was turned the wrong way. In the jostling to correct it, there was a clatter and they both watched as a glass marble, it was Alain's, fell from her pocket, hit the wooden floor and rolled away, disappearing underneath a heavy wooden settle.

"What was that?" Dr. Ambrose asked.

"A marble, one of Alain's marbles," Marion replied thoughtfully.

"Let me fetch it for you." Dr. Ambrose started to move towards the settle, but Marion put out her arm to stop him. He looked at her curiously.

"No, you can leave it. No need to have you crawling around looking for a marble. He has several, and anyway, this one's job is done."

"Job done? What do you mean?"

"Oh, too much to explain but, you know the promise you just extracted from me?"

"Yes, of course I do. I will treasure it."

"I must tell you. If it should be that we were ever to have a future together, if Russell didn't …, well I just have to say, it would have to include Alain."

"Your ward, Alain? Of course it would. And what's more, he must have his marble back."

Dr. Ambrose walked to the settle, dropped to his knees and stretched his arm underneath. On his third extraction he handed the now dusty marble to Marion, who gave him her handkerchief to wipe his hands and which, after use, he pocketed.

Marion gave the marble back to Alain at breakfast and in answer to his unasked question she returned his look with a wide smile, and told him that all was and would be fine for them and that despite her mother's wishes, he was to call Mrs. Drake, Grandmama, from that day forward.

He promised he would.

1918

Little Missenden, April & July 1918

Marion had to admit she was in her element. She was now a firm favourite of matron's and enjoyed responsibility beyond which her years of experience should properly allow. The doctor who replaced Ambrose was dumpy, crusty, and largely deaf and he relied heavily on her during the ward rounds. He was no old duffer though and Marion marvelled at his incisive diagnoses and wise treatments, and felt proud whenever he deferred to her opinion. She was enjoying her morning break. An opportunity to breathe in the spring air, and reread the letter from Russell that had arrived the day before. And one from Dr. Ambrose that very morning.

Four years of warfare and, Marion reflected, her expectations of life had changed, irreversibly. She had been attracted to nursing because the running of wards was a woman's domain, but in many walks of life women now had a firm, if not sometimes upper, hand. Only that morning Nanny had been talking about two of her sisters who were learning joinery in High Wycombe: making furniture, a protected craft of men, and she said they were good. Evelyn and her mother were always talking down about girls working in factories or on the land, as if it was an affront to their own femininity, but Marion understood just how liberating employment was for women, particularly those who had been closeted and unpaid before the war.

Marion no longer assumed there would be an end to the war, or that their lives would return to how they were before.

It was easy to let the patterns of work, family, and shortages dictate her routine, punctuated only by news of battles fought and won or lost, neither outcome seeming to make an iota of difference: the wounded still passed through their wards. Place names in Belgium and France were as familiar to her as Buckinghamshire villages: the Somme, Bapaume, Messines, St Quintin, Arras, fought over so many times, each battle reported as part of a final push. She only really paid attention to the Western Front, battlefields further away remained too foreign for an association, and Russell and Doctor Ambrose remained her conduit to the fray in France. She sometimes wondered at all the efforts by the Americans, who had yet to enter the actual fight. What would happen to their reputations if the war ended without an American firing a shot? How would Russell deal with that frustration, thwarted in his hunt for manhood and meaning?

The whole notion of men squaring up to each other to face off against their differences seemed ridiculous to her and it would have been laughable if the implications were not so deadly serious. Bluff and bluster was all she could fathom featured behind the bullets and the bombs. She had been astounded to learn from her father the evening before, as he read out highlights from the newspaper, that one general had only just been appointed to co-ordinate all military efforts on the Western Front, and he was a Frenchman. Only just! Her father had humoured her astonished outburst until even her mother had joined in. No wonder so little progress had been made: each military force had been fighting their own war with no overall strategy to direct them. Mrs. Drake, who made it her business to chair most of the committees of which she was a member, fully appreciated the need for one clear leader. For the first time Marion understood the need for the liaison role that Russell held: the folly of men and their territorial necessities.

Marion picked over parts of Russell's news in his letter,

crumpled from being in her pocket. They had developed a language to help her understand more of what was going on, without Russell exposing anything military.

"Almost went to a bash. There had been a big party and we were invited, but Papa did not want us to play with the others."

Marion was aware of the frustration in the Press that Pershing had a separatist mindset and would not allow his troops to be absorbed under French or English command, while the English and French doubted that the green Americans would achieve anything on their own. Their own troops may be battle weary, but they had learned from each affray and, Marion frequently read in the papers, experience was everything in war.

"The older boys keep squabbling between themselves. Our girls are manning our phones, post too slow."

Marion had been amazed to read of the infrastructure the Americans were putting in place, which included running their own telephone lines across France. The French military still sent orders via the postal service in some quarters. She had tried to remain calm when she learned that American girls were filling some of the support jobs in France, happier when she pictured Russell in a totally male domain. The fact that Doctor Ambrose was surrounded by nurses and, no doubt, adoring ones, amused, rather than piqued her. He had been constant and regular in his letters to her and their friendship was firm. Expecting Horatio not to flirt was a futile endeavour. When he wrote of the lives he had saved, or lost, she chafed against her more comfortable surroundings and work, but she had made her choice and told herself to stop yearning for more excitement. Her work was fulfilling and Alain a constant delight. She reopened Horatio's letter.

"Tell me more about Alain. You paint such a pretty picture of the two of you together. I laughed at your description of him having a bath and the conversation he had about names for his toes. I quite *agree every big toe should be called Roger,"* Dr. Ambrose had written.

Alain, almost three, with curly blonde hair, puppy fat features, a ready smile or giggle, and piercing blue eyes, never stopped talking, or asking questions.

"Mummy, what holds the clouds in the sky?"

"Grandpa, what colour is water?"

"Nanny, where does the sun live?"

"Mummy, what is war?"

And he was also so calm. He could sit for hours, applying himself to a task or game that he had designed, or sometimes he would sit quietly and look as if he was listening, but to what Marion never deduced. A smile and hug was always ready for her and he could wash away any sadness she might have. Her father called him a ray of sunshine, and he was right, Alain beamed happiness and joy. He was learning choruses, at Sunday school, and although he muddled up the words and tunes he seemed to love singing.

"I am h-a-p-p-y

I am h-a-p-p-y

I know I am, I'm sure I am

Jesus wants me for a sunbeam

I am l-o-v-e-d."

She returned to Russell's letter. *"I hope this note reaches you and finds you all in good health and not suffering shortages too much. Has my mother's parcel arrived? She packaged it with care. Do write to her for more that you need."*

The package from America had indeed been very welcome, containing two tins of ham, a bag of sugar, tinned peaches, and flour. It did not stretch very far in such a large household, a fact that her mother pointed out, but it was appreciated nonetheless. Marion had written a long letter of thanks in reply: her first contact with her potential mother-in-law. She had taken time to describe something of their life, and reassure her that they were not in danger of starving, just missing treats. She had enclosed a picture of her and Alain together, taken in the Amersham studio, and had another ready to send to Russell when she wrote to him that evening. Alain had taken to signing his name too, an unintelligible scribble, but his kiss was always clear.

"Please give Alain a hug for me and save a big hug for you too. I dream of our future together, yours forever, R."

Marion had actually stopped dreaming of their future together; she was usually too tired to dream at all. Her days were packed with nursing, Alain, or chores at home. Relations with her mother had settled to the best they had ever been, and Marion's practical approach to household matters meant her opinion was often deferred to and many arrangements fell to her. She adopted the same stance with the help at home as she did with her colleagues at work and they seemed to respond well to this. Her mother's more officiously autocratic style jarred all the more with help these days.

Marion folded Russell's letter, and reread the end of Horatio's note, then checked the time, stood, straightened her uniform, and made her way to the reception hall of the house. The hospital was expecting a visit from an eminent surgeon that day and she and matron were the welcoming party. Dr. Gillies was keen to meet and assess some of their patients, to see if he might manage some facial reconstruction. Two of Marion's patients had to eat through straws, as they had holes in the side of their faces and no jaw action. One officer breathed through a hole in his cheek as he had lost his nose completely, taken off by a bullet. Each man seemed more ashamed of their looks than angry with their loss, and some had refused visits from their family and loved ones. *Perhaps, after this doctor's ministrations, that might change.* Marion hoped that it would.

His visit was long. He spent two hours with each patient, with Marion in tow, taking notes for him and labelling the sketches that he made. It was a lesson in cranial anatomy for her and she marvelled at what he hinted might be possible. He said more when he had finished with the patients and they were waiting in the staff room for matron.

"They are a poor show. I can't make things any worse for them; that's for sure. Thank you for your help today, most kind, and you know your patients well. None of them would have been as forthcoming without your encouragement and observations."

Marion beamed at his praise. "I'm delighted to be of service, and they do deserve the best we can give them. They will have no life as they are, they look monstrous."

"I can't give any guarantees, and they will always be scarred. I can't replace muscle and they will have livid scars, but I can rebuild jaw lines and noses and realign eyes and brows to some degree."

"I didn't realise such surgery was possible."

"Well, it's early days. Pioneering you could say." He looked to Marion to be in his fifties and she had anticipated he would be an expert in this field. "It is only since the war", he explained, "that we have had such subjects to practise on."

"Practise?"

"Rather. No method is tried and tested, and many approaches have failed." Marion was shocked to hear this. "I need to schedule the surgery with matron."

"She will be along in a moment, she knows you are waiting."

"I shall be here a while for these men," the doctor said as he started pacing. "They will each be under the knife several times. Beautiful countryside though: I shall be glad to escape the smoke of London, and the bombs." The doctor had stepped to the window and could take in the view of the gardens and rolling hills beyond. "My wife can't wait. She has been angling to leave London. I may never entice her back there."

"It is beautiful here," Marion agreed, "and the bombing

seems quite indiscriminate. London one week, Folkestone the next. Scarborough, Ramsgate, Broadstairs. It's so shocking. We are lucky even greater numbers haven't been killed."

"Lucky indeed. Ah, matron, just the person." Matron walked into the room and informed Marion she could take over now.

"I look forward to seeing the results of your work, doctor," Marion said as she took her leave. "I'll note down any questions the men have and keep them for you. It was a lot of information for them to absorb today. I'm sure they'll have more as they think about it." Marion shook his hand.

And over the next few days they did.

"Will I be able to open and shut my mouth again?"

"Will I have lips? If I do can I give you a kiss, nurse?"

"Will I be able to close my eye do you think?"

"Will he replace my teeth?"

Marion had no answers, but made a file note against each man's name, except for Joe, who asked nothing and made no comment. Unannounced, a photographer arrived the following week with a list of instructions sent by the surgeon.

He had described the angle of all the pictures he wanted taken and Marion spent the day holding and pointing his lamps to obliterate the shadows, or the men's heads to keep them still while talking to them to keep their spirits up; Joe seemed particularly self-conscious.

Joe was only twenty. Over the weeks Marion learnt he had volunteered from the upper sixth of his school at Uppingham along with most of his year. He had been an officer in the school's cadet force and was excited to join the show. A top bowler in the school cricket team, it was he who stood up to throw a grenade, above the parapet long enough for a sniper to find a target. The dumdum bullet entered just in front of his left ear, smashing his jawbone and taking out his top row of teeth before exiting out of the side of his face, leaving jagged holes. With the structure of his jaw gone his face had dropped completely on one side, which dragged his mouth down into a shape that channelled a constant stream of dribble down his chin. She had to pay close attention to understand his words when he moved his mouth to speak.

Marion imagined Joe had been a good-looking boy with his clear blue eyes and blonde hair that showed his youth. But the rest of him was haggard. He rarely spoke, but seemed more relaxed around Marion than any other. He hated having his picture taken, wanting no record of how he looked, and he had refused visits from any of his family. Marion had been chipping away at his resolve. She was excited on his behalf about the surgery, but he had expressed no emotion at all.

Marion sat with Joe after the photographer had finished, to help him settle. She held his hand, which he allowed for a while and then snatched it away. When she challenged him he said he found the whole day humiliating and felt patronised, even by her.

"You pat my hand like an aunt would. No girl will ever look at me again. This whole exercise is a waste of time. I wish they would just forget about me."

Marion knew better than to admonish him for his negative thoughts. She passed him a tissue to wipe his chin. It was impossible for her to step into his shoes and see the world through his eyes; it was not her place to chide when his thoughts were black. All she could do was encourage.

"I see you had some post today. Was it a letter from your mother? Perhaps you could tell her about the surgery? She would be delighted to hear about it. It is such a marvelous opportunity, and available to so few."

"No. She mustn't know. I don't want her to know, until …"

"Until what?"

He said nothing and turned his face away from her.

"Until we know that it has worked," Marion suggested. "Is

that what you were going to say? Until you have seen the results?" She picked up his hand again. "It is very kind of you not to get her hopes up, and is that what frightens you? Getting hopes up in case you are disappointed? I can understand that, you are being experimented on after all." Marion did not have to wait any time at all for his reaction.

"Experimented on? What do you mean?" Joe had turned back to face her.

"This is pioneer surgery. They figure they can't make anything worse so why not have a go and perfect some techniques along the way."

"I didn't realise. The doctor seemed so professional I thought he knew what he was doing. You mean it was all bluff: just like the army."

"I can't comment on the army, but there was no bluff about him. He was very frank about what he thought is possible. He can't deliver miracles but he can definitely make improvements. If you're brave enough to let him try, that is. He is talking to a dentist about teeth for you too."

"I am twenty. I don't want false teeth."

"How are you going to smile with no teeth?"

"How am I going to smile with no face?"

"We'll see about that shall we?"

Over the next few months Joe had three lots of surgery and today, St Swithin's Day, 15th July, was the big day when the last of his bandages were to be removed. Marion was excited and agitated at the same time. She was waiting for the doctor to arrive, and he was late.

She had found it hard to relax at breakfast with Alain and he had picked up on her tension.

"Mummy frightened?" Alain asked.

"No, not frightened, Alain. Mummy is thinking about one of her patients who will receive some important news today, and I want it to be good news for him. I am just a bit anxious for him."

"I have a picture for him."

"For my patient, for Joe?"

"Yes. I'll fetch it."

"That is very sweet of you to give him one of your pictures." Alain was an avid drawer of pictures. His enthusiasm outweighed his skill by a considerable amount, but each representation always carried a story with it. She was interested to see which one he would bring. She did not have to wait long and was delighted with his choice.

She was now holding it rolled up in her hand like a talisman. She gave up on the doctor and decided to go and wait with Joe.

"The doctor is late, sorry Joe, but I have something for you while we wait."

"As long as it's not a mirror." His voice was muffled by his bandages.

"It's a present from Alain, especially for you."

"Your son?"

"My ward."

"What is it?"

"Have a look," Marion said as she handed the roll of paper to him.

Joe unfurled the paper. The drawing was of a very large sun with a big smiling mouth on it.

"Very optimistic of him, do thank him. Where is the doctor?"

"Late, but on his way I am sure. Alain isn't an optimist. I am sure he knows things we don't know. He is always spot-on with his messages."

"How old did you say he is? You did tell me."

"Three."

"Three and you have him down as a soothsayer."

"Wait and see. I am sure you will be smiling before the day is out."

"Of course you will. "The doctor arrived breathless, and interrupted Joe before he could reply. "Come along, lad, let's take a look at what I have been doing with my knife and fork."

Between them Marion and the doctor took time to remove the bandages. The lower layers had been kept moistened to help the skin, which had been grafted from Joe's thigh. With the last bandage gone Marion applied Vaseline all over Joe's face. The skin looked raw and taut in places, but compared to the mess it was before, it looked good: the structure was right. She stepped back, smiled, and nodded. Joe, who had been watching for her reaction nodded too and the doctor stepped forward and asked Joe to open his mouth.

"Sorry I was late, I was waiting for these to arrive in the post." The doctor positioned a top plate of teeth into Joe's mouth. "There we are. They'll feel awkward, even sore, for a while, but increase the time you wear them each day and you'll soon get used to them. No sun for you: keep indoors, and keep your face moisturised. In a few weeks the rawness will settle and you'll find some of the tightness will relax. What do you think, nurse? Does he pass muster?"

"Handsome, I'd say. What about you Joe? Are you ready?" Marion asked.

Joe said nothing but without taking his eyes off her face he nodded and she handed him a hand mirror.

"I need to take the doctor to see Lieutenant Roche. I think he might have an infection, but I will be back soon. Take your time." Marion and the doctor left Joe alone behind the curtain screen.

It was an hour before Marion returned to Joe. She peeked her head around the curtain, uncertain as to how he would be and was greeted with a tentative smile.

"Nurse Drake?"

"Yes, Joe?"

"Would you post this for me?" He handed Marion a letter.

"Yes of course. First class?"

"Yes please. It's an invitation. I am inviting my parents and sister to visit."

This time when Marion reached for a tissue it was not to wipe his face. It was to wipe the tears from her own.

France, June 1918

Russell's stomach lurched. The driver of his sidecar combination had lost control of their vehicle. *We're going to crash.* Russell pushed his arms into the sides to brace his body. They had just swerved away from a head-on collision with a truck, and had left the narrow track at speed, flying over a ditch to land violently onto rough ground, slick with mud. His driver was shouting but over the noise of the screaming engine Russell could not tell whether the man was trying to tell him something, or simply yelling in terror. Veering wildly from side to side they hurtled straight for a line of trees, looming in front of them.

The driver managed to regain some control and the motorcycle slowed and turned. *We're going to make it.* And they almost did, but the front wheel hit a rock large enough to twist the handlebars and ruined their chance of avoiding the wall of trees. The driver's valiant efforts had not been enough and they slid into a tangle of branches and brambles just before hitting the first of the tree trunks. Fortunately for Russell, he was on the side furthest away from the force of the impact. Nevertheless he was jolted violently, and his knees smacked into the front fairing before he was slammed back into his seat.

All was quiet. The engine was no longer running, and the only immediate sound was his own breathing as he gasped for air. The driver was still on the bike but propped against the tree trunk they had hit; he seemed barely conscious, deathly pale, and blood was beginning to seep from under his leather helmet and down one side of his face. Russell could see he was pinned against the tree by the motorcycle, with heaven knows what damage to his leg.

"You fellas okay?" a voice asked from behind Russell.

"What kind of dumbass question is that?" another voice answered. "Get those guys out of there. Jeez, I hope we haven't killed a general. You, get over here too." The commands continued.

"Wait. Don't move that driver yet. We need an aider. There must be one with us? Go find one, huh."

Russell turned his head to look behind him, and gasped as a sharp pain shot across his neck and shoulders. He caught sight of familiar American uniforms and then found himself being carefully lifted up and out of his seat. His helpers continued to support him after his feet were on the ground, to test whether he could stand. He could feel all manner of aches and pains, most especially in his knees and neck, and although shaking from the shock of the accident, could remain upright. First the man on his right, then on his left, slowly released their holds on his arms, but they remained beside him, ready to grab him if his legs gave way. He heard that voice again, from beside his driver who had now been laid on the ground.

"Okay, do what you can. Make him as comfortable as possible. Then stay with him until the first ambulance arrives. You can follow us on later. If you run into Germans you've gone too far. Now, how's our officer here? Bit bruised I guess, by the look of it. Damn lucky wasn't a whole lot worse."

Russell recognised the voice. He removed his motorcycle goggles and managed a smile as Walt recognised him too.

"Well, hot dog, would you look at that. I do declare that I nearly killed one of our more intelligent intelligence officers. Bit of a dramatic way to meet again, wouldn't you say, Lieutenant Clark?"

Russell found himself looking into the beaming face of Walter Sheldon.

"Guess you'd like a lift back, Russ?"

In almost a year, since American headquarters had moved from Paris to a new base at Chaumont, Russell had only met up with Walt twice, and then briefly. Now, sitting together in the cab of a truck, they tried to use the opportunity to catch up. Conversation could not flow very easily, as they had to shout to make themselves heard over the noise of the engine and rough lanes, and with every bump of the vehicle causing Russell pain. There were many extended pauses between responses.

"Heard from the others?" Walt shouted.

"Nothing, no. You?"

"Nah, I've been building, buddy. Building like you wouldn't believe."

"No fighting then?" Russell asked.

"Not yet, but looks like it's on its way. You?"

"Yeah, some, Cantigny. More to come I expect."

"Cantigny. The boys had it rough there I heard."

"What have you been building?" Russell was not ready to talk about Cantigny.

"Every damn thing: docks, barracks, roads. Glad we're in the fight now. Thought we might be too late."

Since March the Allies had endured a series of massive German offensives, and had lost much ground. When Russell heard a recent attack that threatened Paris had been thwarted, with the help of American troops, he felt proud to be earning some respect from the French. At last American troops were supporting the Allies to hit back; even Russell had begun to think Pershing was prevaricating.

Russell had been assigned a liaison role in the counter-attack about to be launched by combined American and French forces. They were to force the Germans out of a salient, a bulge in the German lines that ran some forty miles from Soissons to Reims. The exposed flanks of the enemy made them vulnerable to attack and the Allies were primed to take advantage.

"At least I'll get some action now," Walt said and he told Russell he was in command of a support group of engineers and had been driving towards the jump-off point for the 1st Division when his procession of trucks and equipment had driven Russell and his driver off the forest track. "Beats logistics. What's liaison like?"

Before Russell could answer their vehicle ran over a large hole in the road, and lifted them off their seats before thumping them down again. Russell caught his breath and winced. He was unable to speak and Walt carried on regardless.

"The boys back home have been making my life hell, sending the wrong things to the wrong places. When we wanted trucks I'd find some damn fool in Washington had sent them without wheels. Even had one consignment of women's clothes. I've spent as much time sending cables as building; needed you to liaise for me. Hopefully fighting will be much simpler, well, apart from dodging the bullets of course. Cantigny you say. Some battle. What was it like?"

Russell gingerly turned his head towards Walter who, in turn, looked at him. There must have been something in Russell's eyes that gave an answer for Walter just nodded and both men turned back to stare ahead as the vehicle continued to jolt and jar down the forest road, their driver fighting with the wheel. The strain to talk in the noisy and uncomfortable truck became too much and both men lapsed into companionable silence, and Russell's thoughts returned to Cantigny.

It was almost two months since the battle of Cantigny but the memories still plagued Russell every moment he was not occupied or asleep. The Americans and the French had planned meticulously for the attack on the village, not because it was of huge strategic importance but because it was the first serious offensive action by Pershing's army. The Americans were green; they had been in France for almost a year and not yet fired a shot in anger. The American 1st Division was to make the attack, with the French providing the tanks and heavy artillery, and good co-ordination between the two, Russell's liaison role, was vital. This was the first real, and public, test of the American soldier. Russell, one of a number of liaison officers, had to ensure American requests for artillery support were relayed, clearly and concisely, back to French gunners. They had trained repeatedly, and knew that once they had taken ground, retreat was not an option.

"I want no slip-ups, or, by God, there'll be hell to pay. However frightening the Germans might be to you, remember I'm worse," his colonel had barked.

Not many men had ever intimidated Russell, but Colonel Ely did when he addressed his junior officers. A huge, strapping man, with a hero's jawline, made Russell wonder whether their commander had been chosen for his resemblance to a comic book leader of men. But it was only a fleeting thought. He quickly gathered from the regimental officers that Ely, though formidable, was as immensely capable as his reputation suggested.

The night before the assault, together with a French officer, Russell was led to a forward observation post, not much more than a shallow hole close to Cantigny, where they joined two other Americans, one a lieutenant. He passed a fitful night, taking turns with the Frenchman to call up the artillery command, at intervals, to ensure their telephone wire was still intact and functioning. It was impossible to mark any bearings in the dark; he could only hope the original reconnaissance had provided the artillery with the right coordinates. Any adjustments would need gunfire and daylight, a dangerous combination. *Here it comes.*

Russell's mental preparations for the opening barrage planned for dawn proved futile. The whistling scream of hundreds and hundreds of shells passing overhead was paralysing and they were only the prelude to explosion after explosion, which reverberated like rolls of threatening thunder. With the others he huddled down in their feeble shelter, making himself as small as he could. He had stuffed small strips of fabric into his ears and with his hands pressed tightly over the top tried to deaden the noise, but it was impossible.

The fearsome violence was so much more than he thought it would be, and the ground was shaking as if some mighty earthquake was erupting from the depths. He tried to hold his body tight but it was buffeted as shock waves from the blasts passed through and over them. After the longest hour Russell had ever known the gunfire ceased, and then, after a few minutes of silence, began again, but now somewhat lessened and with a more rhythmic pattern. The rolling barrage had begun and he knew the American soldiers would be moving out of their trenches. Slowly the four men unlocked themselves from the foetal positions they had crunched into, muscles stiff.

Russell gingerly lifted his head to peer out. The skyline of Cantigny, on the slope above them, had changed completely; there was smoke and dust hanging in the air above and around the village and, from what he could make out, only a handful of buildings remained standing, and these had no roofs.

"Wow, it's blasted," Russell said as he sunk back down and immediately started to cough, the air was so thick with dust. He lifted himself again. To his right, lines of men, bayonets fixed and bowed down with kit, walked forward.

"The men are on the move," he mouthed to the others, and then instinctively ducked when he heard some loud rumbles close by.

"That's the tanks," the other lieutenant told him.

Russell had not seen these machines in action before and he watched as five French tanks lumbered by with ranks of men walking behind them, and instinctively ducked as two French planes buzzed overhead. Everything was being thrown into this assault. Russell got to work. He passed his, the lieutenant's, and the French soldier's observations, map references, and timings down the line, only too pleased he did not have to work out the detail. Although functioning his head could not clear from the cacophony of gunfire and his wits felt dulled, but it looked like the battle plan was working. And then the resistance started.

Russell saw a gap blasted open in their attacking lines as sporadic German shelling started. He was impressed by his army's discipline as soldiers moved quickly close together again as they moved on, although several men had fallen.

"Some men are down," Russell called out.

"Leave them. The medics will have them covered," the French soldier said and Russell translated for the others. It was hard for Russell to ignore the groans drifting towards them over the breeze. *They need help.* His instinct was to go to them and he felt impotent, a frustrated bystander.

Russell observed and reported throughout the morning as troops made their faltering way into Cantigny. He could hear rifle and machine gun fire, and saw an occasional bright flare where flamethrowers were clearing buildings. He was impatient to move and follow the soldiers into the town, but their orders were to remain in their position.

"*C'est ne pas fini, mes braves. Fait attention. Bientot.*"

Russell felt patronised by the French soldier's words. Of course the battle was not over, but to Russell it looked as if the village was secured.

"Look," the youngest of their party pointed at a group of soldiers who were stumbling and limping down the hill, back towards the American line. Russell feared they were retreating

Americans but they turned out to be German soldiers, taken as prisoners.

"More of them surrender, that is good." The French soldier spoke in English, much to Russell's surprise and annoyance as he had laboured over his translations throughout the morning.

After the prisoners passed there was something of a lull interspersed with occasional bursts of shooting in the village and the odd artillery or mortar explosion. Russell was relieved to spot some aiders working the field, seeing to the wounded, and assumed the worst of the battle was over. He cheerily gave a thumbs-up to the greenhorn soldier, who had said and done little all morning. The French officer shook his head gravely.

"I know this enemy. Just wait."

He was a small morose man, older than the other three. So far he had only spoken to Russell when their work together required it, but Russell had not been offended. However grateful France might be to welcome them into the war, he knew most French soldiers viewed the brash, robust, and well-fed American troops as naïve and hopelessly optimistic. He guessed he would feel the same after four years of privation and nihilistic destruction. And for more destruction they did not have to wait for long.

The German retaliation was fierce and for Russell terrifying. German shells tore down, and clouds of dirty smoke rose again from Cantigny. But then the explosions crept closer to their meagre shelter. All four men huddled down, but there was nowhere for them to hide from the attack aimed on their field guns and troops behind and to the side of them. The onslaught was savage. The ground rocked as shells exploded all around, showering them with clods of earth. Russell's mind was frozen. *This is it, this is it.* He thought his time had come and waited for the bang that meant oblivion, in no fit state to do anything other than accept his fate. The young soldier curled up tight beside him was mumbling incoherently, words that Russell imagined to be a prayer, to spare him from this hell on earth.

The shelling moved away again and then stopped entirely. With the ensuing silence came a gradual movement of limbs and the realisation that no one had been hit. Stiffened by tension Russell was stretching his body when an almighty blast landed nearby covering them with soil. It was the last straw for the young soldier who leapt upright, screaming incoherently before hurling himself out and into the open. Without thinking Russell leapt after him and grabbed him around the waist and brought him down. He held onto him as the soldier thrashed about like a landed fish, his body flat on the ground underneath him. Russell did not move until the soldier quietened, his chest heaving with sobs. The French soldier crawled up next to Russell and grasped an arm of the sobbing man and together he and Russell pulled him back down into their hole. They made the soldier, gasping for breath, his eyes and nose running, sit between them, and held onto his arms to stop him making another impulsive suicidal move. Russell caught the French soldier's eye and received a curt nod.

"Now you understand war a little, mon ami."

The French artillery responded to the German bombardment, and they kept their heads down for the next couple of hours before orders were received to move forward to the edge of the village.

Using a break in the shelling they joined reinforcements, medical officers and supply teams heading for the village. Stretcher bearers passed them going the other way, gasping under the weight of their bloodied, maimed cargoes. Russell was sure some of them were dead. He stumbled on the uneven ground but when he put his hand out to steady himself he found he was touching a severed arm and in front of him was the lower part of a leg, boot still intact. Bile rose in his throat and he took several deep breaths to steady himself. His arm was taken hold of by the French lieutenant who pulled him to his feet and urged him on. The Frenchman was caked in a fine dusty covering of earth giving him a ghostly pallor: the cleanest part of his face was the whites of his eyes. Russell realised he probably looked the same and wiped the back of his hand across his face.

As he approached the back streets he could hear heavy firing on the far side of Cantigny where German infantry were attempting to retake the town. The American forward headquarters were under one of the first buildings he reached in the cellar of a ruined storehouse, where a harassed major soon had him working. For the rest of that afternoon and evening Russell sent spotters out to note artillery positions and details of the German advances and retreats, which he relayed to the major and the French. He was pleased not to be doing the running himself; his legs were still shaky from the earlier shelling. The sound of firing became more intermittent as darkness loomed and Russell was thankful, but then he picked up that the French troops and artillery were being pulled out, leaving them exposed for the next day. They would not stand a chance without this back-up.

"I am sorry, my friend. I have to leave you." The French soldier had come to find Russell and explain. "There has been a German attack south of here; the Germans are coming through our lines. They say Paris is under threat again. This place is not so very important, you understand? We must take our guns and go to help our army. May God go with you."

"And with you," Russell said as they shook hands, both still grimy from the day's battle.

Russell was ordered to rest by the major, who himself was going to try to catch some sleep. "It's all down to us tomorrow, boys," he had said before turning in. "Black Jack's reputation is down to us. Let's see what tomorrow brings."

Russell lay in the dark waiting for sleep to overtake him, but anxiety kept him awake. With the French withdrawing most, if not all, their artillery support, he knew his liaison role was largely redundant for now and he wondered what new orders would await him in the morning, or even for what duties he might volunteer. He surprised himself to think he wanted to fight, to put his effort behind ousting the Germans, and force his will against theirs. It suddenly struck him that his thoughts were not for his own safety, but he actually felt anger towards these aggressors who had spilt the first American blood that day. It was such a waste of life and they had to be stopped. He intended to pick up a gun the next day and hoped his basic training had been drilled into him enough.

He imagined Marion's indignation should she be in conversation with him now.

"Oh, so it's all right for you to put yourself in danger while you wrap the rest of us up in cotton wool."

And she would be right. His own excitement was growing with the recognition that he was attracted to danger and not frightened of it, but he wanted her to shy away from any trouble. For the first time in his life he experienced the thrill of holding onto life lightly. *He was man enough for this.* He felt liberated but in the same instance was flooded by love for Marion and an ache to be with her again and he did not want to throw their future away by taking risks. It was difficult for him to square the two thoughts, but his determination grew to get stuck into the fight.

He reflected on his newfound courage. For the first time since he discovered Marion was hiding soldiers from the Germans in Brussels, he fully understood the dilemma she had faced and the decisions she had made. Putting herself in peril had been a significant bone of contention for him ever since. He had always seen her recklessness as an act of stubborn defiance against his own conservatism and caution, against his control, but now he was struck by the thought, it had nothing to do with him at all. The circumstances demanded a response and she gave it, just as he was going to the next day. The clarion call was bigger than either of them could resist. He groaned when he remembered how he had tried to lay down the law to her about not going overseas again. Luckily for him Alain had carried the day. It meant everything to him to know she was safe, even if he was about to put himself in jeopardy.

Still awake, halfway through the night Russell went in search of some rations and stumbled across Andrews, the private he had thrown to the ground earlier in the day. He could see the soldier was still shaking and sat down beside him. Andrew's sudden jerks and tremors reminded him of Marion's descriptions of the patients whose nerves were shot to pieces. Russell held down one of the lad's arms to steady him, but he could not stop the movement. He and Marion had debated hysteria and shell shock and he had come down quite firmly in the hysterics camp at the time. One day of battle conditions and his mind was changed. This soldier was a wreck. He talked to him and told him he would fabricate a job the next day, which would take him back behind their lines, but Andrews shook his head even more vehemently.

"No sir, I want to fight. I'm not going to run away."

"Well, perhaps you can show me the ropes tomorrow then. It's about time I did more than talking in this war."

"Yes sir, of course sir."

"Now try and get some sleep. Our orders will come soon enough in the morning."

What Russell could not know was that compared to the following forty-eight hours that first day was, if anything, a relatively benign introduction to combat. It seemed the Germans were determined to deny success to the Americans' first offensive action and their army threw whatever it could against the ruined shell of Cantigny. Without the protection of the French artillery, wave after wave of German shellfire crashed onto them, interspersed with infantry assaults. The Americans still had use of their own divisional artillery, and although that did not have the range to deal with the long distance artillery bombardments, it did deter the German infantry. But American casualties mounted quickly.

Before Russell had been able to volunteer himself for fighting duties the next morning, the major had barked at him.

"Clark, comms and telephone wires, down to you. Take three men and arms. Keep those spools turning. Want this town covered, corner to corner." And that was his brief. Over the next two days Russell often found himself in the most exposed of positions as he placed wires and traced broken telephone lines back towards headquarters.

By the third day of the battle Russell had lost the capacity to think and react. He went through the motions of what was required but, sleep-deprived and near deafened, his slow-moving body and mind felt drugged. He had seen sights that belonged to the worst of nightmares. He often came across crazed and injured men huddled among the debris, or, in some cases, wandering around seemingly oblivious to the danger and ignoring their own gaping wounds. He had escaped many near misses, but apart from some minor scratches, was largely unscathed. He put this down to luck: it was nothing to do with any dexterity on his part. All he knew was he had been in the thick of it and had survived and the relief he felt when troops arrived to take over was overwhelming.

"Here you go, buddy," Walt said, jolting Russell out of his reverie and back into the truck. "Guess you're going to have to find yourself a new driver. This is as far as we can take you. It's been good to see you. Sorry about your bruises. You look after yourself and keep your head down. You've already done enough if you were at Cantigny."

"Yes, it was pretty hot there at times. You stay out of trouble too."

Walter got down from the cab and Russell slid across the seat to get down too. He was sore but once on the ground he found he could move without too much pain, provided he did not turn his neck too much, and favoured his left leg.

"Thank you, Walt, I appreciate the lift."

They shook hands with uncharacteristic solemnity.

Russell was given a few days' leave. His bruises looked very convincing and purple, but were nothing compared to his driver who had broken an arm and a leg and cracked his skull. Russell wrote to his family for him, warning them to look out for him as he was on his way home.

Russell had been writing to Marion with his usual regularity, but since Cantigny his letters felt trite. He was a changed man but did not have the words to convey this to her: the censors only permitted bland, and he was still working it out for himself. He had faced death on the battlefield, had held his nerve, and felt stronger for it. He knew he had accounted for himself well enough and had proved he had courage when it counted. He would never carry doubts about himself again and just as important to him was the way he now understood Marion and her fights to withstand conventions and constraints, including his. He wanted her to know that all he wished was for her to be happy and fulfilled, whatever decisions might accompany that. He could only hope she could read between the lines in his attempt to update her.

> "There was an awful lot of noise at Papa's birthday bash. I was blowing up balloons with the rest and best of them. Can now understand why you like parties so much. I liked being a guest too. Fancy dress party planned soon. I will never stop you going to a party again. Your happiness is all that matters. Love as always, Rx."

Little Missenden, July 1918

Something was different. Marion could not put her finger on what exactly but there was a feeling of anticipation in the air, almost as if people were holding their breath. What she could not work out was which way the news was going to go, bad or good. Was it false bravado in the papers that told her the Allies were pushing back, and that the German nation was being starved? Was it true that the tsar of Russia had been shot, and that the Romanov family was missing? Was the feeling of national concern for his children, or for the social order that had been turned on its head? Was Russell different or was she imagining it? It was Sunday morning and Alain had a slight summer chill so Marion had stayed at home with him rather than go to church. He seemed unperturbed and was using the morning to draw a picture. She read Russell's latest letter.

Dear Marion,
    Be careful my darling. There is a dangerous illness afoot that is traveling across countries. Believe the worst of it.

Even though Marion had received Russell's letter some days before, she stood up and went and pressed her hand against Alain's forehead. It felt all right. He had the slightest of temperatures only. She had been alarmed to read this opening line to his letter, having learnt his big news always went into his first paragraph, so this must be serious. News of deaths from influenza had reached the hospital and they had received a bulletin giving instructions for quarantining any patient who showed signs of the illness. So far they were clear, but the rumour was it was being passed through the troops. She feared for Russell.

> There was an awful lot of noise at Papa's birthday bash. I was blowing up balloons with the rest and best of them. Can now understand why you like parties so much. I liked being a guest too. Fancy dress party planned soon. I will never stop you going to a party again. Your happiness is all that matters.

These were the lines she kept rereading. He had obviously been engaged in action of some sort, fighting even and had enjoyed it. Enjoyed it? *And he thinks I like fighting too?* She must be reading the wrong meaning into his lines. *Danger, perhaps he meant danger rather than fighting.* She had stepped into danger without any thought for herself in Brussels, that was what he was always saying to her, when the truth was, she had not actually appreciated the danger was real, until, until it was too late to save Edith and she had to flee. *Oh Edith, poor Edith.* But his dangers were obvious if he was close to the battlefields: bullets and bombs were very real. *But why was he getting involved in the action? He had said he wouldn't have to fight.* But perhaps the truth is, she pondered, there is a part of every man that wants to be a soldier and fire a gun and he had said he wanted to be tested.

> Had an accident. Motorcycle driver lost control and took us off the track into some trees. He was knocked up with some broken bones. I was stiff and bruised, nothing more. Had been enjoying the ride until then, pretty countryside, the parts that have not been blasted to smithereens. Good picnic weather!

Picnic. That was a good idea. If Alain seemed all right after lunch, she would pack a few things and take him off for a picnic tea. Not far from the house, but distant enough for him to rouse his energy and perhaps have a run around. The weather was good, perhaps not as hot as it was for Russell but pleasant nonetheless.

Thank you for the photograph. My mother received hers, very touched, as was I. No home comforts here, but no complaints.

"Marion, are you there, Marion?"
Marion looked up to see Evelyn rush into the nursery.
"I'm here. What's the problem? Are you all right?"
"Yes, no, it's not me, it's Papa. He collapsed in the service. He has been taken to Shardeloes. They want you to come. The doctor has been sent for. Hurry."
"Alain, I can't leave Alain."
"I'll stay with him. Go, hurry."
"Alain, you'll be all right with Auntie Evelyn."
"Mummy, take this for Grandpa." Alain handed her his picture. She kissed him and ran from the room.

Marion was delighted to see the carrier, John, waiting for her at the front of the house.
"I'm to take you to the big house, miss. Your uncle sent his car for the doctor."
"Thank you. What happened? Were you there, at the service?"
"Yes, miss. He collapsed. Clutched his chest. Looked like a heart attack."
"Was he conscious? Did he speak?"
"I can't say that I knows that, miss. Your uncle was by his side in a moment."

Although short in distance, the journey took an age for Marion. To stop her from jumping off the cart and running ahead she took herself through the protocols that she knew she must apply if she reached her father before the doctor. She prayed that he would be there. Despite her nursing experience she was not experienced in emergencies, and all she knew of heart attacks were that they were largely fatal. She started crying at the thought.

"Now, now, miss. They won't want to see your tears. Chin up. Your father is a strong man, he'll make good."

"Yes, yes, of course. It's all so sudden, that's all. He'll be fine." *I hope, please God.*

Marion fumbled in her pocket for her handkerchief and found the picture Alain had given her, now crumpled into a ball. She started to open and flatten it, but had no time to look at it before they pulled up at Shardeloes House. It went back in her pocket and she jumped off the cart, thanking John as she ran up the steps, past the colonnades and to the door, which was immediately opened for her. She was led to the first floor where she met her mother.

"The doctor is with him now. He asked me to leave the room. I was flustering him apparently. Go in, go in, and tell me what is happening."

"Yes, yes I will, but sit down, Mother. Sit here." Marion saw her mother's distress and led her to a chair on the landing. She had just settled her when her aunt appeared with two glasses in her hand.

"Brandy, just the thing. I'll find you when I have some news," Marion said as she entered the room and closed the door behind her.

"Indigestion. All rather embarrassing I fear. And I have caused a lost of fuss and concern. Kidneys for breakfast, too rich for me, and I rushed them too."

Mr. Drake was sitting up in bed when Marion rushed to his side.

"Oh, Papa," was all she could manage before she burst into tears.

"Let us not be too hasty here," the doctor said as he stepped forward. "It might well be indigestion, but I don't like your colour and I think your heart might well be under strain. I insist that you remain here and rest for a few days, if that can be accommodated?" The doctor addressed his question to Marion's uncle William who was standing discretely by the window.

"Of course he can. No need to move him. Poor chap has been doing too much. Just the thing to be ordered to bed."

Marion, who had by this time pulled herself together once she knew he was not at death's door, immediately thought of her mother.

"Mother. I must tell Mother that you are not in grave danger. Do excuse me. She is beside herself."

Indeed, Marion had never seen her mother in such a distressed and agitated state before. There had been no slight taken by her ejection from the sick room; all her concern had been for her husband.

"Tarry a while, Marion. We need some moments to be sure, wouldn't you say, doctor?" Marion's uncle William stepped forward.

"Well, umm, …" The doctor's fumbles for a response were soon interrupted.

"Well, put it this way, without question he needs some peace and quiet wouldn't you say, and not to be fussed over," her uncle persisted.

"Indeed, rest yes, he must stay quiet. Perhaps Miss Drake could attend him." The doctor looked towards Marion.

"Of course. You must tell me what he needs. As long as I won't inconvenience your household, uncle."

"Not at all, and I am sure we can convince your mother to return home, if she knows you will be remaining here. I shall rely on you for that."

"Now, William. She means everything kindly." Marion's father started to speak, but her uncle interrupted him.

"Daphne is a wonderful woman, as you are always telling me, but it will do no harm for you to be removed from her auspices, nor for her to appreciate your qualities from afar for a few days. Don't you agree, Marion?"

Marion, who was never usually far removed from criticism of her mother, found herself at a loss for what to say. Her uncle had strayed, or rather marched, into the domain of her parents' relationship and she did not feel equipped to comment, and was surprised that her first instinct, like her father's, was to defend her mother. She was clearly very distressed by her husband's collapse: Marion had never seen her so vulnerable.

"I am sure Mother can and will accommodate anything the doctor will advise, but perhaps it is he who should lay out the regimen of care, rather than me. She admires the professional voice and might accept instructions more readily from that quarter," Marion offered. "And we really must put her mind at rest about my father's hold on life; it is unfair to prolong her anxiety."

The doctor, who was familiar with Mrs. Drake's capacity to bend the world to meet her will, looked askance at the task. Marion's uncle stepped in again.

"I will manage the conversation with you doctor, we will go together. Marion, why don't you make a list of your and your father's things you require from the rectory. With a job in hand Daphne will more readily depart, and having feared the loss of her husband, if only for a few hours, Bernard may reap the harvest of her greater considerations for some months to come. I will fetch you some paper and a pen, Marion, but take your time. Doctor, let us arrange our conversation."

Marion and her father were left alone when her uncle, and the doctor, moved through the connecting door into the adjacent dressing room. It was the first opportunity for Marion to take in the room, which was large and lavishly furnished, with heavy mahogany furniture and dark blue drapes, its size emphasised by the height of the ceiling and the long drop of the windows. Her father had his eyes closed so Marion stepped to the window and looked at the view, which was admirable. Her father had been taken to a guest suite at the front of the house. The land sloped away from the house towards the river Misbourne, which defined the line of the valley. Fields and woodlands formed the hill on the opposing side of the valley. In between was the lake. The setting was peaceful, and Marion knew would be recuperative for her father, who, she acknowledged rarely had a moment's peace from either his parochial duties, or matrimonial exchanges. It was clear to her that her uncle William was the king of his castle, and despite the lack of crenellations on the building, she did feel she was looking at his kingdom from this vantage point. To an observer, particularly one with the keen eye of her uncle, the rectory could appear more of a fiefdom under the control of Baroness Daphne, and she could see why Uncle William would baulk at that. Until this moment she had thought it had entirely suited her father, but perhaps more tensions existed than she was privy to. It struck her, just how little thought she had ever given to the life of her parents, other than in their interaction with her.

She turned as her uncle and the doctor re-entered the room and took the paper and pen offered. They relayed to Marion and her father the script they had prepared for Daphne and to be given to well-wishers who would no doubt be enquiring after his health: the attendees at the service would all need their concerns managed. Heart strain was to be the diagnosis and secluded rest, no visitors, with attendance by his nursing daughter at the Shardeloes residence, for a week, was the prescribed treatment. Her uncle said he would write to the hospital on her behalf to absent her, and Marion nodded her agreement. *But what about Alain? How was she to be away from him?*

Bernard, who had been silent throughout, cleared his throat and immediately had everyone's attention.

"All of your intentions are kindly meant, but I do feel a fraud. I am sure I am quite well, just dyspeptic, which a tonic will soon address. I have no need of the respite you prescribe. Perhaps after a rest for a few hours Marion can accompany me home, and we will remove ourselves as an inconvenience."

"Tosh," William said. "Come on brother, you know this makes sense. You were telling me just the other day you felt tired. I am pleased this hiatus can be used in this way. Rest is exactly the tonic you require. And it will do my niece no harm either. The two of you should use this time as a reprieve from your work. The world will soon accommodate your duties for the next week. As your employer, brother, I am telling you to take a holiday."

"But then perhaps I should take Daphne away to …"

"From all responsibilities," William interrupted.

"Papa, you do look quite pale and tired. I am sure this is good advice," Marion added her voice to the appeal.

"Very well then, so be it. I must be tired, I have very little fight within me, but on one thing I must insist: that you Marion consider this a holiday too and join me here, with Alain."

"Done," William said. "Marion, I will send the housekeeper to you to discuss all the necessary arrangements. Augusta and I will be away for much of the next two weeks. We are off to Cheshire to review the estates. I have a young chap in charge there and he has some progressive farming ideas he wants the tenants to employ, but they are not behind him yet. I thought I'd go and take a look and smooth the choppy waters. We plan some time at the Boston spa too, so you can have the run of the place."

"Are you sure you don't mind? Will it not inconvenience

your staff?" Marion asked, and then added, "and for Alain to come too, will Aunt Augusta be comfortable with this?"

"Only sorry we won't be here to enjoy you as house guests. Admirable what you have done with that boy. He is a lucky chap to have your attentions. We must discuss his schooling when he is of an age. See what we can do for him. Right, matter settled. Let's draw these curtains and let this man have some of this rest we keep talking about. Marion, bring your list to the morning room when you have it complete, and no worries if something is forgotten, John can fetch and carry for you."

The week with her father became one of the most precious of her life. He was tired, but so, she quickly realised, was she. They breakfasted late, took an afternoon nap each day, and dined early, all with Alain. And, when together, they fell into easy conversation. She tried to capture something of the week in her letters to Russell, but found it difficult to describe the deepening of the relationship with her father; always close, but now so much more informed from their time together.

Their intimacies were endless. They exchanged ancestral and personal histories, hopes and fears, delights and disappointments, family values and perspectives on the world, war and women, her mother being a particular focus.

"She doesn't mean to control, her only drive is to conform," her father explained, "because with that comes acceptance and comfort. Abiding by the rules and having others do the same is security for her." Marion had nodded her understanding. "Those who challenge the order of things, who raise questions, or who threaten the status quo," *in the way I do,* "attack the edifice she has constructed around her place in the world. Her rules are a bit like the corsetry that hold you ladies in place."

Such insight from her father into her mother's motivations knocked for six her own, more derisory, description of her mother's sometimes pompous airs and graces and the rigidity of her narrow tolerances towards her own behaviour; but she did not argue, just listened.

He was content, more than happy. She had more curiosity than ambition. He was more philosophical than spiritual. She was more pragmatic than principled, but on loving Alain, they both agreed.

"Were you disappointed not to have a son?" Marion asked one afternoon while they both watched Alain build a fort with some wooden bricks. The toys he had discovered in the nursery delighted him.

"I thought I might be, at first, and your mother was mortified that she didn't provide one. You were her last attempt."

"And I have been a disappointment to her ever since?"

"Is that how you have felt? Is that how we have made you feel?"

"You never, but Mother, yes: back to her thing about conformity. I have never quite struck the right chord on this. Always feel I have chafed. Staying in her good books requires walking a tightrope and I know I often fail her, Alain being a case in point."

Marion smiled at Alain who laughed as his precarious tower crashed to the floor and he started all over again.

"That one has some tenacity," Bernard said as he watched Alain. "Daphne has stopped correcting him if he calls her Grandmama. Have you noticed?"

"Now you mention it, you're right. But I know she isn't happy about him. I do wish she could accept him; he feels her rejection, you know."

"He is surrounded by love and has the wisdom of a saint. He's a canny boy, quite extraordinary."

"As was his mother."

"I would love to hear about her, and Brussels, when you are ready."

"Yes, Papa, yes you're right, it is time. This evening, when Alain is settled, yes it would be good to tell you."

And she did, tell him everything, from beginning to end, with pauses for her tears for Edith, and apart from a few questions here and there he listened in silence, often with his eyes closed. He surprised her with his statement when her tale was at an end.

"You are your mother's favourite, you know. Never to be spoken of course, but it is clear to me all the same."

Marion had expected recriminations and admonishments, or mild criticism at the very least; she was astonished at his comment.

"I beg your pardon? Mother? Me? Surely you mean Evelyn. She is the apple of her eye? And what has this to do with what I have been telling you? Have you nothing to say about Brussels, Alain, Russell, my escapades?"

"It is because of all of those things that your mother loves you most. She has always known of your propensity to stray into trouble, unwittingly, and with the best of intentions, however impulsive they may have been. She has tried to hold you tight for your own protection and feels she has failed you when things go wrong. When she sees Alain she sees her failings as a mother, not yours. Evelyn, light-headed and light-hearted as she is will always toe the line. She needs few constraints, apart from avoiding fashion *faux pas*. But you are a different kettle of fish entirely."

Marion had never thought of her mother's stance towards her in this way before and found it difficult to accept her father's view, but he was adamant. She had always chafed against her mother's control and had never looked beyond this to see the love and protectiveness that drove it. When she thought of her attitude now she felt quite penitent.

"Does Mother think Alain is my child?"

"No, and she never has, but you have never given her the

story that can turn you into a heroine in other people's eyes. Not in the way you have done with me today."

"But that's the thing entirely. I am not heroic and Mother would boast about my exploits in the most embarrassing way. I was in a set of circumstances and I did what any other person would have done."

"And that is where you are wrong, Marion. Did your friend Gwen do the same things? Did she help the soldiers and return to England with an orphan to bring up as her own? No, and nor would most. Most would consider inconveniences on themselves, but not you. You thought of the soldiers and Alain first."

I was selfish. "Actually, I just did what I wanted to do and gave little or no thought to the social consequences. Russell told me not to bring him, but I went against his wishes and Mother has never recovered."

"Your mother extracts a high measure of her self-esteem from holding the moral compass for the parish, and I must admit your arrival with Alain caused quite a judder for a while. But you heard what William said, they admire what you have done for the boy, and he will have thought about the lad's education. You are admired, more than you are judged, and your mother is beginning to realise this, and that you will never be malleable to her mould. She would feel honoured to hear your story, and would be respectful with it, I am sure."

"I'm not as convinced of this as you."

"When it feels right for you, you will tell her. No pressure from me. I will say nothing. She is used to you and I having secrets."

"I don't want Alain to know the details of his conception, ever. That must remain a secret."

"My lips are sealed. But don't you worry about that one, he weighs up life from a different set of scales to the ones most of us use. I look forward to the time when he can fully converse: I will have plenty to learn from him, I am sure."

"His mother was remarkable, and look at this. This is what Alain was drawing the morning you were taken ill. He gave it to me when I left to come to you. I only found it again yesterday. Sorry it is so crumpled, but you can just make out the crayons."

Marion handed the piece of paper over to her father, who with glasses positioned, looked at the picture and smiled. With no particular skill Alain had drawn three figures, two adult, and a child. One of the adults was a woman and the other a man with grey whiskers. All were looking towards water and there was a tower of wooden bricks at the child's feet. A beam of sunlight shone down on the man. It was a tableau of their afternoon.

"Yes, when he can converse, he will be worth listening to." Mr. Drake repeated. "Now, tell me about your admirers. How many of those officers do you have dancing attendance at the moment, and how is Lieutenant Clark?"

When Marion and her father returned to the rectory, both refreshed after their week of rest, they were welcomed with open arms and her father was soon settled in the lounge, with a blanket over his lap despite him insisting it was not needed.

Marion felt kindly towards her as her mother held forth with the list of visitors she had both enjoyed and endured all week. Apparently the callers had come thick and fast to pay their respects and bring food and provisions to help the family. Never had her mother received so much attention, particularly not of the kind that conveyed such genuine affection and concern for both her and her husband, and she was clearly overcome and humbled by it. These were not traits Marion was familiar with ascribing to her mother. Was she the one seeing her mother in a new light, or had her mother also undergone a metamorphosis?

Marion wrote to Russell that evening, welcoming the solitude of her own room and company that evening.

It is as if a tautness has left my mother's body. She looked the same apart from her usual stiffness, which had somehow softened. She spoke to my father about the fondness his parishioners have for him, as evidenced by the concern they had shown throughout the week. But if my mother had allowed herself to say it, I think she also realised some of that fondness was directed to herself too. In my words, far too extreme for her, I believe she felt loved and perhaps more importantly for her, she felt accepted and liked as well as respected.

I have a feeling she and I will get on better now. Quite a revelatory week for all.

Marion knew it would take some time for the conversations of the last week to settle with her, but she was aware she was already experiencing her mother in a different way, and liked it. Alain had triumphed on their return by running straight up to Daphne and hugging her dress and saying "I missed you, Grandmama. I drew a picture for you," and giving her a crumpled piece of paper. It was a colouring of a big heart with kisses next to it. Marion was convinced her mother's eyes had watered.

> P.S. Father sends his apologies. He should never have refused your proposal and hopes to welcome you to the family on your return. I didn't tell him you have been fighting. Keep safe my beloved. No influenza in Bucks. Mx

France, July 1918

Rain was teeming down and water was soaking through the fabric of his coat. Russell was wet, numbed, and cold. He had been standing in the rain since early afternoon directing traffic at a crossroads of tracks and pathways in the woods. And now it was so dark he could hardly see, the only light coming from a lamp hanging from a low branch. He changed his weight from one leg to another, shook his arms and kept his shoulders hunched, to stop the rain running straight down his neck.

Troops and equipment had come through for hours, but the mudbath was now unusable for infantry. Russell had positioned himself on the only remaining mound of grass to stop from sinking knee deep in the sodden clay. Soldiers forcing their way through undergrowth on makeshift paths unleashed their frustration with breathless curses. Russell could hear them for quite a time before they appeared at his junction and he shared their exasperation. The situation they were in could have been foreseen but the Americans' reliance on French knowledge of their own countryside had let them down. This latest offensive had become a logistical nightmare with thousands of troops, tanks, and heavy equipment blundering through forests and ravines, as they hurried to reach their battle positions in supposed secrecy and on time. And the instructions from the French, in nominal control of this joint attack, had been intermittent, confusing, and at times wholly contradictory.

Russell could hear an increasing amount of crashing in the undergrowth signalling the imminent arrival of more soldiers and soon an officer stumbled out of the trees followed by his men. In single file, they each held on to the shoulder of the man ahead to not get lost in the dark. Looking exhausted, panting hard, many bent over with hands on their knees gasping in lungfuls of air as they gathered in the clearing. The officer spoke to Russell.

"This is crazy. Where the hell do we go now? I'm Mayhew, 18th Regiment."

Russell indicated with a sweep of his arm and shouted over the rain.

"Three hundred yards ahead, sharp right turn and another five or six hundred yards will see you with the rest. Keep to the edge of the track and you'll avoid the worst of the mud. Good luck, captain."

The officer turned back to his men.

"Almost there, fellas. Come on."

They straightened up and Russell watched as they adjusted their packs before moving off. As they passed him Russell heard soft-voiced cursing, none to his face and all mumbled, but he was sure he was called "asshole" at least half a dozen times before the last of them had gone. Though he had nothing to do with the planning he was the embodiment of the staff HQ responsible for the current chaos: he took it on the chin.

Can't say I blame you, boys, I guess I'd feel the same. He peered ahead for the next strays to come his way.

Any gaps in the assault line caused by absent units could undermine the whole assault, so when reports of delays had filtered in to HQ during the previous day and faults in the planning became apparent, the French staff had erupted in a high state of panic. In response, the American command recruited every spare engineer and staff officer they could to guide in their missing men, and that included Russell. Fifty or so were acting as impromptu guides, and were now scattered along key junctions and approaches to the battlefield. He was there all night.

Russell staggered so jolted was he by the deafening roar of the artillery barrage when it started up. The dawn light was slow to reach his spot in the woods and even though he knew an early attack was planned, he was shocked by the suddenness and ferocity of the noise. His muscles tensed and he clenched his jaw to hold his face firm. His right hand started to quiver and he clamped his left hand over it and squeezed tight until he felt the tremors fade. Memories of Cantigny surfaced in his mind, unbidden and unwanted.

He told himself it was the noise he was reacting to and not fear he was feeling, but since Cantigny he'd had concerns about his survival. He hated to think of the grief for his parents and Marion if he fell. He put his hand on his stomach, which felt hollow and slightly bilious. He hated this part of the attack before the advance began and he had no comrades around to distract him. One of the drawbacks of his role was constantly being moved to wherever a go-between was needed, so he lacked the comfort of belonging to one unit and being able to feed off the strength of a clan. Despite his discomfort he was thankful to have been busy all night and now the attack had begun his orders were to make his way to camp for his next assignment.

Relieved to find some dry kit, Russell managed a couple of hours' sleep in the corner of a staff tent and filled up on eggs and coffee in the officers' cookhouse before being finally ready to go to his next posting. He was surprised that he had fallen asleep with the constant shriek of ordnance flying overhead and the rest had refreshed him. He was even more surprised to have a brandy thrust into his hand the minute he was introduced to the officers in the command tent of the Moroccan Division. Russell's orders were to liaise between the Moroccans and the American 2nd Division on their right. They were about to lead their troops as the vanguard of the offensive and Russell was amazed to find the dozen or so garrulous French Moroccan officers in apparent celebratory mood. Small and mustachioed they all enthusiastically pumped his hand. Some even embraced him. Russell was not sure whether their devil-may-care casualness uplifted him or scared him to death.

With his glass of brandy he was pressed into joining a toast to "*l'attaque*". It was obvious this was not the first time glasses had been raised, and his arrival provided a good excuse for another fortifier. Gone were the days when he viewed the consumption of hard liquor as a sign of irredeemable decay. He grinned back at them in the inane manner that seemed to match their mood, and raised and downed his glass in one go, then gasped and choked at the strength of the spirit.

"*Mon ami.*"

"*Mon Dieu!*" The nearest officer slapped him on the back, which made Russell cough even more.

"*Salut.*"

"*Au revoir.*"

"*Adieu!*"

The room filled with cheers and jeers and glasses were refilled but Russell declined, however welcome the afterglow that began in his stomach and quickly reddened his cheeks. After another toast, the officers gave a rousing cheer and, with much back-slapping left the tent: each intent on following their separate orders.

Russell found the French communication officer, who was to be his comrade for the next few days. He had a diagram showing the positions of all the troops, and they soon agreed where to head on his motorcycle. The bike was low to the ground and Russell had to tuck his knees up high, which made balancing as a pillion rider quite tricky. They made their way through the makeshift camp towards the front ranks of men and in the occasional brief pauses of artillery fire Russell heard *"Allez, allez"* being shouted down the line and even the faint sound of cheering from the Americans to his right as they also began their advance.

All were heading across a plateau edged with ravines, with the town of Vierzy as their first objective, but Russell could not get a clear view of the scene. The artillery was firing smoke shells as well as explosives, so the town came in and out of view, depending on the breeze. Luckily the rain had stopped and the ground on the plateau was well drained. The Moroccans nearest to Russell were mostly silent as they advanced in loose, uneven, and seemingly disordered groups. While to Russell's eye this went contrary to his notion of attack procedure they seemed to know what they were doing, and the French officer with him, Lt. Fournier, appeared delighted and cheered them on. Sporadic gunfire quickly followed their departure and Fournier and Russell had to hold back their own advance.

Bumping across the ground behind the second wave of the Moroccan advance the two officers soon came across shallow trenches and dead German soldiers. Moroccan casualties were rare, so far at least. Russell soon realised he had seen no enemy wounded, nor prisoners and the explanation for this became clear when he saw that many of the bodies had, amongst other injuries, knife wounds. He had heard of the Moroccans' merciless reputation and now he understood what this meant in battle: they took no prisoners.

The advance slowed as opposition stiffened. German machine gun positions were holding up their progress, and mortar shells cracked down from time to time, one close call showered Russell in small stones and grit, but did no harm. He tucked himself in behind Fournier, his greatest fear a stray bullet. They spent their time criss-crossing between the Moroccans and the Americans, the Frenchman revving the bike and hollering in excitement while Russell hung on with his teeth gritted and often eyes closed.

There was a competitive edge between the Americans and the French and Russell and Fournier were frequently asked the progress of the other, more than for details of the enemy, but there was no lack of willingness to cooperate when necessary. Russell was frequently called upon to direct American field guns to clear out a stubborn enemy position, which had been delaying the Moroccans.

The attack had lost much of its initial momentum by the afternoon and the line of the advance had become ragged. Russell's back felt stiff from all the jarring over uneven ground and Fournier complained that his wrists ached from holding so tightly to the handlebars. On each trip they made they criss-crossed a regular stream of walking wounded making their way back, including dazed and dirty German prisoners. Some groups of prisoners were accompanied by just one or two lightly wounded Americans, but, in a few cases, they appeared to have been left to find their own way, unarmed, to captivity, and they seemed to do this willingly. They looked dejected and exhausted.

Russell by the end of the day felt the same exhaustion, but the mood of the troops and the command posts was one of exhilaration at the progress made. Russell's legs almost collapsed under him when he climbed off the bike for the last time that day and straightened up. His ears were ringing from the constant explosions and his voice was hoarse. Fournier grinned and grasped Russell in an embrace before kissing him on each cheek, proclaiming the magnificence of the day for their cause. Russell ignored the catcalls and whistles from two American soldiers who happened to be watching.

Russell was surprised to find himself in a tent when he awoke the next morning. His dreams had taken him home to his parents and he half expected to smell bacon cooking when he crawled out from the canvas. Although absurd, he was disappointed.

Fournier cheered him when he arrived but then Russell was soon wincing as his bruised butt bones came into contact with the seat of the bike. They set out towards the town following the first wave of reinforcements. They were halfway across an open area, alongside bands of American foot soldiers and tanks when they heard aircraft approaching. Fournier pulled the motorcycle over into the shade of a tree to give them the chance to watch the plane, still a novelty to Russell, who was at first distracted by the tanks, two of which were trundling past with soldiers walking along behind and to the side of them.

Reconnaissance planes often buzzed the skies. Russell had seen many sets of photographs produced by their cameras, all invaluable intelligence, but he suddenly became aware that the approaching planes, and there was more than the usual one, had more roar to their engines. They were flying fast. He turned to shout this observation to Fournier when he heard the rattle of machine gun fire and the ground around them started to erupt. Men screamed as the area was strafed by gunfire from the attacking German planes. Russell threw himself off the bike and scrambled towards the trunk of the tree, pulling and dragging at Fournier. They collapsed against the trunk and Russell threw his arms over his head as bullets ricocheted in the branches above them. One large shattered branch fell and a large splinter of wood drove into the back of his hand.

He had no time to give his wound any attention. From the sound of the engines Russell knew that the planes were circling around for another attack. He grabbed at Fournier and shouted at him.

"Move, move." But the officer seemed stunned and unable to comprehend what Russell was saying. Russell was trying to drag him to the other side of the tree when two soldiers dived in on top of them, both of them screaming, and then the bullets came again. Russell was struggling to free himself from the soldier who had landed on top of him, who was also floundering to get to his feet, when he suddenly slumped like a dead weight and Russell could not move. The planes came around three more times and it was some minutes after the skies were quiet before Russell was able to release himself from underneath the dead soldier. The soldier on top of Fournier was also dead.

Russell managed to sit Fournier against the tree. For a while they remained silent, too shocked to think until the pain in Russell's hand penetrated the fog of his mind and he looked at his wound. In the melee the shard of wood had come out of his hand, leaving a gaping jagged hole, but it was not bleeding very much. He took a kerchief from the neck of the soldier on the ground next to him and tied it around his hand. He could make a fist and move all his fingers, so he knew the wound was only to his flesh, no tendons were severed. He had got off lightly. He was shocked to see blood all over his legs and started to examine himself for further wounds until he realised it was not his blood. He turned to Fournier.

"Are you hit, are you hurt?" Russell asked. It was impossible to tell as Fournier's legs were also covered in blood. His own or the other dead soldier, Russell did not know.

"Yes, yes my leg."

Fournier had been shot twice in the thigh, but luckily the bleeding was relatively slight, with no arterial bleed. He was obviously in pain and Russell was concerned that he might pass out on him. He gave Fournier some water and propped against the tree they started to take in the scene around them. There were bodies scattered everywhere. The advance seemed to have stalled. He could hear the engines of the tanks, but they were not moving as their paths were cluttered by bodies.

"We need to get the medics, and you need a doctor. Can you stand if I help you? I'll fetch the bike."

Russell stood up and dusted himself off and then put a hand against the tree to steady himself. His legs were shaking. The motorbike was on its side and it took Russell all his strength to pull it up and put it on its stand. It looked unscathed, but that did not mean it was going to start.

Russell helped Fournier to stand on his good leg and he half hopped and hobbled to the bike, leaning on Russell for support and then clambered on board behind him. But when Russell kicked the bike to start it Fournier lost his seat and fell off.

"Wait till I've started it, and then climb on," Russell shouted, and after the fourth kick the engine burst into life. He had only had two driving lessons, but remembered enough of the fundamentals to head back to their camp and straight to the hospital tents, where chaos now reigned. He deposited Fournier and then headed back to catch up with the advance attack party, but he met most them returning, in retreat. He stopped in the area where they had suffered their own attack and set to work helping to organise the collection of the wounded and then later in the day, the dead. He sat for a while with the two dead soldiers under the tree and promised them he would write to their families. He noted their names and regimental details, but did not detach either of their dog tags. In his letters they would be heroes, and for him they were, they had shielded him from death.

As darkness settled on his long and harrowing day, life had never felt more precious to him. He was one of the last to arrive at the dressing station for treatment.

The statistics were bad and continued to be high for the next couple of days, but Russell was moved away from the front.

His bandaged hand had him included in the casualty list, but after a few stitches he considered himself able to work. The number of casualties, over 7,000 by the end of the third day of fighting, was a major concern to Pershing and hospital facilities were clearly inadequate. Russell's new posting was directing logistics to supply the medical teams and offer translations where required.

Despite the protracted battles, after a few days good news started to filter through. The tide had turned: the Germans were being pushed back. The Americans were even being hailed as heroes by the French for their support in driving the enemy out of the salient. More greenhorns had battle honours.

Russell enjoyed the camaraderie of the medics but he did not like the news he was picking up from them about the number of soldiers who had died in transit camps in the States. They were dropping like ninepins, from the influenza infection, which was now storming its way across the Atlantic to Europe. In his next letters home and to Marion he shared his concerns, but on rereading his letter, it read like a list of instructions, and no different from what she would expect to receive from her mother. His handwriting was poor due to his bandaged hand.

> Wear a mask at all times Marion if you nurse these patients, but keep away from them if you can. Disinfect yourself before you go home and get yourself treated quickly if you develop any symptoms at all. The doctors here are very worried, and we will be significant numbers of men down.

Before posting these sentences were cut out of his letter by the censors: no word of weakness was to be allowed through. Marion received none of his advice or caution.

Bachelor House, November 1918

The war was over.

Three more officers had died that day. It made Marion angry. And frightened. The patients had died of influenza and she had not been home for over two weeks. All staff and patients had been quarantined at the hospital. Their medical masks had arrived only that morning, and were much lighter to wear than the makeshift scarves they had been tying over their faces. She was worried for, and missing, Alain, but the good news was the villages were clear, so far. The outbreak was just at Bachelor House, brought in by a new patient.

Marion had been unlucky that the outbreak had occurred on her shift. The nursing staff off duty had been forbidden access to the hospital, and those working were spread thinly and were tired. The illness struck hard and fast. Marion was used to spotting the early signs of infection in patients, but with this illness symptoms were often only visible a few hours before the end. Just the day before two of her patients had complained of sore throats and feeling shivery at breakfast, by lunchtime they were coughing violently, by teatime gasping for every breath, and by evening they were dead. It was the most vicious and rapidly developing type of pneumonia that the doctors had ever seen and it was highly infectious. But the mystery was that not every victim died, and some did not catch it.

She had spent two nights nursing matron who succumbed to the illness within hours of tending the first officer who died.

She had been very ill, but appeared to have come through her crisis. Two nights of bone-shuddering delirium, hacking coughs, and sweats had left her hollow-faced, pale, and so weak she was unable to stand; but she had avoided death's door. So far at least.

The experience of being confined to the hospital was stultifying. News came in each day with fresh vegetables, but it was easy to feel forgotten and out of touch with what had quickly become labelled "out there". They had all been taking in news of the planned armistice when the sickness struck. Marion was dejected at missing out on the celebrations: the streets of London had been crowded with revellers dancing with each other in the streets. The toast they raised at the hospital on the evening of the eleventh had been muted, the loss of those who had survived battles, and then succumbed to the "flu" sat heavily with them.

Marion wanted to join the London crowds, but the eleventh was not her day off, so had intended to attend the local festivities at the weekend, until thwarted by this confinement. Her last conversation with her family had been about the end of the war. Her father had been surprisingly circumspect about the celebratory air.

"It is only a ceasefire that is being arranged," he had said. "We don't know yet whether the Germans can be trusted to turn tail and go home." His sober words had dampened her mood at the family breakfast table.

"No more shooting, no more deaths from eleven o'clock on the eleventh. It can't come too soon," Marion's mother had volunteered. "The soldiers can all come home. James Baxter will be released from prison camp, won't he Bernard?"

"My dear, I have no idea of what will happen, but I cannot imagine when the final whistle blows they all throw down their rifles and walk home, or throw open the doors of the prisons, just yet."

But that was exactly what Marion had imagined. When she heard that talks, rather than more battles, were driving the war to a conclusion she had thought Russell would be back with her by the end of the following week at least. In his last letter he had described his duties away from the fighting and she had been relieved to know that he was safe. Provided he kept away from the influenza.

"How is matron today?" Marion was jolted by the doctor's question. She had stepped into the staff kitchen to make a pot of tea and give herself a rest, but when the doctor startled her she had been staring into space, oblivious of her surroundings, too little sleep taking its effect. She answered automatically and began mashing the pot.

"Oh, yes, she seems fine, sleeping when I last looked in. Her breathing is regular. Shallow, but not rasping, like some."

"Looks like she might pull through then. There is no logic to who this damned thing takes. Is there one in the pot for me?"

"Yes, yes, of course. I'll pour one. Do sit down, you look done in."

Marion had only had a passing acquaintance with Doctor Brown before the quarantine as most of his work was conducted on the second floor. Older than the rest of the medical team, with grey hair and gnarled hands, she wondered at his stamina. His soft manner made him easy company for all the nurses.

"As do you, Nurse Drake. Don't let me interrupt your break. Close your eyes if you need a rest. Have you heard that we are to be relieved?"

"Relieved? How? When?"

"Don't know the details yet, but thank goodness. We all need a break. Apparently we have to remain here in the staff quarters for a couple of days to make sure we are clear, and then we can go to our homes. I can't imagine how they coped in those field hospitals day after day. Relentless."

"Yes, I heard from Doctor Ambrose, now and then. His

letters were always full of crises: short of supplies, or beds and too many patients. But he was saving lives."

"And now we are losing them. Damned rotten luck. Excuse my language, nurse."

"We are doing all that we can, and you could do no more than you have done."

"Yes, well, kind of you to say, but it never feels enough when they die. Are you feeling all right? Apart from bone weary, no symptoms?"

"No," Marion touched the back of her chair, "touch wood. But I smell like a bottle of disinfectant."

"Makes a change for me from burning rubber." Doctor Brown rubbed his hands over his eyes and face.

"Have you been having success, with your ECT treatments?" Marion asked.

"Some, some are quietened. In my philosophical moments I think of the nervous system as the barometer of the soul and these poor souls have been to hell and back. Those memories are hard to expunge, and I'm afraid we dull too much of the mind in the process."

"That's what Doctor Ambrose says."

"Does he indeed?"

"He prefers encouraging his patients to talk. Oh, I'm sorry. I didn't mean any criticism," Marion apologised.

"None taken. It is well known that there are almost as many views on treatments as there are doctors. We know so little about the mind. We are all stumbling around in the hope that we can find a cure, or something that will help. At least we aren't just locking them up in bedlam and throwing away the key. They deserve much more than that. We just have to hope that now the war is over they are not overlooked; they might need treatment for years."

Marion took her cup to the sink to rinse it out and he stood up and brought his over to her.

"It just breaks my heart to think of these officers who survived the fighting with terrible injuries, and were so close to recovery and home, to then lose them to this illness. How much more suffering can be handed out to people?" Marion picked up a tea towel.

"Life is cruel, of that we can be sure," Doctor Brown agreed.

"It is the randomness of death that is cruel." Marion stacked the cups ready for the next break.

"Lieutenant Skelton was telling me," the doctor said, "that it was only when he stopped fearing death that he felt able to lead his men over the top. He felt invincible and invisible to the enemy. Proved wrong when the bullet hit him, of course."

"And what now, does he have it?" Marion asked.

"No, no signs of it in him."

"Yet," Marion said with a deep sigh of exhaustion. The relief team could not arrive too soon.

When the relief team took over, Marion slept for twelve hours, woke to eat some bread and soup, and then slept for a further six hours. Her first question was to ask if matron was well and she was greatly relieved to hear of her recovery. She could vaguely recall having her temperature taken, but all was well with her and after the prescribed two days of rest she, along with the rest of the staff, were allowed to go home. Alain ran down the drive to meet her.

"He knew you would be back today. He refused to go to Sunday school. He has been saying 'Mummy coming' all morning." Nanny was out of breath from chasing after him. Marion swept Alain up in her arms. With tears pouring down her face she hugged him to her, until he wriggled to be put down.

"It's lovely to see you, miss. I couldn't hold him back. You look exhausted."

"I have done nothing but sleep for the past two days," Marion said as she took his hand and walked towards the house, "but it's wonderful to be home, for a few days at least. Now, young man, you and I have a lot to catch up on while I have been away. Are you going to tell me what you've been doing?"

Alain's chatter accompanied them all the way back to the house and up the staircase to the nursery. Marion could not stop touching him and after a couple of shrugs he seemed to give up and let her keep a hand on him. To Marion he seemed to have grown taller in the weeks they had been apart. His hair was longer, his thick blonde curls falling almost to his shoulders. He sounded very sure of himself with everything he told her and became very excited when he showed her his pictures; there was quite a pile of them, and then he gave her her post. There were two letters from Russell and one from Doctor Ambrose, one from Sister Wilkins and another in a hand she was not familiar with. This one she opened first. It was an invitation from Mr. and Mrs. Baxter to Lieutenant James Baxter's homecoming party. Marion saved her other letters to read later. For now being back with Alain was enough.

"Grandmama's coming," Alain said as he looked towards the door.

"No, she wouldn't come up here," Marion said and pulled him into a hug.

"Oh yes, miss," Nanny said, "your mother has been here a great deal, reading stories and watching him draw."

"My mother, here?" Marion was incredulous.

"Don't look so surprised, Marion," her mother said as she walked into the room. "And welcome home. We have been very anxious for your well-being. I am pleased you are out of that place and safely home, very pleased indeed. Your father is downstairs, don't keep him waiting, dear."

Marion could not recall her mother using a term of endearment with her since her childhood and was quite taken aback.

"And I am pleased to find you all well, with none of the illness here," she said with a smile as she stood and moved to pass her mother. Her mother put out a hand to touch her arm.

"Thank you for the time you have spent with Alain, Mother. You must have been a great comfort to him," Marion said.

"Oh no, Marion, you have it all wrong. I wasn't comforting him, he was the one telling me you were all right."

Marion went to find her father. He was in his study and he rose to greet her. She flung herself into her father's arms and allowed herself to shed a tear as they held each other tight.

"I am sorry for giving you all a terrible time," she said when they pulled apart. "But for once it was not of my choosing."

"Not that anyone could have kept you away from the hospital when the emergency broke out, of that I am sure," he said as they sat themselves down.

"I don't know, Papa. This is real. It is the most horrible thing I have seen. We must all take precautions here, and you must stop visiting the sick immediately."

"You know I can't stop doing that."

"You must," Marion urged him. "If there is the slightest chance that someone brings the infection to the village, no one must visit them. That is the way it passes around, it is highly contagious."

"We'll see, we'll see. There is no news of it around here, but the congregation was smaller today. It's in the newspapers, the encouragement to stay at home and not gather with others. Good job the armistice celebrations are behind us or they would have been damp squibs. Not that I was for them anyway."

"Oh, Papa, we have to celebrate that the war is over," Marion said, "even if more people are dying now from influenza. This is black humour from our God. Survive the war to face a plague."

"Don't lay this one at His feet, Marion. As far as I am concerned He kept you protected and safe at that hospital."

"I am sure carbolic soap had something to do with that." Marion and her father were laughing when her mother joined them, with Alain in tow.

"What are you doing downstairs, young man?" Marion asked him as he rushed to her for another hug.

"I thought he might like to join us at the table for luncheon today," her mother said. "Your return is a special occasion after all."

"We mustn't make too much of it, Mother. I will have to go back to the hospital in a few days."

"Yes, well, all the more reason we all share a meal together today. Shall we go through?"

Alain's manners were impeccable at the table. Marion was delighted and touched to see how her mother offered to cut his food for him and place napkins either side of his plate to catch any remnants that he dropped. He did not fidget; his only interruption was to giggle twice at something he found funny about his vegetables, but he did not say what this was and they did not ask.

"Did you see your letters, Marion?" her mother asked as she passed Marion more vegetables.

"Yes, thank you. I haven't opened them all yet, but I did see an invitation from the Baxters. Is James home already? How wonderful for them." Marion saw a look pass between her parents.

"No, James is not home yet, and his mother and I have exchanged words about the gathering she is organising," her mother replied.

"Not home: then why the party? Isn't it a bit premature?" Marion looked at her father and her mother.

"My thoughts entirely, and as your father pointed out, even if he does get home, he may not actually want a party. A POW camp is no picnic apparently. She is getting too far ahead of herself, but won't be told."

"It is not a good time to be bringing people together anyway. All the advice is not to mingle. Perhaps she can be encouraged to postpone it," Marion said.

"I rather hoped you would talk to her, Marion. She has always had a soft spot for you, and I know she still favours you for James." Mrs. Drake raised her hand to silence the remark that she anticipated would come. "If you would speak to her, she might listen. The party is only a way of creating a diversion for herself while she waits for news of James."

"Yes, of course I will. I can go under the pretext of advising them on some sanitary arrangements to fend off this infection, and there are precautions I would like us all to use here, and Evelyn too when she returns from her in-laws."

Marion explained about the soapy mix she wanted to have by the front and back doors to the house, but when she began to describe the washing routines she wanted everyone to follow, including sluicing inside noses, her mother asked her to stop until they were finished their meal.

"William is giving out cigarettes to all his staff at the house. Apparently the smoke can reduce the risks."

"I think I would trust soapy water more," Marion said. "I was telling Father he must stop visits to the sick, Mother."

"And would you listen if we told you not to return to the hospital? I thought not," her mother said, as Marion shook her head. "We all have our calling, Marion."

Marion only allowed herself to open her post when Alain had fallen asleep, and she read them in an order that saved the best for last. Elizabeth Wilkins's letter was about her campaign to have Edith's body returned to England and she was seeking support from Marion to write to the British government and to Hugh Gibson. If they had the Americans behind them

Elizabeth was sure it would happen. Marion would use her rest days to reply and would think about her requests. She still deeply resented the government for not saving Edith and the thought of begging them for help sat heavily with her. She wondered just how many families would try to have their loved ones returned from the foreign fields in which they had fallen. The government had already vetoed this: all dead military personnel were to remain buried in foreign soil. Although entirely practical, in the face of such overwhelming national loss and grief the government stance was pilloried as heartless, and Marion worried as to where the comfort for the bereaved was to come from. She knew her aunt was desperate to bring Jack's body home, and Marion could understand her concern that his soul would remain unsettled until he was once again embraced by the family, but despite her uncle's money and connections he had failed to retrieve Jack for his wife and she was aware their wound remained raw.

Doctor Ambrose's letter made her weep with his descriptions of soldiers being wounded or killed right up to the final hour of the war. He also said they were holding their breath to see if the ceasefire held. No one trusted the Germans to keep their word, even though there was evidence of them pulling out. He had taken an excursion to the front line and beyond and was horrified by the trail of destruction caused by the fighting, with scarred landscapes, towns and villages in rubble and rudimentary crosses marking graves at every road junction.

"When I consider the scale of the fighting, stopping even one man from bleeding to death seems an ineffectual contribution. This war has been a numbers game. Luckily 'your' Americans came good and the Germans did the sums and withdrew. Some say they are regrouping, but our men are hot on their tails, pushing their retreat, without a shot being fired. Hopefully my work will quieten down now, from the wounded at least, but we have had some nasty cases of influenza here; it took out half the men from one corps. A friend who is returning to England will post this for me, the only way of avoiding the censors. They have kept the statistics hush-hush. Keep writing to the same address. I'm not going anywhere for a while, it would seem. The men are straining to get back. The volunteers think their job is done and want the next train home; some are refusing to accept any more orders. They can turn into quite a rabble when roused. I can see some tough weeks ahead."

Russell's letter turned those weeks into months in one short sentence.

"There has been no let-up from Black Jack. The men continue to train and we are still operating as if at war, just no triggers are pulled and all we see are the backs of the German Army as they head home. Pershing would like to deliver the killer blow and quash the invaders and is champing at the bit to do this. No luxuries for us, and the weather is bitterly cold. The mood is hangdog and home seems a long way away for the men. We won't start shipping men back until next year, and only then if there is no trouble. I hadn't thought past the fight, but operations here will take as long to dismantle as they did to build. I will be here six months, at least. Please wait for me."

Marion felt her heart sink. *Six months. Another six months, at least another six months.* The thought made her feel out of sorts, but she knew no sympathy would come her way: at least her man was safe and would be returning. The latest count was that over seventy men from the Amersham and Missenden area would never be seen again. The roll call was read every Sunday in church. Horatio seemed to have no idea when he would be back either. The end of the war, if that was what it was, seemed something of an anticlimax and Marion was pleased to have missed the celebrations, which now seemed premature.

The fear of influenza oppressed and constrained her rest days. She worried for Alain, and decided that he must not go to Sunday school or the village until this local outbreak had passed. She would have to find other ways of keeping him occupied. *Perhaps it was time for him to learn his letters.*

Letter writing dominated her days. She replied to Elizabeth and wished her well for her campaign, but could not find it in her heart to write cordially to the government on the subject of Edith, so thought it best she wrote only to Hugh. Her letter to Horatio was light, apart from when she wrote of the deaths from influenza at the hospital, and she even relayed some sluice room stories to make him laugh. Her mood with Russell was different. Her future was tied with his, and yet his, and therefore hers, seemed to be in limbo because of the army. *How much longer?* She was tired of waiting and found it hard to keep the tone of her letter upbeat and not let her disappointment at his delay seep onto the pages. *Think of him, Marion, and not yourself.* She told him she was missing him and wanted him home, but what she really wanted was for them to be able to get on with their lives, free to make choices, and to be released from the parochial nature of a village community.

The world was changing for women. Marion wanted to expand her horizons, and was impatient for her own circumstances to change. Everyone had stopped making plans while the war rolled on year after year, but now she could be on the brink of something new and was irked to be held back.

She determined to work at Bachelor House for as long as it remained a hospital, but after that, if Russell had not returned, she had no idea what would be next.

Marion signed off her letter to Russell with all her usual endearments, hiding her frustration as best she could.

1919

Bachelor House, Spring 1919

"Do you want to tell me what happened?" Marion asked. She had positioned herself by the side of the bed in the soft glow that came from his bedside lamp. The ward was quiet in the evening. It was unusual for Marion to be at the hospital so late and she was not used to the shadows that formed in the corners of the room and the arcs of yellow that lit each patient. The dusky light of the room invited intimacies and she had stayed back to encourage James to talk.

"Nothing happened. Nothing at all. Nothing. Day after endless empty starving day when nothing happened." Lieutenant Baxter turned his head away from her.

Marion waited, but he said no more. Doctor Ambrose, recently returned from France, had warned her it might take time for him to open up.

"All that one needs is patience, Marion. Coax his story out of him and his appetite for life will return. He's acutely depressed but his nerves are strong. Not like some of the other poor buggers, excuse me."

Marion caught his eye as he apologised for his choice of words, and they both smiled.

"Don't mind me, I've heard much worse," Marion assured him and had to stop herself from laughing.

"I'm sure you have, but I certainly don't want to make it a habit! You're family friends of his aren't you? He'll relax more with you. Spend time with him but don't rush him. Let him know you are there to listen. Perhaps stay behind one evening. He'll let it out soon enough."

James Baxter had arrived home from Germany the previous week, unannounced and emaciated. And had barely spoken since. Mrs. Baxter had been anxiously waiting for news of him since the war had ended but, other than learning that most prisoners of war had been released, no specific news of James had reached them before he turned up. At her wits' end she had turned to Marion who, after talking to Doctor Ambrose had organised his admittance to Bachelor House. With no outbreaks of flu for some months, and fewer soldiers, they had spare capacity. Matron had put him in one of Marion's wards.

Now, suppressing her desire to provoke a response she waited for James to speak again. But he was lost in his thoughts.

I look at my men. We are all nervous. The mayor of Bavay, Monsieur Mercier, has just handed us over to the German Kommandant who is shouting at him in German and appears furious. I can't follow what is being said. Our plan to surrender in the grounds of the hospital, and through the local official, was supposed to safeguard us from any German reprisals, but this officer is obviously very angry. The mayor turns to speak to us. He is the only man present in civilian clothes, and he's rattled. He dabs at the sweat on his brow with a large white handkerchief and turns to me.

"He wants to know where you've been sheltering. He doesn't believe you've been living in the forest all these months without help. He wants to know who has been feeding you. He doesn't like it that you crept into the town under the noses of his guards. He's very angry that his enemy can hide from him. It's good there are so many of you, twenty is too many for him to shoot, I hope. But I fear my days are numbered; he will make an example of me."

"But he can't harm you. That's not right," I protest.

"What is right has nothing to do with it. They are the ones with the guns and they make the rules."

The mayor falters as he says this, and is abruptly interrupted by a shout from the Kommandant who gesticulates that he should follow him. When he is gone the soldiers guarding us indicate that we should sit on the ground with our arms on our heads, which, after some shuffling, we manage. I soon feel the damp ground through my coat. It is a cold November night in 1914 and my breath is visible in the night sky.

"What's going to happen, sir?"

Samuel Elliot is sitting next to me whispering when the guard turns the other way. We had been camping in the Forest of Mormal, in the south-west corner of Belgium, trapped behind enemy lines since the battle of Mons in August, and had relied heavily on local help. Aristocrats, Reginald de Croy and his sister Marie orchestrated our supply of food through a network of help. Two of the couriers, Jacqueline and Isabelle, had taken great risks for us. I was in love with Isabelle. The German searches had extended their coverage and the de Croys no longer considered it safe for us to continue in hiding. Better that we all surrender than be shot in the woods. Reginald had made the arrangements but none of us had anticipated this hot-headed response from the newly-installed German authorities.

"I have no idea. We'll have to wait and see." As Elliot's officer I was sorry I couldn't offer more.

"If it's a nice day tomorrow we could take a walk in the grounds?" Marion interrupted his thoughts, without expecting a response. "It would be good to take some regular exercise.

You've been cooped up for the war and need to build up your strength. Get yourself dressed after breakfast and I'll be along by eleven o'clock. I hope you have a good night's sleep. And make sure you eat your breakfast."

Marion left his bedside to go back home. Her mother would want to give Mrs. Baxter any news of his recovery. The only good news was that he was eating.

We don't sit on the ground for long. Orders come through and we are marched along the empty streets of Bavay. I would prefer to have our departure witnessed, as I have no idea where we are being taken. Perhaps it will be to the woods and a firing squad after all. No one speaks. The tramp of our boots is the only sound that disturbs the dark night.

"But you don't have to go with them. You're an officer," Isabelle had said. "The de Croys will hide you and get you to Brussels. You can return to England. I can come to Brussels with you. Don't surrender, after all this time. Don't just give up and hand yourself over. They might shoot you."

"They are less likely to shoot my men if there is an officer with them."

I now doubted the wisdom of this. What if these Germans really have rewritten the rules of warfare and plan to execute us? And these are not even my men, in a regimental sense. A ragbag of soldiers caught behind enemy lines after the first incursions of the war. But we have survived together and, as the only officer among them, they do follow my lead.

Isabelle carried her disappointment stoically as duty rather than passion dictated its terms for me. Isabelle had guided us to the grounds of the hospital for our rendezvous with the mayor and had disappeared into the night with only the whisper of a goodbye. Our parting, and private embraces, had been earlier at the home of the de Croys.

We come to a stop on the edge of a wood. The soldiers at

the rear bumped into the ones who had halted. There was flurry of nervous whispering.

"Where are we, sir?"

"What's going off?"

"Should we make a run for it?"

I raise my hand to silence them, alert to what might happen next. The German guards appear quite relaxed as they light and share cigarettes among themselves, smoke adding to their steaming breath.

"There's a railway line, sir, alongside the trees. Maybe they are shipping us out?" Elliot had moved close to tell me this.

"Perhaps they are. But pass on to each man: if they start shooting, we must rush them. At least some of us can be spared."

"Yes, sir."

But there is no shooting, just a shuffle onto a train that stops to the German guard's flag in the light of dawn. We are herded into a cattle truck, bare boards, with a bucket of water in one corner and an empty one opposite. The train moves off, destination unknown.

Marion was enjoying one of her favourite moments of the day, breakfasting with Alain in the nursery. She had taken to eating with him, as she was typically on her way to work before the rest of the family gathered in the dining room for their own meal. That Marion chose to work continued to be a bone of contention between her and her sister. Evelyn had challenged her on the subject the previous evening when both boys were asleep.

"Mother and I hate it that you are employed in paid work. It is so unnecessary and brings us all down. A gentleman wouldn't approve you know. The war is over, you can stop now."

"Nursing is very necessary." Marion was really not in the mood for a critical exchange with Evelyn and continued to fold Alain's freshly laundered clothes and put them away in drawers. "The war may be over, but the wounded still need care."

"Nursing may be needed, but not by you. Visiting, yes. Mother's ladies' circle attend the local hospital every Wednesday afternoon. It is a tonic for the men. But more than that is demeaning." Evelyn perched on the windowsill and made no effort to assist with the laundry.

"Demeaning! Nursing is a profession of high standing. The world has changed, Evelyn. The world you cling to is in the past."

"It is you who are keeping the wrong company, Marion. In my circles, the ones that you should also frequent, no gentleman would contemplate his wife working. And I don't expect your American would view it any differently. Where is he by the way?"

"Still in France. Decamping takes a time." *Decamping is taking far too long.*

"What does Nanny have planned for you today?" Marion asked Alain as she buttered his toast. "Did she tell you yesterday?"

"Yes, on our walk today Anthony and I are to find five things that begin with the letter eff."

"The letter f, umm, I wonder what you can find."

"Well, one is easy, and that's a flower, and if I can find one, a fir cone."

"Yes, and perhaps a fungus."

"What's a fungus?"

"A mushroom, or a toadstool."

"That's not an eff. That's a muh or a tee."

"No, not individually, but all together they are known as fungus, or perhaps it's fungi, anyway it's the type of thing they are."

"Nanny might not let me have that."

"No, perhaps not."

"And then we have to draw them."

"Oh, that will be fun. You paint such good pictures. Save them for me to see this evening."

The walls of the nursery were covered in his artwork. She could always tell his from Anthony's. Alain's scenes always contained the sun with its rays beaming down onto one of his stick people.

"All finished?" she asked. "Wipe your face and then you'll be ready for Nanny. She'll be here soon. It's time for me to go."

"I hope the sun shines on you today, Mummy." He smiled at her.

"So do I. I'm taking one of my patients for a walk in the grounds today and he needs to feel the warmth of the sun."

"I'll draw a picture of him with the sun. Is he tall?"

"No, not particularly, he's the same height at me. He's a horseman, like my cousin Jack was. It's easier on the horses if the riders aren't too big."

"I can't draw a horse." Alain frowned.

"Leave the horse out then. Put him in a garden with me on a sunny day. I can take it and show him tomorrow."

"Let's sit here where we can feel the sun on our faces. That was a good walk."

Marion sat down and waited for James to join her on the garden bench with the best view over the Missenden valley. The rolling hills, covered with fields of crops and patchworked by lines of trees, were just starting to take on a colour. More of her time now was spent outdoors with her patients. Even though the war had ended the manorial home continued to support the work of the doctors. The therapies had become less forceful now the race to return able-bodied men to the front was over. Marion was convinced that all many of the men with mental scars needed was encouragement to talk, suet pudding, and time to heal.

"I would dream of days like this. Sitting out, fed, and free." Marion was jolted by his words. Their walk had been in silence. James stretched out his legs and put his hands behind his head.

Marion noticed just how thin he was. His face was gaunt, his eyes deep-set. Stretched out beside her she could see the tautness of the sinews holding his frame in place. He needed building up.

"Were you shut up all the time?" Marion asked and then bit her tongue for rushing him. To her surprise he answered.

"No, not all the time."

"Will you tell me about it?" Marion realised she had gone too fast with her question when he shifted his position and folded his arms in front of his chest. He didn't reply and stared ahead.

"Where do you think we're going, sir?"

"I don't know, Samuel," I shrugged. "If they were going to shoot us they would have done it by now, so I suspect we're on our way to Germany as prisoners."

"No more action for us then. Not that I'm sorry. I only joined the Territorials back home in London to liven up my life a bit. Bank clerking is a bit dull. I hadn't expected to be fighting for real."

"I'd rather see action than all this sitting around," I said.

"No, it's been a bit too lively for me, sir. I'd rather be at home with my Rosie. First littl'un is on its way."

"At least we have our battle scars from Mons."

"We were lucky with our nurses. Those lasses, Isabelle and Jacqueline, saved my leg, I'm sure."

"Yes, they were great girls. Great girls. We were very fortunate."

We have been on the train for two days and one night, so far. Through gaps in the slats of wood that make up the side of the carriage I watched the countryside pass by. On the first day I had been shocked by the devastation I saw across Belgium; houses and barns burnt or shelled and German troops seemed to be everywhere. We had been given very little to eat, spoonfuls of black beans and a drop of coffee for most meals. This changed to black bread and raw smoked bacon, tough and hard to chew, when we crossed the border into Germany.

James turned to face Marion and started to talk. He described being turfed off the train at one station and having to sit on the concrete platform while they waited for a new engine. People from the town threw rubbish at them and called them "*swiner*", encouraged by their guards.

"We travelled for three days and nights to get to … well, we didn't know where we were when we arrived. Just pleased to get somewhere at last."

"This was when you were captured and taken to Germany?" Marion asked. She was bursting with questions, but said nothing more and waited, holding her breath. He nodded and continued to describe the tiny separate cells they were put in for a night and then marched to a prison camp the next day. It was full of French people, about forty thousand he soon discovered; all trapped in Germany at the start of the war. There were a couple of hundred people to a hut.

"We stayed together in one corner, and put down the straw bedding we were given, hessian thin; it was a sack with a couple of handfuls of straw inside; a piece of blanket, already worn, and a small bowl filled with watery soup, but that was still welcome."

Marion acknowledged a wave from two nurses who walked by, pushing a bath chair between them, always difficult on the uneven paths. James waited for them to pass before telling her of the abuse they received from the German guards who would hit them with their rifle butts whenever they could. He paused again, this time distracted as a patient walked past using the arm of an orderly for support. Their progress was slow. Each of his limbs seemed to have a mind of its own, jerking in different directions.

"Is there any cure?" James murmured.

"Too soon to say. The electric shock treatment settles some, but not all."

"Puts me to shame, what some of these buggers went through. They fought the war whilst I, I did nothing. And here I am, taking your time and attention because, what, I feel sorry for myself?" His tone was bitter.

"Now James, you are being very harsh on yourself. You have been through an ordeal too. You were almost starved for four years. That can't be brushed aside by the shake of your head."

"My father thinks it can, and should be. And if I'm honest, so do I." All of a sudden he looked close to tears and Marion waited for him to compose himself.

"But your mother understands," Marion said softly. "She can see that you have suffered. Anyone can. You look haunted and are so thin. You really must eat."

"And what was it all for? What was the point of the war?" Now there was anger in his voice.

"To stop the Germans, wasn't it, and we did that," Marion said.

"At what cost? And I must not take up more of your time." James stood up abruptly and turned away from her, looking out over the valley.

"Oh no, you must take up my time," Marion pleaded. "I'd much rather be talking to you than emptying bedpans. Dr. Ambrose thinks you will respond to some dedicated attention, so please don't turn your back on me, or I shall be deemed a failure. And your mother would never forgive me."

"I'm the failure, not you." James returned to the bench seat. His shoulders slumped, all agitation gone.

"You didn't fail, you survived. All of you here were so brave."

"Brave? I wasn't brave." James put his head in his hands. "I surrendered."

James said no more. After a few moments he brushed his hand across his eyes, wet with tears and blew his nose, then stood up and they returned to the house in silence. It was the following day before they spoke again.

James watched Marion across the other side of the room as she made Captain Starling more comfortable. James had never heard him speak a word. He knew Starling had received a Military Cross for taking out a machine gun at the Battle of the Somme, but shrapnel later in the war had damaged his brain. It was only his body that had returned from France.

She moved to another bed. Her movements were rhythmic as she tucked in sheets and plumped up pillows. He imagined her moving to music; they were in the old ballroom after all. Marion could be crisp and to the point, but her tone and touch conveyed warmth and a sincerity that, despite their forlorn state, drew patients to her. She was popular and he was pleased to see how much she enjoyed her work. Lost in his thoughts he almost jumped when she approached his bed and spoke to him. She took a piece of paper out of her pocket and unfolded it.

"Alain drew it." Marion was holding a picture up for him to see.

"Alain? Oh yes, excuse me, your ward?" James propped himself up on his elbow.

"Yes, it's of you, sitting in the garden, in the sun."

"Mother did tell me something about him. How old is he?"

"He's four years old, coming on five. He draws well, doesn't he?" Marion sat on the bedside chair as James took hold of the sheet of paper. "The horse isn't very good. He said he couldn't draw horses, but at least he tried."

"That's a horse? Well now you've told me perhaps I can see it's a horse. And who is this? It looks like an angel." Marion caught a brief smile on his face.

"That's me. He was carried away drawing my nurse's uniform. Those are my elbows, not wings. He explained it to me this morning." Marion laughed.

"And that's me on the seat?"

"Yes, he coloured you grey."

"Our battledress was khaki."

"It may well have been but he told me he chose grey because you were sad and had lots of tears inside you."

"You told him I cried, did you? Some soldier I am."

"No, I didn't. I wouldn't. Not that tears are a bad thing, in fact I'm sure a good cry usually does people good. There is no need to feel ashamed of emotion."

Baxter looked at the picture and avoided her eyes.

"He gave me the picture when I arrived home from work. He drew it yesterday morning while he waited for Nanny. He'd almost forgotten about it, more excited to show me his flower and fir cones from his morning walk. He and my nephew were looking for things beginning with f."

"F?" James asked with a frown.

"They are working their way through the alphabet. I can stick the picture up here for you. Or you might think it rather silly?"

"It's not silly at all, and that's a good place for it." He smiled.

Marion pinned it to the side of his bedside cabinet. Each patient had one for personal belongings together with two chairs for visitors and a folded screen for privacy when needed. The ward was now only half full of patients.

"I can look at it and remember the day I made a fool of myself," James said.

"To cry is not foolish, but to pretend you're not hurting is."

"Quite the sage today, aren't we?"

"Words stolen from my father. He's the wise one, not me," Marion replied.

"So you told your father I cried?"

"No, James. I haven't spoken of you to my father. He said that to me when Edith, a friend of mine died a few years back and I was so angry about it. I was too angry to cry. I bottled it up for ages and then one day it all burst out and I cried for weeks. Yesterday's tears were the start for you. There may well be more."

"I'll make sure I'm on my own next time, don't you worry."

"You never need to be on your own. Look at the picture. The sun's rays are coming down on you. Just soak them in and you'll never feel alone."

"More of your father's wisdom?"

"No, Alain's."

"Quite the child prodigy."

"I must get on. I'll pop by later when your mother is here to say hello."

"Good afternoon, Mrs. Baxter. James, did you eat a good lunch?"

"Yes, he told me he had, didn't you, James."

"I can speak for myself, Mother."

"Then do, James, do. It is time for me to go: your father needs the car this evening. I shall tell him you have more colour today. Quite a flush to your cheeks, in fact."

"Are you feeling flushed, James? Do you feel feverish?" Marion was immediately alert.

"No, I do not. It is just Mother being Mother."

"Well, I am leaving you now, dear, in the safe hands of Nurse Drake."

Mrs. Baxter stood, pulled on her gloves, and retrieved her

handbag from the side of her chair. Her frame was petite and she was always perfectly dressed.

"Thank you, Mother, and for your visit. Pass on my regards to Father please, if mention of me won't upset him."

"He wants you strong, James. We all do. You must forgive him his ways." Mrs. Baxter rose from her chair and Marion left the ward with her.

"Do you see any physical difference in him?" Marion asked her as they walked along the corridors to the front entrance. The house was looking tired and the carpet they walked on was threadbare, but the grandeur of the place was there in the height of the rooms and the drapes that bordered each of the floor-to-ceiling windows.

"Yes, I do think he is starting to fill out a little. He was always slim; strong though. It's his lack of energy that concerns me. He is mostly lacklustre: but I do see him perk up when he sees you. I think your ministrations are doing him the world of good; you are quite the tonic for him."

"I am delighted you think so." Marion smiled. "Dr. Ambrose is keen on us devoting our attentions in quite an individual way. He believes it is better to draw out the memories and for the men to learn to live with their fears and grief rather than suppress them. Face them and conquer. It makes more sense to me than firing electric shocks and frying their brains. But, excuse me, I am speaking out of turn. I shouldn't question the treatments. I am sure ECT helps many of the patients here too."

Marion and Mrs. Baxter had reached the top of the steps that led from the front entrance to the drive. Mrs. Baxter raised her hand and her car pulled forward. By the time they reached the last step her chauffeur was out of the car and opening the door for her.

"Dr. Ambrose does sound very forward thinking," Mrs. Baxter said as they descended the steps. "James just needs to get strong and have some quiet for a while. He does enjoy your company, brings him out of himself; stops him being too maudlin. Thank you, Marion for all your attentions. Tell me, is there any truth to the rumour you are engaged?"

"No, stop, please tell me she didn't ask you that. I'm appalled. You must accept my apologies for the bluntness of my mother's approach. She is convinced there is something between us. And if there isn't she wants to know why I am not being more forthcoming. Mothers, really!"

James and Marion were seated on their favourite bench in the garden, after their walk. The house was behind them and the vista of the valley was in front. The day was still and the shadows just starting to lengthen. It was a beautiful day and many patients had been drawn outdoors or shepherded there by orderlies, or taken by the arm by a visitor.

"Oh please don't worry, our mothers are entirely the same, in fact mine is worse. After a first meeting she would know your financial means, social connections, schooling, and army rank without you even being aware that you had been asked a question. She works by stealth."

"Sounds like she would make a good interrogator."

"The best. She could trip up the most consummate liar, I'm sure. I give my mother as little information as possible to go on; it has always been the safest way."

"I know mine means well," James said. "Her view for my happiness is simply to see me married, working with my father again, and carrying a few extra pounds."

"Well, I agree with her on the few extra pounds. You still need to eat more, James."

"But you don't see marriage as the existential answer to life?" James looked at Marion and waited for her answer.

"No, I don't," Marion eventually offered. "It can form a place in a life, but I don't see it as the be-all and end-all, which is the opposite of my mother's ambitions."

"So you're not engaged then?"

"That's exactly how my mother does it." Marion laughed. She wheedles the information out of you. I prefer your mother's direct approach." James grinned.

The silence of the garden was suddenly interrupted by a loud bang. A car that had pulled up at the front of the house backfired. Two men on a bench nearby threw themselves onto the ground, their bodies jerking as if they were having a fit. One began to howl.

"Wait here," Marion said to him and she ran across to the men, arriving at the same time as two orderlies, so she backed away and returned to James.

"What did you say to my mother then?"

"What? Oh, her question. I told her no engagement had been announced."

"What does that mean?"

"It means that I am informally promised, but it is a private matter only. A loose arrangement. I will find out how we stand soon though. He is due back by the summer."

"I thought you were going to say you had an understanding with Dr. Ambrose. He definitely has a sweet spot for you."

"James! You are such a gossip."

"But there is something between you isn't there?"

"Yes, we have worked together for several years now; we understand each other very well."

"You know I mean more than that."

"I know you do, but what is this, an interrogation? Dr. Ambrose and I have a close professional partnership and are friends, and that is all."

James laughed and they sat in silence, but it was an easy silence. Marion was delighted to be working with Horatio again. He had made clear he had returned to Bachelor House because of her and after a few weeks of attempting more he had settled for friendship, but waiting, he told her, for his moment, when she had "that American" out of her system. Marion had waited this long for Russell and was determined to meet him with an open mind and hopefully an open heart.

"And what about you?" she turned to him and asked. "What romantic exploits have you kept from your mother? I'm sure you have some secrets."

"Yes. There was someone. I met her in France."

"And? Her name?"

"Isabelle."

"A pretty name. Is she pretty?"

"No, well, yes, attractive. But no, not pretty, not in the way you are."

James dodged Marion's mock punch.

"She looked very young, quite boyish when I think of it."

"Boyish?"

"Let me say coltish. She hadn't rounded out when I knew her. If she had a few of the sponge puddings they serve here her figure would soon blossom. I am sorry. Not an appropriate conversation. Forgive me."

"It is an entirely appropriate conversation, and look at how your face has lit up. You think a lot of her, don't you?"

"Yes, I do. Well I did; she probably saved my life. She was a brave girl, and we were, well, fond of each other."

"Where did you meet? Do you mind me asking?"

"No, talking about her feels surprisingly good, but she does seem a lifetime away. I met her in 1914. She was one of a group of people who kept soldiers hidden from the Germans. It was chaos after the battle of Mons and many of us were separated from our regiments, left behind enemy lines. Some were injured and were nursed back to health. Rudimentary stuff, but I'm sure she saved many lives and limbs. A number of us hid in houses and barns in her village but when the numbers increased and the German reprisals became more vicious, it was decided that we should move to the nearby forest and camp out there. The conditions were tough. Do you remember that really bad winter? It started so early."

"It wasn't so bad in Brussels," Marion recalled. "Shall we walk some more?"

"The food Isabelle and others brought was our lifeline," James said as he stood at her prompting and walked in step beside her. "And I have to admit her visits became even more of a tonic for me than the food. I wonder what happened to her and where she is now? I heard that many Belgians and French suffered at the hands of the Germans. I only hope she kept safe."

"Perhaps you could write to her and find out, or go and visit?" Marion took his arm.

"I'm not sure I ever knew her surname. I could find the village again and her house, but it was her mother's house, not hers. I think she lived somewhere across the border in France. She was a teacher, or at least learning to be one. Perhaps I could write to the de Croys, they might be able to tell me."

"The de Croys?" Marion said with surprise at hearing a name she knew from Belgium.

"Yes they were the local family that …"

"I know who the de Croys are," Marion interrupted him.

"You do? That's incredible. And it's such a small village that they live in, though their chateau was quite the thing locally. Have you been there too?"

"No, but I know them, I mean I know the name. I met Prince Reginald, just once, such a charming man. I know of his sister, Marie, but I have never met her. The war must have been hard on her. I believe she spent some years in a prison in Germany."

"Oh, no, why? What for?"

"Sad to say, James, but it was for helping soldiers like you. She and many in the escape organisation were exposed. She was tried and sentenced to death, but this was waived and she was given a sentence of ten years in prison. I assume she was released at the armistice. Some were not as lucky as her, I'm afraid."

"Isabelle? Was Isabelle caught? How do you know about this?"

"Because my friend Edith was not so lucky. I don't know about an Isabelle, I can't remember all the names. Perhaps you need to go and find out, James."

"Edith, your friend Edith. You don't mean Edith Cavell do you?"

"The one and same. I was training as a nurse in her establishment in Brussels when the war started."

"Oh my goodness. No wonder you were upset about her. Did you know what she was involved with? Is that why you left?"

"No, it was a bit more complicated than that."

"Too complicated to explain? I may be worn down, but I'm not dim." He stopped walking and faced her.

"No you're not, come on, keep moving, and that's enough about me." Marion picked up her pace and James had to work harder to keep up with her. "Do you think you would you like to see Isabelle again?" she asked.

James pursed his lips. He had not allowed that thought for a while.

"Isabelle? Yes, yes I think I would, and Princess de Croy. How awful that she was in prison, she is far too genteel for such a place."

"I am sure she would be able to help you locate Isabelle, if anyone can. Why don't you plan a trip over there? There is no threat from the Germans now. Many people are travelling there, searching for loved ones."

"I read in the newspaper we are still finding and burying bodies in the battlefields."

"But it's safe now and Isabelle might be waiting for you."

"Waiting for me? No, I can't imagine that. Our relationship could only ever be short-lived. We made no promises to each other, just enjoyed a romance. She probably hasn't given me a second thought, but thoughts of her stayed with me through many a miserable day." Baxter sounded wistful.

"I want to hear more about the camps."

"Another day," James said. "It was men at their best and at their worst in prison. When basic instincts come to the fore they quickly devour our parlour-room ways. *'Manners maketh the man'* is my mother's mantra. Not where I've been, let me tell you. Not where I've been."

Bachelor House, Spring 1919

James was dressed and waiting for her when Marion arrived on the ward the next day. She gave him the piece of rolled paper she was carrying. It was a picture from Alain for James.

"Will you give this to the grey man today, Mummy?"
"Of course I will, what is it?"
"It's a picture."
"Oh, he'll like that I am sure. Tell me about it."

As with most children, Alain's thoughts did not easily transfer onto the page and sometimes it was only the position of the sun that showed her which way up she should hold his pictures. This one though was much easier to understand: a ship at sea, and a grey man on the deck, the sun's rays pouring down on him.

James was on his feet as soon as he saw her. He took the rolled paper from her and, without looking at it, put it on the chair he had vacated and asked if they could walk. Marion was delighted. She had never seen him so keen to be outside. The day was clear but there was a slight chill to the breeze. She went to collect her cloak.

"I have just been given a message from matron. Your mother will be visiting this afternoon," Marion said.

"I think I have become her worthy cause, now that the war effort is behind her. No more bandages to roll."

"James, that is unfair! Your mother is very concerned about

you, as well as being delighted to have you back. My sister Beatrice has not let her husband out of her sight since he came back. Not that he can go far; he lost a leg."

"Oh, poor chap. At least wounds are heroic."

"I think he would rather have his leg than his medal."

"I am very sure he would. Sorry, I just feel like such a fraud. The war passed me by whilst I fought petty battles for food and shelter."

"You make too light of your struggles, James. We both know that many, too many, did not survive the prisoner-of-war camps. The more I hear of them, the more horrified I become, and I am sure you have spared me the worst of the descriptions."

"We had no sanitation, no soap, and little water to wash with. Our food was a watery soup of cabbage or beans, or barley, or black peas, or rotten fish. A loaf of hard bread had to stretch over a week to ten days. That was it. My dentist couldn't believe what had happened to my mouth when I came back."

"You still have a nice smile though."

James smiled self-consciously. "Yes, maybe, but I have no teeth at the back to chew with. We were lousy, had skin diseases. And let's not forget the scarlet fever, typhoid, and whatever else that raged through the camp. Dysentery was commonplace."

"I told you not to say you had it easy. You were underfed, malnourished. Look at how hard you are finding it to put on weight and to feel energetic. It is bound to take time."

"We were always cold, our clothes fell apart on us and the German soldiers cut off most of our buttons so our uniforms, or what was left of them, were held together with bits of string. Almost no one had boots: we had to tie bits of cloth over our feet in winter. Five of my men died before spring came and one who was Irish was moved out of our hut."

"Why? Because he was Irish? Didn't he mix?"

Russell told her of the Germans' attempts to persuade Irish POWs to join them and fight against the British.

"And did they?"

"No, but the Irish took their time deciding and ate many good meals while the Germans tried to convince them."

"But aren't there rules that dictate how prisoners should be treated? The German POWs here were treated royally compared to your experience. Shall we sit here?"

James settled himself and then addressed her question. He explained that the British government apparently sent money over to contribute towards costs, but the benefits didn't reach them and by 1916 they were put to work for their keep. No one came out of the sanatorium alive. There was no treatment; men were just left to die huddled on the floor, crawling with lice.

"No wonder you have nightmares." Marion was unable to suppress a shudder.

"We had a visit once from the American minister, Garard I think his name was. Apparently he kicked up a real stink and there were some improvements. We had two burners put into each hut that winter, but the food didn't get any better. Elliot was great at making cigarettes out of the wood ash. He would swap them for food, it helped keep us alive."

"Where is he now, your friend, Elliot?"

"Samuel, he died." James stood up and kicked at some old fir cones on the ground. "He made it through the whole of the bloody war and then damned well dies from influenza before he reaches home."

"And I'm sure it's not entirely behind us yet."

"It hit the Americans hard. Serves them right for leaving it so late to join the fight. It swept through their transit camps. Poor buggers." James threw himself back onto the seat, his fight gone. "I don't really wish them ill."

"My 'young man' as my mother calls him, when she acknowledges his existence, is American."

"American? Did he fight?"

"Well, he has been in uniform but I am not entirely sure what he has been doing. He always seems very keen to tell me he is all right, whenever one of his rare letters reaches me. No doubt he will tell me when he's back over here in the summer."

"You said you left Brussels in '15. So it's been four years since you've seen him. It is four and a half since I saw Isabelle."

"No, I last saw him in June 1917. We only had a few hours together in '17 when he passed through London on his way to France."

"What's his name?" he asked as they returned to the house.

"Russell, Russell Clark." James enunciated the name slowly. He had just interrupted his mother who was once again extolling Marion's virtues.

"Who is called Russell? What are you talking about, James? Are you listening to me? You just go off into your own world; who is Russell Clark?"

"Her fiancé. Marion's fiancé."

"Ah, I see. The American she hints she is promised to. Now don't let that put you off, James. It is not a public engagement, at least not from what I have gleaned. I was more concerned about a whisper from her sister Evelyn of an understanding between her and Doctor Ambrose."

"Mother," James was shaking his head, "please, let this idea go."

"But James …"

"Mother, enough. And anyway there is another woman I want to talk about."

"Here? At the hospital? Who is she?"

"No, not here. She is someone I met in France."

"In France? Why haven't you said anything before? Is she someone special?"

"I thought so at the time, but it was only a brief encounter and not in normal circumstances."

"Who are her family?"

"Stop right there, Mother. This is where it stops." James was struggling to keep his voice calm. "Pedigree is for the horses at the stables, not for me. I am not interested in house parties and the inane chatter of the social circuit. I spent the last four years with the sort of men that muck out our stables and I have more time for them than some of my so-called class."

"Let's not fight, dear. Tell me about her, your mystery woman from France."

"I want to do better than that. I want to introduce you to her: the woman who saved my life. Will you come with me to find her? To France?" James picked up his mother's hand and held it.

"To France? To France? Well, I ... how on earth would we get there? You're being ridiculous."

"By boat." James let go of her hand, opened his bedside cabinet and pulled out a roll of paper. He unrolled Alain's picture that he had found on his chair after his walk with Marion and held it up. By boat."

Marion was starting to fidget. The patient conference had gone on for far longer than she had anticipated and she was aware that James had now been expecting her for the past hour. She had promised him a walk and she had something to ask him. The meeting had been good, full of encouraging reports, but the patients they had been discussing for the last half hour had not involved her, they were not on her ward. If she had not felt so impatient to get to James she could have enjoyed listening to the debate between the doctors. She was in support of Doctor Ambrose and his talking therapies. His approach had worked for James but then unlike some, his nerves had not been shot to pieces. Many were in a sorry state and for these the meeting concluded sedation and ECT were the only treatments. James was on the discharge list, which was also why she needed time with him today. As soon as the meeting finished she hurried to find James.

"You look deep in thought," James said as they walked. "Is everything all right?"

There was such an easy familiarity between them she squeezed his arm and smiled. They had just discussed his discharge and she was pleased that he felt ready to leave.

"Yes, sorry, just making sure we had covered everything about your departure. But there is something I want to ask you today. Edith Cavell's body is returning to England. The Germans refused to release her body during the war and arrangements have just been made to bring her back. Will you come to London with me, to the service at Westminster? I don't think Russell will be back by then, and even if he is I would like you to meet each other. Will you come with me?"

"I would be honoured to accompany you. Is it likely to be a difficult day for you?"

"It will be a very sad day. I couldn't face her memorial service in St Paul's. It was held just weeks after the news of her death reached us here. It was too soon for me. I was consumed with such a rage that they had executed her."

"When is the ceremony?"

"It's in a week's time, May the twenty-second. After the service in Westminster they are taking her body to her home in Norwich."

"Will you want to go on to Norwich too?"

"No. I shall pay my respects in London. That will be enough."

"It will be good to see you before I leave for France."

"So your trip is definitely on?"

"I hope so. My mother is trying to convince my father it is an important part of my convalescence, and that she should come with me. She is trying to smooth the waters between him and me, but I know he is accusing her of molly-coddling me. The truth is he probably doesn't want her making such a trip, doesn't like her to be away from home. He really does have soft insides. Shame the outside is so damned tough."

"That was a sad occasion, very sad. Such a good family," Bernard Drake said as he removed his hat and laid it on the table in the hall. Marion always used the position of his hat as a touch point for whether her father was in the house or out on parishioner duties.

"To bury three at once. It is a tragedy, Papa. What will happen to the little girl? She is the only one of the family left?"

"She has an aunt and uncle in the next village. They were at the funeral and will take her to live with them," Bernard answered Marion.

"But what if she takes the infection with her?" Marion asked.

"There seems to be no rhyme or reason to this disease …" Bernard said.

"And that is why I would not allow the girl to attend the funeral," Marion's mother cut across her husband, "and I really don't think funerals should be held at such times. Bernard, you should not be exposing yourself, or us to such dangers. If this influenza is back, we must pay heed."

"People have to be buried, my dear." Her husband was placatory, but firm.

"Bodies should be burnt to kill the infection. Too many have died across the world from this ghastly influenza already. We do not want more casualties here." Marion's mother pulled off each glove with a flourish to emphasise each pronouncement.

"Have there been more cases at the hospital, Marion?" her father asked her.

"Thankfully not, although several of the patients lost friends to it. They talk of hundreds dying when they were waiting in camps to be demobbed. It seems so utterly unfair to survive the war and then die of this awful condition. James was very upset at the death of his close friend. They had been POWs together. The doctors at the hospital watch for possible symptoms, but I think we all thought it was dying down, until these latest cases. And so local."

"They had been to London. That's where they caught it. A dirty place." Marion's mother led them towards the lounge. "I will call for some refreshment and a lozenge for each of us to take. No, Marion, do not leave us. Your father and I want to talk to you. Come and sit down."

"Oh, I must just go and check on Alain …"

"No, Marion, sit. Please."

Marion judged this was one of the occasions to obey her mother, and that is what this suggestion felt like: an instruction. Marion looked towards her father. She expected him to be noncommittal in his usually distracted way, but he nodded and so she sat in the armchair in front of her parents, who had positioned themselves side by side on the settee.

"We have some news," Marion's mother stated. "Your sister Evelyn wishes to marry."

"That is not news," Marion said.

"Not that she wishes it, perhaps not, but that she now plans to, is."

"Thank you for telling me. I wish her well. I'll go and congratulate her," Marion said and moved forward on the chair to stand up.

"It is not so simple as that," her mother said.

"Why? Is there a problem?" Marion frowned.

"Yes there is. It would appear you are the problem. Please tell her, Bernard."

Marion's mother retrieved a handkerchief from her handbag and patted her nose. Bernard looked at Marion and cleared his throat.

"You see, Marion, the gentleman hasn't yet presented himself to me, and your mother thinks," he stopped and glanced at his wife before continuing, "that is, we think, it is because of your situation. It might possibly be holding him back."

"You mean because I work. Is that deemed to be undermining Evelyn's social standing? Isn't it time to wake up? Some women have the vote already. The world has changed."

"Please don't lecture, young lady," her mother retorted, "and no, we are not referring to the fact that you insist on paid employment. It is your situation as an unmarried woman, with a child. The sniff of a scandal will not go away. No doubt his family have heard of it and have stopped his approach."

"Well, the news of 'my situation' as you call it, didn't deter Mrs. Baxter. She was keen for James to approach you about me."

"Well, why hasn't he?" Her mother said as she raised her arms and dropped her hands back down onto her lap. "Your father would receive him. They are a good family. I consider his mother a dear friend. She put a lot of work into the war effort. As did I." And she looked to her husband for confirmation.

"Yes, dear, you did, noble efforts, and the Baxters are a good lot," he concurred. "The Major trains a good ride. William has had some mounts from him. He's as tough as old boots. Is his son like him?"

"Not by the sound of it. He really suffered in the POW camps. It's a wonder he survived, the little they had to eat. His father sounds impatient for him to recover," Marion said.

"Marion, what exactly are you telling us?" Marion's mother was keen not to have her conversation diverted. "Is James going to approach us? Will you be engaged to him?"

Marion did feel bad about dashing the hopes that had so readily formed in her mother.

"Sorry, no, Mother, we have no affection for each other. Actually that's not true: we have affection as friends, but nothing more. There is no relationship between us of the type you hope for. His thoughts, and I believe heart, belongs to another. He will be heading off to France soon to find her. It's someone he met at the beginning of the war."

"Oh, not another dreamer! Holding out hope for someone from years past. Ridiculous, and just like you. Bernard, you must talk some sense into her, and him too. Where is your American, Marion? Is it him you are still waiting for? Mrs. Baxter must be so disappointed. She had quite convinced herself of a match."

"Have you heard more from Mr. Clark?" Bernard asked. "When is he due to return, and will he be in a position to provide for you?"

"He chose to go to war rather than stick to his studies. The man is a fool if you ask me." Marion's mother now used her handkerchief to fan her face.

"It was me that discouraged him rather too much, my dear," Bernard said.

"Don't worry, Papa, that is in the past now," Marion said, and gave her father a brief smile. "Russell will return this summer and then we shall have the answers to all your questions."

"Will he present himself again, when he returns?" Marion's mother asked.

"I have no reason to think otherwise," Marion said.

"Then can we let it be known that you are engaged. That might be enough to smooth the path for Evelyn."

"Discreetly, yes. I am sure Russell would not have a problem with this."

"Then there is nothing further to be said for now. We look forward to his return."

"I had no idea it was going to be like this," Marion said. She was standing next to a uniformed Lieutenant James

Baxter and they were shuffling forward in a queue of people to enter Westminster Abbey through the west door.

"Do you mean the abbey or the people?" James asked.

"I meant the number of people, but the abbey is very impressive."

"It looks much bigger inside than when you look at it from the street."

"Yes, it's vast," Marion agreed, "and beautiful. I would like to walk around when it's empty."

"It quite feels like a royal funeral today, the way the people have lined the streets. It's extraordinary." Marion nodded and told James she had heard there were people crowding every station platform and railway bridge on the line from Dover to Victoria. Children had been allowed out of school to watch the spectacle.

"Where is she now? The cortege I mean?" James asked.

"Apparently her coffin will be brought to the abbey on a gun carriage. She's getting the lot, military bands and guard of honour."

"Didn't you want to be part of it? You should have a place in the procession."

"That's what Sister Wilkins said when she wrote to me. No, she is there for Edith, that is what matters, and I am in here, that's enough. Elizabeth very kindly organised our seats for us, but I don't want to be part of the show. It's all right for the establishment to own her now, but where were they when her life needed saving? Nowhere. They washed their hands of her. It still rankles with me. I don't want to be part of their charade, thank you very much."

"That's a bit harsh, old girl. Her name means a great deal to many. She has become a symbol."

"Of what?"

"Of fortitude in adversity?"

"What?"

"You know what I mean. Mothers are grateful to the women who helped our boys when they were overseas. In Edith they have a name. She snubbed the Germans and people love that." James looked around. "Look at all the uniforms here. She risked her life for our men. That's what she represents."

"They let her die and then they used her."

They had been shuffling slowly forward, but the queue had stopped moving.

"Oh, look at that." James pointed up to a window where a shaft of sunshine was streaming through, onto a row of seats. "Come on, I bet our seats are over there. Follow me."

They were soon seated and Marion was basking in the sunlight, until her attention was caught by the sight of Queen Alexandra and one of the princesses, Marion thought it was Victoria, being led in by the dean. Faintly, through the west door, she could hear strains of music from one of the military bands approaching the abbey. The music was sombre, a funeral march, she presumed. This was soon interrupted by shouted orders and then a delay until the coffin made its entrance, draped with a Union Jack and topped by a cross of red roses trimmed with white. Marion spotted Sister Wilkins among the nurses in procession behind the coffin. It was not the occasion to wave. The hierarchy from London's nursing establishment, who had adopted Edith as a cause célèbre, were themselves now centre stage. Marion and James along with the rest of the congregation stood as the coffin passed. The theatre of the occasion was perfect.

Intent on her conversation with James she had not paid attention to all those that had filed into their seats around them, but the abbey looked full and was soon reverberating when they sang the first hymn, *The Lord is My Shepherd*. It was enough to lift the lowest of spirits and Marion sang loudly along with those around her. The mood was almost triumphal.

Marion did not know the names of all the pieces of music,

but she was familiar with the choice of readings. Her father referred to *Revelations* when he was officiating and as she listened to the words she imagined Edith taking comfort from them in her final hours. "*I saw a new heaven and earth ... yea, though I walk through the valley of the shadow of death, I will fear no evil, for thou art with me ...*" and then they sang the hymn *Abide with Me*. Marion listened to the voices around her and pictured Edith, in her sitting room at the clinic, warmed by the glow from her fire. James who saw she was not singing nudged her with his elbow and she gave him a watery smile. She hated to think of Edith on her own in her cell, during her weeks of captivity and facing her death, but as they reached the seventh verse – her father only generally selected four – the beams of sunlight returned and Marion felt the warmth penetrate her and the words of the hymn seemed to come direct to her from Edith:

I fear no foe, with Thee at hand to bless;
Ills have no weight, and tears no bitterness.
Where is death's sting? Where, grave, thy victory?
I triumph still, if Thou abide with me.

In that moment Marion felt a heavy weight within her lift. She drew in several long breaths. James mouthed "Are you all right?" to which she nodded her reply despite the tears that were streaming down her face. He thrust a monogrammed handkerchief into her hand. She was grateful he was with her.

It was not long before people all around her were in tears, including her stalwart escort. A drum roll that increased to a crescendo introduced the buglers for the *Last Post*. The silence lingered after the last note faded and for Marion, and as she imagined for everyone there, name upon name passed through hearts and minds. So many had been sacrificed in the war. Today was their day, as well as Edith's.

It took Marion and James a long while to exit the abbey. The throng of people moved slowly and joined the hundreds outside who were lining up to follow the cortege to Liverpool Street. Marion took James by the arm.

"Do you mind if we follow?" she asked.

"Of course not. We must."

"It's quite a walk. We can go some of the way at least, but you mustn't tire."

"I promise, Nurse Drake." James patted her hand. "I will let you know if I need to rest. That was quite a service."

"Yes, it was. I feel much better for it: quite light, despite the tears. I would even use the word blessed. Do you believe we can be blessed?"

"It was you, or should I say Alain, who showed me how I am blessed. You were sitting in a shaft of sunlight for most of the service. Need we say more?"

"No, perhaps it doesn't need words at all. But now I know she is at peace." *And perhaps now I can be too.*

Marion and James had had to run for the train. They collapsed into what was, luckily, an empty carriage, caught their breath, and straightened themselves before either of them spoke.

"It's been quite a day for you, Marion."

"And for you. You are looking tired. I can't believe you walked all the way from Westminster to Liverpool Street, but thank you. I didn't want to leave her."

"Are you sure you don't want to go on to Norfolk?"

"No, I have said my goodbye."

"And to your anger?"

"Yes, perhaps I have." Marion smiled. "And what about your plans, when do you travel?"

"Not for a few weeks, but I wonder if I am wise to go and find Isabelle."

"Of course you are. You want to thank her at least."

"Yes, but riding into town on a charger to make her my bride is a little ridiculous and overly romantic." James laughed at himself. "What are you expecting when Russell returns?"

"Oh, we'll have to wait and see." *Wait and see.* We plan to meet in London when he first arrives. Time together in private is what we need, time together. And that is what you will need with Isabelle. Is it right to take your mother with you?"

"You may be right but I don't think she would let me out of her sight again. And I do want her to meet Isabelle. One step at a time, one step at a time."

Both tired from the emotion and exertion of the day, the rest of their journey passed mostly in companionable silence.

France, June 1919

"Do you have room for this in your bag?" Marion asked James. She was visiting his home with her mother before he and his mother left for France.

"What's that?

"One of Alain's pictures for you. He gave it to me this morning."

"I've kept his others. I'm starting quite a collection. And I look forward to meeting this young artist one day. Can I see?" James stretched out his hand to take the picture from Marion.

"Let me hold it up for you." Marion unrolled the sheet.

"I think it might be upside down." He reached out and turned it in Marion's hands and then took a step back. "That's better. Now let me take a look."

The picture was of a pin man, coloured yellow, standing next to what seemed to be a large rock about the same size as the man, with a shaft of sunlight streaming down. It looked to have something written on the front of it. There were no words to make out, just squiggly lines. To the left of the man were three more stick figures, one red, the next white and the third one blue.

"Now what am I to make of this?" James asked Marion who laughed.

"I have no idea. When I asked Alain what he was drawing, he just said it was for you. I've done my bit and given it to you. It might make sense one day."

"Well, I will be getting onto the boat he drew so I'll keep it with me."

"You are looking so much better. It's the spark in your eye that I'm so happy to see, and you have put on some weight."

"Yes, and my release papers have just come through. I am officially free from the army. I think they gave priority to prisoner of war veterans; they knew we were of no use to them. I've heard there have been riots in some camps and plenty of absconders too. Now the fight is over the men just want to get home. I don't blame them. They're fed up with taking orders and they want their lives back."

"And I heard one of the camps was nearly wiped out by the 'flu," Marion said. "It's still killing thousands and thousands of people. You must be careful where you travel. And we've had more cases locally."

"Yes, my mother told me. You look after yourself too. My father grumbled about the trip, but mother made a good case. It's a busy season for him, so she won't really be missed. She may return before me anyway; we've left our plans open, it's too difficult to say at this stage. But now it's here I am pleased to be going. And I have to say a big thank you for your encouragement, Marion. I do feel I'm ready to grasp hold of life again."

James had been carefully folding the picture and he slotted it between the pages of the book he was reading, a Baedeker's travel guide to France.

"I think suet puddings played a bigger part in your recovery than me. You just needed some stamina for your zest for life to return."

"*Carpe diem* from now on."

"Seize the day," Marion agreed. "That's a good motto for everyone to carry now that the war is behind us. Where are you heading first?"

"To Bellignes, to visit the de Croys. My mother and I will stay in Bavay and head out and visit them."

"Will they be there? Have you made contact?"

"You sound just like my mother. No, I haven't contacted them. I want to wait until I am there to be sure it is the right time. For them and for me."

"And where do you think you will you find Isabelle?"

"I have no idea," James shrugged. "Lille perhaps, but I may not even look for her. I think I am getting more realistic about the chances of a reunion."

"Or perhaps you are feeling cautious," Marion teased. "What happened to being fearless and seizing the day? It sounds to me like you are giving up on the whole notion prematurely."

"Maybe. Perhaps my fearlessness goes no further than my rhetoric. Truthfully I just don't know what we will find. I am happy to keep an open mind."

They exchanged a smile.

"Well good for you. I think it's brilliant you are going. You might find a lot of tourists there, not that tourist sounds the right word. The newspapers are full of stories of people going over to try and find out what happened to their sons who are still listed as missing. The government is asking for the public to wait until their records are more complete and the graves better organised, but you know what people are like; they won't be told."

"And what's the news for you and Russell? Do you know when you will be seeing him?" James asked.

"Well, his last letter said he was waiting for his release papers and had a trip planned to Washington. His letters have been vague for so long now, but I'm always pleased to hear from him, to know that he is all right. I don't think he has received half my letters; he has been on the move so much. He suggests he will be over here soon, but who knows when. The closer it gets though, the more I want to see him. It has been a long time." Marion sounded wistful.

"That's good to hear, and I feel the same about Isabelle. Though I sometimes think I would rather keep the fantasy of her alive than risk the truth of there being nothing left between us."

James put his suitcase down on the floor of the bedroom in the hotel in Bavay and threw himself on the bed. He was exhausted and beginning to regret bringing his mother along on the trip. For one thing their travel had been far more arduous than either of them had anticipated, and for him far more emotional. Flashbacks had started almost from the moment he had stepped onto French soil. His mother was showing her frustration with him: the number of times she had to say his name before she was able to draw him out of his reverie to engage in a conversation about the scenery or discuss their journey plan, or to eat some food.

He was being unfair. He was sure he would have been feeling far more wretched if he had been on his own. For one thing she had been assiduous in her supply of food. He would definitely have forgotten to eat, and he marvelled at how she produced tasty morsels from her travel bag. They must have eaten two fruitcakes between them since the start of their journey. And she had been very patient with his ad hoc approach to their accommodation. He had not known when they might reach Bavay so had not booked ahead, but luckily he managed to secure two rooms in the only hostelry that seemed equipped with an appropriate level of accommodation. His father would not have contemplated staying in such a place, but the hotels of Maubeuge, although probably better, were just too far away for James to consider.

James had time on his hands ahead of dining with his mother at eight o'clock. They had been told it would be simple but wholesome food, which had found her approval. *She really was game.* He determined to be better company for her that evening. Setting out to explore the streets he was drawn as if pulled by an invisible magnet to the grounds of the hospital. It was a small and simple two-storey building and there was no one around, so he found a bench seat and sat down.

Immediately the scene of his surrender and his last sighting of Isabelle replayed in his mind.

"I thought I might find you here."

James was startled by the voice that had interrupted his thoughts and looked up to see his mother standing in front of him.

"Do you mind if I join you," she asked, and James nodded and moved himself along on the seat to create space for her. "I have been watching you for a while. You were lost in your thoughts. Penny for them?"

"I'd rather not talk about them, if you don't mind."

"Actually,' she said, "I am beginning to mind. Your silences and you are becoming a little too long and moody. I thought as your companion I might be of some use and comfort; instead I feel I am in your way, and of no assistance. Your father said as much and you know how much I hate for him to be right."

James collected up his mother's left hand in his.

"You really are a trooper, Mother. I had been thinking how grateful I am that you are here. Truly." He gave his mother's hand a squeeze. "Coming back here is altogether more harrowing than I expected it to be. Actually I don't think I knew what to expect. I have been having very vivid flashbacks. Waking up after the battle, evading the German soldiers, finding shelter and help, hiding in the village and then the forest. The faces of people who helped us; the night we surrendered. Here, in this garden: twenty of us. I wonder if I can find the mayor, Monsieur Mercier, I think his name was. He was in hot water with the Kommandant for bringing us in."

"You could ask the hotel patron for his address this evening and send him a note. I'm sure he would be delighted to see you again. Would he know of the de Croy family, or how to send them a note of your desire to visit?"

"Mother, this is the country, French country. They don't stand on such ceremony as your circles at home. People just visit, and are generally welcomed."

"That may have been how it looked to you when you were here, James, but I cannot imagine arriving at the home of Prince and Princess de Croy without an invitation. I will not do it."

"Very well. I shall talk to the patron and send them both notes, but it will rather spoil the surprise."

"You young people are so casual. It really is quite ill-mannered."

"It will be done your way, Mother, never fear. I am not quite as feral as you think."

James and his mother returned to their lodgings and after writing the two notes, James sought out the patron to organise their delivery. He was pale and shaking when he joined his mother in the dining room.

"James, what is the matter, you seem quite distressed?"

"Monsieur Mercier cannot be visited, Mother. He is dead." He sat down heavily and put his head in his hands.

"Deceased, James, we say deceased. What a disappointment for you."

"No, you don't understand. Because of me. He is dead, deceased, because of me."

"What do you mean? How can you possibly have had anything to do with his demise?"

"He was shot. A few days after we surrendered he was shot. The patron said it was "*a reprysaille.*"

"A what?"

"A German reprisal against the town for harbouring enemy refugees."

"But you don't know that meant you. It could have been any one of a number of soldiers."

"That's kind of you to suggest, Mother, but the story of the twenty British soldiers who surrendered in November 1914 is quite a legend in these parts apparently, and largely because the mayor was executed. The poor man. He didn't deserve such treatment."

"No one deserves such treatment. Those Germans are barbaric. Just look at the state they left you in, you were skin and bone."

"At least I was left alive."

"Yes, yes, of course, dear. I am not intending to draw comparisons. Did he leave a widow?"

"Oh, I don't know, I didn't ask. I was rather taken aback by the news." James was still quite shaken.

"Of course you were. We can enquire after dinner and discuss whether you would like us to make a house call, or you on your own, of course. I do not need to shadow you on all of your visits."

James made no comment, but gradually recovered himself just as *soup du jour* was served. There was no menu and James found it impossible to guess the flavour of the soup.

"What of the de Croys? Any news?" his mother asked.

"Yes, yes. Princess de Croy is at home. The patron told me she has been in poor health after her sojourn in a German prison, but apparently her brother, Reginald, is away in Brussels. The patron will have the note sent to her. Did I mention her mother is English. I didn't ask if she was still alive. She was quite ancient when I met her."

"Then we can only wait until we have replies to see how we plan our next few days. And who else was it you wanted to see? You mentioned a special young lady, did you mean Marie de Croy, or did I gather there was someone else?"

"One day at a time, Mother, one day at a time."

Two notes awaited James in the morning. They were on the breakfast table. His mother was waiting for him, to order her breakfast and to open the notes. He quickly obliged on both fronts.

"Madame Mercier will be available for us to visit her. She suggests eleven o'clock today or three o'clock tomorrow."

"And Princess de Croy?"

"Wait just a moment. She has written a longer note." James settled back into his seat to read her fine handwriting.

"Dear Lieutenant Baxter,

Of course I remember you and the circumstances of your surrender. I will be delighted if you and Mrs. Baxter would care to visit. You will find me in poor health, so our hospitality will be impoverished, but to see you will be a tonic indeed. Unfortunately my brother Reginald is not at home. He will be disappointed when he learns of your visit.

I will send the trap for you tomorrow at 11 o'clock and greatly anticipate your arrival.

With sincerest wishes, *a demain*,

Marie de Croy.

"How thoughtful of her to provide transportation," James's mother said, after James had handed her the note, "but do you think we should visit at all if she is unwell? It is quite an imposition."

"She has willingly extended the invitation, and we need not stay for long if we find her out of sorts. I shall accept on both counts, and to Madame Mercier for this morning."

"Then we must order our breakfast James, or we shall be rushed."

"*Bonjour madame et monsieur. Asseyez-vous s'il vous plait.*"

Madame Mercier pointed to two chairs and James and his mother sat themselves down in a parlour with dark wood panelled walls and a shiny tiled floor. The only softness in the room was a knotted rag rug, but the colours were so faded it did nothing to brighten the decor.

Mme. Mercier was dressed tightly in black, with only the slightest edging of lace on her cap to break up the rigid band across her head, but the smile with which she had greeted them warmed an otherwise sombre atmosphere. James, hesitant at first, was soon speaking French to his host, assisted by Madame Mercier when he struggled to find the right words.

"Thank you for permitting this visit. I was saddened to hear from the patron at the hotel of the death of your husband, and am fearful that I might have been the cause of his demise. I would have understood if you had not wished to see me."

"It is the Germans I have no wish to see, ever again. I hope they are put in their place once and for all. The governments must be tough on them. They gave no quarter here and none must be given to them. To see you gives me hope."

James had not expected to receive a political commentary from the mayor's wife. He was aware of the conferences that had been ongoing since the beginning of the year in which the borders in Europe were being redrawn by the world powers and sanctions applied to the aggressors, but he was relieved that none of her anger was directed towards him.

"Your husband was masterful on the evening we surrendered, madame, but it was clear that the Kommandant was very upset with our appearance. We were lucky to be spared his wrath. I am so sorry that it was directed at your husband."

"You were the donkey that broke the straw's back, but there had been others before you. The Germans wanted to make an example of someone to stop villagers and townspeople harbouring soldiers."

"The straw that broke the camel's back," James found himself correcting her. "The Kommandant was probably frustrated that he couldn't shoot all of us. I am sure he would have done if they had stumbled across us in the woods. Mind you, we would have put up a fight."

"We were lucky that it was only my husband they shot. In

some towns they executed women and children too. For weeks I expected them to come for me as well."

"What a terrible time you have had," James's mother contributed, "and I would like to extend my gratitude for all that you and your fellow countrymen did to provide for and protect our young men. My son would not be alive today without all of you."

The widow bowed her head.

"My son was not so lucky," she said. He died in Ypres. The town was flattened."

"Your husband and your son? My dear lady, how you have suffered." James's mother looked sadly towards her.

"At least I know where my husband lies. He is buried in the cemetery on the edge of town, but I do not where the remains of my son are."

"I would like to pay my respects to your husband. Would you tell me where to locate him in the cemetery?" James asked.

Their hostess rose from her chair and took some paper from a drawer and drew a plan of the cemetery marking her husband's grave with a cross. "I shall go this afternoon," James said.

"We shall go," his mother corrected him.

Having just breakfasted James refused all offers of refreshment and after half an hour he and his mother took their leave, but not before James had promised to return.

"He needs more than this," James turned to his mother as he pointed to the small slab that marked the grave of Monsieur Mercier. "His resistance and fortitude should be commemorated on a much grander scale."

"This is a modest cemetery, James. Look around, there are no grand statements. They obviously don't go in for sculpture here." The cemetery on the outskirts of the town, boxed in by a high wall was full of graves interlinked by footpaths worn in the grass and gravel.

"I wonder if they would let me put a statue to him in the town square."

"James, do you have any idea what you are talking about? That could be an extremely costly venture."

"It wouldn't have to be fancy, it could even be a piece of uncarved rock dedicated to him. It is what it would represent that is important, and could speak for all those who resisted the Germans."

"Really, James, you don't know the ways of these people. You cannot assume this is what they would want. They might wish to put the whole period behind them and forget it ever happened."

"Madame Mercier is never likely to forget her husband and son, and her sacrifice should be acknowledged."

"This is not something to be rushed into. These are not matters for you to meddle in."

"This matters to me a great deal, Mother."

"Yes, I see, well, perhaps a conversation with the princess tomorrow would let you know if this would be appropriate. There is no need to be impulsive. I know you are upset by his death, but you were not responsible."

"That is a good idea, to talk to Princess Marie. But do look at this, Mother." James unfolded a piece of paper that he had in his pocket and turned it for his mother to look at.

"What is it?"

"I think it is me standing next to a commemorative stone and I think it is for Monsieur Mercier. Look there is writing on the rock and the people are red, white and blue. The colours of the French flag."

"Well, you can make out more than me." She looked at him doubtfully. "This looks like a child's scribble. Where did it come from?"

"From Alain, Marion Drake's ward. He drew it for me, for my trip. Quite prophetic isn't it?"

"Well, only if you let it be. It seems a big leap in anyone's imagination to see something in these crayoned shapes. There really is no need for you to become involved in a project here, James. You are only passing through."

"The same could be said of the whole of our life, Mother, we are only passing through. But surely we have to ponder how we want to be remembered. So far in my life I have done nothing memorable other than survive a war when others died. The least I can do is honour this man."

"Your survival was an achievement, James, and by all accounts you set an example for many. You were acknowledged by your men in their letters: your father and I were quite taken by their comments."

"Were you? He said nothing to me." James was surprised to hear of his father's admiration.

"No, well, he wouldn't. He doesn't show his sentimental side to many, nor often. But you measured up for him and that's what counts. He holds you in high regard. You need to start doing the same for yourself."

The thought of his father holding him in high regard was so new to James, that he felt quite unbalanced.

"Perhaps, if I do this thing for Monsieur Mercier, Mother, I will."

"A good life is waiting for you to step into, James. You need to move forward, not dwell in the past. I understand that you want to show your gratitude, but the sooner we return home, the quicker you can re-establish yourself."

"Don't rush me, Mother. I need this time, and to have the drive to actually do something is a new feeling for me. I thought all ambition was lost forever."

This was a big confession to make to himself, let alone to his mother and it discomfited him. He rose and walked away from her deep in thought but after a few moments turned back towards her.

"I have felt numb since Samuel died, but I even think I could visit his wife now. He would like that. Rosie, her name is Rosie. He gave me his address. I think that's when he knew he'd had it."

"Such a loss after you had been through so much together. To die from influenza, and in what, three days?"

"Three days and I could do nothing."

"Thank goodness you were spared."

"To be honest, I didn't think so at the time."

"Oh, James," His mother cried out. "And it is not entirely behind us yet. We must remain alert, although I haven't heard of any cases in this area. Perhaps they've been spared."

"They deserve some good luck after those years under the Germans. Thank you for accompanying me, Mother. I don't take your kindnesses towards me for granted. I'm just finding my way, back from the abyss. I can only apologise for being withdrawn and troublesome."

"Thank you, James. I suggest we find our way back to the hotel and both have a rest before dinner. We have a big day tomorrow, and an early night is in order I believe."

The following morning, breakfasted and waiting for the de Croys' trap, James experienced a flutter of anticipation in his stomach. The trap and his mother arrived at the same time, and with the two of them on board, the horses trotted down the street towards the hamlet of Bellignes and the chateau of the de Croys. James did not remember the lie of the land and was surprised by how little time passed before they turned into the long drive to the house. But he had been lost in his thoughts, about Isabelle. Their last night together was etched in his mind, and as the tower to the chateau came into view he had to brush away tears. His mother caught the motion and gave him an encouraging smile. Princess Marie de Croy was waiting for them at her front door. James remembered her as slight, but now she appeared shrivelled. Her smile was broad though.

James could tell his mother was quite disoriented to be led through to the kitchen and to watch as Marie made and served them a drink. Marie caught her eye and smiled.

"I have been home for four months and am still thrilled by turning on a tap whenever I want to. I had to go to a sanatorium for a few months after my release. I was too frail for such a long journey home."

"You must have had a dreadful time. From the little I have heard from James, prisoners were poorly treated in Germany," Mrs. Baxter said.

"Yes, it was hospitality that had to be endured, and hopefully never have to be repeated," Marie agreed.

"How did you come to be in prison?" James asked. "We know what happened to Edith Cavell, but what about you?"

"Oh, it was such an ordeal, such a trying time, and I was so worried that they would capture Reginald, but thankfully he escaped through Belgium to Holland. He will be back here in a few days and no doubt he'll tell you his story. I do hope you will still be here to see him."

"Yes, we, I, intend to remain for a while at least. But how did you come to be arrested and tried?"

"We had known for some time that the line had been infiltrated and so we hadn't passed any soldiers along for a few weeks, but arrests were being made in Brussels and guides taken in for questioning. We knew it was only a matter of time before they came for us. It was most important for Reginald to get away, but I remained here. I destroyed all items that could have incriminated me. They found no proof here, but still they took me to Brussels for questioning. They said I would be home later that day, but it was three years and three months before I walked back in the door here."

"I'm so very sorry," James said. "How is your mother? Is she still alive?"

"No, sadly no. The shock of the searches and my arrest, and our fears for Reginald, proved too much for her. A couple of days after my departure she had a stroke and never recovered. She died shortly afterwards. There was some talk of letting me visit her, under armed guard, but it would all have been too late anyway."

Distressed, Princess Marie stood up from her chair and busied herself at the sink for a few moments, before turning back to them.

"I'm still adjusting to her absence. The house seems very quiet without her, and of course we are short of servants. At least I am kept busy."

"If you don't mind me commenting, you look like you need more rest. Are you looking after yourself well enough?" James's mother asked.

"I know I should sit down more, but to move is freedom. I was cooped up in a small damp cell for most of my incarceration. I find it very difficult now to sit still for any length of time. I am quite the fidget. Shall we walk outside? I just love being outdoors whenever possible now."

"Perhaps we could sit out there. Is there a shady place where you would be comfortable? James's mother asked.

"Yes, yes, come with me."

One bench seat and two chairs were already positioned underneath the bough of an old oak tree. They arranged themselves with James on the bench and the ladies in the chairs. Marie continued to tell them her story about the farcical trial.

"I blamed everything onto my brother, and I think that and some of our lofty connections spared me from the same fate as Edith Cavell. Titles do come in useful sometimes."

"It is a very grand title," James's mother said. "Most royal."

"A title with no purse, nor purpose. That's the way of it in Europe. You keep your estates intact in England. Very wise. My other brother Leopold's expectations of life have not been met by his title and our chateau. He is a pauper within his set and it doesn't sit well with him. Reginald and I are more alike."

"And nothing in your life prepared you for prison, of that I am certain," Mrs. Baxter sympathised.

"At the start I was thankful for it. Several in our group were sentenced to death, so a prison sentence felt something of a reprieve. In the event only two of the death penalties were carried out. You have heard of these, no doubt."

"We know of Edith Cavell," James said. "I was recently at Westminster Abbey for a service of remembrance for her. Her body has just been returned to England. At the time I understand her death caused quite a stir."

"And thank goodness it did. The Spanish minister, Senor Villobar and Mr. Gibson from the American legation used the furore to have the other sentences commuted. They worked relentlessly on our behalf. They are men to be praised." Marie moved her chair out of the shade. "I knew of the service in the abbey. It was too far for me to go but I went to the memorial ceremony in the hall at the Gard du Nord in Brussels at the start of Edith's journey to England. She enjoyed full military honours here too. It was from the same place that I travelled, under guard, to Germany, to prison. It took days to travel to Sieburg, with little refreshment."

"We were in cattle trucks for our journey," James commented.

"Yes, I want to hear all about your news. I expect you suffered a great deal more than me."

"There is time for my tales of woe later. I am so sorry that you had to suffer at all; so undeserved. Do continue."

"Well, really, when I look back there is very little to say. One day was much the same as the next, until dysentery struck the wing and that carried its own dramas. I had a cell on my own in the hospital wing with an earthenware mug, a plate and a bowl, a small, hard pallet for a bed, one chair, and one pail that I had the opportunity to empty daily. I had a pan of fresh water daily to meet all my needs. My chest will never recover from the damp."

"You poor, poor, lady. You have been so brave," Mrs. Baxter said.

"We had a mug of coffee for breakfast, or so-called coffee. It was hot and brown and sufficed to shake off the chills from the night, so it was always welcome. Soup was ladled into our bowls at lunchtime and for the first months a slice of brown sticky bread. It had an unpleasant bitter taste, but was always eaten. We endured boiled barley at night, sometimes with meat or fish, but towards the end with no such additions."

"So terrible," Mrs. Baxter gasped.

"My uniform was a skirt and jacket in a sort of twill. Very rough against the skin, and they found it hard to find a skirt to fit me as I was so thin by then."

"James has been struggling to increase his weight since his return, but he has filled out some, I am pleased to say." Mrs. Baxter looked as if she might continue, but James silenced her with a look before turning his attention back to Marie, who carried on.

"I learnt that there were several of us there, political prisoners, but we were kept among the criminal fraternity who were the dregs of German society, some no better than animals. It must have been hardest for the nuns. Many arrests had been made as convents had been found to be the safe harbour of many soldiers. The Germans had no respect for God's work or his workers. I suffered from dysentery twice and was so ill from a weak chest that I had to be transferred to a hospital for the last few months of the war. They treated me more kindly there, but my warders remained close by. I doubt I would have survived another winter in the prison."

"The winters were definitely the hardest of times," James added.

"My brothers had both returned home ahead of me, and I

was pleased for this. The chateau had been badly damaged; you can see this for yourself."

The princess waved her arm towards the medieval tower that cornered the front of the house. James had noticed windows with broken glass and shattered frames.

"Furniture had been broken or stolen, most windows smashed. The lawn is pockmarked with craters. When I returned, shell cases and munitions still lay around everywhere. An unexploded shell had been removed from inside the house. If it had gone off it would have destroyed the dining room. I fear we have made little progress since my return. Help is so hard to find."

"From what you describe you have made remarkable progress. The chateau would appear to be largely habitable," James said.

"It is mostly clean, but not secure, and by no means restored. I've been distracted by many memorial services for those who died. Only now does the sadness surface; such loss, so many tragedies. I am glad my mother was spared all this." Marie wiped tears from her face.

"We heard about the death of the mayor in Bavay and we visited Madame Mercier yesterday. I wanted to ask you about a thought I had."

"James really, you mustn't trouble the princess with your impulses," Mrs. Baxter interrupted him.

"No, it's all right, Mrs. Baxter. What is it, James?" the princess asked.

"I would like to position a memorial to the mayor in the town. I feel responsible for what befell him. What do you think?"

"Oh, James, I think it is a splendid idea, but you must not think yourself responsible. If anyone is it is my brother who involved the mayor in the scheme, but none of us anticipated this type of reprisal. What you suggest is definitely the sort of thing we must do. I'll start making some enquiries and will get Reginald onto it when he is back."

"There, James, just what I feared. Now the princess has another task to put her mind to. I asked you not to mention it," Mrs. Baxter said.

"Mrs. Baxter, it is entirely right that this task sits with my brother and me. I only wish I had thought of it myself, but that honour will remain with James. It is easier for something like this to be orchestrated by us. We know how to make such a thing happen, but I cannot say how swift we will be; that will depend on the quarryman, and the town council."

"I am sure there is no need for urgency," Mrs. Baxter said.

"No. Not at all," James agreed.

"And I am sure we have tired the princess enough with our visit today, James. We must take our leave." Mrs. Baxter stood up to brook no argument.

"Right, yes, of course," James said as he stood and offered his arm for Marie to take. "Let me see you back to the house."

"You will come back won't you and will you go and visit Jacqueline, James?" Princess Marie asked as they walked back to the house.

"I would like to call on her and give her my thanks. Is she well, and her mother?"

"They are doing nicely. Jacqueline manages the bakery and the brewery so she has little time for socialising, but I feel sure she would like to see you and hear your news. She remains in touch with Isabelle."

"Isabelle."

"You remember Isabelle? Of course you do."

"Of course," James blushed. "I had wanted to ask about her. How is she? Where is she?"

"I know of little detail. She returned to Lille, to teach. I believe she and Harold run the school together."

"Harold? Who is he?"

"He is the headmaster. I believe they married."

"Married, Isabelle is married? Married?"

"This has come as a surprise. I should have been more gentle with my news."

"No, no, not at all. No need for solicitude. I am delighted for her. She wanted to teach, and she was a bright girl, so I am sure it has all turned out for the best for her."

"Will you visit her in Lille on your return? She would enjoy meeting you again, of that I am sure."

"Well, I don't know. I have some thoughts about my return, but I will talk to you about these on another day. When may I visit again?"

"Whenever you wish, open house. Reginald should be here the day after tomorrow. Why don't you and your mother join us for lunch."

"I shall accept for myself and I am sure my mother would be delighted too. Thank you." His mother nodded.

"And thank you for coming all this way to offer your thanks. Your visit has been a real pick-up for me. I look forward to seeing you again very soon."

James left her at the door and returned to his mother and the trap. He did not speak a word on their journey to Bavay and his mother allowed his silence. His mind was reeling. *Isabelle was married.* The woman whose memory had helped him through his darkest hours now belonged to another.

Bellignes, June 1919

"I would rather go alone today," James said, but not unkindly. He was breakfasting with his mother.

"Thank you for making your wishes clear, James, but I am not inclined to comply. We have only a few days before our return and I do not wish to stay confined in this hotel. Besides, I enjoyed Princess Marie and her eccentricities and would like to meet her again, and she was most welcoming towards me. She did include me in her invitation to luncheon."

James tried again.

"It is just that I would like to make another visit on the way to the chateau and they would be overwhelmed by two visitors."

"Don't be ridiculous, James. My accompanying you does not create an entourage or warrant this fuss, and before you say it, I am quite capable of the walk if that is how you wish to travel."

"No, I have a trap ordered."

"Then if you wish to exclude me, I can remain on the trap. Although you did say that you wanted to introduce me to a certain lady or have you changed your mind? Is this who you are calling on? What time are you expected?"

"I am not expected. It will be a surprise for the family."

"Not expected? A surprise? Where are your manners, James? I will not be party to such a social imposition and will remain with the trap and continue on to Princess Marie's with you. Will that suit you?"

"Yes, Mother, that's perfect. Can you be ready to leave in half an hour?"

"Yes, without any difficulty. I have completed my breakfast. I will meet you in the lobby." Mrs. Baxter rose from the table and took her leave from James.

He was happy enough with the compromise they had reached but he was beginning to feel constrained by the presence of his mother. He had lain awake for most of the night and a plan had begun to take shape but not one that included his mother. He wanted to suggest that she return to England and leave him in France, but it was unthinkable for her to travel back alone. He acknowledged he had needed her at the outset of the trip. He would not have fared well initially, and would have faced some lonely dinners, but he felt more energetic and able to fend for himself now. He had focused on his idea during the night to block out all thoughts of Isabelle: her married status was a disappointment too great for him to face.

The idea he wanted to suggest to Princess Marie was that he remain and help on her estate with some repair work. It was clear to him that there was plenty to do, and from her conversation it was evident that staff were hard to come by and expensive. She still had her old gardener and his wife, but their upkeep was now more an act of charity: she had said they could manage very little work.

James and his mother rode in cordial silence for much of the route to Bellignes. He spotted a tree at the edge of the hamlet that would offer some shade for his mother and the horses and suggested they stop there while he walked further along the road, past a few more houses to Jacqueline's house. His planning was interrupted by a shout and he looked up to see Jacqueline waving to him. She had been standing by a cottage talking to an elderly man.

"Lieutenant Baxter? Is it you? Lieutenant Baxter?"

James jumped down as Jacqueline ran to greet him.

"I had a message that you might be calling. Come along to the house. My mother is there. Princess de Croy sent word yesterday. Is this your mother?"

"Yes, Jacqueline. How good to see you. My mother is going to wait in the shade while I call to see you." James held out his hand in greeting but she planted two big kisses on his cheeks. Jacqueline had thickened out a little since he last saw her, but her face and smile were instantly recognisable and just as welcoming.

"Please, your mother is welcome. Bring the trap along to the yard. We can water the horses. Come along."

Jacqueline took hold of the bridle of the lead horse and led them all along the road, James walking by her side and his mother looking down on both of them. Introductions would wait until they were at the house.

James soon found himself sitting at the table in the kitchen where he had first met Isabelle, and there was a picture of her on the dresser. He tried to avert his gaze, but Jacqueline followed his eyes.

"She is in Lille, Isabelle. This is a picture of her with her son."

"Her son?" James tried but failed to keep the surprise out of his voice. "Princess de Croy told me she is married, but no mention of a child. I thought she said she was a teacher."

"Yes, she married the headmaster of the school where she trained. She is very busy teaching so writes very little, but she visits her mother here from time to time." Jacqueline picked up the photograph and passed it to James.

The photograph was taken in a garden and showed Isabelle and a little boy, probably aged about three years old, beside a tree. Dappled light threw shadows over them so he found it difficult to clearly make out her features, but her son had fair hair to her darker shade.

"May I see?" James's mother asked and he handed the

picture to her. His mother examined the photograph very closely, even asking if she might go to the window for a better look.

"A lovely child," Mrs. Baxter said as she handed the photograph back to Jacqueline.

Lemonade was poured for all and James and Jacqueline shared reminiscences of their various escapades in the woods. Jacqueline was saddened to hear of Samuel Elliot's death. It was her ministrations that had saved his leg.

"You were the last soldiers we were able to help. After Monsieur Mercier was executed the villagers wouldn't permit us to hide any more. That's when Isabelle returned to Lille. Isabelle was very fond of your son, Mrs. Baxter. She will be delighted to hear of his survival through the war."

"I am sure she will be too busy with her husband and family to be distracted by news of James, but do please pass on my gratitude to her, and yourself of course, for looking after James and our other men. You carried great risk and I, and I know James, will be forever grateful."

"It is so rewarding to have you come back, to know our efforts have not been forgotten, and that they weren't wasted. We have often talked about you all, hoping that you survived. Will you go to Lille to visit Isabelle? Is it on your way home?" Jacqueline asked.

"I am sure Mother is right. A visit would be an imposition, but I echo her message of gratitude. Do please pass it on when you next see Isabelle. Now we must be on our way to the chateau, but perhaps we'll meet again before we leave."

"Yes, I am in and out of Bavay all the time, and we have the quarry here for your piece of rock for Monsieur Mercier."

"How did you hear about that?"

"Princess Marie has already asked the quarryman to find a rock. We all think it is a wonderful idea. And if the town won't have it then we will have it here."

"But we only spoke of it two days ago, and it was just a thought." James was incredulous. Jacqueline smiled.

"And it was just the nudge we needed. So much was lost through the war, it becomes too easy to want to turn your back on everything, but there are some actions and sacrifices that should be celebrated. You have done a good deed with this."

"I hadn't realised Marie would act so quickly," James said.

"She may have been exhausted by the Germans, but her spirit will never be daunted. Let me fetch your horses with you, James."

Jacqueline and James left together to bring the horses and trap around to the front of the house. Jacqueline took hold of James's arm.

"Do go and visit Isabelle, lieutenant. I am sure she won't mind me saying but she was very much in love with you when you left. I know she will want to see you."

"Thank you, Jacqueline. I'm sure I was in love with her too, but much has happened since then. She soon settled with another and by the looks of it has established a good life for herself. Better than I have managed. I hope she is contented, happy with her husband and son."

"Did you expect her to wait for you, lieutenant?"

"No, of course not. I was damned lucky to survive anyway. No, we made no promises to each other, but still, I have to admit to disappointment that she is married, and has a child. That possibility had never crossed my mind. Stupid of me really."

"Isabelle made the decisions she had to make to survive. It was very tough here during the war."

"Of course she did, of course. And she will always have a special place in my heart." *I had hoped she might protect me from the English drawing rooms that my mother will now parade me through.*

"She holds thoughts of you dear as well. She named her son after you. Jacques is James in French."

"She did? I didn't take her for being the sentimental type. Jacques? Maybe I should go and visit and meet my namesake."

"Would you like me to write to her?"

"Thank you, Jacqueline, but no. I don't know what my plans will be, and if I do go it will be a flying visit. I wouldn't want to put her and her husband to any trouble, so it will be best if I arrive unannounced, if I visit at all. I might just leave the past alone. My mother keeps encouraging me to move on with my life. Perhaps this is one instance to heed her words."

"Perhaps. But you don't have to decide now. Here we are."

Mrs. Baxter was waiting for them at the front of the house. Her first comment as they left the village was,

"Tell me about Isabelle. I assume she is the young lady you mentioned."

"Isabelle? What is there to say? She is married and lives with her family in Lille. She is living her dream. She always wanted to teach. I am pleased for her."

"Are you? You don't seem at all pleased. In fact I would say you are upset. Was she a sweetheart of yours? Is it her this trip is all about?"

"This trip is about closing a chapter of my life. To thank the people who saved my life, and then as you so rightly say, I need to get on and live that life. To make sure all that they risked and sacrificed was worthwhile. I have been malingering for too long."

"It is nice to hear you agree with me, James, but I was asking about Isabelle."

"Yes, Mother, she is the one. We were very fond of each other. She was a true comfort for me during those bleak winter weeks in the forest."

"And did you make any promises to this girl? Is she likely to look for something from you now?"

"No, no promises were made, from either side. And as we can see she has moved on with her life. There is no place in it for me now."

"As long as you are sure you have no obligations. We wouldn't want any complications creeping into your life in later years."

"Mother, I have no idea what you mean. We were two people caught up in extraordinary circumstances and we found a friendship, and there is no doubt the relationship became exaggerated in my mind. I had reason to hold onto the memory for longer than she did."

"An intimate friendship?"

"Mother!"

"For heaven's sake, James, I do know where friendships lead."

James was saved from making a response by their arrival at the chateau, and was delighted to see Prince de Croy, Reginald, standing at the door to greet him. Much back-slapping followed, and James could see that his mother enjoyed the prince's solicitous behaviour towards her. He had not lost his aristocratic air and looks and was a gentleman through and through.

"I have convinced Marie to serve luncheon in the dining room. It is a good occasion to dust and air the room. Come through, she will join us in a moment."

Reginald led them through to the room where James and Isabelle spent their final private moments together. James looked for the chair where he had sat in the hours before his surrender, with Isabelle nestling in his arms, but it was gone. He did not recognise any of the furniture, of which there was very little. The room was now quite spartan.

His mother was right: he was upset that Isabelle was married and the news of her son today was a body blow. *Jacques*. His dream of them building a life together now had to be consigned to fantasy, and he only now appreciated just how much of his recovery had become vested in this picture of a future with her. He was not ready to pick up all the pieces of his life back at home; he had been ready for Isabelle. He realised Reginald was waiting for an answer from him. "I beg your pardon, what did you say?" James asked him.

"I was asking if you were following the talks, the peace talks. Looks like they have got through all the flannel now and will start making decisions. How the blazes those Germans think they have a right to negotiate terms, I have no idea."

"I refuse to have talk of politics all through our luncheon," Princess Marie said as she entered the room, interrupting her brother's rant.

"When we were released from prison," James said, picking up the conversation, "and were making our way home through Germany, we were surprised to see all the celebrations for the returning troops in the towns we passed through. They were welcomed as heroes. The Germans didn't believe they had lost the war, they had just decided to stop fighting. I suppose this makes them feel they have every right to push for terms," James said.

"Well, they won't get them," Reginald insisted. "The allied powers have their eye on all sorts of solutions to suit themselves. Germany will rue the day it marched into Belgium."

"Enough of this," Marie said. "Peace should mean peace, not the retaking of territories under the guise of an amnesty. They are using barristers now instead of bullets: no good will come from it."

"I thought you didn't want to talk politics, sister?"

Marie snorted. "I don't, let us eat. Come through."

Reginald offered his arm to Mrs. Baxter and James followed the party into the dining room. It had been enlivened with fresh flowers, but the damage to the walls and floor had yet to be repaired. The dark and damaged furniture compounded the feeling of decay. During lunch they heard of Reginald's escape to Holland, dodging capture, sleeping rough, and swimming across canals; and Marie and James shared stories from their incarcerations. Sombre subjects, but they still found much to laugh about. His mother was an attentive listener.

"The countryside is ravaged, skylines are unrecognisable, much of the forest flattened, roads damaged. It will take years to return to its former beauty. We haven't started to think of our gardens yet, we still have the house to put straight," Marie said as they moved out of the dining room back into the salon.

"And that's something I wanted to talk to you about," James said. "I was wondering," he paused as he looked towards his mother, "whether I might be of some assistance to you."

"What do you mean?" Reginald asked.

"You clearly have a lot of work to do around here, I was wondering if I might stay on, or even return to help you."

"That is a very kind and generous offer, James, but one that we couldn't possibly accept. I am sure you are needed just as much at home," Marie replied.

His mother quickly stepped in.

"Yes, his father will be relying on James now he is more recovered." Mrs. Baxter smiled at Marie and Reginald and then looked at James. "But I am sure a few more weeks won't matter to him. The most important thing is for James to strengthen and perhaps some weeks here would do that."

James beamed at his mother.

"But", she continued, "I will not be able to extend my stay. James could return after accompanying me home."

"Perhaps, my dear lady," Reginald said, "I might be of some assistance. I could offer to accompany you."

"Oh no, I couldn't possibly impose on you."

"No imposition. I have to travel to London in two days' time and would be delighted to be your escort. The imposition would be mine."

Within a further half an hour all was agreed. The prince and

Mrs. Baxter would travel together, and James would move into the chateau and start labouring on the work that was to be done.

"Thank you, Mother," James said as they rode back to Bavay later that day.

"I wish I could capture the light that I see in your eyes, James. That is what I have been waiting for all these weeks. You have returned to us at last. Whether I will be able to make your father understand this, I don't know, but I know you are on the road to recovery, and that makes me very happy. Just make sure you don't weary yourself too quickly. Marie is like a sparrow; you both need to put on weight."

"Perhaps my help will reduce her worries. She ate well with us today."

"I am sure it will be a great help. I will telegraph your father in the morning to tell him of our plans. He will blow hot about it, but I can manage him once I am home."

"You are being a real sport, Mother. I am grateful. Would you mind taking a letter back to post for me, to Marion? I want her know how well I am doing."

"And are you perhaps more interested in her, now you know that your peasant girl is married?"

James was quite firm in his reply.

"No, Mother. Marion is a good friend, and you still do not seem to be able to absorb the fact that she is promised to another, and her Mr. Clark is due back in England any time soon. And by the way, Isabelle isn't a peasant girl. Her father was the local doctor. She is a young lady with many accomplishments. Her English is impeccable."

"Perhaps you should have given this more heed, before you compromised her."

"Mother, really!"

"You were irresponsible, James. Thank goodness the young lady, as you call her, was able to secure her position through marriage."

"Isabelle always had her future clear in her mind: she wanted to teach. I am pleased it worked out for her."

"And you definitely want to play no further part in her life? You have consigned her to the past?"

"That decision has been made for me, Mother. I have no intention of being a home-breaker, not that Isabelle would entertain such a thought, I am sure. She is a woman who would be constant and loyal."

"To her husband or to the father of her child?"

"Yes, to her husband and the father of her child."

"But what if these were different people? Where would her loyalty lie then?"

James could not follow what his mother was asking.

"Mother, what are you saying? That her husband is not the father of her child? Don't cast such aspersions on her character. You do not understand Isabelle."

"But I do understand women caught in a predicament."

"Predicament? What predicament? Do you mean the war? Do you think Isabelle was attacked, raped. Where did you get this from?"

"No, on the contrary, I think Isabelle was loved, by you. And that Jacques is your son."

"My son?" James stopped the horses. "My son? Who gave you that idea?"

"He did. His picture. You and he looked identical at the same age. James, Jacques is your son, I'm sure of it."

James pressed his hands to his forehead and when he lifted his head tears were pouring down his cheeks.

"My son? Do you really think so?" he turned to his mother. "Jacqueline did tell me that he was named after me. Jacques is James in French, but I don't think she was telling me he was my child."

"She probably doesn't know."

"It can't be true. Don't all children look the same with blue eyes and blonde hair? Perhaps you are reading more into this picture. You only took a glance at it." James wiped his face and clicked the horses on.

"You may want to think that, James, but I examined the photograph by the window, if you remember. I was looking at you as a child. I know I am right."

"My son. That changes everything." James stopped the horses again.

"Or nothing."

"But if he's my son I ..."

"I what, James?" His mother interrupted him. "When you knew she was married and had a child you consigned her to history. Nothing has changed. That is where she must remain."

James shook his head, unable to gather his thoughts.

"You must not let her make any claims of you, and if her husband thinks he is Jacques's father that is the way history is best written."

"Then why tell me?" James turned on her. "Why put this notion in my head? It would never have crossed my mind that he was my son." He was angry.

"Perhaps not, and then you wouldn't be prepared if Isabelle, hearing of your return, starts to make demands of you."

"Demands? Are you saying she might come after me for money? Is that what you think?" James was incredulous.

"Yes, that is what I think. It is a ruse that has been used by girls for generations. You are quite a catch you know, an English gentleman, and you have a reputation to protect."

"How dare you insinuate such a thing? You are insulting Isabelle without ever having met her. I can't imagine the thought would ever enter her head."

"My point exactly. Women's heads are full of wiles that men could not begin to fathom. To underestimate a woman is a fool's game."

"Then I would rather I remain a fool."

"And that, James, is my fear. Fools rush in without thinking. I merely want to pre-empt you so that your impulses can be controlled. We haven't heard the last from this young lady, I am sure."

"Well, I want to hear nothing more about it from you. The idea that I might have a son, or even a potential blackmailer on my hands is just too ridiculous for words."

Yet again they were riding in silence when they arrived at Bavay and parted, this time acrimoniously, to go to their rooms.

Little Missenden, July 1919

The wait was almost over.

My darling Marion,

It won't be long now before I am back with you and we can build our future together. Our plans to leave France have been significantly delayed by the influenza, but by keeping men separated rather than mustering in large groups we have avoided some of the huge losses. Your boys have been hit bad.

Everyone is itching to get back home. Home, that word holds a special magic for me now. I have had enough of adventuring. I just want you and Alain. But there has been plenty to do and I have made some really good friendships, and Pershing has said he will open doors for me if I want to work in Washington. I will make my home in England though if that is what you prefer.

Thank you for your letters, I received three in one bundle last week. It never ceases to amaze me that we can be tracked down at all. I do hope this reaches you and finds you well.

I have no problem with people being told we are engaged, as long as this sits well with your father. You engaged my heart a long time ago! I hope it smoothes the matrimonial path for Evelyn and her new suitor.

Please tell Alain that I rode in a tank, the most uncomfortable thing imaginable. There are such a lot of abandoned munitions over here. I think much of it will be buried; it is far too costly to try and bring it back, and there are horses everywhere. It is so sad to see the auctions where so many are sold for horse meat, an impossible task to reunite them with their owners and their military use is done. I wonder how many bloodstock lines will be lost through this war. No doubt your uncle will be keeping track.

Must dash this off now. With you soonest,
Your ever-loving Russell.

America. Yes please. The thought of escaping from England excited her as much as seeing Russell again. There was no question in her mind where she wanted to be. The land of hope and glory was subdued by all the loss and calamities that had left no community untouched. Grief on a scale not witnessed before lay like a blanket over the country. It almost felt wrong to be happy and Marion kept her anticipation about Russell's return largely to herself. Only Alain picked up on her growing excitement.

Whenever she could she took Alain out on walks, which for him were runs. He would bound back and forth like a puppy off a lead and she loved to see and share in his exuberance. She would not tell him about Russell's ride in a tank, preferring to keep him as ignorant about the war as possible. Only thankful that it was now over and was never to be repeated. His lifetime would be safe.

The hospital was due to shut down at the end of the year. Doctor Ambrose had once again propositioned her about them working as a team. He had heard of a partnership opportunity in Chalfont St Giles with a Doctor Webber, but she had held his enthusiasm at bay, and he knew better than to press her. She wanted to believe that she and Russell had a future.

Not so for James, it seemed. At least not the future he had

dreamed of with Isabelle. His mother had delivered a letter from him when she came to tell them all about her trip and her rather heady return journey from France with a prince.

> Dear Marion,
>
> I have asked Mother to pass this letter to you when she returns, and by now you will have gathered I have remained here, for a while at least. I want to give a helping hand to the de Croys and it is a good way for me to build up my strength. I am eating well.
>
> I have not met Isabelle but have caught up with her news. She is married and has a son. It has been hard for me to realise that lives have been lived and turned around in the time I was incarcerated, and harder still not to resent this. So no happy ever after ending for me to report, but after some hard graft I am sure my good spirits will be restored. Princess Marie is a wonderful example for me of fortitude. Her resilience is boundless, as was Mother's patience with me on the trip. I have not been the easiest of travel companions.
>
> Do write to me care of the de Croys at Bellignes and tell me your news.
>
> Yours affectionately, James.

She did not reply, deciding to wait until she had her own news to report. The humdrum description of her life held no appeal for her and she imagined would only bore a reader. James was determined to lift himself out of his doldrums so needed no words of comfort from her. She knew he would right himself.

Bellignes, July 1919

Jacqueline had just departed and Marie and James continued to sit on their seats in the garden. He was admiring the difference from the hours of work he had put in over the past few weeks since his mother had returned to England. A pattern of starting early in the garden before the heat of the day built up, and then working in the house for the afternoons and many evenings was quickly established. "Garden" was still too organised a word for the ground where he had been trying to restore order. Marie had helped him mark out where the beds used to be and he had concentrated on removing the debris from the various troops who had attacked or defended in the vicinity. He had filled in shell holes, collected shell casings, barbed wire, helmets, and unidentifiable twisted and rusting metal. He had raked the soil, dug over the areas designated for the beds, and marked out the edges of paths that criss-crossed what would later return to lawn. James shifted his position and folded his arms across his chest.

"A penny for them?" Marie said.

"Pardon?" James replied. "I'm sorry, what did you say?"

"A penny for your thoughts. You haven't said anything since Jacqueline left."

"Oh, I have been admiring my handiwork and thinking of where next to give my attention."

"What you have managed is marvelous. Reginald won't recognise it when he returns. I hope you are not doing too much, though. Your mother would not forgive me if we wear you out with all our demands."

"She will be delighted with the appetite it is giving me. The fresh air and hard work is more of what I need than sitting around waiting for my energy to return. Perhaps my father was right after all." James smiled at Marie. "I enjoy the work and am delighted to be helping you. I shall start on the dining room tomorrow. Bertrand has promised to come over and do some more plastering. I will master that craft before long. I'm determined to. He makes it look so easy."

"It is not a skill a gentleman requires, James," Marie gently mocked. "Your mother will be upset if you turn into an artisan."

"There is always plenty of scope for me to upset my mother, Marie," James laughed. "I'm sure she expects me home any day, so my extended visit here will soon wear thin with her, regardless of what I am doing."

"Yes, we must stop relying on you so much. She is right to expect you home, but I hope you won't now leave before Isabelle's visit. It was kind of Jacqueline to come and tell us that she will be visiting her mother next week. You will see her, won't you?"

"I am not sure that would be a good idea." James was still absorbing Jacqueline's news. "It might be better to stay with the memories and not disturb them. I am sure I'm not the hero she imagined me to be and she already has her life much better worked out than mine."

"Anyone who survived the war is a hero, civilians and soldiers alike."

"That reminds me." James was keen to take the conversation away from Isabelle. "I found three crosses near the poplars. Do you know anything about them?"

"They are nothing to do with the family. Our dogs are buried in the back garden. They must be soldiers, but from which army, who can possibly know? I'll let the mayor in Bavay know about them. We are expecting the British army administrators in the area soon apparently."

To James's quizzical look she went on to explain.

"They are collecting bodies from marked graves and re-burying them together in commemorative gardens all over France. I had hoped to ask one or two from the gardening teams to stay on and work with us for a while here, but you have made that thought redundant now."

"There will be work for a good couple of years to put all this right, I can assure you. I would grab all the help you can," James said.

"There will be no harm in my asking, I'm sure," Marie agreed.

"Wait until you've met and have the measure of them first. You don't need to take a shirker on board. I've known a few of them in my time."

"Do you remember Private Culloch?" Marie asked.

"Private Culloch, that Scots weasel? He's not easy to forget and defines the word shirker. I'd like to meet up with him again and hold him to account for a few things." James did not like to be reminded of the one troublemaker who upset his men when they were hiding in the woods. "Why do you raise his name?"

"I thought he was a shirker," Marie said, "but actually he proved to be a great help. He remained in the area after the rest of you surrendered, and started to call by whenever the area was clear of German soldiers. He would work hard for a meal, until he decided to head home and we passed him along to Brussels via our guides. He'd had such a tough life in the gutters of Glasgow, or so he told me. I often wonder what happened to him."

"And I'd like to kick him right back into the gutter. He was a bad'un. Never mind his sob story. Don't spare any pity on him."

"Apparently he introduced Quien into the clinic in Brussels and it was Quien who exposed Edith."

"Culloch did that?" James's anger flared.

"Yes, but the authorities were already onto us. Culloch was just a stooge and Quien will see his day in court. Reginald is working hard on that agenda."

"Well, if Culloch ever shows his face around here again, set your dogs on him. He deserves nothing better."

"Enough about him." Marie smiled. "We don't want him spoiling our mood. Now tell me, what do you feel about Isabelle, or is it impertinent of me to ask? My brother is forever warning me off my matchmaking?"

"To be totally honest with you, I don't think I feel anything." James stretched his legs out in front of him. "I've felt quite numb since I heard she was married and had a child. I have to tell you." James laughed. "My mother has some foolish notion that Jacques is my son." He shook his head and then clasped his arms around in front of his chest and his tone changed. "I held onto thoughts of her all through my captivity and hours spent planning our new life together kept boredom at bay. But I don't think I ever really believed that was the way things would work out. Too much of a fairy story." James slapped his hands on his thighs and sat upright. "My hopes have been dashed, and I am sad to lose my fantasy, but that's all."

"Bravo. But we'll see," Marie said. "At least you will be meeting as friends."

"Yes, always that I would hope, but for now, if you will excuse me, I must get on with my work."

James rose, stretched his back, picked up his tools and went back to work, but his thoughts returned to Isabelle once his body was working in a rhythm with his spade. He had not been honest with Marie but he was wary of speaking the truth. It was not that he could not admit the truth to himself; it was the shock of it that kept him silent. He was still in love with her, at least with the notion of her and he was not ready to part company with the Isabelle of his dreams. It was thoughts of her that kept that demon loneliness at bay. His nervousness was for what would happen when an indifferent Isabelle, for whom he held no relevance, collided with the woman of his dreams.

James's day was busy and sad. He had accompanied the army administrators around the estate and now, mid-afternoon, had just returned to the house from the nearby woods. It was quite an operation they were undertaking, to locate and identify the bodies. There had been no digging that day; that exercise would come later. Today was just marking the graves. He had taken them to the three crosses he had mentioned to Marie the week before, and they had taken him to seventeen more that they had listed in their notes. It was a bit like being on a macabre treasure hunt. They had certain clues as to their whereabouts, but the lie of the land had changed in some instances, and trees marked on sketches and maps were often missing. In place of two graves in one location in the woods was a shell hole; no remains were found there. The graves were all British soldiers and each one had been identified, some small relief for their families at least, James thought.

He did not feel like doing any more work that day, and sat himself on the bench seat at the front of the house. The sun was warm and he closed his eyes and allowed himself to doze. He was startled by a cough; a child's cough and he sat up, opened his eyes and squinted as they adjusted to the light. He was looking at a miniature version of himself.

"Bonjour, Jacques," James said, but the child said nothing in return, until a butterfly caught his attention and he took hold of James's hand and pulled him to his feet.

"Vite, vite," the young boy said.

James followed the child as he ran after the butterfly and whooped with delight at its erratic flight path. Eventually it settled and James watched as Jacques reached out and gently cupped it in his hands.

"Avec moi," he said as he started to walk carefully back to the house with James obediently in tow.

Jacques went round to the back of the house and James pushed open the back door to enable him to enter without opening his hands.

"Maman, Maman," the boy called as he walked into the kitchen with James at his heels. A woman, dressed head to foot in black turned at his call, her attention on the child until she saw that there was someone behind him and she looked up at the same moment that James saw her.

"Isabelle?" James said hesitantly. "Is it you Isabelle?" He took another step forward. "But you are beautiful." And she was.

The woman standing in front of him, and yes he thought, woman was the right word, was slim, but shapely. She had filled out and he chuckled at the memory of describing her to Marion. The word coltish no longer applied. She was poised and, that was the only word, beautiful. She smiled at him.

"Yes, Lieutenant Baxter, I am she. I am Isabelle, and thank you for the compliment even though you seem shocked to find me so. Am I not as you remembered me?"

"You know that you are not, and neither I'm afraid am I."

"Your suntan suits you better than the winter look I remember," Isabelle said. "Come here, do you not have a kiss of greeting for a friend? You are in France."

James who had stood transfixed, started forward and kissed her on both cheeks, then held both her hands as he pulled back to look at her again.

"It really is you. How lovely to see you. I didn't know we were expecting you today. I would have been better prepared. I'm in my working clothes, as you can see."

"Marie has been telling me how useful you have made yourself." Isabelle turned and smiled at Marie. "I wasn't expected today. I just called by to arrange to visit more properly tomorrow. Is that enough notice to clean yourself up?" Isabelle laughed as James started to answer her question seriously, only to be interrupted by Marie.

"That will be enough notice for us, Isabelle. I shall insist on no work tomorrow," Marie said. "It's so lovely to have you back among us, but I am sorry to hear your mother is unwell. Jacqueline didn't mention this last week when she visited us."

"No, she had kept it from me too. My mother is very frail now and the slightest chill takes its toll. She has been well looked after, in fact I feel slightly in the way now that I am home. She will not miss me tomorrow, but if she should worsen I will send word to you that I cannot come."

"Let us hope for the best on all counts," Marie said.

"Indeed," said James, nudged by Marie's foot.

"Come along, Jacques, say au revoir, a demain, until tomorrow!" Isabelle took her son by the hand and the butterfly took the chance to escape and fluttered up into the air.

Isabelle gasped in surprise, and then laughed as it landed on James's head.

She stepped forward to cup it in her hands, and James had to manage every restraint he could muster not to kiss her on the neck. Instead he breathed her in until she stepped back and asked Jacques to open the door. They all followed outside and she bent down and lowered her hands so that Jacques could say goodbye to the butterfly before she released it.

"Until tomorrow," James said as he raised his hand in farewell.

Bellignes, July 1919

"Did you know Jacques was my son?"

James and Marie were sitting in the kitchen over breakfast. James had scarcely slept that night and fidgeted all through their meal.

"I thought there was a chance he might have been," Marie answered cautiously.

"Excuse me but what sort of answer is that?" James asked, and then apologised as he realised he sounded testy. "I'm sorry. I couldn't sleep last night. What time did she say she was coming, do you think she will bring Jacques?"

"This is not a question you should be asking me at all," Marie said. "Isabelle is the person to speak to about Jacques, or perhaps you ought to wait and hear what she wants to tell you."

"So you do think he is my son?" James asked.

"Well, he is the image of you, I suppose," Marie replied.

"Thank goodness my mother has left. I can't imagine her reaction to Jacques, although she did seem convinced from the photograph she saw at Jacqueline's house. It was too grainy for me to make out anything. I didn't believe her."

"But you are convinced now?"

"Yes, I felt like I was looking at my younger self. I even chased butterflies when I was a boy too. Why did she marry someone else when she was having my baby? Why didn't she tell me, or wait for me? Did I mean so little to her?"

"James, you are torturing yourself with all these questions, and just remember before you start any inquisition, Isabelle does not need to give an account of herself to you."

"What do you mean? She has had my child, of course she has to explain herself."

"Let me remind you of your words, James. You made no promises to each other. I'm sure she made the decisions she thought were wisest at the time. Now are you going to eat your bread, or just batter it with the butter?"

James had been pressing hard butter into his bread in an agitated manner since their conversation had turned to the topic of Jacques.

"I'm not hungry," he said as he pushed his plate away. "I can't concentrate on eating."

Marie stood up and began clearing the breakfast dishes off the table. On her way to the sink she turned back to him.

"If you don't mind some advice," Marie said, "I think you would benefit from a brisk walk around the estate. You are like a coiled spring and need to unwind before you see Isabelle. You will startle her if you approach her in this manner."

"Yes, yes, you are right. I am on edge. She looked so poised yesterday. I don't want to look like a dog yapping at her heels."

"Give her time, give yourselves time, that's my advice. You both have your stories to tell each other. Let her tell you what she wants you to know, in her own time."

"Yes, you are quite right. But her visit is not meant to be with me anyway, it's you she wants to see. It is your trials that she wants to hear about. It is just happenstance that I am here for her visit. I have no claims on her, or on Jacques. Perhaps I should carry on working today; it is a shame to miss a day's work."

"No claims on them, no, but let kismet play its hand," Marie said with a smile and laid a hand on his shoulder. "Forget work today, go on, take that walk."

James followed Marie's advice and took himself off towards the Forest of Mormal. He had no thoughts where he was going, taking turns at a whim each time a choice of path presented itself. It had been dark, back in 1914, when he and his men had made their way to the de Croys the night before their surrender, and, led by a guide, he had not needed bearings. The forest had been thick then but now it was sparse and pock-ridden with shell holes. It looked forlorn and bedraggled, with little or no sign of this season's growth.

Even the earth is scarred by the war. James shuddered as if his body was absorbing shockwaves that still reverberated from the fighting. Marie had been right, the motion of walking had calmed the turmoil in his mind and he was better able to order his thoughts with the rhythm of his steps.

His love for Isabelle had been reawakened the moment he had set eyes on her. She had not just been a fantasy to keep him company through the intervening years. Their love had been real and was the reason for his return. His love for her was alive. He knew nothing of her feelings for him, or, in fact, if she had any at all. Perhaps she considered their relationship as nothing more than a flirtation. She could not have held him in high regard if she married so easily and was prepared to deny him knowledge of the existence of his own child. He felt tortured to be this close to her and yet separated by a gold band on her hand.

James found an area covered with moss, dappled in sunlight and sat down. The dew had burnt off and warmth from the sun was seeping into the mutilated forest.

He could have no expectations of her. Marie was right, he had no claim on her or Jacques. He may have fathered the child, but he had not been a father to him in any other way. He had not known or ever imagined his existence. But regardless of his mother's warnings he knew he would give Isabelle anything she might ask of him: an allowance for the child, anything. If his mother's fear was he would have no backbone to refuse Isabelle, then she was right. Isabelle could claim from him, and his true desire was that she would claim his heart. It was hers for the taking. Acknowledging this made him feel lighter. He now had to accept whatever hand fate dealt him.

A body landed on top of him hard and winded him, and it went dark. What felt like rough sacking was over his face: he smelt mould and bits of mud fell into his mouth as he gasped for air. He arched his back and twisted and tried to raise his arms to push off his assailant, but he was totally pinned. He kicked his legs, but only at the air. He stopped struggling to take some breaths but it was more and more difficult to draw in air. He could feel panic rising as the weight pressed down harder onto him making it impossible for him to expand his lungs and a blackness swirled at the edge of his vision. *What was happening? Was he going to die?* Just before he blacked out he thought he heard a gun fire.

"Are you going to tell James about Jacques?" Marie asked.

Marie and Isabelle were in the garden watching Jacques dig worms up from the earth that had been prepared for a flowerbed.

"I don't think there is any need to do that," Isabelle replied. "He will be rebuilding his life after the war. He doesn't need to be saddled with thoughts of a child. He has his life ahead of him."

"He knows," Marie said after a pause.

"He knows what?" Isabelle turned to her.

"That he is Jacques's father."

"How? How does he know? Who told him? Did you tell him, or was it Jacqueline? She wrote and told me he was here."

"Is that why you came?"

"No, yes, no. It's complicated. I have so much to tell you, Marie, but I want to hear about you. How are you and what did you suffer in prison? I wish I could have taken your place."

"Your place was with your husband and your child. How is Henri? Is all well with him and Jacques."

"Yes, it was, but now everything has changed. How does James know he is Jacques's father?"

"Isabelle, it is obvious. James looked at him and recognised himself. His mother had done the same from the photograph at Jacqueline's. Apparently she warned him away from any responsibilities you might want to foist on him."

"Foist myself on him? How dare she? I am quite capable of looking after my son. I do not need his help with Jacques. I would never come after him cap in hand. But perhaps she would never believe this of me. She would think I had ruined her son."

"Mrs. Baxter is actually a charming and very down-to-earth lady and not ignorant of the ways of women, but she doesn't know you either, Isabelle. You are as much a lady as she. You look so well, Isabelle, but why the black dress? Has there been a death in your family, or Henri's?"

"I can see I am going to have to answer your questions before you will tell me about your ordeal, so let me start."

Isabelle was interrupted by a shout from the back of the house.

"Jacques, wait, come back."

Isabelle jumped to her feet to call Jacques who had immediately started running towards the noise.

"Come here, to me," she shouted.

Jacques turned back and had just reached her when Joseph the gardener stepped into view from the back of the house. He was waving his arms and calling to them.

"What on earth is all the commotion?" Marie said as she rose to her feet and joined Isabelle and Jacques as they made their way towards Joseph. The old man was quite breathless when they reached him and he held up his hands to show he needed a minute to recover.

"What is it, Joseph? Has something happened? Is it Isabelle's mother?" Marie was perplexed.

"It's Lieutenant Baxter, he has been hurt," wheezed Joseph.

"Hurt? What do you mean?" Isabelle burst out. "Where is he? What has he done?"

Joseph, unable to answer gestured them towards the kitchen.

Isabelle was first into the room, where she found James sitting at the table holding onto his side with one hand and his head with the other. His breath was rasping, he looked in pain and he was covered from head to foot in dirt and mud.

"James, what's happened?" Isabelle rushed to him.

At the sound of her voice he lifted his head, but the effort seemed too much for him and he slumped down onto the table. She put her hands on his shoulders as heaving sobs tore out.

"James, tell me, what happened? Are you hurt?"

Marie interrupted her as she walked towards James.

"Isabelle, put some water on to boil. What has the boy done to himself? Joseph, fetch the brandy. Jacques, sit down and keep still. James, can you speak?"

James lifted his head again and gave a slight nod.

"Take your time, but tell us what happened? Are you injured?"

Joseph stumbled back into the kitchen with the brandy bottle, which he handed to Marie.

"A glass, pass me a glass." She poured the golden liquid and passed the glass to James.

James gasped as the brandy hit the back of his throat; the shock of the alcohol made him cough and he immediately grimaced and gripped his side.

"I have hurt my ribs," he managed to say.

"Hurt your ribs? Is that it? Is that what all this drama is about? Really," Marie said as she pulled up a chair and sat at the table. "I think I need a brandy too for my nerves. Really, Joseph, did we need such a fuss?"

Isabelle approached James with a wet cloth.

"Shall I?" she gestured to his face with the cloth. James nodded his reply and closed his eyes as she cleaned the mud from his face and some blood that had congealed around his lips.

"I didn't think I was going to see you again, Isabelle," he whispered and to her puzzled look he said, louder, "Joseph saved my life."

It took some time for the women to extract the details of what had happened. James did not seem to know much himself, but he repeated what Joseph had told him on their way back to the house and Joseph then repeated everything that James said with his own embellishments. He too had been poured a brandy. What they gleaned was that Joseph had been out looking for game and had spotted two men fighting on the ground and one seemed to be getting the better of the other. It had looked to Joseph like the one with his back on the ground was being suffocated by the weight of the one on top who was pressing down on him, pinning the man with a sack. Joseph had been unsure what to do, so had fired a warning shot at which the assailant ran off, deeper into the forest.

"It was only when I approached the man on the ground and drew back the sack I saw it was Lieutenant Baxter," Joseph said. "His face was blue and I thought I was too late, but he started coughing after I thumped him a couple of times."

As Isabelle heard this she sat on a chair next to James and clutched and stroked one of his hands.

"You mean you were attacked?" Marie said, which caused James to raise his head.

"Almost killed, and robbed."

"Oh, James," Isabelle said and burst into tears.

Jacques ran to her side.

"Don't cry, Mama, don't cry."

Bellignes, July 1919

"Do you think they'll find the man?" Isabelle and James were sitting on their own in the garden a few hours later. He had bathed and changed, a slow operation due to his sore ribs, badly bruised, he thought, but not broken.

"Joseph said he had noticed someone skirting the sheds and had the feeling someone was hanging around for a few days," James replied.

"But he hadn't said anything?" Isabelle pressed.

"No, it wasn't much to mention, until today."

"Why were you attacked? Do you have any idea?"

"Yes, he robbed me. Took my pocket watch and my jacket, but it all happened so quickly I am only just piecing it all together."

"Jacqueline had two barrels stolen last week from her yard. I think there are many desperate people about, and no doubt some are sleeping rough in the woods. Perhaps you disturbed one of them."

"Yes, most likely. Well, he'll make a pretty penny from my watch. It was my grandfather's."

"Well, some of the men from the village have gone out to look for your attacker. It should be only a matter of time before they find him," Isabelle said. "Thank goodness Joseph was there and acted as he did."

"Yes, I was starting to black out. I just couldn't take a breath. It was horrible."

Isabelle winced and reached for his hand.

"It's so dreadful. How is your rib feeling? Are you sure it's not broken. Shouldn't we fetch the doctor?"

"No, it is only bruised. I have broken a rib before, falling from a horse. I can tell the difference. This is nothing, it will be fine in a few days, but I won't be lifting a shovel today, that's for sure." He smiled to reassure her.

"I should hope not when we can be spending time together. I assume you want to do that."

"You assume correctly. I want to hear everything about you, your life in Lille, how you have been. Your family. Are you enjoying teaching? I am sure you are very good."

Isabelle shook her head and waved her hand.

"No, no, I want to hear about you first. What happened after you surrendered? Where did you go, what was prison like, how are the others? Elliot, Samuel Elliot, where is he now?"

"Whoa, so many questions." It was James's turn to stem the flow and Isabelle laughed.

"We'll have to take it slowly, telling a piece of our story in turn," Isabelle suggested.

"How much time do we have?" James asked.

"As much as you like," Isabelle replied. "I will not be returning to Lille for some weeks, if at all."

"But what about the school, your teaching, your husband, Henri?"

"Perhaps James, I should start my story here and work backwards."

"Perhaps you should," agreed James.

But before she could begin Princess Marie called for them to join her for lunch, and over lunch Isabelle took the opportunity to catch up on more of Marie's experiences of her trial and incarceration.

"They should have taken me instead. I was much stronger than you. If only I had stayed." Isabelle was quite distressed by the hardship Marie described.

"Thank goodness you weren't here, they would have taken you as well as me. They were out to make examples of as many as they could find. The escape line had been compromised by Georges Quien. He was working as a spy for the Germans; they had first-hand evidence, making denial impossible. But I have news for you both about him. He is going to be tried in court for his crimes, as a traitor and a spy." Marie looked triumphant. "I am going to give evidence against him myself, in Paris, next month."

"I hope there is enough to convict him. He should pay a high price for what he did," James said.

Jacques ran into the kitchen and Isabelle helped him onto a chair. He had been helping Joseph in the barn.

"Have you two caught up with each other yet?" Marie asked Isabelle and James. "I've been dominating our conversation. Why don't you return to the garden; I can keep an eye on Jacques."

"You were going to tell me about your life in Lille," James reminded Isabelle when they had returned to the garden.

"Yes, we have had a very difficult time at the school. The influenza hit the school and we lost pupils and teachers. The school was closed down and with Henri's death, I am not sure it will reopen."

"Henri's death? Your husband? He's dead?" James could not hide his surprise and worked very hard to hide his delight. "Oh, Isabelle, I am so sorry for you." And then her mention of the "flu" hit him. "Thank goodness you and Jacques survived." He felt shaken by the thought of losing her.

"Yes, we were lucky. Actually many of us stayed healthy, even though we were nursing the sick. It is the most horrible disease. It kills so quickly, but not without the person suffering. I had to wait some weeks before coming back here, to make sure I wasn't carrying the infection."

"It was influenza that got Elliot. We were inseparable all through our captivity and then he caught it at the transit camp. I couldn't bear to watch him die. I wished that I had gone with him."

"I'm so pleased that you were spared."

"As am I, now." James reached out and took her hand, but Isabelle slipped it out of his grasp and folded her hands in her lap. James looked at her.

"Henri was a good man, a truly good man. All the teachers revered him and the pupils did their best to please him. He did not deserve such a death. He ran a good school and taught me all I know about teaching."

"And was he a good husband to you and father to Jacques?"

"He was very kindly towards us. We worked together well as a team. We got along well enough."

James was quickly tiring of all this praise for Henri and landed the next question with a jab.

"Did he know that Jacques was another man's child?" James softened his question by picking up Isabelle's hand again and this time would not release it.

"What is it that you think you know, James?" Isabelle asked.

"That Jacques is my son."

"And it would be a waste of my time trying to deny this?"

"Yes it would."

A silence hung between them until Isabelle responded.

"You're right." She stood up and moved away from him, then turned back to face him. "Henri assumed fatherhood of Jacques with never a question. We married as soon as I returned to Lille, and Jacques was a late delivery, so no eyebrows were ever raised. Not that I witnessed anyway. Henri had no desire to have children of his own, but he wasn't disappointed with Jacques. In his way Henri loved us very much and I was very fond of him."

"Surely you felt more than fondness to rush off and marry him the minute I had gone?" James sounded tetchy and got to his feet too.

"Don't censure me, Lieutenant Baxter. I begged you not to surrender. I offered to go to Brussels and beyond with you. I didn't want us to be apart, and I knew nothing about the child I was carrying then." She folded her arms and half turned from him.

"It is entirely unfair to describe surrender as a choice."

"And there is only one choice available to a single woman who finds herself pregnant. She must find a husband and quick, if she and her family's name is to survive, and her child be fed."

"I wish you had waited for me, or told my family: they could have helped."

"Don't be so naïve, James." Isabelle turned on him. "You had gone and I didn't know if you would even survive. I was certainly not going cap in hand to your family to be paid off. I would not seek charity then as I will not seek it now."

She spun on her heel and walked away from him. He was quick to follow her and was soon striding along beside her.

"Enough, enough. We have been through too much to fight. Isabelle, please. We must talk."

After a few more steps Isabelle stopped striding, and then turned to him. "Yes, you're right, of course, you're right." They both returned to the seat.

"Thoughts of you were my constant companion at the prison camps, Isabelle."

"Were they? I thought you said Elliot was your constant companion." But Isabelle softened her words with a fleeting smile. "I am so saddened to hear of his death, and after you and he had survived so much. Tell me everything, please, I want to hear about it."

"But …"

"Please James, tell me what happened to you."

"Well, you brought me back. I came to find you."

"No, don't start at the end, the beginning, take me back to the beginning."

For the next few hours James talked and talked and talked. The stories and memories poured out of him. Sometimes he cried, sometimes he laughed, and sometimes a pause would lengthen into a silence as he faced a memory before putting it into words for her. Isabelle's eyes never left his face, and it was only as the day cooled and the shadows lengthened that he brought his monologue to a close. He felt exhausted and purged and now appreciated all Marion's attempts to make him talk. He had thought her therapy was an indulgence, but the relief he now felt was immense.

"It is amazing that so many of you survived. So little food and such difficult conditions," Isabelle finally said.

"I couldn't have done without Elliot."

"And I am sure if he was here, he would say the same of you."

"Perhaps. Yes, perhaps he would. But all we did was survive. We weren't fighting like all the heroes were. I feel quite ashamed when I think of it."

"Well, that's entirely silly. Surrendering was not the act of a coward, and protecting your men in the ways that you did went beyond the call of duty. You should feel proud of yourself. I am proud of you. Very proud indeed, as Jacques will be when he is old enough to understand this war. And talking of Jacques, we have left him for a long time with Marie. He will have exhausted her. I must take him home."

"And I'll walk with you. It's not safe to be out in the lanes on your own."

"I think you are forgetting you nearly died this morning. You will do no such thing. Joseph can take us on the cart, I am sure."

Joseph had anticipated the request and had the horse ready. And Jacques had worn himself out, as well as Marie. He was sleepily curled up on her lap when they returned to the house.

"If your mother is well enough cared for to be left why don't you and Jacques come and stay here for a few days? I would enjoy your company," Marie asked. "And if you were here, I might actually get some more work out of Lieutenant Baxter." They all laughed.

"Thank you, Marie. That really is most kind and Jacques does find it hard to keep quiet enough at Mother's house. We'll see you very soon."

Goodnight wishes were extended all round, but no kisses exchanged, and within minutes of her departure James was asleep in his small box room at the top of the house and, for the first time since his capture, he had a night of undisturbed sleep.

James could hardly move from his bed in the morning. His heart was singing but every muscle in his body felt bruised and cramped. He gingerly dressed and made his way down the stairs to join Marie at breakfast. He had such an appetite that she cooked him a second round of eggs.

"Joseph tells me the men found no one," Marie told him, "so no more solitary walks for you for a while."

"He will be long gone, I'm sure."

Marie put a fresh pot of coffee on the table and he poured them both a cup.

"I will enjoy good coffee for the rest of my days." Marie sipped from her cup. "How was your time with Isabelle? Did you establish Jacques was your son?"

"Yes he is, and now that I know she is widowed I can't wait to take them home with me to meet my family. I will happily settle into work with my father now to provide for them."

"You did cover some ground then. So Henri has died, I thought as much. When do you all plan to leave?"

"Well, I've yet to discuss this with Isabelle, but I am sure she will see the sense in my plan."

"Oh, I see. James, if I might advise, do tread carefully with Isabelle." Marie paused. "She can be very strong-willed. Coax her as you would one of your father's thoroughbreds. Let her come towards you. If you go charging in with your futures defined you might find her retreating at some pace."

"But surely she will see the sense of such an arrangement?" James had not considered that she would not.

"James, Isabelle doesn't need to be part of any arrangements. I am sure Henri will have left her financially independent. That girl needs her heart spoken to, not her head. Take your time, and I feel confident you will succeed, but don't rush her."

The confidence that James had started the day with began to drain away.

"Now are you feeling well enough for some work today? How are your ribs?"

"Tender, but that's all. Perhaps no digging today, but there's plenty else for me to do. It will be good to keep myself occupied. Isabelle didn't say when she was coming back, did she?"

"No, but I shall see her today in the village and will find out. We are moving the rock for the memorial to Bavay today. The council has agreed to its position and the plaque is being engraved. They will want you as guest of honour at its unveiling, but this won't be for a while yet. Your idea was an inspiration."

"It is your execution of it that is inspirational. You don't let any opposition stand in your way."

"I think that is what those who have suffered the loss of freedoms find. They never want to be thwarted again, or be under another's control. Now watch yourself with Isabelle. Your desire to make up for lost time might rush her."

"Yes, message is received and understood." James nodded his head. "I need to adopt my mother's style rather than my father's. It's she who always seems to get her way while he's left dumbfounded. Your words are wise, Marie, and I will heed them, thank you. Now I'll go and find Joseph and see what tasks I can tackle today." And tonight, he thought, he would write to Marion. Her reply was swift.

> Dear James,
>
> Attacked?! Such horrible news. I do hope the perpetrator can be found and brought to justice.
>
> Isabelle sounds delightful. I am so pleased, and do not be put off by her widow's weeds, she is the same woman beneath them. And to think you have a son, almost the same age as Alain, perhaps they will be friends one day. Alain sends you a picture. He had drawn it the day before your letter arrived. Trust in Marie's tactics, she sounds a wise woman.
>
> All is fine with me. Russell is due back soon, but there have been more deaths from the 'flu here – so remain where you are! Work at the hospital is getting much quieter. Doctor Ambrose has been offered a post at a London hospital. He is making up his mind whether to take it.
>
> Best wishes,
> Marion Drake.

James opened the folded sheet to look at Alain's picture. It was of a man, a woman, and a small boy, all holding hands.

France, July 1919

Russell put Marion's letter to one side and unfolded the sheet of paper she had included with her note. It was one of Alain's drawings and showed a man, woman, and child, all holding hands as they stood on the banks of a stream with stepping stones cutting a path across the water. He smiled and planted a kiss on the paper before carefully folding it away. With some luck it would only be a matter of days before he could be having a picnic with them by the Misbourne. He could not wait.

He had been uplifted by Marion's letter and support for their life in America. He would have settled in England if that had been her wish, but he was very excited about the opportunities that were being mooted in Washington. Pershing had been true to his word and he had three letters of introduction for him to pursue. His status as a Rhodes scholar was guarantor enough according to Pershing, but the personal touch from his sponsor was what gave Russell the confidence to know he would find work in the corridors of power. And this was definitely where he wanted to be. The academic world of research no longer held its appeal; he wanted to be putting his efforts into what concerned people today.

Russell's glimpses of the Allies' leaders at work had often left him dismayed. All too often it was the stubborn defence of an ego that held sway in what ought to have been a rational consideration of a situation to form the best plan. And lives had been lost because of a refusal to listen or accept facts that would have caused one of the bumptious to lose face. It sickened Russell and Walter Sheldon had little time for the power plays either. He and Russell were waiting for one of the last crossings of American troops to England and they were always pleased to have time together and to enjoy omelette and fries in a small café in Boulogne.

"Glad you came over, Russ?"

"Yes, but even more glad to be heading home, Walt. How about you?"

"The same, pretty much the same. Wouldn't have missed it though."

"No," Russell agreed, "but Lester and Eugene were lucky to be away six months ago. I'm mighty tired of inventories and men who are sick of taking orders."

"Apparently many of the French regiments couldn't stop their men disbanding. They just went home, while the Brits brawled at every opportunity and complained whenever anyone would listen. I've been building houses for the French for the last two months. Could have put regiments to good use if they had been more willing."

"Houses?"

"Well, huts, let's call them huts. They come as a pack of wooden planks, and are quick to put together. Tiddlers compared to the barns we raise at home, but it's a good way to get some of the villages back on their feet. I was amazed at how quickly folks returned to the burnt-out ruins of their homes, camping out in all weathers, sticking flags wherever they unearthed another body. It's a mess."

"I've been dealing with the lists of our dead and their whereabouts," Russell said.

"How many were killed?" Walt asked.

"Upwards of 60,000. And at the last count about two thirds of their families want their boys back home. What an operation that is going to be. I'm glad to be handing that job over. It will take years. I've even had British folk asking me to trace their deceased, but it's of no help to them, they can't take them home. They are to remain buried here."

"Doesn't make any difference where I lie when I'm dead, I reckon," Walt said.

"No, I'm sure," Russell agreed, "but it sure matters to the living. They want their men back."

"What next for you, Russ, back to Oxford?"

"Yes, but only to collect my belongings and then to Amersham to collect my girl, I hope, then I shall be heading to Washington."

"Haven't you had enough of massaging egos, and Washington is the place for the biggest of them?"

"I've heard that Hoover has accepted a role administering the food programme at home and abroad. I'd be interested to join his team. He is not one to pander to egos, he just wants a job done and done well."

"So I've heard. And who is this girl you are taking with you?"

Russell told Walt all about Marion and how they had met and was proud to talk of her escapades in Brussels. Walt was impressed.

"And she will understand what you have been through: that makes a lot of difference. My girl Sal, home in Minnesota, doesn't have a clue about this war, or any war for that matter."

"And let's hope it stays that way."

"Yes, but hard to return a hero, when she has no idea of the risks."

"I'm sure you'll convince her," Russell laughed.

When they parted in Folkestone they made promises to write and meet again. Walt was heading straight back to the States and Russell to London and Marion.

Bellignes, July – August 1919

It seemed as if the whole of the region had turned out for the ceremony to unveil the stone and plaque for the late mayor of Bavay. James had had little to do with the project beyond its inception, but he found himself as guest of honour and was delighted to have Isabelle and Jacques standing alongside him. He looked at the flags flying and the memorial and took the by now very crumpled picture crayoned by Alain out of his jacket pocket and showed it to Isabelle. She asked him to tell her about it later as the speeches were about to start. James looked around him at the crowd. Those nearest the front of the crowd were wearing what looked like their Sunday best, despite the heat of the day, and those further back their working clothes. Children were running around being hushed by their nearest related adult and although a serious occasion James could feel a festive spirit waiting to burst through. James had been asked to speak and stepped forward after his introduction had been made. He followed Prince Reginald who had actually left him very little to say so James expressed his heartfelt gratitude on behalf of all the soldiers who had been assisted by the people of the area and kissed the mayor's widow on both cheeks. Isabelle reached for his hand when he returned to her side and gave it a squeeze. After all the dignitaries had had their say, they and their guests retired to the town hall for refreshments.

Apart from the frequent and increasingly impatient letters from his mother asking when he was planning to return, to which he had only briefly replied, life had established a contented rhythm for James. He worked hard for the de Croys and could feel his fitness returning. He had heeded Marie's advice and not made any move on Isabelle, though he had of course paid her lots of attention. "Walking out" is what his mother would call their relationship. No intimacy but easy companionship. Sometimes he laughed at the absurdity of becoming friends with the mother of his child. He wanted more, but, for the moment, was at ease with waiting. His best times were when Isabelle flirted with him. He felt she was testing to make sure of his interest, but she backed off quickly if he became too responsive. He loved having her by his side as they mingled with the functionaries.

The only dark cloud was the health of Isabelle's mother. Her last illness had left her quite debilitated and she had now lost interest in any food and talked incessantly of "going home". Isabelle was largely stoic about her demise, when in his company, but he could feel the strain it put her under. She would arrive at the de Croys' house at different times of the day, as she put it, to "breathe in fresh air". Her mother's house now had the curtains pulled at all times, and it was not a good environment for a young boy.

Jacques was full of life and curiosity and sometimes spent a whole day with James when he was working outside. He reminded himself to ask Isabelle if he could start leading Jacques on the horse. It was such an old nag he would come to no harm, but still he needed her permission.

He looked at her by his side and felt his heart swell with pride. He had seen several arms nudged and heads nodded in their direction. He hoped this was because they made a fine couple standing together, but he was sure word was out about Jacques's parentage. Isabelle appeared not to notice, but he was sure she would be aware of any gossip.

"What was that picture you showed me?" Isabelle asked

him as they walked back to her village later in the day. Jacques had gone in the trap with Marie and Reginald, but they had preferred to walk together.

"It was given to me by the son, sorry ward, of a friend of mine. He's the same age as Jacques, but his drawings are often a picture of the future. I've had a couple of offerings from him. He predicted me coming over to France and standing next to a memorial. Quite uncanny really."

"How unnerving for his mother."

"No, she's definitely not his mother, but calls him her ward. I'm not quite sure what the relationship is."

"And what is her relationship with you?"

"She's a family friend and was my nurse at the hospital. It was she who encouraged me to come and find you. You remember I told you about the nurse who escaped from Brussels when Edith Cavell was captured? That's her, Marion. She will be expecting her beau home to her soon. He's American and fought in France. He's normally an academic I believe."

"Perhaps he will marry her and give her ward a father."

"I think that is what she is hoping for. Anything to keep her mother off her back and the locals from gossiping."

"That sounds just like us here," James said. "You noticed the nudges and nods, did you?"

Isabelle shrugged.

"What I notice more is when conversations stop when I am near. They can talk all they like, it doesn't bother me, as long as my mother is not capable of hearing their tittle-tattle, and she will be gone soon anyway."

"Is she much worse?"

"The doctor said at his last visit it wouldn't be long. I hope she can just slip away in her sleep one night. She's ready to go, and no doubt my father will be waiting for her. They were such a team when he was alive. And what of your mother, have you had a summons recently?"

"Yes, yesterday actually. I really am trying her patience now and must plan my return. It is entirely unfair of me to put all of this effort into the de Croys' estate when my own father is struggling with his business. I should be thankful to have work that I love waiting for me. I do feel fit enough for it now."

"Training horses?"

"Yes, and breeding them too. Oh, by the way, I wondered if you would let me put Jacques on a horse. I would lead him. Just to see if he liked it."

"Is he old enough?"

"Yes, I had my own pony by his age. Always led of course."

"Do you think riding will be in his bones?"

"I would like to think so. I'll ask him and see what he says."

"Believe me, if you suggested he ate dirt he would do it without question, he adores you."

"And I him."

"And what of his mother? What do you feel about her?" Isabelle's tone had become serious. James looked at her.

"Do you need to ask?"

"Not really. I asked Marie and she said you were head over heels in love with me, and that I should put you out of your misery, and wed you. I think she likes happy ever after endings."

James stopped walking and turned to face her.

"Don't we all?" He took hold of both of her hands. "Why did you ask Marie and not me, and anyway, couldn't you tell?"

"Actually James, no, I couldn't tell. You've confused me. You have been so restrained when I thought I would be fighting you off. You were very amorous when we first met, so then I worried your feelings might have changed. You've given me very little indication of wanting me."

"I have been following Marie's advice."

"To play hard to get?"

"To give you time. And I always will, give you time."

"But James, don't leave me to do all the running."

"Believe me, the first step you make in my direction and you'll be swept off your feet." He pulled her towards him and gave her a hug. She did not pull back and whispered in his ear.

"Then follow me."

Isabelle took a path off to her left and he followed her. After crossing a field they entered a copse of trees and she took him by the hand to the bank of a small stream where she sat down and looked up at him.

"Are you sure?" James asked her.

"Are you?" Isabelle asked in return, but received no words in reply.

It was dusk when they emerged and entered the village. The moment Isabelle saw a cluster of people outside her house she knew what had happened. Her mother had died.

James had borrowed a dark suit from Reginald a month before for Isabelle's mother's funeral, but for its next wearing, Marie had insisted on making some alterations to improve the fit.

"I am sure your parents would have sent one of your suits over for you if you had asked them," Marie muttered with a mouth full of pins.

"I haven't mentioned to them that I have need of a formal suit."

Marie finished adjusting the jacket and removed the pins from her mouth before she spoke again.

"You mean you haven't told them you are to get married, that you are marrying Isabelle?"

"No. I thought it easier to present her as my wife when we arrive in England."

"Easier for whom? For you maybe, but not for them. And what about for Isabelle? What will it be like for her to be judged at her first meeting with her in-laws?"

"It may be bumpy for a while, but I am sure they will grow to accept her."

"Accept her? Isabelle deserves better than that. There is still time, James. You must tell them and invite them to your wedding. It is unforgiveable to keep this from them. Let them adore Isabelle on first sight, and love her when they get to know her. And as for Jacques, he will steal anyone's heart. You simply must tell them and invite them here, as my guests. In fact we should write to them together, you with your news and me with their invitation. They may be unhappy with you, but they can't refuse my offer of hospitality."

James had to agree that with Marie's support, facing his parents over his decision to marry Isabelle did feel easier. He agreed they would send the letters and invitation and it was down to them how they chose to react to the news. Once done James found he was immensely relieved, but anxiety immediately piled onto Isabelle instead.

"What if they try and stop you?"

"They couldn't, my mind is made up. It is you and Jacques that I live for."

"But they might create a scene."

"A scene? My father is an English gentleman. He might write me out of his will, but never a scene."

"But to be disowned by your family, that would be a terrible thing."

"You and Jacques are my family. You have no one else and if it is to be the same for me, then so be it."

"You sound very calm about it. I thought you were convinced not to tell them until after we were married."

"My mother liked Princess Marie very much when she was here. I think she will respond well to the hand of friendship being extended to her. My father has given up on me anyway I fear. I returned from the war a big disappointment to him. Men were made of sterner stuff in his day."

"I like you just the way you are."

"Like?"

"Love you."

"And that is all that really matters. Anyway, I know they will adore you."

"Even if your mother will think I trapped you into marrying me?"

"Princess Marie will put her straight on that. And look at you. You are beautiful and accomplished. I am the luckiest of men to have you marry me."

"I wish my mother could have seen me wed. She couldn't come to my wedding to Henri and now she has died before ours."

"Are you sure this isn't too soon for you? We can wait a while longer if you would prefer."

"We have waited long enough, James. Long enough."

The telegram was short and to the point, and addressed to Prince Reginald and Princess Marie de Croy.

"Thank you for invitation. We will arrive on August 15. Cannot manage before" wrote his parents. James's delight that, by the looks of it, both his parents were coming, remained tinged with anxiety as to their mood. He and Isabelle were sent off on errands at the time his parents were due to arrive at the chateau, a situation orchestrated by Marie. She had also arranged for his parents to be driven to the chateau and be made comfortable before introductions to Isabelle were made. James interrupted laughter in the salon when he entered and presented Isabelle.

"Father, Mother, may I introduce you to my fiancée, who will indeed become my wife tomorrow, Isabelle. Isabelle, my parents, Major and Mrs. Baxter."

"Peter and Barbara, please. It is a pleasure to meet you Isabelle," said James's father Peter as he stretched out his hand to shake hers. "A real pleasure." He was almost standing to attention, but brushed his whiskers with his hand, something he did when nervous. "My wife."

Mrs. Baxter stepped forward to take Isabelle's hand, and for a moment James thought Isabelle was going to curtsy, but she bowed her head slightly and flashed one of her wonderful smiles.

Isabelle looked a picture. Poised, mannered, and accomplished in English she was immediately enquiring into their journey and comfort at the chateau and to thank them for making the occasion of their wedding so special by their attendance.

"We've heard little to nothing about you from James, my dear, but Princess Marie has been filling us in with some details," the major said. "I can't think why you want to take my son on, but then, I have never understood women." He looked towards his wife and smiled. James was delighted to see him in such good humour and enjoyed a back-slapping greeting of his own from him and a whisper of "fine looking filly" from him in his ear.

"We were very saddened to hear news of your mother, and of course, your husband," Mrs. Baxter added. "And we have yet to meet your little boy. A lot seems to be happening in very short order for you. I do hope James isn't rushing you. He has always been impetuous."

"Thank you for your condolences and your concerns. It was my mother's dying wish that I should be settled and James has been extremely patient."

"Will you be wearing black for the wedding?" Mrs. Baxter asked, and before Isabelle could answer Princess Marie stepped in.

"I have asked Isabelle to wear my own mother's wedding gown. It needed very little alteration apart from to the length and she will look beautiful. Isabelle is like a daughter to me and to my brother and we are delighted that she and James have found happiness together. There has been too much heartache these last few years; we must celebrate when we can and put grief and loss behind us."

"I see. Yes, yes of course we must, although this does seem to be such a rush," Mrs. Baxter said.

As if on cue, in rushed the youngest member of the family, Jacques. He tripped over the carpet and landed in a ball at Mrs. Baxter's feet and burst into infectious giggles, which soon had the whole room joining in. It was Major Baxter who put down a hand to help him up.

"Come on, lad, let's take a look at you. Oh, yes, you're a Baxter and no mistake. I hear you've been on a horse. Why don't you come and sit with me and tell me all about it." The major looked across and gave his wife a nod.

Mrs. Baxter stepped forward and took hold of both of Isabelle's hands.

"Welcome to our family, my dear. I meant nothing by my question, just nervous to be meeting you. Now tell me about this dress and do you have some flowers to carry: perhaps I could make up a posy for you?"

They moved and sat near to the window and were soon in deep discussion about the arrangements for the following day. James watched in some amazement at his parents and then caught Marie's eye. "Thank you" he mouthed to her nod. Her adoption of Isabelle had certainly smoothed the way for his mother; the rest was down to Isabelle and he had no doubt that she would do nothing but impress everyone she met. James's happiness was almost too much to bear.

The only person who did not shed a tear at their wedding was Jacques. He carried himself perfectly throughout the day, never letting go of his grandfather's hand. When glasses were raised to toast the bride and groom, nudged by his grandfather Jacques stepped forward shyly. The room went quiet for him to speak. He looked to his grandfather who gave him a nod and he turned to the bride and groom, his parents, and slowly and deliberately, in an almost perfect English accent said,

"Welcome home, Papa."

London, August 1919

This was not the return that Russell had dreamt of. He had telegraphed Marion, booked into a hotel, enjoyed a good night's sleep, and had waited for her to arrive. But she had not and he did not know what to do. They had agreed that London was the place for their reunion to be enjoyed in the fullest sense, but what was he to interpret from her absence? On the afternoon of the first day he had sent another telegram, just in case his first one had not got through for some reason, and he kept checking with the hotel reception for messages. By the second day he had gathered enough courage to telephone her home, but the phone rang and rang until the operator cut him off at the exchange.

He did not leave his room apart from his trips to the telegraph office, not wanting to miss her arrival and always convinced that she would be on every train from Amersham. But by the evening of the second day, with no Marion, he did not know what to think. Had she changed her mind? He lost confidence by the hour and tossed his way through a night of increasing despair. The following morning he was woken by a knock on his bedroom door, which he leapt to open.

Russell reacted without thought. The moment he read the telegram handed to him by the valet, he had checked out of the hotel and jumped on the first train out of Marylebone station to Amersham, exactly the opposite of what he had been told to do.

Apologies – just read your telegram – Marion too unwell to travel – stay in London – will contact you soonest – influenza here. Bernard Drake.

Russell paced up and down the corridor of the train, trying any distraction to keep the picture of Marion, sick with influenza, out of his mind. With each rattle of the wheels he recited and repeated: "She must not die, she will not die, she must not die, she will not die," but fear had gripped his whole body the instant he read her father's message.

He left his luggage with the porter at the station and asked for it to be forwarded to The Crown hotel. Regardless of whether they had a room available he knew they would hold his bags, and remembering the route he had taken with Marion he ran and jogged his way to Little Missenden, only stopping to cool himself down with water from the Misbourne before he approached the vicarage. He was surprised to see Alain standing by the gate.

"What are you doing here young fella?" Russell bent to ask him and Alain flung his arms around his neck.

Nanny stepped out from the shade of the tree.

"He is not allowed in the house. We have just come down from his uncle's house. I couldn't keep him away, and he kept saying you were coming."

"What's happened? How is Marion? Where is she, can I see her?" Russell had released himself from Alain's hug and taken hold of his hand as he fired his questions to Nanny. She sounded grave.

"She is upstairs and very ill. This is the third day of her fever. Her mother is insisting on nursing her and the doctor from the hospital has been supervising her care. I believe he's in the house now. They are not allowing visitors, but I'm sure you will be a boost for Marion, if she can know you are here."

"Stay here, little man." Russell handed him over to Nanny by passing Alain's hand to her. "I'll knock on the door and see what I can find out."

"You will learn nothing that way. They are not opening the door to anyone. Go to the back door, wash yourself with the soap and water, and go in. She is in her own bedroom. You may not be welcome, but I am sure you can be useful."

"You must return with Nanny, Alain. Go back to Shardeloes and I will come and find you when I can tell you that Mummy is well again. It is too dangerous for you to be near this infection, do you understand that?"

Alain nodded, but flung himself at Russell again who enveloped him in a bear hug, until he could peel himself away. There was no picture from Alain today.

Russell met no one on his way to her bedroom, having let himself in through the kitchen door. He had just reached the top of the stairs when a bedroom door opened and out came Bernard Drake and Doctor Ambrose. They were startled to see him, and did not recognise him at first.

"It's Russell Clark, Mr. Drake. I came as soon as I received the news. How is she?"

Doctor Ambrose looked at Mr. Drake who answered his unspoken question.

"Be assured, I specifically told him not to come." He turned to Russell. "In crisis, she is in crisis." And he rubbed his hand over his eyes. He looked exhausted.

"What does that mean? Can I see her? Please let me see her."

"She is unlikely to know you are there," Doctor Ambrose said, "but her parents do need a rest, and as you have broken the quarantine anyway we may as well make use of you."

"Tell me what I can do," Russell said. "Anything. I've seen this before, wretched thing."

"Go in, her mother will tell you, and then make sure she takes a rest. I will be back this evening, but call me back if her condition deteriorates."

Russell and Doctor Ambrose looked at each other.

"We'll know in the next twenty-four hours," Doctor Ambrose said to the question Russell was too scared to ask.

With curtains drawn the room was dusky. Marion's mother was beside the bed with a flannel in her hand dampening Marion's face. She looked exhausted.

"Let me, please, let me," Russell said as he gently took the cloth from Mrs. Drake's hand. She let him take it without any protest.

"Time for you to take some rest, my dear," Bernard said as he came back into the room. "We will watch her now, you have been up all night, and as the doctor said, there is little we can do but wait and pray."

Mrs. Drake had tears coursing down her face as her husband led her from the room, leaving Russell alone with Marion.

Marion's eyes were closed, but her lids kept fluttering, her lips had a blue tinge and beads of sweat kept pooling on her upper lip and forehead. Her breathing was shallow and her face was deathly white. She had bruises all over one arm that lay on top of the coverlet. He started to pray, with all his heart he prayed until he realised he was talking to the wrong person. It was Marion that needed to hear his voice, not God. So he began to talk, and he described the life they were going to have together, for hours and hours. She gave no sign that she heard him.

Her father brought him soup and water, and a large brandy, which he left untouched. Marion's mother returned, but did not remove him from the bedside; instead she sat by the window listening to his voice whispering secrets and stories to Marion.

Marion's whole body was limp, but Russell held and stroked her hand all day. But when Doctor Ambrose visited, her breathing was shallower still.

"She is still fighting. Her pulse is stronger than this morning," he declared to the room after his examination.

Russell was astonished with this pronouncement. He was expecting him to be announcing her imminent death.

"But she is so lifeless, hardly breathing." Russell's face was etched with anxiety.

"That's as maybe, but she is still breathing. Not many make it through forty-eight hours. With every hour she holds on, the hope of recovery increases. What sort of day has she had?"

"Sometimes restless and feverish, but mostly still and shockingly pale, apart from the blue tinges around her lips."

"No nose bleeds?" Ambrose asked.

"No, nothing like that," Russell said, and Mrs. Drake agreed.

"Keep up with your prayers, and Russell, let her hear your voice. Talk as much as you can. She can hear you, tell her you want her back, we all want her back. She has waited a long time to hear your voice, we can only hope it does more than mine for her."

Doctor Ambrose turned to Marion's mother.

"You have kept Alain away, haven't you? This is no place for a child."

"Yes, yes, the whole household has gone to Shardeloes. Are there more outbreaks?"

"No, nothing in the area. Marion was unlucky to fall foul of this. He was our last case at the hospital, and she nursed him. I think she was overtired, which is why you must all rest."

Mrs. Drake thanked Doctor Ambrose and Russell rose from Marion's side to thank him too. Stiff from sitting all day he put his hand out towards the doctor.

"Best not, old chap. The fewer direct contacts the better," Doctor Ambrose said. "Keep yourselves quarantined here, and Russell, I rely on you to make sure her parents rest and call me if anyone else starts any symptoms. You rather committed yourself by bursting in here."

"And I am pleased he did," said Mrs. Drake, and she smiled at Russell, which took him by surprise. "Call me a romantic, Mr. Clark, but if you can give my daughter anything like the life you have been describing to her with such love and devotion, she will be a lucky woman indeed. I only hope she can hear you."

"She will be able to hear you, so keep it up," Ambrose said. "The next twenty-four hours will show us how this is going to end."

Russell failed in his encouragement for her parents to go to bed for a proper night's sleep. One or other and sometimes both of them sat in the shadows of the room throughout the night, but they left him to his bedside vigil. The night was long and the next morning seemed to stretch endlessly, but their shared anxiety formed a bond between the three carers and by midday intimacies were being exchanged. Russell told Mrs. Drake of Marion's escapades in Brussels and the genesis of Alain.

"You must think I have been heartless towards him, an orphan?" she said.

Russell was surprised by her openness.

"Not at all. I think you have been rightly protective of your daughter and her reputation, something that Marion has been too casual about by far," Russell replied.

"Kind of you to say so, but such reputation has little meaning at a time like this. She has shown herself to be truly Christian and I have been chasing things of little matter." Marion's mother choked back a sob.

"A secure future for Marion, with or without Alain is a worthy cause." Russell was distressed to see her upset. "It is me who let her down. I showed myself to be a fickle suitor chasing my own dreams of heroism on the battlefield. If I had not been so selfish we could have been a family before now and shared years of happiness."

"Yes, well, I have to admit to my part in shattering that dream, young man," Bernard coughed. "It was rash of me to turn you away when your intentions were sound."

"No, sir, you were quite right to. I was naïve and ill-prepared to provide a home, but I can do so now, I assure you. I have been invited to take a role in Washington, low down of course to start with, but a worthwhile job and then I hope to move into the department that develops social policy. We can have government accommodation in the city."

"Washington?" Mrs. Drake gasped. "You would take her to Washington."

"Only if that is what she wants, and Alain too of course. She must decide."

"One step at a time," Mr. Drake said, "one step at a time."

It was three o'clock in the afternoon when Russell felt a pressure on his hand from Marion's fingers. He was not sure of it at first, but it came again, and he continued his story of the giant redwoods in California with added fervour. He saw that she was trying to move her tongue against her dry lips so he moistened the cloth and dabbed it on her lips, and this was how she took her first drink since his arrival. Some hours later, when able to croak her first words she whispered, "Alain?"

It was two weeks before Marion was strong enough to sit out in the garden and still the Drakes kept people away until they were sure none of the household carried the fever. Russell was her constant companion and nurse, a warm and loving partner to her. He told her everything of his experiences in France, reliving his battles and the sights he had seen, and tried to explain what he had realised about his own and her courage. Marion said very little and asked few questions but her attention was encouragement enough for him to talk and talk. He repeated his descriptions of the life that awaited them in

America, and was delighted when she appeared to share his enthusiasm for this, but he was aware she was lacking in the energy to fight or disagree with him, so he assumed nothing, and was just happy to enjoy their harmonious relations. She even easily accepted the news that he had told her mother about Therese and Alain. Their only difference of opinion was concerning Alain and his return to the house.

"We must leave his return until we are certain influenza has left the area," Russell insisted.

"We must ask him when he wants to come back," Marion countered.

"He is a child, he won't understand the risks. We must wait."

"Oh, Russell, you don't yet know this child." She shook her head. "He will know before all of us. You will learn about him and his ways."

Alain decided it for both of them, by joining them in the garden one day, followed by a flustered Nanny.

"He said he wanted to bring you a picture, but he refused to stay at the gate. He can be very determined when his mind is made up." Nanny was breathless.

Neither Marion nor Alain was listening to Nanny as they were hugging and kissing each other before he settled on her lap for a few minutes, but tiring quickly she shuffled him over to Russell and he hugged him, until Alain became restless and slipped off his lap onto the ground.

"What picture have you drawn for us, Alain?" Russell asked.

It was Nanny who unfolded the sheet of paper and handed it to them. The picture was of a very tall tree with a red bark and high branches. Russell recognised it as a giant redwood and told Alain about them in California.

"So you have been thinking of America, have you Alain?" Russell asked and winked at Marion.

"No," he said, "Uncle William has one at Shardeloes. It's his biggest tree," Alain replied.

"Nothing prophetic in this picture then," Russell said to Marion, and was surprised at how disappointed he felt.

"He drew that the day before we heard your fever had broken," Nanny said, "but it was only today he made a fuss about bringing it over. He has another one in his pocket that he hasn't let me see. Are you going to give it to Mummy, Alain? Don't forget it."

"In a minute, when you've gone," Alain replied, and received a tap on the hand from Marion, for being rude to Nanny.

"No, he's right, I must go. Evelyn is due back from her in-laws soon, with Anthony, and I must make some preparations in the nursery. It is so good to see you are on the road to recovery, miss, and to meet you again, Mr. Clark. Don't tire your Mummy, Alain. I'll go and inform your parents that we must return. They can't carry on managing like this any longer. Do you think they'll mind?"

"Not at all," said Marion. "It's time to put this solitude behind us."

As soon as Nanny left and it was just the three of them Alain pulled his picture out of his pocket and laid it on Marion's lap. She looked at it and smiled at him, before handing it to Russell.

He could make out a man, a woman dressed in white, and a child standing in front of a church with a steeple, like St Mary's in Amersham.

"Is that lady a nurse?" Russell asked Alain. "She looks like Mummy in her uniform."

"It is Mummy, but not in uniform," Alain said. "She's at her wedding."

Marion and Russell looked at each other. He raised his eyebrows and she gave a slight nod, and they both smiled.

You must excuse me, Alain, but I need to go and speak to your grandfather for a moment. Stay with Mummy, and don't tire her. I won't be long."

"I'll look after her," Alain said.

Russell bent down and gave Marion a kiss on her cheek and walked towards the house.

Alain called to him when Russell was only a few steps away. He looked back to see Alain waving.

"Welcome home, Daddy, welcome home."

Seven months later, London, 17th March 1920

Marion gasped as the cloth was pulled away to reveal the statue of Edith Cavell. Here she was, a VIP on the steps of St Martin's church, to the side of Trafalgar Square, among royalty and robed dignitaries with masses of people thronging the streets. Heads craned to look at Edith's likeness, her face high above the crowd.

Marion remained bitter towards the Germans, who had judged and shot Edith, but she was no longer swamped by feelings of sadness and remorse, and was now able to feel thankful for her own escape.

With the speeches over, last hands shaken, and final note played, Marion walked slowly around the statue. She read the inscribed words aloud: *"humanity, devotion, fortitude, sacrifice"*, and each word was echoed by Alain, who was holding her hand. They remained, a solitary pair with Edith long after the crowd had dispersed, and Marion told Alain the story of her friend, until they were approached by four people, one a young boy.

"There's Daddy," Alain shouted. She released his hand and he ran towards Russell who bent down to pick him up and swung him around. The other young boy was watching them laughing and jumping up and down in front of his own father, wanting the same.

"Now look what you've started, Russell," James said, bending to pick up Jacques.

"Boys will be boys," Isabelle said as she hugged Marion in greeting. "I hope it wasn't too difficult for you."

"Not at all," Marion said, "I felt entirely proud of her, and of the small part I played."

"The next statue you folks will be looking at will be the Statue of Liberty. What time do you sail tomorrow, Mr. and Mrs. Clark?"

"At noon," Russell replied, out of breath as he restored Alain to his feet. Alain and Jacques immediately started to chase each other around the statue.

"Jacques will miss his playmate," Isabelle said, as she watched the boys and listened to their shrieks and giggles.

"Then, Mr. and Mrs. Baxter, all the more reason for you to come and visit us, and soon," Marion said as she took Isabelle's arm. But for now I'm famished. Where are we going to eat?"

"The Ritz, I thought, and it's on us," James said. "Think of it as a belated wedding present. In fact, as we missed each other's weddings, this can be our celebration as well as your *bon voyage*. Alain, Jacques, come along and take our hands, we're off for some lunch."

As they waited for the traffic to pass, before crossing the road into Trafalgar Square, Marion turned back towards Edith, and said a silent goodbye.

Postscript – twenty-three years later Leuven, Spring 1944

The bombardment was over, for now at least, and parts of Leuven were on fire. Alain brushed down his uniform and followed the soldiers he had been sheltering with out onto the street.

"Looks like the convent caught it. They're your lot Al. Shall we head, there first?"

Alain nodded and thanked the lieutenant and then ran with the squad across the square in the shadow of St Peter's church, unscathed from the last attack, towards the convent. Black smoke was billowing out and as Alain reached the front of the building the door burst open and nuns started to stumble out onto the street. He helped one to her feet.

"Merci, merci, monsieur le cure."

Alain had to remind himself that his chaplain's cross and stole made him stand out from his armed colleagues. He was more used to being called Al by the company of soldiers he had travelled with from America than having reference made to his role as priest.

He directed the nun and those who followed away from the fires and towards the crypt of St Peter's. As each nun passed him she bowed her head and said "thank you father", and 1st Lieutenant Clark felt humbled by their respect. He was about to turn away, job done when one further sister emerged from the convent. Instead of passing by him she stopped to read his name on his left breast and then bowed her head and said "thank you, my son."

With his slip in status from father to son Alain assumed the person facing him was the mother superior, addressed her as such and asked her if there were any more nuns to be evacuated.

"No, I am not mother superior, and I am the last to leave." She looked into eyes and smiled. "Tell your mother, when you next see her Alain that you met sister Therese, and take my blessings with you, always.

Alain took her hands in his and walked with her across the square to the safety of the church.